Ethea

By A.C. Salter

This novel is a work of fiction. Names, characters and events are products of the author's imagination. Any resemblance to actual persons, living or dead is entirely coincidental.

Copyright © 2017 by A.C. Salter

All Rights Reserved
No part of this book may be used or reproduced, in any manner whatsoever without written permission except in the case of brief quotations embodied in critical articles and reviews.

Other books

The Daughter of Chaos trilogy

Eversong
Shadojak
Ethea

Winters End – Grimwolf's revenge

Dylap

Darkest Wish

Ethea

Prologue

Rescue

It was a dark bitter night. Ben turned the collar of his coat up against the rain before he protectively wrapped his arms around his girlfriend and son. The baby slept peacefully in Nelly's embrace, the opposite to the scene unfolding before them.

"This is the second time I've caught you in the forest," an imperial soldier shouted at them, spit flying from his mouth. "And my last words to you were if I caught you here again, I'd kill you."

Nelly cringed away from him, her frightened face following the large sword that he swung around the clearing before levelling it at them.

"Please," Ben pleaded. "We're sorry..."

The slap sent him reeling into the mud, his face an agony of hot pain as he shook the dizziness from his vision. He heard Nelly scream but it was Zilabeth that offered him a hand back to his feet, before confronting the soldier.

"We're doing nothing wrong," she argued, folding her arms and fixing the man with a hard stare. Beside her stood Teaselberry the wood troll. She folded her own furry arms and mimicked Zilabeth's stance.

Ben touched his sore mouth then wished he hadn't. It throbbed, but he guessed the pain he was feeling was the least of their worries as his gaze scanned over the other soldiers who were ransacking Zilabeth's cart. They were throwing clothes and supplies into the mud whilst helping themselves to the last of the food. One of them was smashing the kettle against a large oak, beaming with pride as it fell apart.
They had spent the last few weeks in Wales, searching for an old friend who it seemed had upset the Emperor. Elora had been made an enemy of the state and was to be killed on sight. She had eluded the Imperial Army since Earth and Thea collided a couple of months ago. Her likeness had been drawn on posters and leaflets and put up in every village and town they had travelled through. It had been made known that it was she who had caused the worlds to merge together, spreading chaos, killing millions and forcing everyone else into confusion and war. Only the deeds of the Emperor himself as he strived to create a new order and unite the two peoples, could make civilisation work once again. Or so the new world Ethea, is led to believe. But all Ben had experienced was the Empire's harsh rules and punishments, dealt out to anyone who stood against them. Now it seemed they were to receive these harsh punishments first-hand.
    Zilabeth was sure that Elora was hiding in the forest, but every time she felt they were close, they seemed to ride around in circles. Passing the same stream, reaching the same tracks as if something other-worldly had been turning them about.

They had set up camp to shelter themselves from the rain, that was when the patrol had found them and begun the interrogation.

Ben watched helplessly as Zilabeth was dragged over to an open fire that hissed and steamed in the rain. She was shoved roughly to the ground before another soldier. His face was set in grim fascination, a smile curling his lips as he watched her struggle to her knees.

"I demand to speak to the commanding officer," Zilabeth ordered, brushing dirt from her long leather jacket. "Who is in charge?"

The soldier laughed as he drew the largest sword Ben had ever seen. It was almost as tall as the man himself and was made from a dull green metal. Its edge caught the reflection of the flames, appearing razor-sharp and as deadly as the man gripping the hilt.

"You know what this is?" the soldier asked, resting the tip on the ground and twirling the blade for all to see.

"It's god-created, a soul reaver," Zilabeth answered, frowning in confusion.

The soldier's grin widened. "That's right, which makes me a Shadojak." He laughed when her jaw dropped in shock. "And there isn't anybody higher in command than a Shadojak, apart from the Emperor himself."

Ben followed the conversation using the tinker's tongue charm Zilabeth had given him. It fitted snuggly into his ear and used magic to translate other languages into his own.

"What's he saying?" Nelly asked beside him as she gently rocked the baby.

"Something about a Shadojak," he replied, although not knowing what that was, he guessed it wasn't good.

The soldier with the huge green sword, gripped Zilabeth around the throat before flinging her into the men who were watching. Their dirty faces leering as they caught her.

"Hold her steady," he growled, raising his weapon and aiming the tip over her chest. "I missed the last traitor's heart."

Teaselberry lunged at him but was easily kicked away before being held down by another man, this one wearing a police uniform, yet acting no differently to the other soldiers wearing chainmail and armour.

Ben knew that the police and the British Army had been enlisted into the Empire. They had little choice as the Emperor had his grip on the monarchy and the church. Anybody who wanted to leave was free to do so, but with the country and the rest of the world in turmoil it was safer to stay within the protection of the Empire.

"Leave her alone, she's not a traitor," Ben demanded, taking a step towards the men holding Zilabeth. He was yanked back by firm hands.

The soldier with the large sword regarded him with a dismissive glance. "We'll soon find out," he growled. "Her soul will reveal all her secrets to me. Then you will be next."

Nelly began to cry as did the baby who must have sensed the terror from her mother. Ben clenched his teeth and put his arm around the pair – please God, don't let them get hurt.

He felt helpless as he watched Zilabeth's arms being bent behind her back. The huge imperial soldier gripping his sword with both meaty hands, ready to thrust the blade into her heart.

Ben closed his eyes, not wanting to bear witness to the murder of his friend, yet her pleading and the men's laughter reached his ears.

"Let her go."

The voice was female, the words spoken with authority.

Opening his eyes again, Ben wanted to see who had spoken. See who this person was that wanted to help, even though they would probably be the next to be branded a traitor and butchered for their trouble.

Standing on the other side of the fire was a slim woman, the hood of her cloak covering her head, her face hidden within the shadow beneath.

"Who are you?" demanded the executioner, surprised. When the newcomer didn't answer his question, the soldier approached, swaggering the way a bully does when about to inflict violence on a victim.

"You're a slight little thing," he said, his eyes alive with menace. "I reckon I could cut you clean in half with one swing."

The men around the camp laughed, some taking steps closer to get a better view of the stranger that appeared from nowhere.

Although a lot shorter and far outnumbered, Ben thought the girl was calm and her stance relaxed. These facts seemed to unsettle the larger man as he cocked the broadsword onto this shoulder, his expression becoming less sure.

"You're with these traitors, are you?" he asked, standing toe-to-toe with the cloaked woman. "I take your silence as a yes. Then, as the Shadojak I find you guilty of treason and sentence you to death."

He turned slowly to his men, lifting his chin and grinning once again. "What do you say lads? Do you think I can cut her in two?" He laughed along with his soldiers before turning back to the girl. "Any last words?"

The stranger's covered head rose as she stared up into the executioner's face. "Yield and you may still live," she offered, and Ben thought he caught the glimpse of twin smouldering coals burning from inside the hood.

The camp went quiet and eerily still as the soldier absorbed her words. His grin turned to a snarl as he spat into the fire.

"I'm the Shadojak. I yield to nobody," he said. Then swinging his huge body to the side, he brought his sword arcing through the air.

To Ben, the weapon seemed to move in slow motion, cutting across the body of the stranger. She remained still and he screwed his face up waiting for her to be butchered in two. Yet as the blade neared her stomach she twisted her waist and ducked beneath the sword.

As the momentum carried the bigger man over, the stranger thrust her arms out. One hand slapping the hilt of the sword, sending it spinning up into the night while her other curled into a fist and punched her attacker in the throat.

The Shadojak's face turned bright red as he thudded to his knees before falling back into the mud. A whistling noise escaped his mouth as he struggled to breath; desperate hands reaching for his injured throat, but the damage was already done.

Ben watched the stranger as she remained relaxed, disbelieving what he had just witnessed. As did the rest of the camp who still looked on in silence. Then his gaze fell on the sword which was still tumbling end over end in the air. It reached its zenith and began to drop. The broad green blade catching the flames momentarily before striking the fallen soldier. The tip entering his chest and the weight of the weapon pushing it through until it stuck him to the ground.

The Shadojak coughed up blood as his hands slipped along the partially exposed blade, yet the act was futile. He gave one last wheezing breath then went still. The executioner becoming the executed.

Zilabeth stumbled out of reach of her captors as they drew their own swords. One began to crank his crossbow while the policeman fidgeted a pistol from inside his coat and shakily pointed it at the cloaked figure.

"Yield," the girl said, calmly.

The soldiers gave each other nervous glances as they waited for somebody to make the first move. Their gazes falling on their dead leader, his sword standing erect from his chest, then back to the stranger.

It was the bowman who moved first, firing his crank bow.

The bolt passed harmlessly through the cloaked figure and stuck into the tree behind her.

Ben's mouth fell open, was she a ghost? The stunned question was barley tumbling through his mind before the entire camp erupted in chaos.

The policeman supported his shaking hand with his other, ready to take the shot, but the moment he squeezed the trigger, his chest filled with bullet holes and his body was flung backwards.

Before the dead policeman hit the ground a large animal leapt over the fire and landed before the soldiers. It roared at the men, displaying sharp vicious teeth and flexed its huge muscles.

It was the largest dog-beast Ben had ever seen. He backed away and turned his head as the beast pounced on the soldiers. Their screams cut short by the clattering of steel and the tearing of flesh.

The soldier who had slapped him earlier, turned and grabbed Nelly's arm. He pulled her in front of himself and used her as a human shield.

Nelly screamed and almost dropped the baby. Ben swiftly grasped the wriggling bundle before he fell amongst the stamping feet. He held him tightly in his arms as he searched for a way to help his girlfriend.

Other men began to step into the clearing. British soldiers dressed in camouflage with rifles aimed into the shadows. They moved amongst the dead, checking for survivors before adopting defensive stances around the cart. One of them stroking the large horses to calm them.

By now the dog-beast had finished attacking the men he had leapt upon. He left their mutilated corpses as he padded towards the soldier holding Nelly. His mouth was pulled back in an angry snarl, teeth bared and sticky with blood.

The soldier pulled Nelly closer to his chest as he raised his sword towards the monster; fear shining brightly in wide eyes.

Ben edged closer and looked to the British soldiers for help, but they watched on in silence. He glanced to the cloaked stranger, expecting her to help, yet it was another who stepped between the beast and the imperial holding Nelly.

The newcomer was tall with wide shoulders, dressed in a similar black cloak to the hooded girl although his face was on show; a pleasant smile held upon a solid jawline and the most piercing green eyes Ben had ever seen.

"I'd drop your sword if I was you," the tall man offered, pulling his own blade from thin air, like a magician pulling a rabbit from a hat.

The imperial's arm curled around Nelly's stomach and held her tight. "Stay back, I know who you are," he screamed, his sword flashing between the man and the huge dog who had settled at his feet. "You're Bray, you're the Shaigun to the daughter of Chaos."

"I can't deny it," the man admitted. "Now, if you drop your weapon I'll make sure Weakest here won't tear your throat out." He nodded to the monster beside him, its hungry eyes glowering at the, soldier.

The imperial let his sword fall and fell to his knees before the man. "Please, the Shadojak made us do those things," he pleaded as Nelly rushed into Ben's arms once again.

"Having a soul reaver doesn't make him a Shadojak," Bray stated. Then lifting the man by the arm, flung him towards the soldiers with rifles. "Bind and blindfold him. We're taking him with us."

Ben watched all that was happening and still couldn't decide if these people before them were friendly or were as bad as the others. After all, they had just killed over six men in a matter of seconds.

"Thank you," Zilabeth coughed as she came to stand beside them. Teaselberry giving the ferocious dog a wide berth.

Bray nodded as he slipped his sword back into thin air. "You're safe now, although I wouldn't stay here long. The imperials will arrest anyone found in the forest."

"We're here to find the daughter of Solarius, Elora," Zilabeth explained. "Do you know where she is?"

"What are your reasons for seeking her?" the hooded girl asked as she stepped through the fire to stand beside Bray.

It seemed to Ben that she drifted through the flames, momentarily becoming smoke as the fire licked against her body.

"My name's Zilabeth," she answered, straightening her coat. "I believe Elora has need of my help and…"

"Zilabeth? Are you a descendant of Zalibut, the God of inventions?" the stranger asked.

"I am."

"Then we've been expecting you."

Ben felt suddenly conscious of himself as the hooded figure inclined her head towards him.

"But I wasn't expecting to see you," she said.

Almost too stunned to speak, Ben stammered, "We're here to find a friend."

The girl raised her hands and removed the hood.

She was strikingly beautiful. Jet-black hair flowing over her shoulders with a lock of blonde teased to the side. She fixed him with a welcoming smile; her violet eyes catching his shocked expression.

"Hello Ben," Elora said.

1

Rams Keep

Elora couldn't help but smile as Ben's jaw dropped as if on a loose hinge. He was as stunned to see her as she was to see him.

"What are you doing here, Ben?" she asked.

"It's a long story," he answered as he handed the baby to the lady beside him. "This is Nelly and my son. We were rescued by Zilabeth and Teaselberry a few months back, when the Molly sank."

"You were on the Molly?" Elora asked, as she shook hands with Nelly and stroked the blonde curls of the baby. She wondered what had happened to the barge once she had left it.

"Yeah, we were living on it for a time. We wanted a place to hide from the monsters and stumbled upon her along the canal. Thought you and your uncle Nat had succumbed to the insect creatures that attacked everyone."

Elora gave him a brief hug. "Well, I'm glad you used her and I see you salvaged some of my old clothes too," she said, eyeing the jeans and jacket that Nelly was wearing. "Don't worry," she continued as Nelly's face became flushed. "They're yours. I wear mostly black these days anyway."

"Are the rumours true?" Ben asked, his face becoming serious once again. "Is all that has happened to the world your fault. You seem to be a different Elora to the one I remember – not including the badass fighting you just did."

Elora offered them a sad smile. "It's true. Pretty much all of it. Who'd have thought I was the daughter of Chaos."

"At least you haven't got a fire-breathing dragon. Even after all the strangeness we've witnessed, I never believed that lie."

Elora shrugged. "Grycul is in the Shadowlands at the moment. She's a bit temperamental to be wandering around the forest."

"It's true?" Ben asked excitedly.

Elora nodded and turned her attention to Zilabeth. "I'm not sure how you're going to help us, but I'm glad you came. And who's this?" she asked, offering her hand to the wood troll.

"Teaselberry, she's a friend and my apprentice," Zilabeth replied. "And I'm not sure how I can help. I only know that I'm supposed to find you. How did you know I was coming?"

"Incredibly, it was the God Minu who gave us the message. I don't suppose you've seen The Green Man on your journey?"

Zilabeth shook her head. "The Green Man, father of nature? Is he involved in all this…Chaos? Sorry, there isn't any better word for it."

Elora chuckled. "Chaos is exactly what it is. And there are a lot of small gods that have being tangled up in it."

"Gods?" Ben asked, astonished.

"Don't worry about it now, I'll try to explain once we're safe. And I've got a friend at the inn who'll be interested in meeting you," she said, giving Teaselberry a wink. "But we can't linger here for much longer. There'll be another patrol party sent out to search for this one. Now if you'll climb in the cart, Captain Brindle there, will guide you back to Rams Keep Inn."

"You're not coming with us?" Ben asked.

"No, we've got to clear this mess up," Elora explained, waving her hand over the bodies of the soldiers. "If it's found the imperial's will have a clue as to where to search for us."

Within a few minutes the cart was jostling along the track, Zilabeth treating Elora to a concerned glance before they disappeared from view. As she watched them leave, Bray stepped beside her and interlaced his fingers with hers.

"The reaver belonged to Gunwahl," Bray explained as he led her towards the lifeless body in the dirt.

The large broadsword was sticking up from the body's chest, the blade slick with blood. Elora knew that it had absorbed the soul of the previous owner; the tip having run through his heart. The next person who picked it up and cut themselves, allowing their own blood to soak into the blade, would gain the skills and memories of all the souls it had slain.

"It's yours if you want it," Elora offered, placing a kiss upon Bray's chin.

Bray let her fingers drop and gathered up a discarded cloak from the ground. He wrapped it around the hilt of the sword before pulling it free from the corpse. It made a grating sound as the blade rubbed against ribs. Once the long sword was free, he bundled it up in the cloth.

"No," Bray replied, hefting the heavy weapon onto his shoulder. "The broadsword isn't a discipline I've mastered and I wouldn't just take it because it's a soul reaver."

"We'll bring it back with us. Maybe we can find somebody worthy – there are no more Shadojaks alive - apart from the twins of course."

"Quantala and Quantico?" Bray snorted. "They aligned themselves with the usurper Flek. No true Shadojak would put themselves before the people. You Elora, are the last Shadojak."

Elora offered him a sad smile, there were four more soul reavers taken from the previous Shadojaks and handed out to the meanest thugs who could wield them. They could be anywhere in the Empire now, doing who knew what damage.

"We better destroy these bodies before they're found," she said as she gripped the corpse before her around the collar of his jerkin and dragged him onto the fire.

Bray placed the broadsword down and began to gather the rest of the bodies. Weakest also helped to drag the carcasses closer to the pyre. Once done, they stood back and allowed the fire to do its work. Dark red flames burning clothes and blackening flesh. The smell was sickly sweet and made Elora feel nauseous although she noticed Weakest beginning to drool.

She watched as smoke curled around the mouth of the leader; open in a silent scream that only the dead would hear, wondering how many more bodies she would burn before this war was over. Unless Neptula had her way, then the world would be under water.

They gathered up the rest of the rubbish, clothing and weapons and threw them into the pyre. After the clearing was empty, Elora began to whisper to the flames, enticing the element of fire and it instantly brightened.

Hungry flames engulfed the dead, burning so hot the surrounding trees began to hiss with steam. The fire twisting in a violent whirling vortex and consuming everything within reach.

The maelstrom lasted until Elora stopped chanting. The flames gutting out with nothing left to burn, leaving them in total darkness. Darkness as black as the pile of ash at her feet.

"It's time to leave," she whispered, taking Bray's hand as they walked to where they had left their horses.

Daisy whinnied as they neared. Elora placed a calming hand along the mare's neck before mounting the Gypsy Vanna.

"I'll race you," Bray offered as he climbed upon his horse. "If I win you've got to run me a hot relaxing bath."

Elora knew he was trying to lighten the grim experience they had endured. "And if I beat you back?" she asked, raising an eyebrow.

Bray chuckled, his moss-green eyes alive with mischief. "Then you get to join me."

"Not fair," Elora laughed as she kicked Daisy into a canter.

They raced through the dark forest, Elora pressing her knees into her horse's flanks to spur her on. Her hair whipped in the wind as they darted between the trees and jumped roots and shrubs. They reached the bridleway together, Bray pushing his mount level with her own as he leaned over his saddle. Steam billowing from the horse's nostrils into the cold night.

Elora knew his thoroughbred was faster than her heavy-set hunter and guessed he was holding back to let her win, but as the inn came into view she slowed to allow him in front.

They broke into a trot as they passed the well before Bray turned back to face her, his smile lighting his gorgeous face.

"So," Elora said, matching his smile. "You beat me."

"Yep," he replied, beaming with delight. "You came second so you've got to run me a relaxing bath." He chuckled before continuing. "Don't worry, I'll let the runner-up join me."

Elora nodded towards the inn. "Weakest arrived first," she said, smiling at the bulworg who was panting by the door. "You'd better ask him if he wants your company in the bath, after you've run him one."

She laughed as Bray's grin fell from his lips. "Don't worry Elf boy, I'm sure Weakest isn't the bathing kind."

They walked the horses to the stables and groomed them before entering the inn, hand-in-hand.

It was close to midnight and the majority of the inn's occupants were in bed. Only Ejan and Ragna sat beside the open fire while Otholo strummed a soft melody from his lute. He paused as they entered.

"You smell of smoke. Have you been burning corpses again?" the bard asked.

"Aren't we always," Elora replied. "Only this time we've brought some friends back." And as if on cue, Captain Brindle stepped into the inn with the new arrivals. Weakest following in behind.

Elora gestured for them to sit down at the large table in the centre of the room, Ben's baby son sleeping peacefully in Nelly's arms. Zilabeth helped Teaselberry climb onto the tall chair where she stared around the room, her large eyes darting apprehensively at Weakest. As was Ben's.

"Does he follow you everywhere?" he asked, frowning at the bulworg.

"Pretty much, but he's of his own mind, he can leave if he wants to," Elora answered.

"Funny, I always thought you were a cat person."

Once they were settled, she introduced them to the others. Ragna and Ejan made them feel at home and set about preparing a meal.

"You can stay here tonight, tomorrow I'll take you to the Keep itself where we'll have a more permanent home for you," Elora explained.

"Permanent?" Otholo mocked. "You mean until the war reaches us?" His fingers began to pluck the strings of his instrument once again. "Unless we're all swimming."

"What does he mean?" Nelly asked, her eyebrows drawing together.

Elora felt like swatting the bard around the back of the head. "I'll explain things tomorrow. Tonight, you can rest."

And you won't be able to do that if I tell you what Neptula has planned for the world, she thought.

"Where's the prisoner?" Elora asked, changing the subject before more questions were asked.

"He's being locked in the dungeon with a guard on the door," Brindle answered. "He's not saying much now, but I'm sure he'll start talking after a few days down there."

Ejan and Ragna returned with plates of bread, cold meat and a flagon of ale. On their heels were Norgie and Gurple.

Gurple, always eager to meet new arrivals, bounded over to the table but halted when his gaze fell upon Teaselberry. Elora watched the two wood trolls stare at each other before they glanced away.

"Oh, another wood troll. How delightful," Norgie said as he introduced himself. "This is Gurple," he turned around to include his friend but he had already run from the room, the door slamming shut behind him.

Zilabeth chuckled, "Maybe he's a little shy. And you're being very quiet, Tease."

Teaselberry stared at the door Gurple had departed through and folded her arms.

"Love at first sight is as blinding as light," Otholo sang, picking a new tune. "-yet try as they might it will end with a fright."

"What's that supposed to mean?" Bray asked, helping himself to a tankard of ale.

Otholo shrugged. "Who can say? Some little ditties are wise and hold some hidden meaning, while others are just random words that rhyme."

"Nice guitar," Ben remarked, admiring Otholo's instrument.

"It's a lute," Otholo replied, "But thank you. Are you perhaps a man of the arts?"

Ben puffed his chest out proudly. "I'm a kind of bard myself."

Elora bit back the laugh she wanted to bark out as she shared a knowing look with Nelly. It had been months since she had endured Ben's attempts at singing.

"Maybe you could teach Otholo a thing or two," Elora chuckled. "But for tonight - what's left of it, I think you ought to rest. Tomorrow I'll show you around."

Elora awoke to the cry of a cockerel letting the inn know that morning had arrived. She rolled over and reached an arm out for Bray, but she was alone in bed. He must have risen early to check on the newcomers, she thought.

Pacing to the leaded window she stared out into the grey dawn, shaking the lingering remnants of a bad dream from her mind. The soul memories from her reaver still plagued her nightmares. Having to relive battles and fights from the swords previous owners was something that all Shadojaks accepted, yet she doubted she would ever get used to.

Frost coated the grounds outside. It clung to the well and cobbled courtyard, encrusted the picket fence and covered the willow by the frozen lake. It was hauntingly beautiful and as the sun began to rise above the black canopy of the forest, it cast everything in a shade of pink.

Movement brought Elora's attention to the corner of the stables where she saw Zilabeth, entering the forge. The tall woman had her long-tailed leather jacket buttoned up tight as she carefully opened the door with fingerless gloves.

Gathering her clothes, Elora threw a cloak around herself and rushed out into the crisp morning.

She found Zilabeth leaning against a battered anvil, tapping a hammer against her palm as she stared into the cold ashes of the fire pit. When her eyes fell on Elora she smiled.

"I don't know what I'm supposed to be doing," the descendant of Zalibut admitted, laying the hammer down carefully on the anvil. "I lost most of my specialist tools and equipment when my home fell into the river."

Elora recognised a sadness to Zilabeth's expression. "I can't pretend to know anything about being a metalsmith or inventions. But at the Keep there's and an army engineer that knows his way around tools and workshops. I'm sure if there's something you need, he can help."

Zilabeth sighed as she glanced around the dark forge. "I don't even know how I can help or why I was sent to you."

"Don't worry about it, maybe you'll have some inspiration once you've seen your workshop."

"This isn't it?" Zilabeth asked, opening her arms to the dark room.

Elora shook her head. "No, this is where Ragna and Jaygen make the shoes for the horses or nails to fix fences. When I was told to expect you, we began to create a proper working workshop and I'm sure you're going to like it."

Elora was glad to witness Zilabeth's face lighten. "Come, you've yet to experience one of Norgie's breakfasts. They're really something."

They entered the bar room as Norgie and Gurple was setting down plates on the large table. The smell of freshly baked bread and frying bacon drifted from the kitchen door. Elora knew that her mother and Ejan would be helping. Nelly already occupied one of the chairs, rocking her baby while chatting to Cathy who was pushing the cutlery out of reach of Genella; the baby was now able to sit up and wanted to grasp everything.

"How's your new room, Cathy?" Elora asked as they joined the women at the table.

"It's perfect," Cathy replied, wrestling a spoon out of Genella's fingers. "Smudge has been busy making everyone comfortable at the Keep. He's even made a nursery room for all the little ones to play in when the weather's not nice."

"Good, and I see you've met your new neighbour," Elora smiled at Nelly.

"That's the reason I came to the inn, to welcome the newcomers."

Norgie chuckled as he placed a large wheel of cheese beside a steaming pot of tea. "And my breakfast of course," he said.

"Of course," Cathy agreed, then startled as Gurple dropped a plate.

The wood troll's eyes widened as everyone's attention turned to him, including Teaselberry who had just entered the room.

"She won't bite," Zilabeth reassured him, as Gurple remained rooted to the spot, nervously wringing his paws within each other.

Teaselberry stepped closer to the table, her large koala-bear-like ears unfurling as she pulled a chair out. Elora noticed that the wood troll wouldn't glance at Gurple as Norgie began to brush the broken pottery into a bin. Her gaze wandered over everything else but skipped him entirely as if she couldn't see him at all. Yet as Gurple bashfully backed away and then padded from the room, she caught Teaselberry staring after him.

No sooner had the kitchen door closed than it burst open again. Ragna came stumbling out, a large board of crusty bread balanced in one arm while carrying an enormous tray of meats and eggs in the other.

"I said take one at a time, you five-bellied lout," Ejan bellowed from the kitchen.

Ragna set the food down on the table. "What's the point in doing two trips, wench?" he shouted back, although a grin was cracking his beard. He sat beside Cathy and tickled Genella under the chin, making her giggle.

Otholo sauntered into the room and joined them at the table as did Ben who sat next to Nelly. Bray came in behind, carrying an arm-load of logs. He placed one into the fireplace, sending a wave of sparks up the chimney before sitting down beside Elora.

"You left early," Elora broached, giving Bray a kiss on the cheek.

"Yeah, I've still to keep my Shaigun training up. I don't want to upset my Master," Bray replied as he cut himself a slice of cheese and began to eat.

Ben leaned closer. "What's a Shaigun?" he asked.

"He's like an apprentice who's training to be a Shadojak," Elora answered. "A warrior judge who protects the people and balances the wrongs."

"What, like the police or something, a good guy?" Ben asked.

Ragna chuckled. "Not always. Sometimes a situation calls for them to be really nasty."

"But only for the greater good," Bray added. "Cut out the rot to save the tree."

"Or burn the tree to save the forest," Elora corrected. "A Shadojak must solve the problem and be as ruthless as necessary. Even if a king needs to be executed."

Bray lay a hand on her thigh. "Or even a god."

"That's some badass dude," Ben said, shaking his head. "Wouldn't like to meet one. So, who is your master?"

Bray grinned. "Elora."

Ben's hand was on the way to picking an apple from a fruit bowl when he paused. "Oh."

"Don't worry," Elora laughed. "You're under my protection now. If you behave yourself, I won't need to do any…balancing."

"That's good to hear," Ben breathed as he grasped an apple. "I always thought you were a little odd." His eyes suddenly widened as he realised what he had said. "Odd in a good way."

Ejan and Athena joined them, each carrying more food and placed them down on the table before sitting.

"Get stuck in," Ejan offered as she broke apart the freshly baked bread, steam still rising from the warm crust.

Elora smiled as everyone helped themselves to the feast before them. It was clear from the way Ben, Nelly and Zilabeth piled their plates that they hadn't eaten a large meal in a while. Yet as big as their breakfasts were it paled in comparison to Ragna's, who had emptied his plate twice before Ejan slapped his hands away from filling a third.

"Sometimes I wonder if Odin sent you back to me because you ate all the food in the Halls of Valhalla," Ejan teased, rubbing her husband's belly.

Ragna laughed. "You're probably right," he admitted, pinching her cheek lovingly. "Although I don't remember much about the afterlife."

"You died?" Zilabeth asked, her elbows resting on the table as she leaned closer.

"I was killed twenty times over by the imperial guard. I died a Viking's death, steel in hand and fire in my belly. But Odin had other plans. There's a war coming – well it's already here and he wants me swinging my hammer to a bloody tune."

"War, with the Empire?" Ben asked.

Elora hadn't planned on explaining things to them, just yet. But now was as good a time as any, she supposed.

"Yes, a war with the Empire, with the small gods and in particular, with Neptula," she explained.

"The Sea Witch?" Zilabeth asked, incredulously. "But she is a god of the oceans. She can't harm us on land."

"She can and she will," Bray added. "She used Flek, once the Voice to the Shadojak Supreme, to kill the Emperor and sit himself on the throne. He is her puppet to make dance to whatever song she wants."

"And, that's not all. Her bigger plan is to rule this new world of Ethea by melting the ice caps and flooding the planet," Elora added. "A world of water."

"How?" Ben asked, placing a protective arm around Nelly and his son.

"With the help from other gods. Volcaneous is already manoeuvring his volcanos to the Antarctic, while Hades attacks the frozen lands of the north. His demons are breaking the ice into smaller blocks to be melted."

"And the Emperor know all this?" Zilabeth asked.

Elora shook her head. "No, he is a means to an end. Neptula is using him to hunt me down or at least keep me busy until she succeeds. Although, Flek is trying to bring some kind of order to the Empire, even if it is by an iron fist."

"Or a god-created one," Bray added.

Elora fixed Ben and Zilabeth with a hard stare. "Be under no illusion, Flek knows where to find us. It's only the fairy protection around Rams Keep that prevents his forces from entering – which they eventually will."

"You've certainly got your work cut out for you," Zilabeth said, a slender hand curling around her chin in thought. "Have you got any plans on how you're going to defeat them?"

Elora sighed. "No plans, but some ideas." She rose from the table, "Come, I'll show you your new workshop and living quarters."

Elora and Bray rode their horses along the frozen lane to the Keep. Zilabeth followed on behind, her cart rocking from side to side with Ben and Nelly wrapped in a blanket in the back, while Teaselberry snuggled up to the baby. Cathy also rode in the cart with them, explaining how people lived in the Keep, where they got the water or food from and where to go for clothes.

"It's magnificent," Zilabeth remarked when the gate house came into view. The imposing stone structure rose hundreds of feet above the canopy of the trees with tall battlements stretching out to either side.

Elora nodded. Smudge had done well at rebuilding Rams Keep. Using bricks and cement to construct the castle to something like its original size. He worked from the foundations and the outlining of the ruins to remodel the shape, and built with modern materials, using steel girders and reinforced concrete to strengthen the older stone work.

Bray waved out to the guards that stood atop the battlements, their rifles slung over shoulders within easy reach. They waved back then gave a signal to the gate guard who began to raise the heavy portcullis.

Passing below the ancient iron mechanism, Elora always felt a little apprehensive. The gate weighed around eight tonnes and would crush anybody should it fall.

No sooner were they through than the gate was lowered into place, sealing them inside with a solid thunk as it settled once again into the ground. Elora nodded to the four huge grimbles whose job it was to winch the portcullis open. They grunted back, huge tusks protruding below boar-like snouts.

"Are those part of the Dark Army?" Zilabeth asked, her mouth open as she gazed at the grimbles who now stood back to attention, tall pikes grasped in meaty green fingers.

"Yeah," admitted Elora as she raised her arms to the Keep in general. "It is only with the help of the dark forces that this was built so swiftly."

Elora could see how imposing it may seem to somebody new to the place. Rock trolls patrolled along the top of the twenty-foot-tall wall that ran the entire perimeter of the Keep. Bulworgs walking along-side them, sniffing the air for any threat. Scraw-harpies circled high above the tallest towers, scanning the surrounding grounds which were constantly being watched by pockets of soldiers who were spread out through the thick forest. Nothing could get close without being spotted and nothing could escape without her knowing about it. She didn't want any of the Dark Army deserting and wandering around Ethea. They were trained and seasoned killers, the lot of them.

They rode along a cobbled pathway that wound around a central well. Three other paths fed from the other large towers which were situated to each corner of the Keep and crossed at the same place. To either side of the paths were a network of barracks, shops and work houses. A patchwork of materials were used for the roofs; thatched straw gave way to tiles which fed onto walkways and narrow bridges that spanned between the higher structures. Stone staircases spiralled around wooden posts that were fixed into the ground, supporting pipework which carried water from the natural spring to the homes and main hall.

They passed a large blacksmith's shop, a dwarf sat outside sharpening a sword against a thick stone wheel. Sparks flew from the metal as an ogre crouched over a connecting cog, turning the gears with a large handle. He paused, scratching one of the horns which sprouted from a flat forehead as it grinned at them. His yellow eyes sparkling with mischief as it took them in.

"Don't stop turning, you clumsy oath," the dwarf snapped at the ogre.

The ogre cringed away from the sharp tongue of the blacksmith, who was easily four times smaller. He stuck a thick bottom lip out in concentration and began turning the sharpening stone once again.

Ben glared after them. "But, they're monsters," he exclaimed as the cart came to a halt next to a courtyard that sat in the middle of a horseshoe-shaped building.

"I can't argue that fact," Elora admitted as she dismounted and handed her reins to a soldier dressed in black boiled leather. "The entire Dark Army is mine to command, I'm the Queen of Darkness after all. But it will be my monsters, fiends and demons that will save this world and the people in it."

She waited until they all disembarked the cart before walking towards the central door of the building complex.

"This is your new home," she explained, holding the door open for them. "You'll have your own private quarters, a comfortable bed and running water. Cathy will help get you settled in and show you around."

"Thank you," Nelly said and followed Cathy into the three storey high structure.

Ben halted on the threshold. "I didn't mean anything by calling them monsters," he said sheepishly.

Elora chuckled. "They are what they are," she said and gave him a final hug before he disappeared inside.

"I'm not living here?" Zilabeth asked as she stared after her friends.

"No," Elora replied as she gestured for her to follow. "We thought you might like your own space, a little closer to your workshop."

They walked to the back of the complex and down a small staircase that gave way to another cobbled courtyard. A separate well stood in the middle of the stone ground and beyond loomed a lone tower. It wasn't as tall as the Keep's towers on the outer wall but was still imposing.

"Your sleeping quarters will be in there," Elora explained, pointing to the upper section of the tower. "Smudge, our engineer, lives on the ground floor."

To one side of the tower lay a hangar-like barn, its wide doors open, revealing row upon row of shelves inside.

Elora entered and found Smudge wheeling in two large acetylene bottles and placing the tall canisters in the corner. When he noticed them he smiled and approached, wiping his filthy hands against his apron before taking out a notepad and pencil and jotting something down.

"Zilabeth, let me introduce you to Smudge, our chief engineer and the man behind rebuilding Rams Keep," Elora said.

"I didn't do it alone," Smudge admitted. "If it wasn't for trolls and grimbles, we would never have lifted those girders into the bigger towers. And the thousands of men who lay brick by…"

"Yes," Bray interrupted. "But it was you who was in charge."

Smudge reluctantly shrugged.

"Smudge, this is Zilabeth. She'll be taking over the workshop," Elora explained.

"Oh," Smudge replied, wiping his hand once again before shaking Zilabeth's. "Glad to meet you. I hope we catered for everything. If we've missed something just say and I'll try my best to get it for you."

"Thank you," Zilabeth replied as she gazed around the room with wide eyes.

Teaselberry's mouth fell open as they slowly walked around the shelves full of springs, cogs and gears of all sizes – nuts and bolts, screws, pins and nails, copper wiring curled and hung on the wall on pegs next to piping and plastic tubing. Engine parts were stacked up next to sheets of metal and plastics. The pair glanced inside boxes and ran fingers along worktops and over tools and equipment.

"I don't know what to say," Zilabeth admitted. "This place is amazing." She slowly turned around, a subtle frown creasing her brow. "Yet I fail to see a forge."

Elora smiled. "Follow me," she said, leading the woman and the wood troll to the rear of the workshop.

The entire back wall of the room was a sliding door on steel runners set into the ground. Elora nodded to Bray and he grasped a silver bar and slid the door open. Runes that were etched around the frame suddenly glowed white and crackled with static.

Red light shone through the crack in the opening, lighting up Zilabeth's face. A sudden wave of dry heat followed, filling the room as the door was fully opened.

From his apron, Smudge produced two identical stopwatches. They were old and relied on springs that needed to be wound. He passed one to Elora and kept hold of the other.

"Time works differently in the Shadowlands," Elora explained as she and Smudge set the stopwatches going at the same time. "Come, let me show you the rest of your workshop."

She stepped through the sliding door and into the Shadowlands. Zilabeth and Teaselberry were close on her heel, their mouths still agape as they soaked up the vast scenery before them.

They emerged onto a large stone platform that had been cut into a mountainside, high above the cracked plains that spread out in all direction. A sea of black bodies covered the vista below; the Dark Army as they waited patiently for a war they knew was coming.

Wind tore up the mountainside and buffeted around the stone platform, coating red dust upon the many steel tables and forming drifts against several cars and vans that Elora had stored to salvage metal from.

Beyond the vehicles was a large brick structure, oval in shape and had a thick square base. It was twice as tall as Bray with a large opening and a tall fluted chimney. Elora approached it and pulled a cord that was attached to the steel opening. It slid down to reveal a vast fire pit.

Zilabeth stuck her head inside. "Amazing," she said, her words echoing inside the structure. "But why is there a hole in the other side?"

"This forge is like no other," Bray explained. "It's flamed by dragon fire."

"Dagon fire?" Teaselberry asked, her bulbous eyes bulging wider.

Elora had already taken a large hammer from the workshop, just for this demonstration. She held it up for them to see, before handing it to the wood troll.

"This was made in a factory on Earth before the merge. It's a strong solid steel. Put it in the pit," she gestured.

Teaselberry reached inside the forge, standing on the tips of her paws as she placed the hammer down. Once she was done, Elora released the cord and the steel shutter came down.

"Grycul?" Elora whispered, questing with her mind and finding the dragon close by.

"Yes, my Queen," the dragon replied, already knowing what Elora wanted her to do as their minds were linked.

Grycul had been resting on a ledge below the stone platform, hidden from view. Yet Elora knew where she was as she could see through the dragon's eyes and when she raised her large reptilian head, she startled the small group gathered beside the forge. Zilabeth gasped as Teaselberry stepped back and tripped over Bray's feet. He caught her before she fell.

Elora sensed that Grycul had intended to make them jump and experienced the satisfaction the dragon felt.

"That was mean," Elora scolded, although she couldn't help but grin. The colossus beast was a thing of wonder. Huge dark green scales reflecting the brightness from the sky as she yawned, displaying large sharp teeth. "Now put your fire to the forge, if you please."

Grycul proudly nodded before filling her lungs with air. Then putting her mouth close to the opening on her side of the large oven, she breathed fire into the pit.

Black smoke instantly billowed out of the flute-shaped chimney as white flames licked the top. Even through the steel shutter Elora felt a wall of heat hit her. She couldn't imagine the temperature inside.

Once her breath was expelled, Grycul craned her head back over. She treated the group with a glare of indifference before lowering herself back to the ledge she was perched on.

Bray pulled on a thick pair of leather gloves and pulled the shutter door open. Black smoke spiralling out into the baking air as he reached inside and pulled out a thick bowl-shaped vessel with liquid metal bubbling at its centre.

"The hammer?" Zilabeth asked amazed.

"Yeah. Grycul's fire will melt anything you put inside," Bray replied, fishing out the blackened wood of the handle and tossing it onto the ground.

"And the bowl?"

Elora tapped the side of the large green dish. "It's one of the dragon's scales. From her leg I think. It's the only material that is resistant to the heat."

"It's perfect," the inventor replied as she stared around the platform. "I only wish I knew what it was I'm supposed to be creating."

"Don't worry, it'll come to you," Elora reassured her, walking towards a large cavern carved out of the mountain. "Let me show you something else."

Inside the cavern she placed her fingers against a lantern and concentrated on the element of fire. She felt heat leave her fingertip and the wick of the lamp suddenly flamed, flooding the cavern with light.

Before them were shelves full of charts, books and scrolls. A large wooden desk was set into the corner, writing equipment and drawing apparatus neatly stored in draws and trays. Elora lay her hand against a comfortable chair. "It would be best if you did any thinking and planning in here or at least in the Shadowlands."

"Why?"

"Time is still against us. We don't know when Flek will attack, but I doubt he's going to wait for long. While Neptula is already putting things into motion. In here," Elora indicated to the cavern and the outside platform. "Time works differently."

Bray nodded. "Smudge will be exactly where we left him on the other side of the gate, only a few seconds will have passed for him."

"How very peculiar," Zilabeth remarked, "so I could spend weeks in here and only hours would have ticked by on Ethea?"

"Exactly, time is relevant to where you are," Elora explained. "And in here you won't feel hungry, thirsty or tired. That's why my father...that's why Solarius created it. A realm where he could build the Dark Army over thousands of years without it ever ageing."

"Incredible," Zilabeth chuckled, seemingly delighted at the prospect.

"Of course, when you come back into Rams Keep you will need a place to sleep," Elora said as she made her way out of the cavern, back across the platform and through the gate into Rams Keep.

Smudge was still standing in the same position in the workshop, staring at the stopwatch.

"Five seconds," the engineer said.

Elora pressed the button on her stopwatch and handed it to Zilabeth.

"Twenty-seven minutes?" the inventor said, eyes going wide. "Incredible."

"Incredible," Elora agreed. "And our best weapon against fighting Neptula and the Empire. I hope you find everything you need - if not, Smudge here will help out."

"I don't know what to say," Zilabeth said, her face brimming with excitement as she turned to Teaselberry. "What do you think, Tease?"

The wood troll's grin spread from ear to ear as she stared around the workshop. "When do me tart?"

"We can start straight away," Zilabeth laughed then embraced Elora. "This is perfect."

"Great," Elora replied, smiling at the pair. "And it seems your other things have arrived."

Elora stood aside as two grimbles pulled Zilabeth's old cart and belongings into the workshop. The inventor reached into the back and grasped a thick utility belt and strapped it around her waist before handing Teaselberry a smaller one with matching tools. They were both grinning as they each pulled a hammer from their belts and clinked them together.

"Come Tease, we've got a new project," Zilabeth said excitedly as they marched purposefully back through the sliding door and into the Shadowlands.

"She's keen," Smudge commented as he smiled after the inventor.

"Yeah," Elora agreed. "I think she's had an idea."

She weaved an arm through Bray's and they both left the workshop. Stepping back out into the cold and the snow which had begun to fall from the grey sky.

2

Skagwangles

The air smelt bad and tasted worse. The stench of humans and land-beasts permeated the upper part of the well they were climbing and seeped into Timoshi's gills. He hated humans and despised all things that lived out of water – it was wrong but the Goddess Neptula would put that right.

His webbed fingers clung to the brick wall of the well, searching for purchase in the green slime that had formed over thousands of years. Long nails digging into the ancient mortar as he climbed hand-over-hand to the surface; his tentacles curling around the well's bucket and rope. His forked tongue passing eagerly over his many rows of teeth as a human unknowingly began to hoist him up.

The membrane which covered his eyes thickened as Timoshi touched the daylight. He sensed the human struggling with the unsuspecting weight, tugging hard at the rope. He watched him lean into the opening above, the land-man reaching to grasp the bucket itself.

Timoshi wrapped a tentacle around the human's neck and yanked him into the well. The movement so swift that the land-man was unable to scream.

He grinned as the body fell passed and splashed into the dark water. Timoshi's brother skagwangles caught him and dragged him deeper into the watery depths. Starving the human of air, crushing him and then tearing into his blood-rich flesh. It had been a long while since Timoshi had tasted human, but he would need to wait a little longer. First he would see the mission through.

The journey to Rams Keep had been far - swimming through an ocean and two seas, then through a river system to the stream and finally the spring which fed into the well. He longed to be back in the deep blue but Neptula wanted her message delivered to the daughter of Chaos. The message and an offering.

The putrid atmosphere above the well attacked his senses as he focused on the other land-beasts. He peered above the well's rim and counted three other humans. A soldier, a woman and a human pup that wriggled in her arms, all with their backs to him.

Tall pointed land-buildings surrounded them with cobbles stone pathways leading off in four directions. Timoshi thought he saw taller tower-like structures further away but they appeared as shapeless smudges as his vision weakened when he was out of the water. And the longer he remained in the foul air, the worse it would get.

He checked for any further threat and when he saw none produced his blowpipe. Aiming the pipe at the soldier, he put his drying lips to the end and blew.

The dart hit the land-man in the neck and he instantly fell to the snow-covered ground. The puffer fish poison would have reacted immediately, stopping his heart and killing him outright.

The woman, still oblivious to Timoshi's presence, set her pup on the ground and rushed to the soldier in a futile attempt at helping him.

This was his opportunity.

Silently, Timoshi slipped over the rim of the well, his tentacles bunching and sliding over the cold snow as he reached out and grasped the wriggling pup.

It screamed in his arms, hurting his ears and alerting the mother. She instantly dropped the soldier's limp wrist as she turned to them.

"Genella!" she cried, rushing towards him.

Timoshi remained calm, smelling the fear from the female as she tried to snatch her offspring back. With a tentacle, he shoved hard against her and sent her reeling into the snow.

"Bring me the daughter of Solarius and I won't harm the child," Timoshi ordered, the human words feeling wrong inside his mouth.

The woman rose on unsteady legs and attempted to reach once again for her child, but two of his brothers chose that time to climb from the well and stand beside him. Each grasping a sharp trident.

"Go now and I promise not to hurt the baby," Timoshi continued, sweeping his webbed fingers over the pup's head as he grinned at the mother; displaying his many rows of teeth.

Other beasts from around the Keep had heard the commotion and had come to investigate. Bulworgs, men, grimbles and dwarves. Stinking creatures of the air the lot of them. All with bristling weapons and death in their gazes. He focused his eyes on the panicked mother before him.

"Bring me Elora, Queen of the Dark Army and you will have your child back," he offered, then addressed the soldiers who began to surround them. "I am a messenger sent by the Goddess Neptula. We are not enemies. Yet any harm that befalls me will be considered an act of war."

The woman made a final attempt at reaching for her child, but was ushered out of the way by tall soldier that pointed a long-barrelled cannon at him.

"She's at the inn," the soldier told the mother. "Take a horse from the stable and go."

"But…" the female began, tears now running down her cheeks, yet the soldier placed a hand against her arm.

"Go, I'll watch Genella. If he so much as raises his voice, I'll put a bullet in his skull, war or not," the soldier explained, bringing his weapon to bear and aiming down the long pipe.

Unsatisfied, yet unable to do anything else, the mother picked up her skirts and began to run away from the crowd.

"Pudding, go with her," ordered the soldier.

"Yes, sir," replied another and chased after the woman.

Timoshi sensed his brothers tense as they gripped tighter to their tridents, tentacles spreading wide, ready to strike.

"Steady," Timoshi ordered them in his own tongue. "These stupid land-beasts won't attack while we hold this pup. They're too weak and pathetic."

His brothers agreed, chuckling as they grimaced at the growing crowd, although Timoshi recognised the hate from the soldier holding the gun as he closed the eye lids of the man he had killed with the poisoned dart. He may be full of hate but he was still weak, he thought as he trailed a wet finger over the pup's head and set the baby to screaming for her mother.

Elora set her mug of tea down and placed her hands on the smooth surface of the table. She listened to the logs crackling in the fireplace as they spat sparks up the chimney, Weakest lying beside it soaking up the heat, his head resting on huge paws. The Vikings and Bray sat at the table with her, waiting for her to come to a decision.

"I still think we should wait for The Green Man to make his appearance," she suggested.

Ragna sat opposite, his huge fingers curling around the beads in his beard as he shook his head.

"And if he doesn't come? It won't be easy making the clans work together. The sooner I can reach the north the better prepared they'll be," Ragna explained.

Elora knew the Viking was right, yet didn't want to make a move until she knew where all her allies were. Not knowing how The Green Man would help was also another mystery. That was of course, if he turned up at all.

She leaned back into her chair and felt Bray's arm slide around her as he joined her at the table.

"Maybe Ragna's right," Bray offered. "Small gods are unpredictable at the best of times. It may even be that The Green Man has aligned himself with Neptula."

Elora didn't want to think about that. She had too many enemies to begin with, without adding another god to the war against her.

It was Ragna that had suggested taking Ejan and Jaygen and heading north to align the Nordic clans. Vikings have a strong dislike for the Empire and he believes they'll come together to fight against them, although they may not align themselves with the Dark Army.

Through the eyes of scraw-harpies, Elora had seen the demons and golems that Hades was summoning to the Arctic Circle. They numbered in the hundreds of thousands and beginning to cut into the great ice shelves and forming rivers from blocks they had already melted.

Elora knew that she commanded the largest army the worlds had ever known, but if she split them in two to defeat both gods at Ethea's poles, it may leave her exposed if Flek brought the Empire to Rams Keep. Not to mention whatever Neptula had planned. If Ragna succeeded in uniting the clans it would take some of the pressure away from her.

"Can you wait a few more days?" she asked.

Ragna puffed his cheeks out and blew through his lips. "Can we afford those few days? We're in no better position than what we were last month or the month before that. And Zilabeth is yet to create this machine or whatever it is that will help us."

"She will," Elora said firmly, wishing she felt as confident as she sounded. The inventor had spent a lot of time inside her workshop, designing and crafting, testing and scrapping. But so far, the only thing practical that has been produced was a large steel bin that Zilabeth apply named the 'chuckit-bucket,' which she used to throw bits and ends in that she felt were useful.

"And Jaygen?" she continued. "Is he as keen to leave?"

Ejan nodded. "He's never been to the north before. Never been amongst his own people. It will do him good."

Elora couldn't argue with that, but if Jaygen left, so did Grimwolf.

"And we still don't know what's going on with the Empire," she said, attempting to change the subject. "The soldier we captured a couple of days ago, still isn't talking."

"You want me to tickle him?" Ragna asked, his large hazel eyes sparkling with mischief.

Elora chuckled. "No, your kind of tickling would probably break his face up so he wouldn't be able to talk."

Weakest suddenly raised his head, ears pricking up as he turned towards the door and the sound of horses as they clattered into the courtyard outside.

A moment later the door was flung open and Cathy stumbled into the bar room with Pudding at her heels. The woman was red-faced, tears running down her cheeks as she fell to her knees.

Elora rose from the table and went to her. "What is it Cathy? What's happened?" she asked as she knelt beside her.

"They've got Genella," Cathy stuttered between sobs. "Horrible creatures at the Keep. They climbed out of the well and killed a soldier, then snatched my baby." Cathy squeezed Elora's hand, panic thick in her voice. "They want to see you or they'll hurt her."

Elora glanced at Pudding, the large soldier nodding, his expression solemn. "It's true. Captain Brindle is there, but won't react until you arrive."

"How many?" Ragna asked as he reached for his war hammer.

"Only three," Pudding replied. "Ugly bloody things. They've got octopus-like tentacles but also a pair of arms."

"Skagwangles," Bray suggested. "They belong to Neptula."

Elora searched for the memory that was provided by the soul blade. She only touched her thoughts before the image of a skagwangle came to her mind.

Ruthless, uncaring and savage. The skagwangles could survive out of water for a few hours, only needing to return to hydrate their scaly skin. The sea creatures were spawns of Neptula, bred in their pods that numbered in the hundreds. And the Sea Witch could have tens of thousands of these aquatic soldiers. Maybe more.

"I promise you, I will not let any harm come to Genella," Elora reassured her, then leaving the grieving mother in the capable hands of Ejan, she ran out of the inn.

She cast a glance at the horses that Cathy and Pudding had ridden from the Keep, but it was clear that they had been pushed hard, snorting great plumes of vapour from wide nostrils. Elora raced passed them and pushed herself into a sprint, hearing the inn door clatter open as others came to join her.

By the time she was out of the courtyard she had reduced herself to smoke and began to spiral down the lane, gliding above the frozen dirt and weaving between the trees and shrubs as she cut across the bends.

She travelled faster than Bray and Ragna who had mounted the horses and come after her, but Weakest kept pace; the bulworg bounding across the ground and appearing to gain speed.

Elora hit a pocket of fog that had formed from the cold air. It slowed her progress as her smoke form found it hard to penetrate and instead she attempted to flow around the obstacle. Yet when she collided with it, her body began to materialise momentarily before becoming smoke once again.

The thudding hooves of the following horses grew louder as her progress was slowed by more fog. She glanced ahead and saw a wall of it, growing thicker amongst the trees and blocking the view ahead.

Elora became solid as she entered the vapour, sprinting through the cold wall and losing ground to the bulworg. She felt desperate, the thoughts of Genella in the hands of the skagwangles stoking her anger.

Weakest leapt ahead and as he passed he nudged her with his head. "Ride," he growled.

Elora dodged to the left, jumped against the low branch of an oak and vaulted onto the bulworg's back.

She clung to his fur as Weakest sped up. He charged faster than a racehorse as he darted lithely through the fog, ducking below any branches and bounding over tree roots and bushes.

It wasn't long before the Keep came into view. The portcullis was already raised as Weakest pounded across the cobbles and through the heavy gate. They rushed through the small citadel, the people jumping out of their way until they reached the growing crowd that had gathered around the well.

"Make way for the Queen," a rock troll bellowed as he noticed their approach.

The crowd parted, leaving them a clear path to the skagwangles, Captain Brindle aiming his rifle at the one holding the baby.

Before Weakest halted she had already launched herself from his back, drawing her soul reaver from her smuggler's pouch as she landed before the spawn of Neptula.

Two of the skagwangles levelled sharp tridents as she approached, yet made no move to throw them - awaiting the command from the creature in the middle, his arms holding Genella and a wicked grin displaying his teeth.

"Elora, daughter of Chaos, I presume," the leader said, his voice cracking as if dry and parched.

Elora raised her sword and pressed the point against the wet ribcage of the skagwangle, his many tentacles curling and weaving about the snow covered floor – always moving and shifting, turning and writhing within each other. She gave the briefest of glances at the baby that cried in his arms, her bottom lip sticking out as she paused wailing, seeing somebody she recognised. She raised her chubby little arms towards Elora, wanting to be taken away from the foul smelling stranger, Elora offered her a smile as she spoke softly to the Skagwangle.

"Give me the baby or I'll burn you where you stand," she threatened in a soothing voice, so as not to alarm Genella.

The skagwangle's grin grew wider as his long webbed fingers stroked the child's head.

"My name is Timoshi. I am but a messenger. If you harm me it would be considered an act of war against Neptula," he explained, regarding her with contempt.

Elora recognised a smugness in his black shark-like eyes and fought the temptation to run her blade through his chest. She knew the violent tendencies belonged to that other her and slowly breathed in, to calm her rising anger.

"As a token of trust, I will hand you the child," the messenger offered, whilst holding the wriggling Genella out to her.

Reluctantly Elora slipped her sword away and grasped the baby who instantly buried her head into the crook of her neck while her fingers grasped her hair.

From behind, she felt the crowd part once again as Bray and Ragna arrived, their sword and hammer already on display as they stood beside her, glaring at the sea-beasts.

"A trust for a trust," continued the skagwangle, a mocking smile parting his lipless mouth as his ever working gills fluttered behind the holes he had for ears. "Now order your men to lower their weapons."

Elora turned to Bray and nodded. He lowered the tip of this blade to the ground but kept a firm grasp of it. She then placed Genella in the huge Viking's arms, forcing him to set his hammer down.

"Take her to Cathy, I want her out of harm's way," she ordered, thinking that giving Ragna this task would be safer for all, knowing that the Norseman would be itching for a fight and ready to swing the Fist of the North.

Ragna held the baby, who began to tug at his beard and sighed. "But I would rather…" he began.

"Cathy will be worried and besides," she opened her arms to the ever growing crowds around them. "I think they're pretty much outnumbered."

"Tis, a shame. The Fist hasn't been bloodied in a while," Ragna remarked. He heaved the hammer onto his shoulder, while Genella sat in his other arm, hiding her face beneath his beard. He gave a final glance to the skagwangles then began to stride though the crowd, his tall frame towering above the rest.

Once he had gone Elora returned her attention to the water creatures. "What is the message you've been sent to deliver?" she asked, her fingers hovering above her smuggler's pouch.

The skagwangle's chest seemed to rise as he straightened his back. "The Goddess Neptula wishes to offer you an olive branch," he croaked. "She offers you peace and a safe sanctuary for you and your followers."

"How very generous," Elora chuckled, arguing with her inner self not to wrap her fingers around his throat and choke the life from the foul creature. "And what of the rest of Ethea's population? Will she cease her attempts at melting the ice shelves to create a world of water?"

Timoshi laughed. "She will not. Ethea is destined to be a world beneath the waves. Yet the Goddess has seen fit to offer you a place in the highlands; an oasis where you may live out your existence, free from war, from the Empire and from a watery grave."

"And kill everyone else?" Bray asked, the point of his sword rising once again from the snow. "What about the false Emperor, does he not serve the Sea Witch?"

"He is a pathetic puppet, nothing more. His use has long been passed. They will all inevitably die. What land-dwellers can survive without land?" The messenger asked rhetorically before diverting his attention back to Elora. "The Goddess Neptula has seen it in her heart that you may survive. Never let it be said that she is not compassionate. She could drown you, with every other air breathing creature on this planet, but she has given you this one chance." He held up a webbed hand, open so the blue membrane in between stretched to make the skin transparent. "In honour of your father, Solarius. Don't accept the offer and…" he snapped his hands closed into a fist. "You will perish and be food for my brethren."

The crowd of men, bulworgs, grimbles and trolls became silent as they listened to the words. Even a grumpkin had sidled to the front, his fists pushed up into his sagging face to stop it from flopping from his skull.

Elora glanced around at her people. The Dark Army had been created for war, for violence and each and every one of them would die for her if she asked it. Intent on evil with a blackness in their hearts they were some of the nastiest, foulest beings on Ethea, but they were hers.

She stepped closer to the skagwangle, his slit of a mouth still fixed in an annoying smirk, and placed an arm around his clammy shoulders; her fingers brushing over cold scales as she mimicked his smile.

Elora gently shifted his body as she inclined her head to the dead soldier on the ground, the dart still visible in his neck.

"You say that if I hurt you in any way it would be an act of war?" she asked, keeping her voice as soft as the snow that began to float down, to lay across the dead body.

"It would be in the eyes of my Goddess, I am but a messenger," the skagwangle said, his smirk slowly sinking as he was led away from the well.

"Interesting," Elora remarked, feeling her anger begin to rise and this time she allowed it to go unchecked. She witnessed the reflection of her violet eyes upon his scales as they began to turn red. "Yet you have killed one of my men."

"Two," Captain Brindle added as he lifted his head above his rifle. "They dragged another into the well before they climbed out."

"Two," Elora repeated, now speaking sickly sweet. "You've killed two of my men and that, in my eyes, is an act of war."

Increasing the pressure on his shoulder Elora whispered to the element of fire and felt an intense heat leave her hand.

Flashing his teeth, the messenger suddenly felt the pain as flames began to devour his flesh - scales turning black as they peeled away, the stench of cooking fish filling the air.

As the water-beast began to scream his brothers moved. They came at her, rising their tridents before them as they shouted in their own tongue. The steel of their three pronged weapons sharpened to razor points.

With a subtle nod of her head, her army moved as one.

Bray dodged below a trident and severed the arm that held it, closely followed by Weakest who pounced upon the creature to bury his fangs into the rubbery throat.

Simultaneously there were several rifle shots and an axe hurled at the remaining skagwangle. He died before his hole-filled body hit the ground. Dark green blood oozing from a hundred different wounds spread into the white snow.

With his brethren dead, Elora removed her hand from the messenger's burning shoulder and turned him around to face her, the bodies of his comrades lying dead at her feet. Thick tentacles spread in all directions like lifeless eels.

"She will kill you, crush your…" Timoshi stammered, the words so cracked and dry that it sounded like sheets of sandpaper being rubbed together.

"No, she won't," Elora cut in, shoving the messenger towards the well where he slammed into the old stonework. He must have jarred his teeth and bitten his own mouth as dark green blood ran down the lipless slit. "I, will kill her."

Timoshi spat blood as his webbed hand fumbled at his wound. "She will destroy you all. The tide of death is coming and nothing can stop it."

Elora watched him struggle over the wall, slippery tentacles curling around the stone and the winding mechanism as he pulled himself into the hole.

He hung suspended for a moment, his shark eyes regarding her with hate. "There are monsters of the deep that will be rising to drag you down. Leviathans are only a small part of Neptula's army. And the Goddess has created her own dragons that will quench Grycul's fire. The sea will conquer this world and your Dark Army."

Elora put her hands against the windlass that secured the bucket and leaned towards Timoshi, until her face was within inches of his foul breath. "Darkness spans the deepest of depths, beneath the waves," she said, glowering at him and matching his hatred. "And wherever the darkness whispers my name, Chaos will be there."

Elora released the catch on the windlass and watched as the bucket suddenly dropped, the added weight of the skagwangle causing the pulley to spin wildly.

His body crashed into the water in a tangle of limbs and tentacles. Timoshi thrashed around to right himself before giving her a final accusing glance. Then slipped from view leaving only a trail of inky blood.

Bray joined her at the well and put a hand upon hers. "We should have killed him," he said.

"It wouldn't have mattered," Elora replied, squeezing his hand. "The war has already begun. This was her way of attempting to keep me out of the way. But it only proves that she feels threatened."

She turned from the well and began to pace back the way they had come, feeding an arm through Bray's as the crowds parted for them. "It's time to put our plans into action."

"Ragna?" Bray asked.

"Yes, Ragna can leave tonight," she replied. "But first, I've got a prisoner to interrogate."

She paused beside the grumpkin, who was having trouble holding his bloated nose in place. The hideous creature cowed beneath her gaze, kneeling like a dog before a cruel master.

Elora despised grumpkins. They were the lowliest, foulest most devious of her father's creations. But they were hers. She had thought of executing them all, yet on some level felt guilt as the grumpkins never asked to be created. Instead she had put them all under supervision and any that were caught taking the skins of others would be killed on the spot.

That also came with problems as grumpkins needed fresh skins to stay alive, replacing the ones they were wearing as they rotted away. Forcing them to stay in the Shadowlands made it a little easier. Their flesh stayed in the same condition as when they entered and wouldn't age. Although some, like the creature at her feet, had rotting flesh to begin with.

"Rise," she ordered him.

The grumpkin rose on unsteady legs, his entire body shaking with fear and causing his puckered skin to shift until one of his eyes stared through his decaying nostrils.

Elora nodded towards the bodies of the skagwangles that had begun to freeze on the icy ground. "Harvest what you can from them," she said, imagining what a grumpkin might look like with rubbery scaly flesh and tentacles hanging from them. She shuddered at the mental image.

What was left of the grumpkin's face formed an elongated frown as her words sunk in. Then he bowed low, lank hair brushing the snow. "My Queen is truly great," he said. "This grumpkin is honoured."

Elora watched him hobble over to the dead sea creatures, a knife having already found his bloated hand. "Don't cut them up here," she snapped, beginning to walk away. "Bring the bodies to the dungeons. We have need of a demonstration."

The grumpkin's face was now shifting from startled, to confused and ending with nothing remotely in between. He shrugged, then pointing at the closest grimble, ordered him to carry the bodies and follow on.

"What are you doing?" Bray asked, seeming amused.

Elora could only smile as she paced away from the well towards the tower which held the prisoner. A gruesome line of her underlings following. A boar-headed monster carrying two octopus-like fiends under thick green arms, being pushed around by a rotting grumpkin. Weakest padding by her side as hundreds of the Dark Army's finest watched on from the many windows and battlements. Had she become the daughter of Chaos unintentionally? She felt like the old Elora, yet she was Queen of the darkest creatures to ever roam Earth.

"I've got a prisoner to interrogate."

3

Casters, Binders and a Warlock

The prisoner was shackled by the wrists and ankles. Thick steel bracelets attached to chains and secured to the dungeon walls. He sat on a stool, head hung low and shaking from fatigue although his bruised face was set in grim determination.

"He still hasn't talked," the guard informed her as he unlocked the heavy door.

"I'm not surprised," Bray whispered so only Elora could here. "He's a Shade or was. The training involves dealing with torture, should they ever be captured."

Elora inclined her head as she swept into the dark cell. "He hasn't been tortured…yet," she said as she drew up another stool and placed it directly in front of the prisoner.

She sat down and folded her arms, glowering at the former soldier they had captured while rescuing Ben and Zilabeth.

His clothes were dirty, greasy hair matted and he gave off the most dreadful smell. Elora realised that he had been given barely enough water to survive and constantly bombarded with questions while denied sleep. The man before her was ready to collapse, but not broken.

She wanted answers from him, a clue as to what was happening outside the Keep and the Empire's intentions. The incident with the skagwangle only added to the urgency. It was time to get rough, although she hated the prospect of having to torture somebody who was merely following orders – however cruel their actions had been.

Captain Brindle stepped into the dungeon, followed by the grumpkin, his eager hands rubbing together as his face sagged into a wicked grin.

"Sets them down here," the shrivelled little man ordered, pointing to a space on the floor beside the prisoner.

The grimble pushed into the cell, breaking the arm of a dead sea creature as he squeezed through the opening, then dropped his gruesome bundles on the ground. The bodies fell with a wet thud, tentacles slick with green blood as they slipped over one another like eels before settling.

Elora watched the prisoner as he turned his head to stare at the dead creatures before glowering at her.

"What is this?" he demanded, his dirty face screwing into disdain.

"Take a look," she replied. "This is the true enemy of the Empire. Creatures of the Sea Witch, Neptula."

The prisoner shook his head. "Neptula has sworn to protect the Empire, she serves the Emperor."

"No, she serves herself," Elora explained. "She used Flek to bring Earth and Thea together so she could flood the world."

"Lies," the prisoner spat. "It was you who joined the worlds, you that has killed millions and made many more suffer. It is you who is the daughter of Chaos." He glanced at the grumpkin and turned his nose up in revulsion. "Why else would you be commanding these creatures of the Dark Army?"

Elora sighed. "I brought the worlds together. That much is true. But I was forced and it was only made possible through the actions of both Neptula and your false Emperor, Flek."

"Lies," the prisoner repeated.

"Believe what you want, it doesn't matter. I've got a world to save and need answers and very soon."

She inclined her head to the grumpkin and nodded.

The grumpkin drew a sharp knife from his belt. It was long and thin with a curved blade. It was a knife for delicate work, for slicing and for paring. He twisted it in his hands, testing its edge with his thumb and grinned manically as he nodded back.

"I won't talk," the prisoner stammered as he leaned away from the knife and the grumpkin wielding it.

"No?" Elora replied. "We will see."

The grumpkin brought the knife within an inch of the prisoners face. Close enough for him to see his own fear reflected in the razors edge and close enough to mist it up with his foul breath.

"Begin," Elora commanded, as she watched the prisoner's eyes widen.

The grumpkin twisted the blade, raised it high above his head then drove it down.

Elora kept her face expressionless as the prisoner shrieked in terror. The knife already imbedded to the hilt in the skagwangle's navel, a little above where the tentacles sprouted from its waist.

The prisoner snapped his lids open and glanced down, his shocked expression turning to puzzlement, then relief as he realised it wasn't himself that was being torn open. Then when the grumpkin began to drag his knife up the belly of the sea creature, he winced.

"Too much blubbery for this grumpkins," the butcher said, as he worked his blade up the thick flesh, sawing up and down to cut through the thick hide.

A putrid vapour seeped out of the gaping wound, followed by handfuls of intestines that burst out like wriggling worms. The wet sticky inners slopped to the floor and spattered up the prisoner's leg. Elora fought the urge to gag as the grumpkin sunk his arms into the belly of the beast and pulled everything out.

"This grumpkins not wanting these squirmy squirms," he said as he tugged out more organs and unceremoniously dropped them atop the growing pile of offal.

Elora averted her gaze as the grumpkin once again began to drag his knife up the torso and over the rib cage. Instead she concentrated on the prisoner whose ashen face had gone a shade paler before he threw up on the floor.

The acid stench of bile mixed with the already foul air in the cell. Elora doubted she would ever get the smell out of her clothes.

"By the Blessed Mother…" the prisoner began before emptying his belly once again, his complexion now going a shade of green.

Elora forced a grin on her face as her periphery vision caught the grumpkin slicing around the base of the skagwangles neck, before placing the knife down. He then gripped the skin either side of the chest and in a practiced movement, tore the skin off the torso.

Smiling to himself, the grumpkin folded the square cut of flesh and placed it delicately at his feet before teasing at the edges of the sea creature's shoulders and began to de-glove the arms.

"No use is webbed fingers, will give this grumpkin extra flappies," the hideous little man explained as he struggled to work the flesh off the now skeletal hand; long strands of pale green muscle joining the bones together.

Once he had removed the skin from the arms he picked up the blood soaked knife and lifted the skagwangles head. He inserted the knife under the chin and began to edge the blade beneath, pulling the face away from the skull.

After he worked the knife around the entire head, he pushed his fingers beneath and wiggled the thick skin while lifting it away from the bone. It slipped before being rolled above the flat bridge of the nose and made a wet popping sound as it came away from the cranium.

Elora clenched her teeth as she stared at the ground, hoping that the prisoner didn't witness her unease but he was too busy retching, the cords in his neck standing out as he strained.

"This grumpkin will be swapsing now," the vile little creature said as he removed the rags he was wearing and dropped them beside the skinless corpse. Then he grasped his own face, the rotten skin falling away as if made from putty. The skull beneath grinned back, the jaw muscles restricting tightly as he snapped his teeth shut. Then he reached around his back and tore at the stitches which gave easily through the decaying skin.

He gripped the fleshy part of his shoulder and yanked the hide off himself. It came away in three pieces and flopped to the floor along with the skin around his arms and hands which he pulled off like a pair of hideous gloves to a human suit.

Now the grumpkin stood before them, void of any skin at all. Elora could see that his skeleton was similar to that of a bipod, only thinner than any human and had a concave rib cage. She didn't see any internal organs, no stomach, heart or lungs. The creature was truly god-created.

The prisoner also watched on in horror as they grumpkin began to slip the face and scalp of the skagwangle over his own, adjusting the eye holes so he could peek out. The nose didn't sit right, nor did the mouth and after several moments the grumpkin gave up fiddling with it. He slipped his spindly arms into the rubbery gloves provided by the corpse and held them before him, working the webbed fingers. Once he was satisfied that the gloves wouldn't come off he picked up the last piece of hide and slipped it on. He held it in place while he signalled for the grimble to hand him a large needle and thread.

The flesh puckered and twisted as he sewed himself into his new skin, muttering as he worked. Elora watched the prisoner as he watched the grotesque scene unfold, his shaky hands held over his mouth and jostling the chain links. She didn't blame him; the whole ordeal was gut retching, yet if she wanted answers she must remain strong.

"It will mouldy mould to this grumpkins soon," the grumpkin explained through the slit of his new mouth. He kicked the discarded tentacles with his skeletal foot. "But those will be no good for my legsies." The yellow eyes peeped through the holes in his skagwangle mask and swivelled to the prisoner's legs. The gesture wasn't lost on the chained soldier.

"No…no!" he screamed in a high pitch voice as he rose from his stool and pulled as far away from the creature as his chains would allow. "No…"

Elora slowly rose and folded her arms, the former Shade was close to tears.

"I don't know," Elora grinned as she rubbed her chin. "I did say that no grumpkin would ever use human flesh again." She studied the prisoner, making a show of staring at his legs, then at the grumpkins fleshless bones. "But you do need legs from somewhere…"

"No, please." The prisoner pleaded, "Don't let him take my legs."

"It's just the skins this grumpkins will be needing," the grumpkin chuckled, as he poked a finger through a sword gash in the hide he was wearing. "Although, these new wrappings are full of pokey holes and it smells of rotten fish."

Elora cocked her head to one side as if coming to a decision. "You may have his legs…"

"No, I'll tell you anything you want," the prisoner blurted out, his tear-filled gaze locked on the grumpkin. "Anything."

Elora paused for a moment, feeling relief that the prisoner hadn't called her bluff, yet she kept the expression of indifference.

"We will see," she said, nodding for the petrified soldier to sit back on his stool.

She gave the prisoner a moment to calm his breathing before interrogating him.

"We already know you're from the main garrison some thirty leagues east of here. We also know that the garrison holds ten thousand and has imposed martial law on the surrounding lands. What we don't know is why you were patrolling this far into the forest and why you had a Shadojak with you?"

"Not that he was a real Shadojak," Bray added.

The prisoner cleared his throat and wiped his nose on a dirty sleeve. "We knew you were hiding in the forest and so regular search parties were sent to seek you out. It was suspected that you were using some kind of magic barrier – fairy protection or something. Our orders were to find the barrier."

"Why?"

"Because in the garrison we have a spell caster and a spell binder. Sent by the Emperor himself, they were to penetrate the barrier or remove it completely. But…"

"They couldn't break it," Elora finished for him, feeling relief. If the fairy protection failed, they wouldn't last long.

The prisoner nodded. "And we couldn't find where the barrier began."

"But if the spell caster and binder found the barrier could they break it?" Elora asked, still feeling that they posed a threat.

"Maybe, I don't know," the prisoner replied.

Elora leaned back, studying him. "Is that it?" she asked, "What else can you tell me?"

The prisoner nodded, his hope filled face flicking between her and the grumpkin who began to tap the ground impatiently with his bony foot.

"There isn't anything else, I'm just a lowly soldier is all. They tell me nothing that doesn't concern me."

Unsatisfied, Elora blew air through her lips. "What you've told me is useless," she sighed as she rose from her stool and paced across the room. She paused at the door and looked back over her shoulder. "Take your legs," she said to the eager grumpkin. "And anything else you can harvest…"

"No! Wait, please," the prisoner blurted, once again on his feet and stretching away from the advancing grumpkin. "I do know something,"

Elora raised an eyebrow.

"A warlock," continued the prisoner. "The Emperor is sending a warlock; he will be arriving at the garrison in the next few days. That's why we had a Shadojak with us, to make sure we found the barrier before he came."

"Warlock?" Bray asked, his brows coming together in concern. "That's not good. Who is it?"

"I don't know for sure, but the rumours speak of Dethtil."

Elora was too slow to stop Bray as he advanced on the prisoner, grabbing him by his shirt. "Dethtil, the impaler? Dethtil the punisher, the torturer; High Warlock of the Twelve Councils of Magic and the enforcer of the archaic rule?"

The prisoner cringed beneath Bray's hold. "Yes," he wheezed, "Dethtil."

Elora's mind rushed through her reaver's memories. A previous Shadojak, his soul trapped within the sword had met with Dethtil a long time ago - centuries even - as Dethtil was such a great master of the archaic arts that he could deceive even death. The memory caused her to involuntarily shiver. He was as infamous for his brutality as he was famous for his abilities with magic. She knew, as did Bray, that if the warlock came, the barrier wouldn't even be a challenge for him.

"Yes, the same," the prisoner continued. "He will be under armed escort, not that he needs it."

Bray dropped the captive and came to join her. "We could set up an ambush," he whispered. "Kill the warlock miles before he reaches the forest."

Elora was thinking along a similar plan of attack, although her mind was now worrying if the defences of the Keep would hold against such a threat. She doubted it.

She stared once more at the prisoner. "Is there anything else?"

The dishevelled soldier glanced at her and then at the impatient grumpkin, knife still in his hand and dripping with green blood.

"No," he said, and cringed away from the grumpkin.

Elora believed the prisoner, he still believed she would kill him. The thought had occurred to her but if she wanted to rid the world of evil tyrants, she couldn't go around acting like one herself.

"You were a Shade once?" she asked.

The soldier shook his head. "I failed the shade training, so I'm just a regular imperial guard," he answered.

"Do you still serve the Empire?"

Without hesitation the prisoner gave a single nod.

"Then your services are still needed," she informed him. "You may join my ranks and continue soldiering. Unless," she inclined her head towards the grumpkin. "You still wish to serve the false Emperor, Flek."

The soldier slowly sank, the chains around his wrists clanking as he knelt. His head hung low, greasy hair brushing the floor.

"Captain Brindle," Elora began, noticing that the SAS soldier had remained silent throughout the whole ordeal and had watched from a corner. "See to it that he is cleaned and fed, then find him a place amongst the Keep's guard."

The Captain nodded. "And if he tries to escape?" he asked.

Elora smiled as she glared at the prisoner. "Then the grumpkin can make a fine spring suit from his body."

"I won't try to escape," the prisoner said quickly, gratefully holding out his wrists for the Captain to unlock the steel bracelets.

"And what about this grumpkins legsies?" asked the grumpkin, pointing down at his fleshless thighs with his knife.

"Make what you can from the other skagwangle," Elora replied. "Then go back to the Shadowlands. Your body will last longer there than in Ethea."

"But this grumpkins...Yes my Queen," he finished as Elora glared at him, feeling irritation that always plagued her when in the company of such nasty creatures.

She followed Bray out of the room and they began to make their way from the dark dungeons, leaving the foul stench of the cell behind. It was still snowing when they emerged onto the upper levels of the tower and began to walk through the cold weather, arm in arm.

"This Warlock is going to be trouble," Bray explained as they stepped across the pristine snow, leaving footprints. "Dethtil will show no mercy if he breaches the barrier."

Elora sighed heavily as she leaned into Bray's warm body. He pulled his cloak wide to envelope her in the fur lined garment and kissed her on the top of her head.

"Things are moving too swiftly," Elora complained, worrying how she would handle everything that was happening. It wasn't that long ago that she was only a simple girl living on a Dutch barge with her uncle. It was hard to believe that singing that one song outside Gloucester Cathedral, had caused all this. Starting a chain of events that led her into another realm, led her to kill her own father and become the Shadojak. Eversong began as an innocent gesture that day, but had ended with another world slamming into Earth, killing millions and spreading chaos.

"Swift or not," Bray said, "you're the only one who can save us."

Elora wished she shared his confidence, but the more desperate the situation got, the more out of her depth she felt.

They had spent the time since Minu's warning, planning, building and more planning for the coming war. Christmas had been and gone and winter would soon give way to spring and they were still discussing the finer details of their tactics. In truth, she doubted they would ever have a solid plan.

"Ragna will leave for the north today," she said. "I don't think we have a choice. I should have sent them ages ago when Ragna first suggested it. We've lost a lot of time already, especially if Dethtil begins to work magic against the fairy protection."

They passed a patrol of men, grimbles and bulworgs, each creature saluting with fist, claw or paw. Elora nodded back, although remained cuddled up to Bray.

She was cold and not just because of the weather. Dread was seeping into her bones and beginning to fill her with the feeling of impending doom.

"We didn't know Neptula would move so quick. And we thought Flek was too busy struggling to rebuild his Empire. You weren't to know."

They skirted passed the buildings which housed the families, Ben was leaning out of an upper balcony, waving to them as they walked beneath. Elora waved back, forcing a smile on her face.

"I should have planned for it happening so fast," she admitted. "How long do you suppose it will take that skagwangle to return to the Sea Witch?"

"A few days, a week at most. Once he reaches the strong currents out to sea, he'll be pulled along at speed."

The white courtyard that led to Zilabeth's workshop was shrouded in a white blanket, the snow having buried everything. It caused drifts against the tower and sat thickly upon the window ledges and clung to the icicles that hung from the battlements above.

"We all thought we had more time," Bray continued. "But we didn't sit idle. Just look at what we achieved with Rams Keep and we do have plans."

"No, we have a few ideas and theories. I wouldn't call them plans as such," she admitted, gloomily. "I only hope Zilabeth has come up with something."

Bray lazily ran his hand along the top of a low wall, gathering snow in his hand. Elora's mind was so preoccupied with the coming war that she hadn't realised what he was going to do until she felt the sudden icy chill of a snow ball being shoved down the back of her shirt.

"Hey!" she gasped as the unexpected cold sent a shiver through her body. However, she couldn't help but smile as Bray jumped away from her as he gathered up another ball of snow.

"No, you won't," Elora laughed as she darted away from him, scraping a handful of snow as she went.

She managed to dodge the first ball he threw, ducking instinctively as the projectile passed harmlessly above her. Bray had thrown it half-heartedly, his idea at being chivalrous. Elora didn't feel the same as she launched her own snow ball.

It hit him in his grinning face, showering white powder over his dark hair. He was still spitting some of the ice from his mouth as he began to pack another ball into his hands.

Elora laughed as she danced out of the way of the next shot, it struck the wall behind her but no sooner did she spring back to throw another than Bray had crossed the distance between them and tackled her to the floor.

Giggling, she managed to curl her foot around his ankle and twist his body so she landed on top of him. Bray gripped her by the arms and using his weight flipped her onto her back and pinned her down.

Dimples formed in his cheeks as he childishly laughed. Elora couldn't help but laugh herself. She knew he was doing this to try and cheer her up and it was working.

She stuck out her bottom lip, mocking a sad face. "You wouldn't let your Queen get cold, would you?" she asked teasingly.

Bray smiled then pressed his lips to hers. "Who says you're my Queen?" he said.

Elora opened her mouth in shock, then grinned. "I do."

Then raising her head, she kissed him.

As he closed his eyes to kiss her, she shoved the snow she had been holding, down the front of his chest.

"Right," Bray blasted, laughing as he wriggled his shirt to release the cold powder that had begun to melt. "Time to make you the Snow Queen."

"No," she protested through giggles as he filled her hood with snow and threatened to pull it over her face. "Don't you dare."

He held the hood playfully, some of the cold seeping down the nape of her neck and making her squirm. "I dare, but what are you going to pay me, not to do it?" he asked.

"A kiss," she answered.

"Hmm, let me try your wares before I decide," he laughed and brought his lips to hers once again. "I don't know," he teased once he pulled away. "I think Ejan might be a better kisser."

"Really?" she laughed. "Then you're welcome to try. But don't blame me if she pulls a knife on you. She's a one-man girl."

"True," Bray admitted jovially. "Then I suppose you will have to do."

He leaned down for another kiss but Elora turned her head to present her cheek. They both laughed as he gently grasped her chin in his strong hand and turned her face forwards. "Love you," he said, then gave her a kiss. This one, longer and more passionate.

When their lips parted again, Elora stared up into his gorgeous face, "Love you too, Elf boy."

He stood and helped her to her feet, then brushed the snow out of her hood. They continued the walk through the courtyard hand in hand, Elora feeling warmer and both their faces were a little flushed.

As they neared the workshop the huge hangar door swung towards them and Gurple crept out, his back to theirs as he gingerly closed it behind him.

When he turned and saw them approaching he gave a nervous wave and scurried away, giving the building apprehensive glances before disappearing around the corner.

"What was all that about?" Bray asked as he stared after the wood troll.

Elora shook her head. "I could be wrong but I expect it has something to do with Teaselberry."

They let themselves into the workshop and shut the door behind them, leaving the cold for the warmth of the warehouse.

"Zilabeth? Teaselberry?" Elora shouted into the large room, but nobody replied.

"They'll be in the Shadowlands," Bray explained as he pointed to a china vase of flowers left on a steel bench. "You might be right about Gurple. I think those are meant for Teaselberry."

"How cute is that?" Elora asked as she picked up the vase and walked towards the sliding door at the back of the workshop. "We can give her them when we find Zilabeth."

The warm dry air hit them like a solid wall of heat, instantly reducing any snow or dampness on their cloaks to steam.

Elora stared about the platform that was carved from the mountain. It was much how they had left it, although some of the cars were missing doors and bonnets. A long steel bench had been made, with hundreds of tools, scrolls and odds and ends laid out upon its surface. Zilabeth had been busy, but building what? Elora couldn't say. Towards the end of the bench was a large circular drum, the words 'chuckit bucket' were etched along the side. Peering inside Elora saw that a lot of scrap chunks of metal, rubber and plastics had been thrown in, along with a couple of devices which most probably hadn't worked.

"Do you hear that?" Bray asked, cocking his head and glancing about, "It sounds like a small motor, an engine maybe."

Elora didn't hear anything above the wind but trusted Bray's elf genes which gave him more sensitive senses.

"I think it's coming from inside the cavern," he added as they made their way across the platform to the cave where Zilabeth's other workshop was.

The tall entrance now had a front door made from wood and easily swung inwards when Bray pushed on it.

"Hello?" Elora called into the cave.

Zilabeth was working behind a desk and raised her head when they entered.

"Morning Elora, Bray," she greeted them, her eyes appearing overly big as she stared at them through spectacles which had several lenses overlapping each other on silver hinges. "Or is it the afternoon or the middle of the night?" She removed her spectacles and set them on the desk beside a clock; its back was off to reveal a network of whirling wheels, cogs and springs. "You know, I really can't tell."

Elora chuckled. "It's about midday and snowing in the Keep. How are you getting on in your new workshop?"

Zilabeth shrugged and pushed away from the desk. "Nothing much to report really, I'm still attempting to create a device that will help against the Emperor, but I'm having trouble finding inspiration. Nice flowers," she said, staring at the vase which Bray held.

"Oh, these. I think they're for Teaselberry," Bray admitted as he placed them on the desk. "Gurple left them in your other workshop."

At the mention of the wood troll, Teaselberry appeared through another door and paused in the doorway. She glanced once at the flowers then looked away as if taking no interest in them in the slightest. Then came into the room and removed a bulky machine which had been strapped to her shoulder and placed it on the ground.

It was box shaped, with a hose that came over the top into a long funnel which Teaselberry coiled up and placed neatly in the corner. It was then that Elora began to recognise parts of the device. It had the body of a petrol lawnmower with the handle and wheels missing. The hose was attached to one side of the engine which had two small cylindrical bottles welded into place. Sprouting from the top of the bottles were a pair of silver pipes which ran from one side of the engine to another.

"I thought I heard a machine when I was outside," Bray said. "Like a motor or something."

"Oh, that was just the dust blower," Zilabeth said, waving a hand dismissively towards the mower device that Teaselberry had set down. "It gets dusty in here so

I adapted that grass cutting machine and turned it into a blower. Simple but effective."

Brays mouth fell open. "You managed to start the engine? That's impossible - nothing works anymore."

Zilabeth's eyebrows drew together. "I studied books on the combustion engine not long after I first came here. Fascinating machines, if not a little cumbersome. They just needed a little tweak."

"A tweak?" Bray asked as he approached the mower-come-dust blower. "There's no electricity, no battery life and no sparks to make the engines work. That's why all those cars outside are just scrap metal."

Zilabeth shrugged again, as if it was no big deal. "Basically the combustion engine has the same principles as a steam engine. Energy in: petrol or coal or liquid fire which transforms into pressure as it becomes energy out: carbon or steam while creating movement from the pistons. Quite simple really. Show them Tease."

Teaselberry scooped the contraption up and slipped the straps onto her shoulders. Zilabeth turned her around so she could adjust a wheel on the back which released a hissing sound from inside. She watched as a needle on a gauge spun into a red mark before pumping a bicycle pump.

On the third push the engine fired to life and filled the room with a noise far louder than that of a simple lawnmower.

Steam spiralled out of the top of the contraption while Teaselberry pointed the hose at the floor causing a cloud of dust to billow away. Once she chased it out of the door she pulled a cord and the devise wound down then stopped.

"But I still don't see how?" Bray asked as he helped the wood troll to remove it.

"Like I said, it really is quite simple," Zilabeth explained as she pulled a screwdriver from her utility belt and pointed it at the silver bottles on the side of the machine. "Instead of petrol mixing with air and supplying the spark to make the combustion. I used liquid fire and water." She tapped both bottles. "All I needed to do was install a primer." She tapped the bicycle pump. "Once it's started the mixture is fed through the carburettor. The instant the water touches the liquid fire it causing an explosion of steam which pushes the pistons – thus exchanging torque to the blades of the mower."

Elora thought she understood what was being explained, but she knew that this thing which Zilabeth had created was the key to why the inventor had been sent to her. This was it, she had a gut feeling that Zilabeth was meant to make the engines run again.

"Do you think you could make the cars outside work?" Bray asked excitedly.

"I don't see why not," Zilabeth answered, raising a sceptical eyebrow. "Although, nothing modern. Anything with a computer or injection system wouldn't work. Only the older kind with carburettors."

"We'll find you the cars," Elora said, embracing Zilabeth. "I think this is it. This is what you're meant to do."

The inventor beamed, then slowly the smile faded to a frown. "But there is one small problem. The only bottle of liquid fire I have, is that," she said, pointing at the back of the mower-blower. "And that won't be enough to run a full-sized car."

"But you can make some more?" Elora asked, feeling her heart sinking.

Zilabeth breathed in deeply, shaking her head. "I brought that with me. Liquid fire is quite rare and very expensive. The only people who can make it are strong spell casters and spell binders."

Elora stared at the machine then felt herself grinning. "If I get you a spell caster and binder, can you do the rest?"

Zilabeth was still frowning when she answered. "They won't be easy to find and they will most probably have to be forced against their will. Liquid fire is dangerous stuff."

Bray joined Elora and placed an arm around her waist. "It just so happens we know where to find a pair of casters and binders. And we will persuade them that making liquid fire is for the greater good."

"Then yes," Zilabeth answered, the smile returning to her face. "It shouldn't be too hard making you your vehicles."

"Thank you," Elora said, embracing Zilabeth for a second time. "Then I'll leave you too it."

From her periphery she noticed Teaselberry standing beside the vase of flowers, reaching up on the tips of her toes so she could smell them. Her wide mouth spread in a grin as she inhaled the scent, but as she caught Elora watching her, she immediately straightened and pretended to wipe dust from the desk.

Elora hid the smile as she fed her arm though Bray's. "Come," she said, pulling her boyfriend around and headed for the door. "We've got a pair of wizards to capture."

4

Thatch and Thud

The Necrolosis was packed tight with bodies. Apart from Zionbuss and his crew, the decks were full of rock trolls and grimbles, bulworgs and men. They were crammed into the hold, pushed up against the masts and hanging from the rigging.

The large patchwork of sails listed gently in the buffeting winds of the Shadowlands, as it hovered against the platform carved out of the mountain.

"We don't need this lot," Ragna protested as he stared at the confusion of bodies teeming over the floating ship. The green sea of souls partially drifting over the rock, tortured faces twisted and dissolving while they writhed amongst silent screams.

"I hope you're right," Elora said. "But they're still going with you. It's better to have them and not need them, than need them and…"

"Yes, I know, but the other clans won't like it. Fighting alongside creatures from the Dark Army; it's just not right," Ragna grumbled, lowering his chin on to the Fist of the North which he rested in the red dust.

"Stop complaining," Ejan snapped, as she slapped him playfully on the stomach. "You're only feeling put out because there are trolls on the ship with more bellies than you."

Ragna grumbled something unintelligible which might have contained the word 'wench,' before puffing out his cheeks and blowing air through pursed lips.

"They'll remain hidden until you call for them. Zionbuss will bring others once he has dropped you off in the north," Elora reminded him.

"And you've got Grimwolf with you," Bray added, slapping Jaygen on the arm.

The young man stared wistfully at the Necrolosis as he shifted a large sack on his back. "Yeah, there's always Grimwolf," he said.

Ragna positively beamed at his son, then grasped Elora into a rib-crushing hug. "We best be off then. It's not going to be easy persuading the clans to fight. And they may be more inclined to fight the Dark Army than the demons in the north."

"Take care," Elora offered, as she was released and allowed to breath once again. The moment was short-lived as Ejan wrapped her arms around her and squeezed her tight.

"Take care of yourself," the Norsewoman warned. "It won't be long before we're all sat around the table at the inn, sharing stories again."

"I hope you're right."

Elora let go of Ejan and went to give Jaygen a hug, but the tall boy had already begun to cross the bone plank to the overcrowded ship. He paused halfway across to shout bye over his shoulder, then pushed his way through the throng of grimbles and trolls.

"He's keen," Bray remarked, staring after Jaygen.

"Aye," Ragna replied. "He's got fire in his blood and wants the chance to prove himself."

The large Viking gave them a curt nod and followed his son onto the Necrolosis.

"He's already proven himself," Elora remarked, feeling dejected at not having said goodbye to him properly. They had gone through a lot together and there was a slim chance that they may never see each other again.

"He's not good at goodbyes," Ejan chuckled. "And I think he's still got a thing for you."

"Oh," Elora said, as she caught a brief glimpse of Jaygen before he disappeared into the crowd of soldiers. His hazel eyes were on hers as he melted away.

Elora fed her fingers into Bray's as they watched Ejan follow her husband and son onto the ship.

"Are we doing the right thing?" she asked.

"Sometimes the only answer left is steel," answered a deep rumbling voice from behind them. The tall demon stretched his wide shoulders, the muscles bunching up and causing the thousands of symbols and scriptures on his skin to shift in and out of focus. He grinned, showing his sharp filed teeth as his hands settled on the pommel of the scimitar soul blade, he wore at his waist.

Elora turned as a huge shadow of a man with long horns sprouting either side of the head, crept over them both. "Zionbuss. I wondered where you went to."

"I was briefing the Dragon Guard, my Queen," Zionbuss explained. "They will begin to march north with the contingent of bulworgs and men I've selected to reinforce the division under Ragna's command."

"But the march would take months," Elora said, glancing down at the black squares formed up and spread as far as the eye could see.

"In the Shadowlands it would seem that way, but on Ethea only a couple of days," Bray said, reminding her how time worked here.

"That is so," Zionbuss agreed. "Although manoeuvring so many over a vast distance will hold its own perils. Another flying ship would make things easier."

Elora stared at the huge floating ship of bones that sailed on a sea of souls. "I'm afraid there is only one."

"True," Zionbuss remarked. "Then my Queen, I best be on my way."

Elora stood aside to allow the demon to cross onto his own ship. He gave them a final wave as the plank was pulled away and he issued orders to the skeletal crew who began to busy themselves about the ship.

Bray dropped an arm over her shoulder as they watched the Necrolosis rise high into the red sky. Its gruesome sails snapping tight as they caught the winds and propelled away.

They remained on the platform until the ship was a smudge on the horizon, then made their way back to the Keep. They had plans to make and a spell caster and binder to kidnap.

It had been a cold night and seemed to be getting colder as the dawn drew on. Elora lay on her belly in the snow in between Bray, who was dressed in an imperial uniform and Captain Brindle, black and green cam cream smudged across his face. They were beneath a row of ferns, their leaves shedding frost as they gently swayed to sporadic gusts of wind.

"The prisoner said that the caster and binder have chambers in the tower of the east wing," Brindle offered as he passed Elora a pair of binoculars.

She put her face to the eye piece and stared down at the huge garrison.

A full moon and clear sky provided enough light to reveal the colossal structure. It was similar to the shade garrison she had been judged at in Rona. Thick stone walls surrounding tall buildings with an open parade square and practice field. It had fared well during the merge, the perimeter and main buildings staying intact. Yet it was clear that a farm had been there before the joining of the worlds. The original welsh cottage was now partially buried inside the stone hall, its chimney smoking from one end of the thatch roof while the other had been crushed beneath the heavier stone wall. A thick crack fractured up the side of the bigger building while the half of the farm house lay in a pile of rubble at its feet. Two worlds merging together, two buildings occupying the same space and forced to become one. Usually, this ended with the weaker of the materials becoming rubble. Elora had witnessed this everywhere she had been.

A steel silo lay on the snow-covered floor. It had at one time contained grain, but had since been emptied. Now the silo had been cut open and provided shelter for two sentries who stamped their feet against the cold while rubbing warmth into icy fingers.

Fire burned from many torches that were set at intervals around the wall which was patrolled every hour by an armed guard. Towards the eastern end of the garrison lay a tower. Dark windows ran vertically up the centre, one for each floor with a larger window at the top with a balcony. Another two sentries stood on the roof facing down into the grounds and the surrounding lands. They had rifles which meant they formerly belonged to the British Army that had absorbed into the Empire.

Elora swept the binoculars down and observed the lowest window which was at least ten feet above the perimeter wall. A subtle glow of a fire flickering against the leaded glass.

"Is everyone in position?" Elora whispered.

The Captain nodded. "My platoon is hidden within the tree-line before the main gate. Pudding and his team have machine guns trained on anything that may rush out. Slater and a second sniper have taken over watch above that hill to the northeast." Brindle pointed at a dark mound with trees dotted around the base. "They'll have most of the garrison on the eastern side covered."

"Good," Elora said. "But only kill as a last resort."

She knew that the imperial soldiers were only following orders and believed that she and the Dark Army were the enemy. Not seeing through the lies of their false Emperor.

"Understood," the Captain replied. Then crawled back into the shadows before silently moving off to join his platoon.

Weakest slipped from behind the deep white foliage to join them, sitting down in the position Brindle had just left.

"Are they ready?" Elora asked him, referring to the large contingent of bulworgs that lay to the south of the garrison. Weakest nodded, his hot breath coming out in plumes of white vapour. "Then we're all set to go."

Bray's hand slipped into hers as they waited patiently for the allotted time. The plan was as simple as it was daring. A swift 'snatch and grab' using the minimal amount of people. Elora knew they had the numbers and strength to seize the garrison if they wanted to. But that would mean a lot of deaths and they risked the caster and the binder being hurt. Not to mention that it would add legitimacy to Flek's accusations. She was determined to only use the Dark Army if absolutely necessary.

The grey sky slowly dissolved into a pale pink, the few clouds becoming purple as the sun began its accent above the forest.

"It's time," Elora whispered. Weakest bowed his head before stalking away, leaving huge paw prints in the snow. "Good luck."

A few moments later, the haunting call from a large pack of bulworgs howling together, echoed around the icy landscape. The sound was followed by a row of explosions as Captain Brindle detonated several grenades from the opposite side.

Elora closed her eyes and concentrated on the scrawharpy that circled high above. The bird's mind linked briefly with hers as she watched the garrison come alive from a hundred feet up.

Guards suddenly rushed from buildings to form ranks in the practice grounds. Thousands of men scrambling to slip on armour and ready swords, spears or guns as they were commanded into groups. Archers ran onto the battlements and surrounding walls, drawing bows or cocking rifles as they scanned the grounds outside.

Within minutes the main gates were thrown open as a large contingent of horse riders trotted out and formed a base line. Steel helms and gauntlets glistening in the rising sun as they searched for the source of the noise. Then under the command of two flags, one group galloped in the direction of the howling bulworgs, while a second contingent rode out in the direction of the explosions.

From where they hid beneath the trees, Elora could hear the many shouts and orders being thrown around the garrison. Panicked voices bellowing that they were under attack, that the Dark Army were upon them – that the Queen of Darkness had come to deliver them through the last door.

From the mind of the scraw-harpy she watched as wave after wave of troops marched out of the gate. Manoeuvring into battle formations like a well-oiled machine, the practiced movements showing the discipline that came with being an imperial guard.

Row after row of sharp steel standing beside riflemen kneeling with eyes trained through sights. Elora studied the new way in which the old Empire worked with the British Army. Men of Earth and men of Thea, modern camouflage and steel armour, swords and guns. They were from different worlds but had formed a brotherhood, coming together to become the new imperials of Ethea.

Elora couldn't help but admire the way in which they adapted to work with each other so easily. Yet knew that beneath what they wore and what they yielded or how they spoke, they were all soldiers united against a common enemy – her.

"Impressive," Bray remarked as he stared through the binoculars. "I'd say there's about two hundred on horseback and a thousand on foot."

"And a thousand more inside," Elora shrugged, grinning as an excitement began to build within her. "Is now a good time?"

Bray smiled. "Now is the perfect time," he answered as he rose to his feet and brushed snow from his uniform. He placed a steel helmet upon his head and gave a mocking bow. "How do I look?"

"Like the enemy," Elora replied. "You make a gorgeous imperial guard."

Bray chuckled as he hefted the spear and stretched his neck. "Is she close?"

"She's close."

Bray knelt to give her a kiss then began to stride out beyond the security of the tree line. When he was clear of the ferns he began to run towards the garrison, shaking his spear as he went.

"Be careful," Elora whispered, praying that her boyfriend wouldn't come to any harm. Yet which god would she pray to? Who would listen to the God of Chaos? She only hoped this plan would work.

As Bray neared the imperials, he began to shout. "Dragon!"

From her vigil, Elora watched as the closest ranks from the garrison turned to face him, the commanders who had been discussing tactics between themselves suddenly hushed as they gazed upon the approaching figure.

"Dragon," Bray repeated as he stumbled through the deep snow. "It's Grycul. Grycul is coming."

By now the entire division turned their attention on Bray as he pointed his spear behind him, panic thick in his voice. "The Queen of Darkness has sent her beast. She is coming - Grycul will kill us all," he screamed as he threw himself before the commander of the horsemen.

Even from her hiding place Elora could hear the murmurings of the name 'Grycul,' being passed along the lines of men and many nervous faces turned to the sky.

"Calm down soldier," the commander shouted at Bray, not seeing beyond the imperial disguise. "What have…"

Elora chose that moment to link minds with Grycul and project her wishes.

The howls of the distant bulworgs quieted as a new sound pierced the sky. It ripped through the silence, louder than a banshee and cut deep into the rising dawn. Elora felt that the screech cut deeper still into the men spread out before her.

"The dragon is here!" Bray shouted as he thrust his spear into the air. "Run!"

The horseman fought hard to control their nervous mounts as some of the men in the ranks began to move, heads now flicking in all directions.

"Remain in your formations!" The commanders shouted, reminding the soldiers that they were disciplined men.

Another scream tore through the air as the formations began to loosen once again.

Then a sudden flash split the heavens, Grycul riding the thunder which followed.

She banked high before swooping into a dive. A tortured shriek proceeded her as she spat balls of white flames.

Elora was impressed by the imperials. They remained steady until the white fire exploded near the front ranks, the closest trees becoming engulfed in flames.

A few of the younger, less battle-hardened men began to scramble away from the burning wood. The ranks behind falling back until the neat rows of soldiers became a shamble of frightened men and all the screaming of the commanders couldn't hold the units together.

Grycul swept around the front of the garrison, screeching and spitting fire at the archers on the walls as the army below lost control and began to run back inside the gates.

Elora picked out Bray as he joined the chaos and disappeared into the crowd to be jostled along with the rest of the soldiers. Once he was inside she made her move.

Dissolving herself to smoke, she drifted down the slope and along the ground, staying close to the trees that were already burning. Entwining with the black smoke as it curled about the feet of stamping hooves and rushing men. She flowed through the throng, slipping between flesh and steel, sweat and panic.

Some of the soldiers stared in awe as the dragon arced around the garrison. One brave determined man raising his rifle to fire at the beast, then others began to copy him. Before long, rifle shots and arrows began to rain up into the sky. Yet the projectiles were harmless. Grycul was god-created and only another god-creation could harm her.

From the images running through Elora's mind, she sensed the scene unfolding from a thousand angles. The hysteria spreading as men fought each other to reach the safety of the gate.

She drifted to the wall by the eastern tower and ascended. Flowing between the cracks and the mortar until she was above the battlements. The archers didn't sense her as she weaved between the men, their attention was fully on the flying beast that was attacking their army.

Elora poured over the other side and rose up the circular tower, spiralling around its stone surface to an open window.

Two men stared out. Fear filled expressions on their faces as they watched the scene below.

She flowed over the windowsill and between the men. Then reformed behind them, her soul reaver held before her.

The men had watched her enter and slowly turned, raising their arms as they focused on the blade.

The pair were middle-aged. One taller with long curly hair and a neatly trimmed goatee while his companion was short and portly with scruffy straw-like hair that stuck out in all directions.

"Are you the spell caster and binder?" Elora asked, staring over their clothes for any signs of weapons.

The taller of the two raised his hand to push round spectacles up the bridge of his nose. "I am a caster, yes," he answered. As he dropped his hand he whispered in an old language and sparks shot from his fingers.

At the same instant Elora realised what had happened, she was thrown backwards against the chamber wall, jarring her teeth and knocking the breath out of her. But before she could react to the attack, the shorter man began to mumble a strange incantation and slammed his hands together.

The clapping sound produced a visible rupture in the air and a wave of ripples suddenly hit her body, pinning her to the wall.

She was paralysed, only able to moan as the two men advanced on her. Did she really think it would be that easy to capture a spell caster and his binder? It seemed foolish now that she was trapped. She should have known they would have been able to protect themselves.

The taller of the men, which Elora realised had been the spell caster approached. Rubbing his goatee between thumb and finger as he inspected her.

"The girl was smoke," he remarked, addressing his short friend. "The girl has a soul reaver and the girl has the eyes of a demon."

"The girl is the Queen of Darkness," offered the other, rubbing his huge hands together. The hands that bound the spell which trapped her.

Elora attempted to speak, but her tongue wouldn't move and she could only produce a wet gurgling sound. Even her sight was locked in the same position. Only able to stare at the pair as they studied her.

"The Emperor will be pleased," the spell caster said, smiling.

"He will be delighted," the binder agreed.

"Charmed," they both said together.

Elora fought to close her eyes, to move anything but couldn't. Even her chest struggled to rise as her breathing slowed.

White spots began to flash in the corners of her vision as Elora reached out to the dying embers in the fireplace. She concentrated on the element of fire and stroked the rhythm to alter it.

Sparks began to glow brighter from the black ash, racing each other as they flew up the chimney. Then the ash itself ignited. A dark cloud exploding, showering the room in hot dust.

The caster spun around, his small eyes growing wide with surprise as Elora turned her attention to the elemental power of air. Enticing a wind to swirl into the chamber and gather the burning dust, spinning it into a cyclone.

Mesmerised, the caster and binder watched the phenomenon spin about the room, weaving a destructive path towards them. It pulled at their robes and tussled their hair, yet Elora couldn't find the strength to force it into the maelstrom she wanted.

Her powers began to ebb away with her vision. The cyclone winding down to nothing as she gave over to unconsciousness. The room shrank as her oxygen starved brain began to shut down.

"I believe she's dying," remarked the binder.

"I believe you're right," replied his friend.

The voices of the caster and binder seemed miles away as other, more recognisable voices began to whisper to her.

Elora...Elora...the darkness whispered.

Elora...Kill...Kill.

Darkness filled her world, its haunting beauty singing to her. Elora felt the lifeless void taunting her back to wakefulness, sensed the Chaos it brought with it and relished its power.

Elora heard laughter. Deep and guttural, it ruptured about the chamber, tugging her back to wakefulness.

When she snapped her eyes open, she realised that the laughter was coming from herself.

"See," the binder said, pointing his finger at her face, "The violet is turning red."

Elora was still laughing when her hand clenched into a fist, feeling delight as the men watched on in horror as she raised her legs and pushed against the wall she was pinned to. Her thighs and calves strained and then all at once she broke through the invisible restraints.

Both men backed away as she levelled her sword at them once again.

"Try and cast another spell and I'll remove your heads," she threatened, breathing more deeply and willing to calm the rising darkness within herself.

The men raised their hands as they cowed against the wall. Elora recognised the fear in each of them and knew they wouldn't attempt to fight her again.

A subtle knock came to the door moments before it swung open. Then Bray slipped inside, closing and bolting the door behind him.

"You took your time," Elora remarked, winking mischievously.

Bray laughed as he slipped his sword back into his smuggler's pouch. "I was recognised a couple of times. There are Shades down there that I've worked with before." His attention went to the two men with raised arms. "Are these the right pair?"

Elora nodded. "They already tried to kill me. They're pretty powerful." She glanced back at them. "What are your names?"

The taller of the two spoke first, brushing hands through his curly hair. "Thatch," he replied.

"I'm Thud," offered the other. "What do you want from us?"

"I want you," Elora said, offering them a shrug. "Both of you." She inclined her head to Bray. "Can we still leave through the gate?"

"No," he answered. "They'll have the gate closed and we can't risk getting recognised." He paced to the open window and looked outside. "Maybe we could climb down."

"We'd be spotted from the wall and shot," Elora explained, searching the room for inspiration for an escape. The original plan was to kidnap the pair and escape through the confusion but Bray being recognised had put an end to that.

Suddenly the door crashed open as an armoured guard rushed in.

The imperial paused as he stared about them, his face a mask of bewilderment as he took in the scene.

"What…Guards!" he bellowed out into the hall as he drew a sword.

Bray crossed the space in an instant, drawing out his own steel.

He ducked the first swing of his attacker then struck the guard across the temple with the pommel of his sword.

The impact made a dull thwack as the body collapsed to the floor, the imperial's sword making a clatter as it fell beside him.

Bray turned to her. "That's the element of surprise gone," he said as the sounds of many more men began to clatter from the corridor outside. "Any suggestions?"

"Surrender?" offered both Thatch and Thud together.

"The roof," Elora shouted, making for the door. "I'll clear the path. You bring these two." She glared at the frightened pair. "And keep quiet; nobody need get hurt."

The corridor was dimly lit by oil lamps, but bright enough to reveal the armoured men rushing up the staircase towards her. Spears pointing the way as steel clattered against the stone walls.

Without hesitation Elora yanked a lamp from its hook and threw it on the floor.

The cylindrical glass shattered and flaming oil ran across the path of the advancing soldiers.

Whispering the element of fire, Elora enticed the flames to rise and form an impenetrable barrier.

"Run," she shouted at Bray as he emerged from the chamber, guiding both the spell caster and binder in front of him. "Up the stairs," Elora ordered, nodding towards the spiral staircase that continued to the upper levels of the tower.

A spear was thrown from the other side of the fiery wall. The shaft bursting through the flames and struck Elora in the thigh.

The pain was slow in coming, giving her mind time to realise that she had three feet of sharpened steel rising up from her leg and three feet sticking below. But when it did come, it brought tears, and she fell to one knee.

"Go!" she shouted at Bray. Her boyfriend having paused to come to her aid. She waved them on before grasping the shaft of the spear with both hands.

Nausea brought a wave of dizziness as she concentrated on the weapon. No matter how hard your constitution was, it made you feel queasy having a foreign body imbedded in your own body.

Laced with anger she screamed at the men she had trapped on the staircase as another spear and a dagger were thrown through the fire.

Elora turned to smoke and felt the steel pass through her being before clattering to the floor, along with the original spear that was imbedded in her.

She rematerialised beside a second lamp and wrenched it from the wall, her injured leg having healed the instant she became smoke.

Spinning twice on the spot, she gathered momentum before hurling the lamp through the hot barrier.

The sound of shattering glass erupted from beyond the wall of flames. Along with the urgent screams of the men who had caught the impact of the burning oil.

Elora grinned at the destruction, yet the expression belonged to that other her. The Queen of Darkness, God of Chaos. She let it fall as she ran after Bray and their captives. The flames would hold the imperials for a few moments more. But without her there to control the element, the fiery barrier would begin to dwindle.

She caught the others as they ascended onto the circular roof. Bray was already advancing on the imperial soldiers who were leaning out over the battlements, firing rifles and arrows at Grycul.

"Look out!" Thatch bellowed, warning the soldiers as Bray struck the closest over the back of the head with the pommel of his sword.

Before the unconscious body hit the ground, the remaining men turned in the direction of the shouts and quickly retrained their weapons on Bray.

Elora counted six of them, not including the body at Bray's feet. Two with rifles and the rest with bows.

Slamming the trap door closed, she launched at the nearest riflemen, reducing to smoke before he pulled the trigger.

The bullets passed harmlessly through her as she materialised a fist to strike the man below the chin, sending him stumbling back into a bowman.

They both clattered against the battlements, an arrow flying loose to hit an imperial guard on the opposing side of the roof. The arrow imbedding deep into his shoulder.

Before the others had a chance to untangle themselves, Elora struck one against the temple and the other on the back of the neck. Their bodies slumped to the floor as more bullets tore into her side.

Fire erupted from her wounds as her blood touched the air, adrenalin feeding her body as she turned on her attacker.

The soldier raised his rifle and aimed at her face, but his body suddenly jerked. A large hole blasting out from his chest.

"Thank you Slater," Elora hissed through the pain. The sniper would have taken the shot from his hiding place on the hillside.

Elora took the opportunity to become smoke, long enough to heal her wounds before diving to Bray's aid. Her Shaigun simultaneously parring and blocking the short swords of the remaining bowmen.

Elora snaked her arm around the closest and choked him, only releasing her hold as the imperial slipped into unconsciousness.

She let his body fall as Bray swept the legs from under the remaining soldier and drove a winding blow to his sternum.

He crumpled into a heap, struggling to breath, eyes bulging out in pain.

Elora kicked his sword out of reach before shoving him back against the wall.

"We're not going to kill you," she said, glaring at him. "Unless you attack us."

She stared at the dead body of the rifleman, blood pooling around the chest where Slater's bullet had exited, then turned on Thatch.

"His death is on your hands," she said coldly. "I told you to keep quiet."

Thatch backed away, hands raised before him. "For the love of the Empire, you're trying to kidnap us. How could we not protest?"

"I am serving the Empire," Elora snapped. "And you will serve it better in my care."

The trap door suddenly burst open and an imperial soldier poked his head out, teeth baring below his steel helm.

Bray kicked it shut, the clattering sound of the soldier falling down the ladder, reverberated from below.

"Serving the Empire?" Thatch asked sarcastically, pointing at Grycul as she spat fire at the gate. "Your dragon is destroying it."

Elora shook her head. "Your false Emperor is doing a fine job of that. Yet the true enemy is neither me nor Flek. It's Neptula."

"I don't understand," Thatch admitted incredulously, pushing his slipping spectacles up the bridge of his nose.

"You will, once we arrive at Rams Keep. I'll explain everything then."

"Rams Keep?" Thud cut in as he stared at Bray and the sword in his hand. "We're trapped. We can't go anywhere. It may be better that you surrender now and save more bloodshed."

Bray began to rise as the trapdoor was forced up an inch.

"He has a point," he said as he jumped up and slammed back down on the wood, trapping fingers in the crack.

Elora stared up at Grycul, projecting her mind's thoughts to the beast. She grinned as the huge reptilian's head turned in their direction and angled her large wings to bank towards them.

She approached the spell binder and caster, putting her arms around their shoulders. "Ever ridden on a dragon before?" she asked, and felt the pair stiffen.

"Might be best you close your eyes and pray to whatever god you believe in," she said, then drew them to the wall and pushed them both over the battlements.

Their cloaks billowed out while limbs thrashed wildly. Both screaming as they plummeted down the tower.

Grycul swooped low and caught them in her talons before they struck the ground. She raised them before her as she glided above the crowds of men, sweeping in a long arc as she cleared the perimeter wall. Thatch and Thud screaming like frightened children.

"That was cruel," Bray chuckled.

Elora laughed as she watched the dragon swing about and begin heading back towards them, the legs and arms of Thatch and Thud kicking wildly through her grasp.

She offered Bray her hand. "Shall we?"

Bray took it, entwining his fingers within hers as they climbed up onto the battlements.

Without any weight holding it closed, the trapdoor crashed open and men began to pour out onto the roof; spears and swords held before them. They looked about the top of the tower in confusion before focusing on them. Then as one they charged.

Elora gave them a mock salute before falling back and letting gravity pull her from the wall.

She spun over as they fell, twisting her body so she was already in a riding position as Grycul passed.

They landed on her back, Elora gripping onto the dragon's slender neck while Bray held tight around her waist.

"Rams Keep," she ordered, shouting above the screams of the men held in the beast's talons.

Grycul obeyed, flying high above the garrison. But not before spitting a final fireball at the Empire's flags that flew above the main gate. The material was instantly devoured by the hungry flames which reduced the flag pole to ash.

The morning sun shone brightly over the white landscape below them. The dragon-shaped shadow skimming over the fields and trees as it followed them home. As they flew above the large pack of bulworgs, Elora waved her arm to signal for them to fall back.

She heard Weakest howl, his voice echoing from the Welsh countryside as the huge body of bulworgs began to dart across the open fields; leaping snow covered hedgerows and fences as they flowed as one into the forest.

"That went easier than I first thought," Bray shouted above the noise of the wind as he planted a kiss on the back of her neck.

Elora leaned back into his strong embrace. "I only hope Ragna has the same luck in the north."

5

North of North

It was a northerly wind that battered across the frozen lands. Relentless in its determination to strip any heat from the three of them as they ploughed through the snow. It tore at clothes, whipped against faces and drove ice into any exposed skin. Jaygen pulled his hood tighter, but the chill still stroked bitter fingers down his neck.

Forcing his frost-coated lids open, he glanced to his father. The great Viking strode out ahead, snow building up a drift against his furs as he grinned through a white encrusted beard. Every so often Ragna would hold his arms out, allowing the weather to batter him as he sang old Nordic songs about battles from the times of his forefathers. Jaygen's mother on the other hand, paced behind her husband and allowed his huge frame to block out the blizzard. She gave Jaygen glances now and again and reassured him that this was only a light flutter compared to what weather the north could offer in the deepest of winters. Jaygen attempted to return the smile and prayed to Odin that he wouldn't experience anything harsher than what was already cascading around him.

When they had stepped off the Necrolosis and passed through the portal, Jaygen's heart had almost stopped beating with the shock of going from the dry heat of the Shadowlands to the sub-zero temperatures of his homeland. His father had slapped a meaty hand over his shoulder and told him that no true Viking blood would ever freeze, yet the numbness which settled over Jaygen had him wondering if he was truly a Viking.

"Not much further," Ragna bellowed above the howling gale as he pointed ahead.

Jaygen could only see a wall of white as it peppered his vision. White against the ground, battering through the sky and a veil that descended over everything.

He was about to ask how much further when his foot pressed down on something more solid than powder. The sudden change of ground caused him to topple against his mother who caught him and pushed him back up.

"We're here," Ejan offered. "Craggs Head is just below us."

Jaygen stamped his feet against the rock beneath him as his mother's words sunk in. Yet he still couldn't see any village, not even a single building, or had Craggs Head been devoured by the blizzard and now lay beneath a blanket of northern snow?

He was wondering if he would ever feel his fingers again when his father halted and Jaygen walked into the back of him. The Fist of the North strapped to Ragna's back suddenly appeared at face level; Elora's sunken hand print packed tight with snow.

Shaking his head, Jaygen attempted to rid his mind of Elora. She had been plaguing his thoughts and torturing his heart. He had found life at Rams Keep unbearable, that was why he was keen to come north, a way to push her out of his head.

Peering around his father, Jaygen saw that they were on the crest of a hill, the slope of which swept down into a deep valley. Several stone and timber buildings were built into the rock. Torches burned from inside some of the doorways and black smoke was spiralling up from stone stacked chimneys. The sloping ground was only partially hidden beneath a thin layer of frost as the village was protected from the elements by the valley itself. Only the thatched roofs were thick with snow.

Ragna led them down the steps which wound around a finger-shaped rock, delivering them before a small wooden hut. Jaygen's father banged loudly on the door and waited for a response.

When it creaked open, Jaygen got his first ever glimpse of a Viking, other than his parents.

A wiry man, buried in furs came to the door. The furs were the same colour as his grey beard so Jaygen couldn't tell where his clothes ended and his beard began.

"Who goes there?" the aged man asked, raising a double-bladed axe in shaky hands. "Friend or foe?"

"Figit? Is that you, you old goat?" Ragna replied, pulling the startled Viking off his feet and into a tight embrace. "You're still acting the village protector?"

When his father released the old man, he staggered back and glared up through watery eyes.

"Ragna? Has the son of Bowen of the red path come home?" he asked, thick grey eyebrows disappearing into his wild hair. "I thought you were lost to the Empire raids, years ago."

"It's a long story and one that will need plenty of ale to tell," Ragna laughed.

"Odin, knows it's good to see you. And you've brought Ejan too," continued Figit, smiling at Jaygen's mother who grasped hands with the old man. "And who is this?" he asked, turning his attention on Jaygen.

"This is my boy, Jaygen." Ragna replied proudly, dropping a heavy arm over his shoulder.

Jaygen nodded, yet he was staring passed the man and at the brazier that burned from within the hut, drawing him in. He could feel the heat touching his face and longed to hold his hands over the flames.

"Well met, friend," Figit greeted jovially, before his face became serious once again. He offered Ragna a sad smile. "These are troubled times you've returned to us with."

"I'm afraid I'll be bringing more trouble with me," Ragna replied. "But first I will seek out my brother, Eric."

"Eric is some of the trouble," Figit explained. "He and some of the other clansmen have been taken prisoner by the Empire."

"What?" Ragna shouted, his huge hand curling into a fist and seeking something to punch. When he found nothing close enough but the old Viking before him, he took a calming breath and uncurled his fingers.

"You better come inside," Figit offered, stepping aside to allow them in. "I'll explain what I can."

Jaygen was only too glad for the invitation to come into the warm hut, but Ragna set a hand against his chest.

"Go to the tavern," his father ordered. "Owen's Rest - you'll find it towards the bottom of the valley. Make sure they've a couple of rooms. We'll join you shortly."

Jaygen wanted to protest, but by the time he came up with an excuse the door had closed, shutting him out with the howling wind once again.

Clenching his teeth and drawing his hood tight, he set off down the valley, descending the stone steps as they weaved between the square buildings.

He felt eyes following him from the dark windows and saw the silhouettes of large men glaring from doorways, sharp objects held in wide arms, yet none ventured out into the cold to challenge him.

The path led to a small wooden bridge that humpbacked over a bubbling stream. The planks were slippery and he crossed with his arms held out either side for balance. On the other side was a tall statue carved from the trunk of a tree. Snow sat atop the grim figure, his hands coming together to hold the shaft of a long war hammer.

Jaygen paused to take a better look. He brushed frost from words that had been carved into the base of the statue. 'Black Owen – protector of the north', it read.

It was his great grandfather. The familiar family features slowly becoming recognisable with the firm jawline and deep set eyes of his father, although the stern expression of the imposing statue was unlike Ragna's, whose - more often than not - was full of mischief.

He trailed a cold finger along the head of the hammer, the wood aged and cracking in places. The Fist of the North hadn't changed since the carving had been done over three generations ago.

Jaygen gave a final glance at the Protector before shuffling on, his great grandfather stared at him judgmentally. But whatever Owen thought of his descendent, he kept it to himself.

The thin layer of snow crunched beneath his boots as he followed the path around a rock and came to a tall square building with a large heavy door. Made from thick logs, the structure was half built into the valley wall and had a thatched roof which, like the rest of the village, was covered in white powder. 'Owen's Rest', was carved above the door on a whale bone which hung from a chain.

Jaygen straightened his fur coat, took a deep breath and entered the tavern.

Smoke coughed from the hearth of an open fire as a draft followed him inside the large hall. It flowed into the thick rafters in the sloping ceiling until the door slammed shut behind him. The sudden noise inviting three men to pause in their conversation and turn their heads his way.

They were elderly, beards gone grey as they leaned over a round table, knobbly hands cradling tankards of ale. They stared at him, eyes narrowing as if suspecting trouble. Jaygen noticed the hilts of swords poking above the rim of the table and one of the trio had a bandolier of knives belted across his wide chest.

He gave them a nod as he strode towards the bar, lowering his hood and offering them a smile. Their expressions didn't change. Untrustworthy lot these Norseman, thought Jaygen as his gaze fell on a fourth man sitting alone in a quiet corner. Different to the Vikings, this man was earth-born. He was cleanly shaven and wore the bright colours of a snowsuit and had a pair of modern skis propped up against the logs of the wall. A map lay open on the table before him which he was studying with great interest and only briefly looked up as Jaygen walked by.

The bar itself was a simple slab of rough wood sitting atop two barrels. Beyond were two shelves full of cups and tankards and a large axe hanging from the wall above. Standing with her back to him was a woman, cloth in hand wiping a tankard clean.

"Hello," Jaygen offered, greeting her in Norse.

The woman turned to face him, eyes narrowing as she looked him up and down before offering him a weary smile. She was maybe three of four years older than himself with a kind face yet seemed strong enough that she wouldn't take any trouble. The axe hanging above her within easy reach, only adding to her strength.

"We've got ale or ale," she offered, placing the tankard she had been cleaning on the bar and filled it with an amber liquid from a large jug. Some spilling over the rim to soak into the coarse wood. "My names Carmelga."

"Jaygen," he replied, glancing at the ale; a thirst working its way up inside him as he reached for the tankard. He gripped the tin handle, but stayed his hand. His mother wouldn't be happy with him drinking alcohol.

"Have you any rooms to rent?" he asked, letting his hand fall from the bar.

The woman shook her head, "None vacant," her eyebrows drew together as she stared into his face. "Are you from around these parts? You look familiar."

"No," he replied, sensing that the three Vikings in the room had gone quiet again to listen to him. "I'm from the south."

"And what brings you to Craggs Head in the winter, Jaygen? The only thing to do up here is fish and the sea is still mainly ice, so you won't be doing much of that."

Jaygen cleared his throat. "We, that is my parents and I, are going north," he answered, unable to think of anything better to say.

"North?" Carmelga asked, chuckling. "You're at the furthest point north. What's north of north?"

Jaygen felt his gut tighten as he searched desperately for an answer, but came up short of anything tangible. "More north," he answered and realised from the way the woman frowned that he sounded less than convincing.

He was about to try an add that they had family in Craggs Head when the tavern door suddenly burst open.

Two burly men and a girl strode into the room, not bothering to shut the door behind them. The men were similar in appearance, one older than the other - possibly father and son. Yet it was the girl which drew Jaygen's attention. About his own age, tall and rangy with the brightest red hair he had ever seen. She may have been pretty, even with a notch missing from one of her eyebrows, but the scowl she was wearing made her seem as hostile as the weather outside.

As they stalked across the room they sneered at the three Vikings sat at the table, who quietly picked up their drinks and sauntered over to the back of the tavern. Jaygen noticed that they averted their gazes from the new trio, as if expecting danger and attempted to distance themselves.

"Carmelga," growled the older of the three. He was a huge beast of a man, his brown furs thick with frost, seeming to make him even bigger. "I've come for the debt."

Jaygen saw anger flash across the barkeeper's face as she folded her arms.

"You'll get your gold, Byral, when my Da comes back," Carmelga snapped.

"Eric isn't coming back, the Empire have him. No, I'll take my gold now and the rest of your ale to make up what's owed." Byral sneered as he reached for the tankard that was set down before Jaygen. "It shouldn't be a wench running the tavern anyway."

In a blur of movement, Carmelga grasped the axe above her head and brought it down against the bar, the sharp blade biting deep into the wood an inch from Byral's reaching fingers.

With her free hand, Carmelga picked up the tankard, put it to her mouth and tipped her head back. Beads of ale ran down her chin before she slammed the empty vessel next to the axe.

"If you want ale, you'll pay for it," she spat, wiping amber liquid from her cheek. "And a wench can run a tavern just as good as any man." She yanked the axe free from the wood and held it between her and the imposing characters. "Or I'll take your stones and see what kind of wench you'd make."

The red haired girl smashed her fist into the wood and leaned over the bar, towering over Carmelga.

"How about me and you go up to the Tooth and settle this the Viking way?" she hissed, her nose almost touching the other woman's.

Carmelga snarled, baring white teeth and not backing away. "I'll meet you at the Tooth and leave your body there for the crows."

"Nobody's going to the bloody Tooth," Byral snapped, taking the girl by the arm and pulling her back. "Now calm yourself Fieri; you've got your mother's temper."

Fieri tugged her arm free and stepped away from Byral. It was then that her piercing blue eyes locked on to Jaygen's.

He had been quietly watching the exchange, keeping as still as possible so as not to draw attention to himself and wishing he was somewhere else.

"What are you staring at?" the red haired girl demanded, glowering through her scowl.

Jaygen averted his gaze and stepped away. The girl seeming so angry that she might vent some of it out on him.

"And anyway," Carmelga continued, gripping Byral's furs and pulling him closer. "If you and your clan had any stones you'd be attacking the Empire and getting my Da out!"

Byral stood straighter, puffing his chest out but said nothing. After a moment he uncurled Carmelga's fingers and shrugged.

"You know we can't attack the Empire. Odin knows how big they've got and with that other world merging with Thea, there's all kinds of nasties around," he explained. "Times like this that you've got to look after your own."

"No," Carmelga replied. "It's times like this that the clans should come together to fight."

The man that came in with Byral nimbly snatched the axe from Carmelga and cocked it onto his own shoulder.

"My Da's right," he sniffed, turning the shaft of the axe over in his hands so the blade caught the firelight and reflected flames along the shining tankards. "So pay up wench. Isn't anyone big enough in your clan left to stop us."

"Happens that there is," came a voice from behind them.

Byral and his son spun, a dull blade finding the hands of the elder as they confronted the speaker. Then as one they paused, Byral's lips mumbling something unintelligible as he quickly lowered his weapon and then placed a hand on the axe in his son's hands.

"Uncle Ragna?" Carmelga squealed with delight.

Jaygen watched his father as he loomed over the pair before him, his grin parting his beard as he chuckled to himself; thick fingers rubbing the woven strands beneath his chin.

"Ragna?" Byral muttered less enthusiastically. "I thought you'd passed through to the halls of Valhalla, years ago."

Ragna laughed as he lifted the jug of ale from the bar, brought it to his lips and drank deeply.

"Aye, been there," he said, holding the jug to his chest like a prized treasure. "But the ale there is a little too sweet if you ask me." He swallowed another mouthful before laying the jug back on the bar. "Now what's this about debt?"

Jaygen noticed the mischief sparkling in his father's eyes and stepped cautiously back - he knew that look.

"Erm…Eric owes me," Byral muttered, shrinking away from Ragna. "For the ale we delivered before winter and for oxen he borrowed to plough the fields and the labour of…"

Ragna rested a meaty hand on Byral's shoulder as he pulled him around so they were both facing Carmelga.

"My niece is right. You should have stolen Eric back from the Empire instead of stealing from her," he said.

Jaygen felt the tension in the room rise, edged with the oncoming violence. Two of the Vikings that had been sat in the corner ignoring the exchange before, were now squaring off against Byral's son while Fieri stepped towards him, pulling a short sword from its scabbard.

Jaygen stared at the blade, cringing from the sharpness of the weapon and the intent in her eyes. There was no doubt that when the fight began she would attack him. He wished that he was wearing the wolf suit instead of it being in the pack on his back.

Fieri, her name was. To Jaygen she certainly appeared fiery. Her face was close enough for him to see the scar that cut through the notch in her eyebrow and the desire for violence in her glower.

A knife suddenly appeared at the girl's throat, the blade indenting the soft skin as his mother's face appeared around the redhead's shoulder.

"Easy now," Ejan whispered, increasing the pressure and forcing Fieri to wince. "My son may be less than happy fighting a girl, but I wouldn't think twice about removing your head."

Byral nervously laughed, the veins on his temple rapidly pulsing as he held up his hands in surrender. "It appears I made a mistake," he admitted, anxious eyes darting between his son and daughter.

Ragna slapped him on the shoulder, the grin still present. "Aye, we all make mistakes. And now is the wrong time to begin another clan war when we have more than enough common enemies." He grasped the jug and poured ale into the empty tankard, then placed it in Byral's shaking hands. "Besides, there'll be more than enough bloodshed to come before too long." He drank from the jug. "After we've taken my brother back from the Empire."

Ejan eased the knife from Fieri's neck and patted her on the cheek, none too gently. "You can put your sword away now," she informed her.

Jaygen still received the full piercing glower from the red-haired girl as she slipped her sword expertly away into its scabbard. If looks could kill, he guessed he would be a hundred times dead by now, from her alone. He made a mental note to stay clear of her from now on.

Byral lowered his tankard. "I'm not fighting against the Empire. Not for your brother, not for anybody," he said. "The world's gone mad and it was a mad place to begin with, without this spawn of Chaos running amok with the Dark Amy."

Jaygen felt his fingers clench into a fist at the mention of Elora, but he kept quiet, trusting his father to do the right thing by his people.

"And the rumour is she's freed Grycul and is burning towns and cities in the south," Byral continued. "For the love of Odin, there's even been talk of Grimwolf joining forces with her."

Jaygen's breath caught in his throat. He had forgotten that Grimwolf was a Viking myth that belonged in folklore and stories meant to frighten children.

Ragna drained the jug and slammed it onto the bar. He absently wiped drops of ale from his beard before slowly turning to the Viking.

"Grimwolf?" Ragna chuckled, sparing Jaygen a sly glance before patting Byral on the shoulder. "Wouldn't have marked you as the superstitious type and I'd never take you for a coward. But there comes a time when the choice for fighting will be taken from you. When the only answer left is steel."

"Nobody can force me or my clan to fight," Byral snapped.

"No, they can't," Ejan agreed, resting her elbows against the bar. "You can let yourself be killed. You can allow your clan and your people to get slaughtered without raising a sword."

"Or you can be a Viking," Ragna finished.

"You expect us to fight this demigod, this daughter of Chaos?" Fieri cut in, standing by her father, raising her chin as if attempting to stare down her nose at the taller man before her.

"No, she's not the enemy and neither is the Empire," Ragna continued.

Byral shook his head, the beads in his beard swinging with the motion. "You're not making any sense. Your words are as mad as you."

Ragna grinned, "I'd couldn't agree with you more, but the words are the truth. Odin sent me back to bring the clans together. To lead them north to fight a battle against the small gods themselves."

"North?" Fieri asked, shaking her head. "We're as far north as you're going to get. What's north of north?"

Carmelga reached for the tankard discarded by Byral. "That's exactly what I asked this young one before you lot barged into the tavern," she said, before putting the tankard to her lips and tipping it back. "I take it, he's yours?"

Ejan smiled proudly, eyes beaming and Jaygen felt his cheeks flush as everyone's attention turned to him. "Carmelga, meet your cousin, Jaygen."

Carmelga laughed. "Thought you reminded me of somebody," she said and slid the ale towards him. "It's on the house, cuz." She turned back to Byral's son and snatched her axe back from him. "So, who are we fighting?" she asked, tapping the flat of the blade against her open palm.

"Neptula," Ragna answered. "And Valcaneous and Hades."

"Mad," Byral stammered. "How do we even fight the gods, if what you say is true, which I doubt?"

Ragna reached over his shoulder and slipped the Fist of the North onto the bar, the wood creaking beneath the weight.

"With this," he replied, tapping the huge war hammer. "And with every Viking from every clan. Uniting the north as my grandfather, Black Owen had done."

Carmelga drove the axe into the wood beside the Fist, the weapon sticking up by itself as she snatched the tankard from Jaygen and downed the ale in one. "Odin!" she shouted. "I'm going with you. About time I got to swing some steel."

Others around the tavern muttered in agreement, except the earth-born skier who Jaygen noticed was still hiding beneath his table.

"Odin!" shouted the two men who had squared up to Byral's son.

"Odin!" Ejan shouted and before the single syllable had been finished Jaygen had joined his mother in saluting the god of the Vikings.

"Odin!" he yelled.

The tavern turned silent as Byral scratched at his beard. "I still see no proof of your claims, other than a man once born to this village returning after a long absence," he said, slapping the grey metal of the war hammer. "I want to see some truth to your words before I commit my family to this folly. Show me how it is that you stand before us now after passing into the halls of Valhalla. How does a man killed, take a breath again?"

Jaygen witnessed the indecision on the others, saw the hesitance in the men who had already sworn to Odin and a scowl on Fieri as she watched the scene unfold.

Ragna chuckled. "Proof?" he asked, shrugging out of his fur coat. It fell to the floor with a thud. "Truth?" he queried, slipping the leather vest from his body. "I died on a narrow pass in Aslania," he unbuttoned the top of his jerkin and pulled it over his head. "I had steel in my hand and fire in my blood. I died a warrior's death, a Viking's death."

Gasps escaped Carmelga and Fieri and the men present as Ragna turned his naked torso so it caught the firelight.

"But I was dying already. Had my five bellies dragged up the God's Peak Mountain with death as my constant companion," he explained, prodding a puckered mess of flesh on his stomach. The rough skin was dark grey against his white skin. "I was stuck by an arrow, the head was buried deep inside, it tickled my innards something bad," he glanced to Ejan. "If it wasn't for my wife and the help from the daughter of Chaos, I would have been left where I was. Instead they dragged my dying carcass with them, hoping that I might survive. But nobody gets stuck in the belly and lives."

The older men around the bar nodded in agreement.

"And Odin it seemed gave me the chance to prove myself," Ragna continued. "We made it as far as the pass before the Empire caught up. The others crossed the bridge to Aslania, but only because I held the soldiers back."

Jaygen noted that his father held the entire tavern captive, each face open in astonishment, gazes falling on the giant before them as he relived his own demise.

"I killed ten score before I fell," Ragna explained, pointing to a star-shaped scar on his wrist. "This is where a bolt stole my grip." He twisted his arm to show the damage on the other side where the bolt had passed all the way through. "And I've a matching scar on my leg, where the shot had brought me down. And this," he continued, tapping a long ugly line that crossed his ribs and ended at the armpit. "Is where I was carved open by a sword when they fell upon me." He lifted his head to reveal the grey jagged gash that ran over his throat. "This is wear a blade found my windpipe and damn near took my head off." He opened his arms up and slowly turned to display the network of scars and blemishes that criss-crossed his entire body. "When I went down they butchered me in earnest. It was by sheer luck that they didn't cut up my pretty face."

"Or shave one of your bellies from you," Ejan chuckled, but nobody in the room seemed in a humorous mood.

"Never in all my days have I seen such scars," Byral murmured, whistling through his teeth. "Very impressive and a grand tale – you always were a storyteller. Yet it still doesn't prove you went through the last door."

"Proves nothing," Fieri agreed, yet her gaze was still wandering over the damaged flesh, her face screwed up in morbid curiosity.

"Thought you might say that," Ragna chuckled, sounding unperturbed by the disbelievers.

He approached Byral and nimbly slipped a dagger from the clansman's belt. "When all is said and done, you can always put your trust in steel, no?"

Byral frowned, but said nothing.

"Sharp, ugly and cold," Ragna continued. "But steel has an honesty to it."

Jaygen's father flipped the dagger around his large hand with the practice of a seasoned fighter, then reversed the grip and set the sharp tip against his chest.

"Raggy?" Ejan asked, a tinge of panic lacing her voice.

"Da, what are you doing?" Jaygen demanded, sharing the anxious foreboding of his mother and feeling fear sinking into his gut.

Ragna ignored the pair of them, his amused gaze fixed on Byral.

"Drive the blade home," he ordered, taking Byral's hand and placing it over the handle of the blade. "Pierce my heart."

"No!" Jaygen and his mother said together.

What was his father doing? Jaygen didn't think he could lose him all over again.

Ragna held his free hand up to halt Ejan's advance. "Fear not wench," he said. "If Odin wanted me dead, he wouldn't have gone through all that trouble to send me back."

Byral stared at the dagger beneath his hand, his fingers trembling upon the hilt as he gripped it tighter.

"Do it," Ragna ordered, his face twisting into a cunning grin. "Thrust it deep and true."

The grey-bearded Viking put his other hand upon the handle, squeezed until his knuckles turned white and glared up at Ragna.

"You're a mad bastard," he said as a single bead of blood formed around the tip and began to run down the sharpened steel.

Then all at once he let his arms fall and stepped away from Ragna, dropping the dagger onto the bar where it clattered against the war hammer.

"Bloody mad," he repeated, shaking his head.

Ragna picked up his leather vest and slipped it on, the wild grin still on display while Jaygen's heart was thumping. He let go the breath he had been holding and reached for the ale. He thought Byral was going to thrust the blade into his father and could only thank Odin that he didn't try. He doubted he was immortal.

"Proof if ever there was," Ragna laughed as he patted Byral on the cheek. "I told you that I couldn't be killed by steel alone."

"But he didn't stab you," Fieri argued, putting her hands on her hips and scowling.

Ragna turned the smile on her. "Then you do it," he offered, parting the vest to show his chest again.

"No, she won't!" Ejan snapped.

Fieri turned on Jaygen's mother and hissed through her teeth, her lip curling up into a snarl.

"Enough," Byral snapped, placing a firm hand on his daughter. "They'll be no fighting between Vikings. Not while we're bringing the clans together and not until after we've destroyed this new enemy."

"What?" Fieri exclaimed. "But you didn't prove anything. Why are we joining our clan with this lot?" she demanded, her face going as red as her hair.

"Because Ragna is right. We should never have let the Empire take Eric. And besides," Byral looked sideways at Ragna, a cocky grin parting his beard. "I'm curious to see what Odin has in store for this one."

"Stupid old farts," Fieri spat as she wrenched her arm free from her father's grasp and stormed out of the tavern. Leaving the door swinging on its hinges and letting in the cold.

"Old farts?" Ragna chuckled.

Byral laughed with him. "I've been called far worse. She has a mean temper, Fieri."

Carmelga refilled the tankards on the bar and pushed them before the aged warriors.

"So, when are we going to free my Da?" she asked.

"Where is he held?" Ragna asked.

"The fort near Gellingly," Carmelga replied.

Ragna grinned. "Then we can do it at sun-up. Dawn raids seem to be fashionable these days."

Byral laughed. "They always were. I'll fetch a few men from my village. It won't take much to break him out of that ram-shackle of a fort. There's barely twenty imperials stationed there. It's more of an outpost really."

"I'll take the heads of every southern soldier," Carmelga shouted as she lifted the axe once again and swiped the air before her.

Ragna caught the weapon around the shaft before lowering it to the bar.

"No, we need to do things a little differently from now on," he informed her. "No killing of the imperials, not unless it's absolutely necessary."

"But…" Carmelga exclaimed, mouth opening wide, mimicking the expression that Byral and the other Vikings were giving.

"New rules for a new world. Our enemy is Neptula and anything that wriggles out of the sea," Ragna explained as he glanced around at the men now turned thoughtful and sullen. "Yet it doesn't mean we can't rough the southerners up some. Nothing says we can't do a little bit of imperial tickling."

Jaygen noticed that some of the men perked up at that. In truth, he felt a little excited himself. He dreamed of going on raids with his father. Fighting side by side against the Empire, like in the stories he used to tell him when he was a child.

Now feeling the warmth and growing camaraderie of the men around him, Jaygen approached the bar and wrapped his fingers around a cup. He drank the bitter ale as he listened to his father issuing out orders to the men.

"Figit, collect as much rope from the village as you can," he then pointed to the Viking with the bandolier of knives. "Gwet, bring a tall ladder…"

Jaygen felt proud as the men enthusiastically set about their tasks and more came to receive orders. He muscled his way through the throng to reach his father.

"What do you want me to do Da?" he asked. "Shall I use the suit?"

Ragna smiled down at his son and placed a hand on his shoulder.

"Sorry, Jaygen. I'll need you to stay here and help your mother and cousin. Craggs Head will need organising before the other clans arrive."

Jaygen swallowed the words rising in his throat. Instead he stood there dumbly silent as the other Vikings busied themselves. Then quietly slipped out of the way as tables were pushed together and his father began to discuss how they were going to rescue Eric.

He watched them for a time before his emotions became too much. Then, like Fieri earlier, he stormed from the tavern and went back out into the icy chill of the north. He thought he caught snatches of his mother's voice calling him back but the door slammed shut, closing him out with the white wilderness and with his sullen mood.

6

The Tooth

The blizzard had relented with the rising sun, leaving the barren landscape a pristine white against a sapphire sky. Jaygen perched on a rock high above the valley, admiring the vast unspoiled land before him.

Craggs Head was below, smoke curling from the few chimneys that lay nestled in the crack that swept down to a frozen beach. Salt reached his nose, travelling on a steady wind that carried inland from the sea. Icebergs lay scattered along the peninsula, the splintering sounds of cracking ice piercing the tranquil world as they rocked against the surface of the water. It echoed around the mountain range behind him, scaring an eagle into flight which cried back in complaint.

The bird soared higher, large wings spreading as it circled above the rocks, floating on the breeze that carried up the valley.

Magnificent, Jaygen thought as he watched the eagle fly, then it suddenly plummeted. It folded its wings as it dropped, snatching a smaller bird that had been preening itself on a tree stump. He marvelled at the sleek attack as the eagle carried its prize aloft, gliding directly overhead.

A lone tear of blood fell from the pair and spattered against the ground at his feet, bright red against the white. Jaygen stared at the kidney shaped stain and wondered if it was a sign of things to come.

His father had left the village last night with a twenty-man strong team and had yet to return. Then the struggle would come of attempting to join all the clans in the north together. There may be a little blood spilt in that alone, before they marched to the battlegrounds to defeat Hades and his demons. He guessed there would be more than a little spilt then too, but he would be there amongst it. Or at least Grimwolf would.

A dark shadow in the shape of a bird silently passed over him. When he searched the sky he saw a large scraw-harpy flying in fast and striking the eagle mid-air.

The two bodies came together in a violent attack, the eagle crying in pain as the larger bird's talons pierced its body. Then in the same movement, the scraw-harpy closed its hooked beak down on the exposed throat of the eagle, snapping its neck.

More tears of blood fell to Jaygen's feet as the Dark Army's flying eyes wafted its huge wings to bear its fresh prize into the mountains.

Jaygen sighed as he stared down at the spreading redness on the ground, the new blood merging with the first as the eagle became the prey.

He hoped it wasn't a sign of things to come.

Movement from below forced him to raise his gaze. Floundering up the valley towards him was the earth-born skier he had witnessed hiding beneath the table at the tavern. He was trudging through the snow, waving his arms to get Jaygen's attention and appearing flustered.

He stopped at the rock beside him, stuck his skis into the snow and spoke in a foreign language while pointing up at the mountain.

"Slow down," Jaygen said, trying to calm the man by holding up his hands. "I don't understand you."

He knew that Earth, much like Thea, had hundreds of different tongues and dialects and he could only understand northern or the common language of Thea, and only one of Earth.

"Can you speak English?" Jaygen asked.

The man halted his gesturing as a large smile brightened his face.

"Yes, yes, English yes," he replied, excitedly.

He screwed his face up for a moment as if working out what it was he needed to say before he continued. "It is good to be understood. Nobody in the village can speak English."

Jaygen offered him a sad smile, "Nobody in the village is earth-born. They're Vikings."

The man nodded, "They do look like Vikings or Saxons. After the joining of the two worlds I learned to not get surprised by anything that I came across."

"That's probably wise, there's a lot of strangeness from both worlds. And I expect still more to come from this new Ethea. How can I help you? You seem a little out of place."

The man nodded in agreement. "Out of place and in place at the same time. Very confusing. My name is Peter, I'm from Finland, a country south of here. My friend and I came north to ski," Peter explained, patting his skis proudly. "Near the summit of this mountain is a famous ski resort, or at least it was famous before the merger. We trekked up there a few days ago, expecting things to be how they were before. But…"

"It's all changed?" Jaygen suggested, staring up the imposing mountain and not seeing any sign of a ski resort.

"Changed," agreed Peter. "When we found what was left of the resort it was in chaos. Buildings collapsed or buried in snow, trees growing through the cart house and bodies everywhere."

"They died in the merge?" Jaygen asked, witnessing Peter's face becoming ashen as he relived the trauma.

"Some, either been struck by rocks or crushed under buildings. But in one case we found a man that had merged into a tree, his entire body missing with only a leg and an arm protruding from the trunk," Peter explained, shaking the memory from his mind. "Then there were the others. Ripped, torn and half devoured by ugly creatures."

"What creatures?"

Peter was silent for a moment, rubbing a shaking hand through the blonde stubble of his chin.

"They were a kind of bear, only with horns and tusks. We were so shocked by the devastation that lay around the resort, that it took us a moment to realise that we may be in danger. By then the bear things were all around us."

"They killed your friend?" Jaygen asked, seeing how difficult it was for Peter to talk. When he did speak again, he was so quiet that Jaygen had trouble hearing him.

"I was still wearing my skis. That's what saved my life," Peter explained, staring out to sea. "But my friend was a snowboarder. He didn't have time to take it from his pack before they set about him. Sometimes, when I manage to sleep I can still hear his screams in my dreams."

"I'm sorry," Jaygen said, about to place a consoling hand upon Peter's shoulder, but paused – he didn't know this man. "I think those creatures were mountain ogres. There was nothing you could have done."

Peter gave a dry sob, biting his lip as he regained control of himself.

"Trouble is, there is something in my friend's pack which I need and soon."

Jaygen shook his head. "It isn't worth going back up there for. You've seen what mountain ogres can do."

"No, you don't understand. I'm a diabetic and so was my friend," Peter explained as he withdrew an object from his pocket. It was a small needle inside a plastic bag and a tiny medicine bottle. "This insulin," he said, holding the bottle up so he could see that it was empty, save from a dribble of liquid in the bottom. "Will only last to the end of the day. If I don't get more, my body will start to shut down and I will die." He inhaled deeply before placing the bottle and needle back into his pocket and zipping it tight. "My friend carried a box of spare bottles in his pack, should I drop or lose mine."

"And you need somebody to fetch his pack." Jaygen finished for him.

The scraw-harpy returned, screaming into the sky. Its cry echoing around the mountain range. Peter watched it, narrowing his eyes at the large flying beast.

"I tried to explain things to the people in the village, but you're the first person I came across that understands me. If I had found somebody sooner I would have gone with them, but I'm afraid that now I am too weak to reach the resort."

Jaygen looked away from the hope in Peter's face. Instead he glanced down at Craggs Head and then back up at the scraw-harpy that circled above. What would

Elora do? She wouldn't have thought twice about helping the man. Maybe her mind was up there now, linked with the huge bird and watching him through the beast's eyes.

He sighed, ready to turn down the offer to help. He would have his work cut out when his father returned and his mother wouldn't let him go on some fool's errand up in the high places. So, he was as shocked as Peter when he answered, "I'll do it."

The snow crunched under foot as Jaygen ducked beneath the branches of an evergreen, using the tree roots to pull himself up above a bluff. He stole a moment to catch his breath and drink from the canteen he filled before leaving some few hours ago. He put the bottle back in his pack and checked the map Peter had given him.

Judging that he was almost halfway up the mountainside, he orientated the map so he could pick out the features around him and pinpoint his exact location.

The mountain itself wasn't hard to climb with varying slopes of different angles of steepness. There were patches of trees, some were marked on the map while others, probably from Thea, were not. He found the cable cars lying scattered on the western slopes, broken and crushed. The cable itself lay in the snow and twisted its way upwards like a steel snake, showing the way to the resort. This was also marked on the map. The only other feature on the mountain that tied in with what he saw before him, was a large rock that jutted out away from the mountain. The slab of granite, the length and breadth of a horse and cart, poked out over a sheer drop. 'Devils Horn', it said on the map, but Jaygen recognised it as the Tooth. A place where a pair of Vikings would settle a score. A place where two would step upon it and only one would return.

Jaygen stared at the strange rock jutting out at a right angle from the slope. His father would tell him stories of the Tooth. A place that was known to have been a part of the Viking culture for as long as there were Vikings. His father had never fought on there but his father's father, Black Owen, had stepped upon the Tooth plenty of times.

He folded the map and placed it away into the folds of his furs before setting out towards the strange rock, wanting to see the imposing jut of granite from up close.

The ground before the Tooth was flat with logs set around the perimeter, forming a perfect circle. Snow layered the floor, pristine and untouched and Jaygen felt a pang of shame from trudging through it, leaving his boot prints and spoiling the effect.

To the cliff side, where the circle gave way to the sudden drop, was the Tooth. Jaygen had been expecting something magnificent. A large carving or statue depicting the famous Viking location but he felt disappointment at seeing that there was nothing except the rock itself. Simple, harsh and ruthless. It was as unassuming as it was final. Ragna would have said it was honest, like the Fist of the North; you didn't need fancy thrills and gold to kill someone when ugly and brutal always worked best.

Slowly he placed a foot upon the rock itself, the wind having blown any snow away and reduced the ice that was left to smooth glass. He could imagine how people might fall off from the slippery perch by themselves, without the added violence of battle to aid them.

Putting his arms out to either side for balance, he edged out onto the small platform, a breeze teasing at his hair and drawing him to the brink of emptiness. He took small shuffling steps until he reached the end of the Tooth and glanced down.

Vertigo forced him to hold his breath as his legs suddenly felt weak.

The dark trees far below seemed so small that they could have been part of a toy model and he could capture the entire village and small peninsular beneath his thumb. If he was to drop off the end it would take an age before he struck solid ground, where he guessed he would be pulverised beyond recognition.

Shuddering he stepped away and turned to leave, but somebody had stepped onto the Tooth and blocked his way to safety.

"Strange place to come, don't you think?" Fieri asked, raising her notched eyebrow and looking him up and down.

She leaned over the edge, hand resting on the pommel of her sword; red hair billowing out like flames from an angry fire. She spat over the side and watched its progress with interest before glancing once more at him. "Long, long way down."

Jaygen made to step passed her but she folded her arms and blocked his way, a wicked grin forcing her lips into a grimace.

"What's your rush to leave? Don't you want to tussle?"

Jaygen folded his own arms and acted as if he wasn't intimidated while attempting to push thoughts of the vast void from his mind.

"Not really," he replied, staring right back into those piercing blue eyes. "Why did you follow me?"

Fieri shrugged, "Nothing better to do and I was curious. You ever killed anybody before, Jaygen?" She said his name with child-like disdain as if the word left a bitter taste in her mouth.

"No," Jaygen lied. When in truth, he guessed, the number was in double figures. "Have you?"

She stepped closer, forcing him to take a step back. "Maybe," she replied, teasingly.

"Then why did your Da make you stay behind? They may have needed a hardened killer like yourself," Jaygen suggested before realising that now wasn't the best place to make her angry, not when his heel was touching the brink of nothing.

Fieri glowered, her hands clenching into fists as she snarled. Any prettiness she had dwindling with her rising anger, her face flushing the same colour as her hair.

Jaygen raised his arms in surrender. "My Da made me stay too. But soon enough they'll have no choice but to let us fight."

Fieri glared at him without speaking, as if measuring his words and deciding whether to simply push him off the Tooth or not. At least she could claim she had killed somebody if she did.

Jaygen prepared himself to shove her onto her back if she came any closer. She was equal to him in height but he had the weight advantage. Yet as he braced she let her arms fall; her fingers un-clenching as she once again rested them on her sword.

"Is what your Da said last night true?" Fieri asked, "Is there a war coming?"

Jaygen nodded as he breathed out. She didn't seem so inclined to throw him over yet.

"What? And the part about the daughter of Chaos?"

Again Jaygen nodded. "Elora," he answered and felt the familiar pull in his stomach as his thoughts drifted towards her. He really needed to put her out of his head before it drove him to fling himself into oblivion.

"I'm going further up the mountain; do you want to come with me?" he asked.

"You know there are mountain ogres up there? Large cats and snow jubs? And you're not carrying any steel. Not to mention the avalanches that are common this time of year, before the spring. There are a hundred ways to die on the mountain."

Jaygen shrugged as if it was no big deal. "So, are you coming?"

For the first time since he had met her, he witnessed a genuine smile on Fieri's face. "Of course, I'm coming."

Jaygen was relieved as he stepped off the Tooth. His heart had raced as Fieri forced him to clamber passed her and laughed when he almost dived to the safety of the circle. At least, he mused, she seemed in a better mood.

They picked their way through the trees until he found the fallen cable cars again. From there they followed the steel rope as it ascended the mountain.

"Why are you so keen to put yourself in danger?" Fieri asked him as they climbed over a flattened cable car. The metal frame was crushed against the rock and only one glass window remained intact. As she scrambled along the body of the car Fieri slipped her sword free from the scabbard and smashed the surviving pane, then grinned at the destruction.

"I'm fetching medicine for the earth-born at Craggs Head. Without it, he will die."

She leapt from the car and smoothly slipped her sword away.

"Aren't you the hero. Why do you care if an earth-born lives or dies?" she asked. "He isn't part of your clan and he isn't even a Viking."

Because that's what Elora would have done, he wanted to say but chose to tell half of another truth.

"I wasn't about to stay and help my mother do chores around the tavern, waiting for my Da to come home. Besides, I've never been here before and I wanted to take a look around."

He watched Fieri as she stalked ahead, pushing a snow-laced branch out of the way and holding it for him. He was about to say thanks when she let go of the branch and it sprang back, whipping him in the face.

"Ouch," he yelped, placing his hand to his stinging cheek. Although the shock of the slap hurt more than the pain itself.

Jaygen cast his angry gaze on Fieri but she had already scrambled ahead, her childish giggling resonating off the evergreens as she ran between the trees. Shaking his head, he set off after her, his pack bouncing on his back as a grin found his lips.

He pushed through the trees and bounded up the steep slope, half climbing and half pulling himself along with the taut cable that lay on the ground. Fieri was using the same method as she climbed over a rock that lay ahead, her breath visible in the cold air. She jumped from the end and landed in a forward-roll before springing to her feet once again and sprinted on.

Jaygen skirted around the rock, attempting to catch up but instead caught his pack against the rough edge, lost his footing and stumbled into the steep slope. He couldn't work his legs through the deep snow quick enough to prevent himself from falling.

"That pack of yours is making you clumsy," Fieri exclaimed through bouts of laughter. "What are you carrying in it anyway?"

Jaygen pushed himself up from the ground leaving a perfect imprint of his face in the snow.

"Nothing," he replied.

"Doesn't feel like nothing," Fieri remarked, grasping the pack as he rose and unceremoniously shook it, making the contents clink together.

"It's pots and pans and cleaning equipment," Jaygen lied unable to think of anything better.

"And this?" she asked, gripping his sword which was wrapped in cloth.

"It's a spare shaft for my Da's hammer."

Fieri shook her head. "Why drag it all the way up here?" she asked, seeming unsatisfied with his explanation.

Jaygen cursed himself. He was never good at lying and the more lies he gave the deeper he was digging himself into a hole. In the end he couldn't think of an explanation so shrugged and attempted to change the subject.

"You ever been south?" he asked as he began to trudge upwards once again.

"South?" she repeated. "Why would I ever go south? Vikings need the high places where the men become as hard as the weather."

"And the women?" he asked.

"Harder than the men," she laughed and threw a snowball at him.

Jaygen had seen her packing the ball tight in her hands as she was speaking and so was ready for it. He ducked in time to see it smash into a white shower against the tree beside him.

Before he stood straight again his hands were full of snow and packing a snowball of his own. He turned to throw it, but paused. She was staring at him with a sad face, puckering out her bottom lip.

"You wouldn't throw snow at a girl would you?" she asked.

Her expression caught him completely off guard. It was the first time he had seen her look anything less than vicious and he found the timid appearance endearing.

"I don't know," he teased, tossing the ball and catching it in his palm. "You did say women in the north were harder than the men."

She stepped closer, keeping her eyes locked on his until she was in touching distance. Close enough for him to notice a subtle freckling over her nose and cheeks.

"We are harder," she admitted in a soft tone. "And smarter."

As she finished her last word she kicked her boot through the snow and showered him in white powder.

Before he had the chance to spit the snow out of his mouth she careered into his side, knocking him over and began to charge up the slope once again.

Jaygen half-heartedly threw the snowball at her, yet she was too swift. It fell harmlessly to the ground as her laughter carried back to him. He began laughing himself as he chased her up the slope.

Fieri weaved between the trees, ducking branches and slipping between the white brush. Her long rangy legs giving her an advantage as Jaygen struggled to keep up. But as the slope levelled out the red-haired Viking skidded to a halt and he almost ran into the back of her.

They were both gasping for breath as they stood before the wreck of the ski resort – or what was left of it.

A long wood and brick building stood proud at the top of a row of log cabins. The roof was missing from the main structure, a thick evergreen rising high and spreading branches where the roof should have been. Its dark red trunk disappearing inside the frame and dislodging bricks from one of the walls. Shattered glass lay amongst the detritus of masonry and splintered logs, along with abandoned skis, torn snowsuits and boots. A child's glove that had become snagged against a thin branch, bobbed and waved with the breeze, adding an ominous tone to the scene – the glove had belonged to somebody.

Another building lay in ruins at the foot of the slope. The cable they had followed up the mountain ran inside and was wrapped around a large steel wheel that was buckled and twisted around rock. A dark brown stain streaked down one side of a crushed cart that had also merged with the granite. A bright green ski jacket flapped against the misshapen metal, the owner still wearing it; the jaw of his skull hanging loose in a silent scream as the rest of his body lay buried beneath the cart.

Other skeletal bodies were scattered around the devastated complex. Curled up and decimated, missing limbs and left for the snow to form drifts against them.

"Mountain ogres?" Jaygen suggested, his voice seeming overly loud as he absorbed the dead.

"No, the daughter of Chaos did this," Fieri remarked, her hand gripping the pommel of her sword. "The ogres finished them off."

Jaygen wanted to defend Elora and was even forming an excuse on his lips when he realised that there was no such defence. The merging of the worlds was by Elora's hand.

"We better be quick," he suggested instead. "It'll start to get dark soon and I don't like the idea of spending the night with mountain ogres."

"Mountain ogres might not be the problem," Fieri replied, pointing further up the mountain to where an immense shelf of snow, sat perched on the summit. The bottom of it sagged thickly over the ledge directly above them. "One snow flake too many and that lot will be coming down. Even the noise from a snapped twig could trigger an avalanche."

Jaygen stared at the looming weight of white death above and all the snow that would come down. It would instantly devour them, crush and leave no sign of their passing.

"Then we best be quiet as well as swift," he whispered as he gently stepped across the open ground towards the ruined ski resort.

He winced with every footfall, his large boots making a crunching sound as he darted glances at the snow shelf, sure that it would topple at any moment.

"What are we looking for?" Fieri asked, joining him at the wood and brick building.

"Peter, that is the earth-born, said his medicine would be in his friend's pack. He's probably one of these," Jaygen whispered, pointing at the mounds before them.

"But how will we know which one is his friend?"

Jaygen shrugged. "Peter said he was a snowboarder so hopefully he'll have a snowboard."

Fieri nodded that she understood, then paused as she began to dig snow away from the closest body.

"What's a snowboard?" she asked.

Jaygen shrugged again, "I don't know. But it must be for going down the slopes with. That was the reason they came here in the first place."

Fieri shook her head. "Why?" she asked. "Why come here and why all this?" She waved her hand at the resort in general.

"I don't know, for fun maybe?" he answered as he knelt beside a mound of snow and began to brush the white powder from the top to expose a body.

"Fun? Earth-borns have a crazy sense of fun. What's wrong with good honest fighting?"

Jaygen didn't reply as he revealed part of a shoulder and head. A large gash had been opened across the throat exposing a windpipe. The frozen blood having formed into black pearls which beaded down the rest of the torso.

He heaved the carcass into a sitting position and searched about him for a pack but found none. It wasn't Peter's friend and besides, this man had a grey beard and was a lot older than the earth-born.

Resting the body back down, he moved onto the next but with the same result.

"This one's missing both his arms," Fieri said, lifting the mutilated body of a man in a blooded ski suit. She shoved it over to reveal a long flat object that was stuck to his back.

It made a cracking noise as she pulled it away, the item having been frozen in place.

She let the body topple over as she lifted the flat article and flexed it. Jaygen thought it resembled Marvin's skateboard which he had seen him using back at the inn, but without the wheels.

"That's it. That's the snowboard," he explained excitedly as he went to her. "His pack must be here somewhere."

Fieri glanced at the board, shook her head and unceremoniously dropped it. "I don't think the pack's here," she said. "His arms were torn off for a reason. The ogres wanted his pack – maybe it contained food."

Jaygen ran his hands along the ground where the body had been but soon realised that Fieri was right. The pack had been taken.

He glanced once more at the darkening sky and realised that time was running out, they would need to begin heading back if they didn't want to spend the night up here.

"We'll search for a few moments more, maybe it's still here somewhere," he suggested glancing to the broken building. "I'll check in there, see if they've dragged it inside."

Fieri nodded as she pulled her sword free and began to randomly poke it through the snow while Jaygen made his way to the building.

The entrance was a large double door, one of which was jammed open by a snow drift. Jaygen glanced inside but saw only darkness.

He breathed deeply then stepped in, holding his arms out before him and finding the trunk of the thick evergreen.

Snow had fallen through the opening in the broken roof and covered the floor. Jaygen used his feet to search the ground, tapping his boots against the solid wooden planks which had splintered in places to accommodate the tree roots and rocks.

He worked his way around the evergreen, tripping over another body which was partially buried inside the tree. As he stumbled a hand slapped his face.

When he regained his footing he found that a single arm reached out of the trunk. The skeletal limb was bent at the elbow and disappeared into the bark below the shoulder.

Jaygen nudged the arm and watched it swing on its hinged joint, the only indication that the person buried inside had ever existed. He guessed that this kind of death had happened all over the world, thousands – possibly millions of people being in the wrong place at the wrong time.

He pulled his gaze away and made a silent prayer to Odin as he forced himself on. No good would come of brooding over the dead, his Da would have said.

To the back of the ruined building he found a pile of human bones, damaged skulls with hair still attached and broken bodies. The flesh had been stripped and the bones gnawed for the marrow.

The ogres had done a methodical job of removing anything edible from the bodies, even crunching through the smaller bones and ribs. They would have taken full advantage of the merge, preferring to eat carcass's that were still warm – that's why they had left the others that had stiffened in the cold.

Amongst the pile he found an orange pack stained brown with old blood. It had been torn open and the contents scattered on the macabre pile before him. Ski goggles, gloves and a compass lay broken and torn but a smaller red pouch with a white cross on it, still sat inside.

He lifted it out and unzipped it.

Inside he found six boxes of small bottles similar to the one that Peter had shown him in the morning.

Jaygen felt himself smile as he re-zipped the medicine pouch and tucked it inside his furs. They could now head back down the mountain. He made his way the door, about to indicate for Fieri that he had found what they had come for, when the smile vanished.

Fieri was standing where he had left her, her sword drawn and arcing in front of a large ogre that was swiping a crude but deadly club at her head.

The Viking ducked and rolled out of the way, moving quicker than the horned beast but it was soon joined by two others.

Without hesitation Jaygen removed his own pack and set it on the ground. He undid the buckles and wrenched it open before frantically pulling the items out.

His mother had wrapped each piece of armour, gauntlet and greaves in separate cloth so it wouldn't make a noise when he carried it, yet the extra protection slowed him in putting on the suit.

Only seconds could have passed until he finally snapped the visor closed on the snarling wolf helm, but seconds would be all Fieri would have against the ogres.

Swiftly Jaygen stalked out of the broken building and stormed towards the fighting beasts, his red cloak instantly catching the rising wind and billowing out.

The closest ogre turned its horned head his way, sensing his approach. Its small black eyes went wide before gathering itself together and raised a thick club.

For a beast the size of a bear it moved with surprising agility. Heavy muscles bunched in its arms as it swung the club towards Jaygen's head.

Predictable, Jaygen thought as he stepped into the attack. He caught the descending club in his gauntlet – the god-created suit absorbing the impact as he clenched the gauntlet of his other hand into a fist and drove it into the ogre's jaw.

Teeth shattered along with the jawbone. The beast rocked back, arms flailing wide as one of its horns spun away.

Jaygen dropped the club and it fell to the ground at the same instant as its owner, both now void of life. He turned to Fieri in time to watch her sidestep her attacker, missing a killing blow from its club. She used the momentum to thrust her sword into its gut, the sound of metal scraping against bone as she forced it further in.

She held firmly to the blade as the ogre sank to its knees before slowly, almost peacefully, sinking onto its side. As he sank, Fieri pulled her sword free to face the final beast.

Having her back to him, Fieri had yet to notice that he was there, her full attention given over to the ogre before her. Yet the beast had seen him and began to back away, its gaze brushing over its fallen comrades before locking on him.

"Had enough?" Fieri spat at the beast.

In answer the ogre turned and fled, flinging the club away in its haste to leave. It struck an evergreen and made a dull thunk that echoed around the mountain. As it tapered off Jaygen heard a deep groan followed by a cracking sound.

He glanced up to the immense shelf of snow and ice above. A large crack splintering up the centre and stretching to the summit.

He held his breath, unable to move – anchored to the spot as he watched thousands of tonnes of white death suddenly slip. It moved like a huge blanket sinking from a bed, as if he was no bigger than an ant on the floor and the bed was made for the heavens.

Jaygen clenched his teeth and was about to grab Fieri and run when the groaning ceased and the slipping paused, only a small powdery shower dropped from the ledge.

It had stopped.

Releasing his breath, he turned to face Fieri as she turned to face him.

Their eyes locked.

Her piercing blue stare caught him off guard, perfect cold circles amongst a tangle of fire red hair.

"Grimwolf?" she asked, her voice sounding tight as if restricted by fear.

Jaygen nodded.

She briefly glanced at the broken building before staring once again at him. "You killed Jaygen and now you're going to slay me?"

It took a moment for her question to sink in. Of course she would think him a cold-hearted killer. Grimwolf was a folk legend, a myth from long ago; a demon sent to kill Vikings and butcher entire clans. Fieri thought him a monster.

Before he had chance to say anything, not that he had anything to say, she attacked.

"Odin!" she screamed as she threw herself upon him.

Her blade was a silver blur as it came down and he was as surprised as she was that he caught it in his gauntlet.

Jaygen closed his claw shaped steel glove over her blade, preventing her from any further attack.

"I…" Jaygen began, but quickly lowered his voice. "I mean you know harm," he whispered throatily.

She said nothing. Just stared at him, puzzlement creasing her brow as her salute to Odin still bounced around the summit.

Jaygen felt more than heard the deep rumbling groan that resonated from his feet and filled his chest. He still held Fieri's blade as he turned his snarling wolf's helm towards the shelf above.

The entire blanket of snow suddenly dipped forwards, breaking from the previous crack and the entire mountain began to shake. The sliding sound screeched through his head as thick ice scraped against rock. Then all at once the mountain rushed towards them, gathering speed and momentum as it picked up stones and trees on its way down.

The reaper was coming.

Turning to Fieri, her face filled with terror he shouted, "Run!"

"Run?" she repeated, incredulously. "Run where? It's a bloody avalanche."

Jaygen saw her point. How could you outrun that? He glanced once more to the rushing death and then down the mountain which in a few moments would be flooded with an entire winters worth of snow.

Then his gaze found the snowboard that had been discarded and left on the ground.

"Do you trust me?" he asked, having to shout above the ferocious tide that was descending on them.

"No," she shouted back. "You're Grimwolf, for Odin's sake."

Jaygen once again saw her point.

"Then I'm sorry," he offered.

"Sorry for what?"

Without another word Jaygen grasped Fieri and unceremoniously threw her over his shoulder. She instantly began to rain punches against his armour but he felt nothing beneath the suit.

He placed one of his feet into the foot loop of the snowboard, gave a silent prayer to Odin and pushed himself off.

The movement caught him off balance. He hadn't expected for the board to skim over the snow with such ease, but was thankful for it as he kicked on once again before placing his other foot on the board.

"Will you keep still," he barked at Fieri who kept throwing punches against his back while thrashing her legs; threatening to throw him off balance. She paid him no heed as they slid further down the slope, rapidly picking up speed.

From behind them Jaygen heard the tortuous crashing as the avalanche devastated the ski resort, the noise rising to a deafening crescendo as it closed in on them.

The snowboard cut down the slope and he found himself having to lean over to steer it around trees that were rushing towards them at a dizzying rate. Twice he almost struck an evergreen, his outstretched arms slapping away branches as he ducked lower to the board.

Fieri had ceased striking him and was now swinging her legs around his waist and holding onto his neck for all she was worth.

"Can't you go any faster?" she screamed into his visor, her eyes going wide as she stared behind him.

Jaygen felt the board shake as he struggled to keep it under his feet, the cold air rushing inside his helm and flinging his cloak out.

The roaring turbulence of the tide caught them up and he became aware of the tumbling snow rushing passed on either side of them; like long arms extending ready to pull them into a deadly embrace. The avalanche had caught them up and was beginning to overtake.

He steered the board in a desperate attempt to stay above the flow, to get caught under or to even fall off would mean the death of both of them.

Jaygen's calves and thighs burned with the effort to keep them upright, he frantically bobbed and weaved; correcting the board's path but it was rapidly becoming clear that he was fighting a losing battle.

Ahead lay a cable car, its smooth roof appearing like a glistening beetle shell amongst the snow as it angled up.

Jaygen leaned harshly to one side, his gauntlet digging into the cascading powder like a canoeist driving his oar deep into the water's surface for a tight turn.

Fieri screamed as she buried her head into his neck, strands of her red hair flying wild and catching against his armour.

Snow flowed over his foot as it poured against them and he fought desperately to keep the front edge skyward.

They hit the roof of the cable car with such speed that the metal shell dented instantly, the avalanche slamming into the back of both them and the steel frame. The added weight gave them lift as they slid up the makeshift ramp and hurtled into the sky.

Jaygen had often wondered what it would be like to fly and felt that this was as close to being airborne as he was ever going to get.

The tumultuous moving ground rushed up to meet them. Tumbling trees, spinning rocks and tonnes upon tonnes of snow all roaring in the downwards storm.

Jaygen wrapped his arms protectively around Fieri as they landed.

For a moment he managed to ride the white wave like a surfer mastering the sea, then all at once the board got sucked down and they followed.

His chest struck the ground and then a trunk rushed into view and struck his head, his teeth jarring inside the helm. His legs were wrenched one way and then the other as his body was thrown over and over until he couldn't decide where up began or down ended.

Amongst the confusion of spinning and slamming he heard Fieri cry out before her voice was snatched away and the growling white avalanche was all that filled everything; drowning out every sense apart from sound and pain – then they too faded out as he lost consciousness.

7

Steam Power

The ice across the surface of the lake had begun to crack and Elora watched with interest as a duck landed clumsily upon it. Feet slipping beneath itself as it began to tap frantically at the frozen water with its beak. It didn't take long to break an area large enough for it to slip into, bobbing up and down as it preened itself.

Elora shivered, the mere thought of being immersed in the freezing waters made her teeth chatter. It was hard to think that spring would be upon them in the next few weeks. The warmth it would bring would be a welcome comfort to Rams Keep. The lives there had been made harder with the harsh winter they had to endure. She only hoped that they survived long enough to experience it.

She pressed her cold fingers to her lips, kissed them and touched the colder rock of Nat's gravestone.

"Miss you," she whispered, seeing the words form white clouds in the air. Through them she spotted a lone figure walking towards her from the direction of the inn.

Silently she slipped beneath the canopy of the large willow, the shroud of thin branches parting for her as she hid behind the trunk.

Bray was dressed in his black cloak, the hood pulled over his head against the cold as he breathed against his fingers.

"Elora?" he ventured, pushing the branches aside as he entered the veil of the willow.

His footfalls crunched in the frost as he came around the tree, searching for her. Elora matched his steps as she circled away and sneaked up behind him.

She placed her finger against the pad of her thumb, found the subtle tug of the smuggler's pouch and pulled them apart. The pouch opened and she slid her soul reaver from its invisible scabbard. The dull red blade caught the morning sun through the willow's fine branches and for a moment the sword appeared to be on fire.

Bray, unaware of her silent approach, paused and rested against the trunk. He folded his arms as he stared out over the lake.

Elora's breath caught in her throat as she watched him lower his hood, his gorgeous green eyes widening with curiosity. A puzzled smile creeping upon his heart-warming face, forming cute dimples above the strong set jaw. He wasn't only handsome, he was beautiful.

She felt incredibly privileged to be able to call him her boyfriend. To be able to feel the same love she felt for him, returned. They had a bond stronger than anything she had ever felt before and doubted would ever feel again.

Stilling her breath, Elora admired him for another moment before stepping closer and thrusting her sword into his back.

Bray's cloak swished as he spun, the black material hiding his own sword as he ducked low and easily parried her blade.

She had been expecting the move and was already hooking her foot around his ankle, ready to shove him onto his back. But he had somehow twisted his free hand over her sword arm and turned the shove into a spin – each of them holding onto the other and pirouetting for a turn before coming away.

"You didn't warn me the lesson had begun," Bray pointed out, adopting a defencing stance, a cocky smile on his face.

Elora circled him, appreciating the swiftness in which he had dealt with her surprise attack. That would be his elf genes, she guessed. Giving him a heightened sensitivity to all of his senses.

"You wouldn't get a warning from the enemy," she replied, matching his cocky smile. "Would an assassin tell you his intentions before shooting you in the heart?"

Elora swiped her sword across his midriff, waited for his counter-block then stepped into him, driving her elbow into his sternum.

Bray doubled over and she felt a pang of guilt for hurting him. Although as he reversed his grip on his sword and struck, she realised that his pain had been an act.

Their blades met again as the steel spat sparks against each other above their heads. Bray's hand curling into a fist as he sought to punch her in the kidneys. She brought her knee up to counter-block it.

Fist struck harmlessly against knee and they came apart once again, dancing out of reach of each other's swords.

"You're the only assassin I would let near my heart," Bray admitted, chuckling as he rubbed his sternum. "But that move did tickle some."

Elora laughed, "I'm just warming up."

She spun away from him, slashing her sword through the branches above and watched as they rained down on Bray. He swatted them away and Elora used the momentary distraction to strike him with the hilt.

Bray grunted as she hit him in the chest, then followed it through with a back sweep, her foot connecting with the back of his calves and taking his legs from under him.

As he fell he had the foresight to raise his own blade to catch hers as it descended upon his neck.

Elora stepped back as he crashed onto the hard ground, his head bouncing on an exposed tree root. She fought the urge to go to him, to press the wounds she had inflicted but this is what she had wanted. It was what Bray needed.

Months ago, before the merge they had duelled in Zalibut's machine – the god-created contraption that kept the worlds apart. She had been that other her then, the daughter of Chaos and had overpowered Bray. She would have killed him if she hadn't needed him to operate the device that brought the worlds together.

Elora had been reliving the memories ever since and knew that if it came to another fight, the daughter of Chaos would kill him. This was the reason she fought him now, urging him to fight back to strike her as if she was that other.

Bray raised himself onto his elbows and rubbed the back of his head, his sword lying on the ground.

"You remind me of Diagus," he remarked as he struggled to his feet.

"At least you tried to fight him back," Elora answered, swishing her blade around the air before pointing the tip at Bray. "Now pretend I'm the Pearly White and try to kill me."

Without warning she raised her reaver and sprung at him, cutting an arc towards his head.

He ducked and rolled, gathering his sword up before adopting the scorpion stance, feet apart with his blade held high above.

Elora let the experience from her reaver flow through her. The thousands of soul memories rushing over her actions as they guided her movements, some she guessed from Diagus himself – no other had fought with Bray as often as he did. Through his memories she recognised Bray's intentions, his patterns and found the weak points.

Their blades met again, the clash of steel ringing across the lake and startling the ducks into flight. Elora caught, held, parried and pushed but felt that Bray still wasn't committing to any real attack. He was holding back.

She dodged the next lunge and struck him in the stomach. As he bent double with the wind knocked out of him, she drove her knee up into his face.

The force thumped him against the tree, his arms flinging wide yet he still held his sword and brought it about in time to parry her slash.

"Kill me," she demanded as she feigned a strike to his shoulder, masking the intentions to punch him across the jaw.

Bray's head whipped back, striking against the willow, yet at the same instant his free hand darted towards her sword arm, knuckles jabbing into the nerves in the crook of her elbow.

Reflexes jerked and the soul reaver spun away from her grasp. It hit the ground and skittered to a stop as

Bray pressed his sword against her neck. Her sword was out of reach.

"Yield?" he asked, wincing as he worked his mouth.

Elora shrugged, "Do you?" she replied as she tapped the barrel of her pistol against his ribs.

The SIG Sauer had been hidden on her leg, the holster hanging low and strapped to her thigh beneath her cloak. She had slipped it free as she allowed him to render her sword arm useless. It still tingled with numbness but she didn't let it show.

"Better," she informed him, withdrawing her gun and placing it back into the holster on her thigh. "But plenty of room for improvement."

Bray smiled as he slipped his sword into his smuggler's pouch. "I'll accept better," he said, rubbing his mouth.

They left the veil of the willow hand in hand. Elora felt gratitude that they could do such a thing now, that there were no longer any Shadojaks to prevent them from showing signs of affection. Although the price of not having them was to not have lethal allies against Neptula. She would even appreciate having Sibiet. The Shadojak that had stood against her in her trials and had used every moment spent in her company, making her out to be a traitor. Yet she knew he would stand against Flek and fight for the Empire.

They paused at the well. Elora leaned against the stonework as Bray brought the bucket up and they both drank the icy water, Bray wiping his mouth with his sleeve. She wondered where Sibiet was now. The rest of the Shadojaks, including the Supreme, had been killed by Flek and the brothers Quantala and Quantico. They had destroyed the league of protectors and balancers that had existed ever since the original eight had brought the God of Chaos down, thousands of years ago. She wondered if there would ever be more Shadojaks or had their kind been wiped out altogether?

"How well do you know Flek?" Elora asked as they continued the path that led them to the inn.

"I thought I knew him pretty well, but now he's turned traitor, I don't think I know him at all. Why?"

"Timoshi will reach the Sea Witch soon and deliver my message. When he does she will have no reason to wait any longer. She will attack."

Bray nodded. "I expect so, and she will enjoy it. But why ask about Flek?"

"Neptula won't be attacking just us. She'll begin with the Empire – anything on land."

Their steps slowed as Bray spun her to face him. "You're planning on making a truce with Flek?" he asked.

Elora sighed. "It's worth a shot. With the coming battle in the far north and the god I must face in the south, it will leave the Dark Army thinly stretched. We'll have barely the numbers here to defend the Keep once the warlock has arrived to break the barrier down."

"If the warlock arrives," Bray cut in.

"I can't rely on ifs," Elora said. "We must be prepared, which will mean leaving a strong force at the Keep. The rest will be marching against Neptula and whatever beasts she'll be summoning from the sea. We don't have the numbers to fight the Empire as well."

"There's always the takwiches," Bray suggested, raising his hands as if the thought didn't sit right with him. "I don't like it, but they'll provide you with millions of soldiers to add to your armies."

"I hate the idea of setting them loose upon the world once again," Elora admitted. "I won't do it."

"You might not have the choice."

"Which is why I'll be going to Rona. I will speak with Flek."

Bray let his arms fall. "I hate that idea more."

"I'm not exactly thrilled with the notion, but if he can be persuaded to turn against Neptula before it's too late – then we may still succeed."

"If you can persuade him."

They continued walking towards the inn when Teaselberry and Smudge rode along the track to meet them. Teaselberry brought the trap to a halt. Smudge; round face beaming, greeted them.

"Zilabeth has done it," the army engineer said enthusiastically. "She's reinvented the combustion engine using steam."

"She has gotten the cars going again?" Elora asked, feeling hope rise inside her.

"Come, you need to see it for yourselves," Smudge replied.

The enthusiasm was contagious, she felt herself smiling as she climbed aboard the trap.

Bray joined her and Teaselberry pulled on the reins to set the horse trotting back the way they had come.

"How are the new recruits?" Elora asked, as she snuggled up to Bray.

Smudge chuckled. "Thatch and Thud? Those boys were quite disturbed by the trolls and grimbles but it turns out they are great admirers of Zilabeth's work. They had worked with her some years ago, before the merge and so didn't take much persuading once they were in her company."

"That's good," Elora said. "I didn't want to recruit another grumpkin to help bring them to our way of thinking."

As they rode to the Keep, Smudge filled in more details of how he, Zilabeth, Teaselberry, Thatch and Thud had spent many weeks working alongside each other in the Shadowlands. And the hard hours and days put into bending and shaping the machines to Zilabeth's design without having to stop for sleep or sustenance.

By the time, they had gone beneath the portcullis and wound around the cobbled lanes to Zilabeth's workshop, she had a good idea of what to expect.

The hangar doors were wide open and as the trap rolled to a stop, two large grimbles pushed a vehicle out into the courtyard.

Elora gazed at the huge machine, recognising it as once being an old Land Rover, similar to the kind the British Army used. The original bonnet was missing, replaced by a sheet of riveted metal – a large rectangular hole at its centre. Poking out of the hole were two rows of thick pipes forming a V shape. Behind the pipes were four silver tubes which came out of the engine and ran along the side of the truck, splitting into two as they disappeared beneath the machine.

"It's just a prototype," Zilabeth admitted as she sauntered out of the workshop, slipping large gloves onto her hands. "It will need tweaks here and there but it goes."

"It's remarkable," Elora said as she climbed from the trap to take a closer look.

"It's a V8," Bray added, sliding his hands over the pipes poking from the bonnet.

Zilabeth nodded as she came to the front of the machine and began to work a hand pump which was bolted to the grill.

"We used the original engine, but stripped away the spark plugs and leads," the inventor explained as she finished priming the pump and began to twist a small metal wheel that cranked a cog, compressing several springs. "I rigged the distributor up to the crank itself, which will feed the liquid fire into the eight chambers in the engine block." She tapped two of the tubes which fed into the engine. "The liquid fire comes through here and is shot in series so the chambers combust in sequence." She tapped the other two tubes. "And these feed water through the twin carburettor at the same instance, making the explosion of steam and forcing the pistons down. Quite simple really."

"Amazing," Elora remarked, impressed by what Zilabeth had explained if not fully understanding it.

"Stand back," Zilabeth warned as she climbed into the driving seat. She began to pump another lever that had been bolted beside the handbrake as she watched a needle on a copper dial rise. "You've got to prime liquid fire from here until the pressure reaches this mark," she explained, pointing to a red line on the glass. When the needle strayed over the mark, Zilabeth stopped pumping and pulled her goggles down over her face. Teaselberry climbed into the passenger seat beside her and pulled her own goggles down over her bulging eyes.

"Ready?"

Elora nodded, feeling a rising excitement as she watched the inventor press a large red button.

Instantly there was a loud bang from under the bonnet that shook the entire vehicle, followed by a large cloud of steam that mushroomed from all eight pipes. Elora expected the Land Rover to shake to bits but it soon settled down and the steam began to puff out in regular chugs.

Zilabeth experimentally revved the engine and the vehicle growled, the sound scaring birds from a nearby tree. Then the inventor slipped it into gear and the truck began to roll forwards, her face beaming with thrilled pleasure.

"You did it," Elora shouted above the noise. "This is perfect."

Zilabeth drove the Land Rover in a circle around the courtyard before stopping. She turned the engine off and climbed out.

"And I've another surprise," Zilabeth admitted, waving her arm towards the workshop.

Thatch and Thud exited through the barn doors, the former carrying a large cylindrical tube while the other pushed what resembled a motorbike.

Elora stole her eyes away to glance at Bray and watched with delight as his mouth fell open. She knew he had a fondness for motorbikes and this one looked as mean and as dangerous as his last one.

"We haven't fired her up yet," Thatch admitted as he kicked out the side stand and rested the bike.

It had a black cylindrical fuel tank strapped by metal bands to a thick frame. It resembled a miniature steam train with wide handlebars. A single row of pipes poked out beside the engine with similar tubes to the Land

Rover, feeding from another tank beneath the seat. The wheels and suspension were taken from a modern bike and judging by the thick rear tyre, it was from a sports model.

Bray approached the bike and trailed his fingers over the large circular lamp which was bolted to the front. His wide grin beamed with excitement as he looked towards Zilabeth.

"Be my guest," Zilabeth invited, nodding towards the bike. "You'll need to prime the pump first. It's on the side of the crank casing."

Bray knelt beside the bike and began to work the lever on the side of the engine. A needle on a dial began to crank up with each pump until it hit a red line. Then he swung his leg over the bike, kicked the stand away and pressed a silver button at the base of the tank.

There was a prolonged pause when everything went quiet, all eyes were upon the bike as they watched with keen interest.

When nothing happened, Elora thought it hadn't worked until there was a loud bang and the engine roared to life.

Bray revved the throttle, causing the bike to growl angrily before letting out the clutch, causing the back wheel to smoke against the cobbled ground. A second later he launched forwards.

Steam billowed from the pipes as he raced around them, making a circuit of the courtyard. The bike moving at a frightening speed yet Bray appeared like a child with a new toy.

"I think he likes it," Elora said to Zilabeth who looked concerned both for Bray and her invention.

"I worried that it may be too heavy, that the water tank made the contraption too cumbersome, but Bray is throwing it around as if he and the machine were one," she answered, seeming to relax as he rode the bike before them and skidded to a halt.

He pressed another button and the engine became still, a cloud of steam chugging a final cloud from the pipes before going silent.

"What do you think?" Zilabeth asked as Bray leaned the bike onto its side stand and climbed off.

He patted the tank before stepping away, his huge grin becoming impossibly wider. "She's perfect," he said.

"And that's before we've added the extra fire bite," Thatch added as he placed the cylindrical tube on top of the bike.

"Extra bite?" Bray asked, as he watched the spell binder screw the tube into a slot beside the crank case.

"Extra bite," repeated Thud as he tapped the bike. Elora noticed that his hair was singed in places and he was missing both eyebrows. "It wasn't easy but we've managed to create an accelerant using dragon fire."

"You turned Grycul's fire into liquid?" Elora asked, staring at the device which he had screwed into the bike.

Thatch nodded. "We had some minor problems to begin with," he admitted, lifting his own singed hair. "But yes, we spell cast and bound the dragon's fire and reduced it to liquid. It's pretty potent stuff."

"Extremely potent," Thud agreed. "That's why it should only be used for a brief amount of time - in case the engine overheats or throws a valve into the pistons."

"And we've another for the Land Rover," Zilabeth added.

Elora hugged the inventor, then wrapped her arms around Thatch and Thud. "They're perfect. It's exactly what we need."

She stared from the truck to the bike, already thinking up ways they would help and how she would use them. Wondering if the Empire would try to build their own cars and trucks.

"Just a thought," Smudge said as he came to lean by the Land Rover. "Do you think you could adapt any engine to work?"

"No," Zilabeth answered. "Nothing modern. Anything that needs a computer can't be adapted. Only older vehicles."

"That's perfect because what I have in mind is old, but I think it would be a great asset towards the cause."

Elora raised an eyebrow. "What are you thinking?"

Smudge grinned. "A Spitfire."

It was Elora's turn to chuckle. "Where are you going to find a Spitfire around here? Even if you can get it working."

Smudge rubbed his chin. "I've an old friend. He's ex RAF and a plane enthusiast. He had a working Spitfire that he used for pleasure riding. If we can get to him, then I'm sure he would donate it and let the old bird fly once more."

"If he's still alive," Bray added.

"Aye," Smudge agreed. "But Terry's an old war veteran. He served in World War II and I wouldn't be surprised if the old rogue has an air-raid shelter or bunker to hide in while the merge happened."

Elora thought about having a Spitfire in her arsenal. It would be a great advantage to have another weapon in the air apart from her dragon. Especially if what Timoshi warned was true; that Neptula had her own gliding sea dragons.

"Where will we find this Terry?" she asked.

"If he's still alive, we'll find him in Gloucestershire, in the Cotswolds," Smudge answered. "If it's alright with you I'd like to use the Shadowlands, if it will allow us to arrive close enough."

Elora nodded. "It's a good idea. We'll put a team together – maybe Captain Brindle will help."

She was about to suggest taking the Land Rover when a bright flash crossed her vision and a sudden sense of vertigo brought her to her knees.

Bray rushed to her side as the image faded and the courtyard swam back into focus.

"What is it?" he asked.

Elora gripped his arm as she pulled herself back to her feet. "I'm not sure," she said, struggling to recall her mind's depiction. "I was seeing through a scrawharpy's eyes. I think it was Dethtil the warlock."

She felt Bray go rigid as his gaze locked on the horizon. "Where? Is he close?"

Elora shook her head as she worked through the short picture in her mind and gathered what details she could. "I'm not sure. I could see a bridge, a big bridge with long steel cables and tall concrete frames spanning a vast river. He was with hundreds of imperial guards and soldiers, camping on one side of the bank. Then I lost the link."

"That'll be the Severn Bridge that links England to Wales," Smudge explained. "It's one of two that are near Chepstow."

"How far away is that?" Bray asked.

Smudge shrugged. "Fifty, maybe sixty miles away, but it's the last major obstacle they'll encounter before reaching us."

"Then we better catch him before he crosses," she said, attempting to reach out to the scraw-harpy that had been circling above the bridge.

Bray grasped her arm. "What do you see now?" he asked.

"Nothing."

Bray struck the side of the Land Rover and the vehicle rocked back on its suspension. "We've got to head out there now to block him before he crosses."

"Yeah," Smudge agreed. "We've got plenty of P4 plastic explosives in the armoury, but we would need to plant them at the base of the bridge's support structure."

Elora attempted to link with the scraw-harpy once again, but she couldn't find the bird or any other close enough to have eyes on the warlock.

"Something doesn't feel right," she noted. "I can't sense the scraw-harpy anymore. It's as if it's just vanished."

"Or killed," Bray said as he swung a leg over the steam bike. "I'll find Brindle and the P4, then I'm heading out for the bridges."

"We don't have time," Elora argued as she walked into Zilabeth's workshop. "I'll take Grycul. I could be there in moments and destroy the bridge before he crosses."

Bray climbed off the bike and followed her into the workshop and through the sliding door into the heat of the Shadowlands. Before she had chance to summon her dragon he grasped her by the arm.

"Elora, you can't go alone - Dethtil is too powerful. It could be a trap, you said yourself that it doesn't feel right."

Elora sought Grycul's mind and beckoned her to come, before removing Bray's hand from her arm.

"I know, but I must try," she said as her dragon landed. Vast wings blasting red dust around them as they buffeted the ground.

Grycul gracefully lowered her head and Elora climbed onto her back. She offered Bray a reassuring smile.

"I'm the daughter of Chaos, remember. I'll tear this warlock apart," she said, hoping that the confidence she lacked didn't show in her voice. "Besides, you'll be following on your new toy."

She tapped her heels into the dragon's flanks and held tightly to Grycul's neck as she crouched low. Then her powerful legs sprung them in to the air.

As they began to rise into the red sky she glanced down at Bray. He was already running back into Ram's Keep. He wouldn't take long to reach the bridge on the bike, she thought. She would need to destroy the bridge before he got there and put him out of the warlock's reach.

8

Crows

Grycul's screech pierced the silent sky as it echoed around the dead land. The columns of the Dark Army – her army, raised their heads to gaze at them as they soared above. The sea of men and demons, trolls and grumpkins stretched as far as the eye could see. Some raising weapons in salute to their Queen. Elora raised her arm in reply but pressed on. Even in the Shadowlands time was against her.

The dragon screamed once again before folding her wings tight to her body and dived out of the red world.

Hot to cold – red to white, Elora squinted against the sudden brightness as she guided Grycul to the wide body of water and steered the dragon down the River Severn.

They descended and glided inches above, so their approach would be hidden from the large contingent of imperials who were escorting the warlock. The tips of the dragon's wings touched the smooth surface, ripping white lines along the tranquil water and leaving a large wake behind them.

Elora caught their reflection riding parallel along the glassy surface and wondered if Neptula's creatures were hidden beneath, watching from below. Was there a host of skagwangles with tridents prepared to be thrown? More likely than not, this was the route Timoshi would have swum up to reach Rams Keep and probably the same one he used to escape. The river fed directly into the sea.

Exhilaration rushed through Elora as she soaked up the scenery. Trees and shrubs coated in snow whooshed by in a blur. Rapidly coming into focus then vanishing out as they banked left and right as they followed the course of the river. Her cloak snapped with the wind, thrashing behind her as Grycul shifted her huge body in tune with the way ahead. Dipping her head to subtly change direction, stretching her neck to compensate for an approaching curve and when they startled a swan into a panicked flight, the dragon made to snap her huge jaws upon the bird. Elora recognised her intentions and pressed harder into the scales.

They left the swan floundering in the waves they created, its orange beak opened wide in complaint as it watched them leave. Elora couldn't help but laugh, the thrill of the flight raising goose bumps along her arms. She prayed for a time when she could experience this for fun and not as she headed into danger.

Elora searched again for the scraw-harpy, probing the area ahead in hope of linking with the bird that had first shown her the bridge, yet found nothing. Had the creature been killed by an imperial with a rifle or had Dethtil himself brought it down?

They rounded another bend in the river and the bridge suddenly loomed ahead.

Two tall support towers rose out of the Severn. Waves crashed against the reinforced concrete as it climbed high above. Thick steel cables swept between the towers and the road which spanned the vast body of water, linking England to Wales. It was immense. Possibly the largest bridge Elora has ever seen, yet as she drew nearer to the huge white and grey structure, she saw no army attempting to cross, no guards or even a single soul.

Grycul wafted her wings, buffeting the river and causing a shower of droplets as they ascended for a closer look.

The Severn Bridge was eerily quiet with only a few abandoned vehicles scattered along the road and a truck poking precariously over the edge; its front grill having pushed between the cables. The only movement came from a group of crows feasting on a carcass on the trucks bonnet. The collective noun for a group of crows is a murder – Elora thought the word suited the black-feathered fiends, well.

When Grycul's shadow passed above the feasting birds, Elora recognised the dead animal to be a scraw-harpy. Most probably the very same which had given her the vision of the imperials. That's when she sensed something was wrong.

She searched her memory for the vision once again and thought the bridge appeared different. Then when she raised her gaze she saw another bridge a few miles further along the river.

Grycul cried into the white clouds as they glided higher, the stealthy approach now forgotten as an ominous feeling crept into Elora's mind.

They headed for the next bridge which was similar in size and stature to the first, although a subtly different shape. This structure was more modern and had an altogether more rounded look to the supporting towers.

It was the one that she saw in her vision.

The bridge was as empty and quiet as the previous one. With similar abandoned vehicles scattered along the lanes and a large bus that lay on its side, crushing a small car beneath it.

Elora searched for the imperials or the warlock but found no sign that they had been there.

She sighed with relief - she wasn't too late.

They flew passed and made to sweep back. It was then that Elora noticed the huge body of men suddenly swarming along the wide road.

They surged as one. The large contingent of imperials advancing on the bridge, charging out into the open in an attempt to cross. Rifle fire suddenly rippled across the heavens as Elora swept lower. A stray bullet hitting Grycul's exposed chest but harmlessly ricochet off her scales.

They knew she was there to destroy the bridge and fought to cross the river before she did so.

She applied pressure to her knees and directed the dragon to the closest of the two towers. Grycul reacted instantly, her mind acknowledging her wishes as she thought them and landed hard against the tall structure.

The impact cracked the painted brickwork as Grycul dug her talons into the masonry. Stones and loose chippings fell onto the bridge below, bouncing off the cars and smashing windows and some even finding the water.

Loud metallic pings rippled along the thick cables that supported the road hundreds of feet down but held firm to the extra weight of the dragon, although the tower swayed back and forth, the crack beginning to widen.

Elora kept her eyes on the approaching men, shields raised as they began to step onto the bridge from the English side. Amongst the throng was a large coach pulled by a team of six horses. She guessed that inside the coach sat Dethtil. The warlock was as keen to reach the other side as his escort. Her soul memories informed her that the warlock, like some demons and wraiths, had trouble passing over running water.

She studied the coach for a moment, but sensed nothing from within. No immense power, no great threat of magic – nothing. Did the warlock sense her?

Reaching for her smuggler's pouch, Elora drew her sword and raised it above her, gripping tight to Grycul's neck with her free arm. The blade briefly caught the sunlight before she brought it down.

The soul reaver cut through the steel cables as if they were no more than paper chains.

The heavy grey threads fell away to crash against the vehicles below, making whipping noises before cascading over the edge. One stray cable, ripping entirely through the bus.

"Send them a warning shot," Elora shouted into Grycul's ear as she watched the men advancing.

The dragon craned her neck and her head shot forward as she spat a white ball of flames.

The ball exploded at the foot of the bridge, melting a section of the central barrier while spreading flames the entire width of the road.

The imperials slowed but didn't halt. Instead, holding shields before them, they beat at the flames with cloaks and sheets, dampening a portion of the flaming wall wide enough for the coach to pass through.

"Idiots," Elora muttered as Grycul clawed her way to the other side of the tower, the bridge groaning in protest. "They won't make it."

With her gaze firmly fixed on the coach she slashed her sword through the cables on the other side and the entire structure suddenly jolted.

Everything turned silent. The eerie stillness broken by a deep growl as the foundations of the bridge slowly twisted. The reinforced concrete beginning to crumble in large chunks as the entire structure warped out of shape.

The imperials halted in their tracks and turned back to the safety of the English side. A group of armoured men struggled to turn the team of horses around as the coach began to slip towards the edge.

Elora watched as the road began to fall away from the other tower, the cables pulling tight and then snapping against the weight they were now burdened with. She glanced once more to the horses and felt a wave of relief as the they were righted and began to clamber off the disintegrating bridge.

She felt the tower they were perched on suddenly drop. Grycul raised her wings to catch the air, lifting them out of harm's way as it toppled sideways and fell into the water. Twin plumes of water spouted up as huge waves battered the mud banks to either side.

If there were any skagwangles hidden beneath, they would surely have been killed. She watched the rest of the bridge crumble and fall. The cars sliding from the bridge, no longer hindered by the cables and the broken bus, to fall the hundred feet into the river.

The bridge had been a wonder of engineering. Elora doubted that Ethea would see such things constructed in the near future, if ever. Without electricity in the world such creations would be hard to master.

The imperials, now safely back on hard ground, began to fire rifles at her once again.

Grycul screamed back in anger as the bullets struck her scales. They fell harmlessly away yet still aggravated the dragon. Elora could feel her irritation and so steered the beast away from the attacking men.

They dived towards the fallen bridge, the remnants of it poking above the water line. Plummeting at speed before swinging out over the surface and gliding up river.

As the second bridge came into view the ominous feeling returned. Should she have attacked the warlock while he was over running water and weak? While he was halfway across the bridge?

It may have been prudent to do so but Elora couldn't feel any threat from the carriage. She sensed more menace in the crows that were still picking at the remains of the carcass on the approaching bridge. A murder of crows that feasted upon one of her own, one of the Dark Army's.

Sending her intentions to Grycul, they ascended so they would fly above the hungry carrion birds. Repulsion seeping into her nerves as she watched them feeding on the bonnet of the abandoned truck. It wasn't right.

The dragon picked up on her emotion and screamed at the crows below. Yet they carried on with their meal and showed no sign that they had even witnessed their approach. Or if they had, they didn't care.

"Take the scraw-harpy," Elora ordered and held tight as Grycul swept low to the truck and snatched the decimated bird.

The meat had already been devoured. The scraw-harpy was little more than feathers and bone yet the crows incredibly still fed from the carcass.

Grycul jostled her talons in an attempt to detach the pesky black birds but they held on, grey beaks locked onto the body, determined to not let their prize go.

Elora felt uneasy. The crows didn't act like normal birds.

"Torch it," she muttered to Grycul.

The dragon flew to the safety of the Welsh side of the river and dropped the scraw-harpy onto the snow covered bank. She landed heavily beside it, her talons sinking into the soft earth.

She threw back her head and spat a ball of fire at the carcass.

This time the crows flew away as their feast suddenly burst into white flames. Yet Elora noticed that they didn't fly the way they should.

The crows circled together, gliding in a tight formation as they weaved in and out of the smoke. Their high-pitched cries mixing with the crackling bones and smoking feathers.

They curled about and suddenly came at her. The small black bodies packed so closely together that they formed the shape of a spear. The leading bird's beak seeming as sharp as its sparkling eyes.

Elora ducked the attack and drew her sword, watching as the spear broke apart into the several birds that formed it. They weaved together once again as they turned about, their cries becoming cackling and then a single voice. A mocking laugh.

The crows suddenly began to fly in ever tightening circles. Weaving, darting and mixing within each other.

The image becoming one single black blur, like a small dark tornado. Then the blur became more solid and took on the shape of a man.

Elora knew that this was the warlock.

The man continued to laugh, deep azure eyes shining with the same mischief that were like those of the crows. Several of which were perched upon his bare shoulders.

"Easy," he remarked, his voice soft and gentle. "So very easy."

Elora levelled her reaver at him and felt Grycul's muscles shift beneath her, readying for an attack.

"Do you yield, Dethtil?" Elora offered as he approached, a tall staff clutched in one hand.

His crow-black hair hung in ringlets down to his slim frame. It made his pale skin appear paler, giving him a haunting quality. She felt surprise at seeing how young he looked. For somebody supposedly hundreds of years old he appeared to be of an age with herself.

"I would offer you the same courtesy," he replied through full red lips, "but you would only refuse."

He stepped closer and lay a hand upon Grycul's neck. The beast hissed and displayed her teeth, ready to bite him. "I know your mind, Elora. You leave it open."

She was about to drop from the dragon to confront him when she felt a jolt of pain pulse through her brain. Icy fingers probing her inner thoughts and pushing into deep memories.

In her mind she shared the same throbbing ache as Grycul, and felt her shudder before lowering her head to the ground.

Elora half slid and half fell from the dragon, one hand clutching her own head as she struck the snow.

Her arms shook with fatigue as she attempted to raise her blade, but she lacked the strength to wield it and the blade dipped to her feet.

"And if you're planning on turning to smoke," Dethtil added amusingly as he drove his staff into the snow. "You'll never become solid again."

Sat atop the warlock's staff was an orb. It spun to life as he whispered to it and began to revolve. The sound of mechanical whirring, spun from within.

"I designed this myself," he said proudly. "It will draw smoke and vapour towards it and bind it to the charm that's whirling about inside." He spun a delicate finger in front of Elora's face, forming small circles. "Like a Djinn, you will be trapped for eternity."

Grinding her teeth together, Elora forced herself upright, fighting against the ache throbbing inside her head. Turning to smoke was her next course of action, right before she unburdened him of his head.

"Ah," he chuckled playfully, reading her intentions. "I see that a demonstration is needed."

He turned to whisper to a crow.

It hopped from his shoulder to land upon Elora's arm. Black beady eyes regarded her for a moment before it stabbed its beak into flesh.

Fresh pain brought tears to her eyes as drops of her own blood fell to the ground.

The drops instantly flamed when it touched the air and began to melt the snow where it hissed amongst the steam.

"Watch," Dethtil commanded as wisps of the steam curled up and drifted towards his staff. It unnaturally spiralled around the shaft as it rose towards the spinning orb at the top - where it dissolved into the translucent surface, momentarily brightening as it disappeared.

"Clever, isn't it?" he boasted. "You've Thatch and Thud to thank for helping me bind the charm. I sense that you're not too pleased with that. Even though you have stolen the pair from the Empire."

"Get out of my head," Elora screamed in rage, feeling Grycul writhe in the snow beside her.

The warlock laughed. "Drop your sword."

"Never," Elora replied through clenched teeth as the ache rose in strength. It was like her brain was filling with rocks that battered at the inside of her skull, attempting to break out.

The pressure suddenly erupted and she involuntary screamed, the reaver falling from her grasp.

She slumped onto the floor, her hands going to her temples as Grycul roared; her large reptilian body stretching to its full extent before going rigid.

Then all at once the pain vanished.

The sudden release was a shock and Elora slumped back, her shoulders resting against the dragon's heaving chest as she too relaxed, her head sinking into the snow.

When Elora forced her gaze to Dethtil, she saw that the warlock now held her sword, balancing the blade amusingly in his palms. When he turned his azure eyes upon her, she saw only sadness in them.

"So, simple," he said, softly. "The daughter of Chaos shouldn't be so easily caught."

Elora sat up straight, her strength returning now the tormenting pressure had left her mind. Although fear began to replace it.

In a single stroke the warlock had taken away her ability to reduce to smoke, exhausted her dragon to the point where she couldn't raise her head and now held her sword.

"You could have killed me on the bridge, it was my weakest point," he admitted without any trace of arrogance.

"It's a shame I didn't," Elora said, reaching inside her smuggler's pouch for the sapphire dagger it contained.

The warlock stared, his sad blue gaze penetrating deep within her. "That is why I created the distraction. It was I that sent you the image of the bridge. I linked with your scraw-harpy and through it I had access to your mind." He pointed to the other bridge which she had destroyed. "There is no imperial escort. No horse-drawn coach. Even the bullets which struck Grycul were figments of your imagination."

Elora's hand gripped the hilt of her dagger and she slipped it silently out, her gaze still locked on the warlock's.

"You put the pictures in my head, all of it?" she asked.

Dethtil nodded. "It was the only way I could be sure that you would pass directly above me and allow me to strengthen my bond. Then when you came back for your scraw-harpy, you gave me a further chance by carrying me to the safety of dry land. And for that, I am grateful."

Elora couldn't believe how easily she had been manipulated. It had all seemed so real, the men on the bridge, even the team of horses pulling the coach. No wonder she didn't feel any threat from within. It had all been a dream and she had destroyed the bridge for nothing.

"Keep your gratitude," she hissed, flinging the dagger underhand.

She had aimed for his exposed throat but the goblin silver passed harmlessly through him, his flesh momentarily becoming black feathers until the blade landed in the snow.

"You're a fighter," he remarked, his ruby lips forming a melancholy smile. "But if I wanted to kill you Elora, you would be dead already." He handed her the soul reaver, then offered a hand.

Gingerly, Elora accepted the hand and allowed him to pull her to her feet.

"What is it you want?" she asked, keeping a firm grip on the reaver, not understanding the reasons he gave it back. "Did Flek not send you to root me out?"

"He did, but I already knew where you were and how to gain entry to Rams Keep. Believe it or not, I once lived there, long ago before it was destroyed in a forgotten war. No, my reasons for coming for you are quite selfish," he explained as his hand lingered on hers, cold fingers stroking her palm. "I want you, Elora - need you and I shall not be denied."

Elora snatched her hand away and held her sword above her head. The defensive stance brought a grin to Dethtil's face. This time when he smiled she noticed that there was a sharpness to his canines and a hunger in his eyes.

"Whose side are you on? Is Neptula your master?" she asked.

"The Sea Witch and I have an understanding," he replied. "As you know, Flek is just a means for keeping the Empire from her doors until she has flooded the world."

"But you will drown with the rest of us."

Dethtil shook his head. "No, I won't. Not now that I have you."

Elora tightened her grip. "You don't have me," she said defiantly, attempting to link her mind to Grycul's once again, yet finding nothing of the sleeping dragon. Instead she sensed a devious intelligence that lingered on the edge of her thoughts.

"I wouldn't try to link again," the warlock warned. "If Grycul wakes it would only be to an overwhelming pain."

Elora shut her mind off and refocused on the semi-naked man before her, the crows upon his shoulders staring unblinking and accusingly at her. She realised that he was in control. The fact that he had given her the reaver back, was proof of that.

"What do you want?" she demanded, unable to think of a way to attack him. The moment she would advance he would fill her head with the crushing pain and render her useless again.

"A song," he answered. "To start with. Something passionate, full of emotion. Sing me the Eversong."

Elora lowered her blade to the ground, about to ask why he wanted a song when a sudden wave of pain flashed through her head. A flash of heat in time to a single beat of her heart. Over almost as fast as it began. It was a demonstration to show what he was capable of.

Realising that she had no other option, Elora began to sing.

It felt odd singing the familiar words which hadn't passed her lips in the few months since leaving Aslania. Yet the same static feeling from the pit of her stomach, rose through her being as the verse progressed. Her voice carrying on the wind and causing the top layer of snow to rise from the ground and begin to circle around them, forming a dome with them at its centre.

Elora watched the phenomenon unfold and wondered if it was her doing or the warlock's.

When the song came to an end, she felt the magic slowly ebb from her chest but the snow still carried on swirling - forming a solid barrier between them and the outside world. Dethtil stared at her, his face a mask of peaceful bliss

"It's a powerful song, the Eversong," the warlock remarked. "Yet I wonder if you even understand the words you were singing. Do you?"

"No," Elora admitted. Strange that she had sung it so many times and yet had no real knowledge of what it meant.

Dethtil chuckled. "Few do. The words are intended for true gods only. The likes of even demigods lack the meaning of the song."

"And you know what they are?"

The warlock nodded. "It's a simple but powerful lullaby. Bonding gods to bodies, or in your father's case – trapping him in his."

Elora didn't know where this was going, yet needed to keep the conversation going while she worked out how to defeat him.

"Interesting," she remarked. "But what does that have to do with me, with this situation? Why ask me to sing it?"

"Because I need the power of the song if I am to become more," he answered as he stepped closer, his gaze consuming her eagerly. "I found immortality long ago and have mastered both the magic of casting and binding. I have roamed both worlds freely and have taken anything from them which I have desired. But I grow bored. What does a man want after he has had everything?"

"The only thing which his out of his grasp," she replied. "To become a god."

Dethtil opened his arms to the swirling white globe. "Selfish I know, but yes. My desire is to be a god. And you Elora, are the key."

"Never," she snapped, raising her blade once again.

The warlock laughed. "I won't be denied. You will bond your blood with mine and you will sing to me with each new day."

Elora was about to turn to smoke, only remembering the mechanical orb at the end of his staff, at the final moment.

"Don't fight me Elora, you will be mine. Either come willingly as my wife or be my slave."

Frustration built within her and she heard the whispers beginning to call her name, the sound carried on the wind that danced around them. She let in the power, feeling her anger rise; the other her demanding more from the darkness as Chaos grew within.

"How fascinating," Dethtil remarked, "your eyes are going red. The daughter of Chaos ascends."

Elora felt that other her struggling to take control of her body, insisting that she devour the man before her, burning him in flames and spreading destruction.

She let just enough of the other her in, to give her the strength but not take control.

Fire welled within her veins as Elora sprang into action.

She reversed the grip on her sword and jabbed Grycul in the fleshy part of her muscular thigh, hoping that it would wake the beast. Then turning her attention on the smirking warlock, she launched herself at him.

Flames erupted either side as she unfurled her fiery wings. Driving them down she gave herself enough lift to fly over the pale man and swing her sword down upon his head.

Long ringlets of black hair whipped aside as Dethtil spun away from her attack, his body becoming the murder of crows as he flew to the other side of the snow dome.

He reformed, sharp teeth bared back in a vicious snarl as Grycul screamed; now woken from Elora's thrust, she craned her head around to snap her jaws upon him. But before the large teeth came together she screamed again and her entire body began to convulse. Pain forcing the dragon's body to thrash like it had before.

Elora landed, turned on her heel and sprinted at the warlock, blade held before her. Yet as she came within feet of him the excruciating pressure returned to her brain, driving her to her knees.

She screamed as her legs gave way and she fell into the cold snow.

"Tut tut," came Dethtil's voice from somewhere on the edge of her senses. Elora closed her eyes as the pressure took over everything, reducing her world to only pain. "I told you Elora, I will not be denied. Be my wife or be my slave. Either way, you will be mine."

Elora wanted to scream, to claw her way out of the agonising place she was trapped in. But she couldn't. She was at the mercy of the warlock.

The whispers pushed through the agony. Her name being repeated by a thousand voices. Kill…Kill…Kill.

She felt her heart quicken, sensed the fire in her veins rage – the heat rising into an inferno.

A scream ripped from her lungs as she lunged at Dethtil. His blue eyes widening with shock as she dug her fingers into either side of his arms and pinned him in place.

"Chaos, is nobody's bitch," she growled, her voice forcing out an entire octave lower. She folded her flaming wings together and engulfed the warlock.

The crows leapt from his shoulder, wings catching fire before they fled. Their pained screeches filling the day as Grycul's cries, ceased. The dragon shook the stunned feeling from her head as she turned to face them, teeth snapping angrily together.

Elora felt Dethtil strain against her grip, his slim arms tensing as he pushed, shoving her back. His attention now given fully to the situation, he no longer had the concentration to keep the swirling wall of snow up and the flakes floated to the ground.

He was stronger than his physical appearance portrayed. His red lips curling in determination as he fought back. Yet it was clear he lacked the strength to defy her as she opened her wings and slammed them together once again. The flames scorching his body and reducing the snow to steam. The vapour being rapidly absorbed into the warlock's staff.

With a final effort Elora put all her anger and hatred into her attack. Her wings beginning to turn white with the fury she released. Attempting to make ash of the warlock.

When he didn't burn she opened her wings and drove her fist into his chest. The impact sending him reeling back into Grycul's open mouth. But before the dragon brought her teeth together, Dethtil spun and turned into many crows, loose feathers falling as they fluttered out of the dragon's reach and flapped skyward.

"No," Elora yelled in frustration as she watched the birds fly out of harm's way. Yet there was nothing she could do. Dethtil was already disappearing over the tree tops and vanishing from view.

Her anger beginning to ebb away, she marched over to the staff he left, picked it up and hurled it into the river.

She watched it sink beneath the grey surface, being dragged down by the current and its own weight.

Now the orb had gone, she had the ability to turn herself back to smoke, should he come back for a counter-attack. She watched the birds as they became small black dots and realised that the chances of that were now slim.

The danger now gone, Elora slowed her breathing and pushed the daughter of Chaos back. It was a job that she found was getting easier. The more often she called upon Chaos, the more they were becoming one - each of them coming to terms with the other. In the future, she supposed, they may become whole. A being that wasn't all Elora and not all Chaos, but something in between.

When she felt in control she approached Grycul and gently pressed her hand against her head. Sensing that the dragon was still feeling some of the pain she had endured as it slowly slipped away.

"We should have killed him," Elora admitted, sensing the same frustration from the beast. Then felt the dragon project mild amusement. "What's so funny?"

Grycul opened her mouth. Caught between her teeth was a single bird. The crow's beak working slowly as it struggled to lift its body.

Elora reached in and grasped it, holding tight around its neck so it couldn't escape.

She brought the bird close to her face and peered into the small black eyes.

"I've got a small piece of you, Dethtil," she said and began to pluck feathers from its wings. The crow shrieked in protest, jabbing her hand, flames darting from the wounds before they quickly healed. "If I've got to take you bit by bit, I will."

The bird opened its mouth and cried in panic before Elora closed it with her finger and thumb. Then paused as she heard the sound of an engine approaching.

The motor was being tortured for all it was worth. The noise of tyres harshly scraping against the icy ground closely followed by the squeal of brakes. The revs kept high as plumes of steam suddenly chugged into the air over the next rise.

Elora's heart soured as she watched Bray come over the hill towards them. His steam powered bike leaving the ground momentarily before slamming back down, the suspension absorbing the impact as he came at them at a frightening speed.

He pulled in before the dragon, his rear wheel locking up as he skidded to a halt. He kicked the stand out and climbed off the bike.

Elora felt the love as she was crushed in his arms.

"Where is he?" he asked, green eyes searching the area. "Where's Dethtil?"

"He got away," she admitted, hugging him back. "Well, most of him did." She showed him the crow in her arms who began to wriggle in her grasp. "Give me one of your boot laces."

Bray undid his boot and passed her the lace. She wrapped it around the bird's beak and tied it shut.

"Dethtil knows where Rams Keep is and I think he has the strength to destroy the fairy barrier," she explained, leaning into her boyfriend as she glared at the crow. "We'll take the crow back with us and see if we can learn something from it."

"Or use it against him," Bray suggested. Then he planted a kiss on her head. "I was worried about you. The Warlock is extremely powerful."

Elora sensed tension in him. An anger or irritation, so offered him a smile. "He is," she agreed, trying to keep her boyfriend talking. "And he has his own agenda."

"Don't they all?" Bray asked rhetorically, shaking his head. "Flek wants the Empire, Volcaneous wants to melt the South Pole, while Hades wants to melt the north. Neptula wants everything under water. What does the Warlock want?"

"Me," Elora answered and felt Bray's embrace tighten. "He wants to make a wife of me. To feed from my veins and make himself a god."

"Is that even possible?" he asked, his fingers tightening into fists.

Elora shrugged. "He seems to think so. If he binds my blood to his body with the Eversong."

"It won't happen," Bray growled, clenching his teeth.

"No, it won't."

Elora felt suddenly weary and wanted to be back at the inn.

She linked minds with Grycul, long enough to tell the dragon that she would be travelling back with Bray. Then watched as the huge beast crouched low to the ground before springing into the air. She beat her wings several times to climb altitude and then in a flash, disappeared into the Shadowlands.

"Come on, Elf boy," Elora said, after slipping the bird into a leather bag which was buckled to the side of the bike. "Show me what this bike can do." She swung a leg over the powerful machine and slid back on the seat.

Bray's scowl never left him as he climbed on. He primed the pump and was about to press the ignition button when he paused, glancing over his shoulder, his face becoming grave.

"Don't ever fly off like that again. I couldn't bear the thought of losing you. Do you know how worried I was?"

"I handled it."

"But what if you didn't? What if Dethtil had defeated you and there was nobody here to help?" He ran his fingers through his black curls. "If you died it would have killed me."

Guilt soaked into Elora's stomach. She had left him at Rams Keep to make sure he wouldn't get hurt, yet wondered how she would feel if it was the other way around.

"I'm sorry," she offered and watched the frown slowly dissolve.

"Maybe it's not such a bad idea making a wife of you," he suggested.

"Marry Dethtil?" Elora blurted out, unable to comprehend why he would say such a thing.

"No," he chuckled, his gorgeous smile forming dimples in his cheeks. He leaned closer and kissed her on the lips.

"I mean, marry me."

Elora didn't know if she'd heard him right. Was it a proposal or was he just toying with the concept? She would marry him in a heartbeat of course, but was he being serious?

"That wouldn't stop him, you know. Dethtil wouldn't care if I was already someone else's wife. He would take me regardless," she said, trying to calm her rising emotions.

"Marry me anyway," he said, then fired the bike to life.

The engine roared wildly but was unable to drown out her thumping heart.

"I love you," he shouted over his shoulder before letting out the clutch, propelling them forward.

Elora threw her arms around him, gripping tight to his narrow waist as he put a foot down and spun the bike around to face the way he had come. Snow shooting from beneath the spinning back wheel.

As the bike accelerated, Elora leaned closer to his ear. "Yes," she answered, pressing her face into his shoulder to dab at the tears. "I'll be Mrs Bray."

She held tight, feeling the thrill as the bike lurched on at a frightening speed, bouncing over the ground and leaving a trail of steam behind. Bray's grin spread wide as she felt an overwhelming joy. Although the world was on the brink of devastation and the hardest battle ever fought was ahead of them, Elora could never remember feeling so happy.

9

The Joining of Clans

Jaygen threw another branch on the fire and watched the sparks rise to the stars. The grey tinges of a cold dawn beginning to touch the sky. Smoke curled around the snow before being snatched away in the harsh wind that battered down from the mountains. Wood crackling in the fire was one of only two sounds that breached the silence that settled after the avalanche. The other was the chattering of Fieri's teeth as she shivered beside the flames, lids closed as she faded in and out of consciousness.

He pulled the red cloak tighter around her shoulders, then sank alongside her, resting his back against an upturned tree trunk and lifting her head onto his lap. The movement drawing a moan from the girl.

She mumbled a name that may have been Jon or Jarn, before her teeth took up the incessant chattering that had been continuous since he had found her.

The unpleasant memory of the previous hours came back to him. The avalanche chasing them down the mountain. The snow snatching Fieri from his arms before burying him under the crushing weight. Then waking into complete darkness, not knowing which way was up or down. The panic as he lay trapped in the cold before digging himself out and the terror that shook him as he realised that Fieri was nowhere to be seen.

After floundering in the snow for what seemed an age, he stumbled upon his red cloak, the tip of which protruded from the surface. After scrambling through the icy whiteness, his gauntlets shovelling quicker than a burrowing polar bear, he pulled his cloak free and found the young Viking still gripping the cloth with rigid fingers.

The same violent snow slip that had almost ended them, provided enough wood pulp and branches to supply an endless blazing fire. He had lit one, then rolled a ruined tree closer to protect her from the elements before he ran to the village for help.

They were close to the Tooth, so he guessed if he ran he could make it in less than an hour.

It was only as he returned to Craggs Head that he realised his dilemma.

He couldn't be seen as Grimwolf, nor could he take anybody back to Fieri without raising the suspicion of how he managed to survive the avalanche himself.

The party that had set off to break his uncle free had returned and everyone was in the tavern, drinking ale and celebrating the rescue. Including his mother and father. If he was to walk in as Jaygen, he would get caught up in the revelry and wouldn't escape any time soon.

Instead he removed the armour and concealed it behind a stack of logs at the rear of the tavern. Then found Peter in the sentry cabin at the foot of the village. The skier had been roped into standing as watchmen, while the others joined the celebration.

Peter was pale and weak, his white skin appearing waxy beneath the glare of the torches. Yet became excited as Jaygen handed him the medicine.

He left Peter to fix himself with the draught and hastily gathered up a thick fur blanket and made his way back to Fieri.

"Jorn," Fieri mumbled again, bringing him back to the now. Her lids flicking open long enough to reveal her bright blue eyes before drifting shut again.

Jaygen pulled her closer, holding her in his arms as he rubbed life back into her fingers, her teeth set back to clashing together.

He couldn't help but wonder who this Jorn was. If he was her friend, or lover. The pang of jealously that flared up was a surprise and he swallowed it back down. Why did he care who she loved? Fieri was nothing to him. She wasn't even a nice person.

His gaze settled on her face. Her notched eyebrow drawing down in a frown as she gripped the red cloak that was almost of a colour with her hair. He had tried to pull it from her grasp but she wouldn't release it, not without force and he hadn't the heart to wrench it from her.

She seemed so fragile and at his mercy, a totally different girl to the one he shared the climb with yesterday. It was hard to believe that she had held a sword against his chest on their first encounter.

"Fieri?" he ventured as he gently pushed her red hair to one side.

Her only answer was the chattering of her teeth beneath blue lips. He placed a hand upon her forehead and felt how cold she was.

"Fieri?" he continued, rubbing warmth into her hands and then her wrists. He worked his hands up and down her arms to keep her circulation moving. Then wondered how he would keep her blood pumping to her toes. Frostbite could so easily set in when the heart wasn't pumping blood to the extremities.

He lifted her leg onto his own to remove her boots, when she spoke.

"What are you doing?" she asked as she stared at her leg in his arms.

"I…" Jaygen began, having to clear his throat to continue. "I was going to remove your boots to…"

She suddenly sat up straight and yanked her leg free. Her glare darting to either side of them.

"The avalanche!" she said urgently. Then after resting back against the upturned tree asked, "Where's Grimwolf?"

"Grimwolf?" Jaygen replied. "You must have knocked your head in the fall."

"He was here. He saved me last night," she snapped, then softened as she held up the cloak she was wrapped in. "See? This was his. He was at the summit. Don't you remember?"

Jaygen shrugged, then hunkered down and placed his hands close to the fire, but Fieri didn't give up the argument.

"Didn't you see anything?" she held up her hands, palms facing the sky. "Not even the ogres that attacked me? He came to my rescue, although I thought he was there to kill me."

"If you say so."

"But…" Fieri began, then slammed her fist into the snow. "He was there. He came right out of the building you were searching."

Jaygen didn't say anything, he thought it best to stay quiet.

"What happened to you, anyway?" she asked.

Jaygen finished warming his hands and sat beside her. "Like you said, I was searching inside the building when the avalanche started. Luckily for me I was beneath a door frame and remained safe."

He had prepared the lie earlier, readying himself for the question. Yet it still tasted foul as he spun the yarn.

"After the avalanche had passed I came out of my shelter and spent the night searching for you."

Her gaze searched his, as if she could smell the untruth of his words and knowing she had no way of proving it.

"Then it was you who found me?" Jaygen nodded and threw another branch on the fire. "Not Grimwolf? Then he could still be buried. Or dead."

Panicking she attempted to stand, throwing the blanket aside as she made to stride off, yet her legs buckled and she fell into Jaygen's lap.

"Easy," he said, helping her sit back down. "You've just been thrown down a mountain. Your body will be sore."

"It's nothing but pins and needles," she snarled, dismissing his words with a wave of her hand. "It's Grimwolf I'm worried about. What if he's dead?"

"He's not dead," Jaygen replied, fighting the smile that wanted to curve his lips as he thought about the concern she was feeling towards him. Well, towards Grimwolf anyway.

"How do you know?"

Because he's me - he was desperate to say. But she couldn't know who the man in the armour was, nobody could.

"He's god-created. Even if he was here."

"Which he was," Fieri corrected.

"Ok, was. But even then he would survive the avalanche."

Fieri relaxed back, resting her head against the ruined bark of the trunk. Yet still seemed less than satisfied.

Jaygen stretched his aching shoulders and stared into the brightening sky, hoping that the conversation about Grimwolf had ended.

"Do you think you could walk if I helped you?" he asked, realising that they hadn't any food with them. "We're near the Tooth, so Craggs Head isn't far."

Fieri sighed as she shifted her weight onto her elbows and once again attempted to stand. Jaygen rushed to her side and placed an arm around her, allowing her to hold onto his shoulder for support. Together they stood and the tall Viking girl took a tentative step forward, then another.

"Think I'll be fine," she said.

Together they shuffled down the mountain, stopping every so often to allow Fieri to catch her breath. They moved slowly, Jaygen sensing resentment from the girl as she relied more on him the further they went.

After a while of shuffling in silence, Jaygen asked, "Who's Jorn?" He attempted to sound indifferent as if he didn't really care and only wanted to make conversation. "Is he your lover?"

"Why do you ask?"

Jaygen cursed himself for even broaching the subject. "No reason, it's just that you were mumbling it in your sleep."

"Why would you care if he was my boyfriend?"

Jaygen noticed the teasing tone in her voice and the jealous feeling he was experiencing brought a warmth to his face.

"Your cheeks have gone red," Fieri remarked, barking out a laugh.

"It's the cold wind, is all," he snapped, feeling self-conscious.

It was a while before she answered. Jaygen guessing that she sensed the tension and cruelly wanting to drag it out.

"Jorn, shares my bed most nights," she admitted, staring ahead. "Jorn, is the only one that my Da allows to kiss me."

"Oh," Jaygen muttered as he fought the sinking feeling in his stomach. He stared at his feet and wished he hadn't asked the question. He wished he hadn't dragged Fieri up the mountain with him.

"Jorn is the name of my hound," she finally answered and elbowed him playfully.

After a moment, allowing her words to sink in, Jaygen felt relief. But couldn't understand why the answer made him feel better. Not that he had any interest in the girl in the first place.

Jaygen realised that she must have walked the pins and needles from her legs by now, yet her arm still lingered over his shoulder and he thought he caught the faint outline of a smile at the side of her mouth.

They paused as they crested the final rise, the village laying before them, smoke curling from the chimney of the tavern as a large group of men stood around talking outside.

"Who are they?" Jaygen asked. He hadn't seen them earlier.

There was possibly fifty of them, all wearing dark furs and bristling with weapons. Steel helmets held in arms as they talked amongst themselves.

"By the black bears painted on their shields, I'd guess it's the Crimlock clan," Fieri answered. "Although I don't see Crimlock himself. Maybe he's in the tavern talking to your Da."

Jaygen nodded. His father had sent a scout to the neighbouring village the previous night. To spread news of the coming battle and to seek help from the clans. These men would be the first of the great army that would be descending on Craggs Head, ready to march north.

"Ragna did it then," Fieri suggested as they continued their way down the winding track that led to the village.

Jaygen already knew the answer. He'd watched his uncle Eric laughing and dancing with his mother while Carmelga danced with his father in the celebration earlier. Now the party had finished and the men were planning for battle.

"It appears so," he said.

They walked on in quiet contemplation. Jaygen wondering what Fieri was thinking about and when he might see her again. Then she suddenly gripped his arm.

Ahead of them a tall man approached, a large dog at his heel.

"It's my brother," Fieri hissed. "If he sees me with you, my Da's going to think we spent the night together."

Jaygen glanced for somewhere to hide but the dog had already begun to bark and Fieri's brother glanced up.

"Listen," she said urgently. "He can't know I was at the summit or caught up in the avalanche."

"Fine."

"You keep my secret and I'll keep yours."

"I don't have a secret," Jaygen whispered harshly, worried that she had worked out that he actually was Grimwolf.

"It's alright, I won't say anything," she reassured him. "I know what you are."

Jaygen's blood went cold. "And what's that?"

"A coward."

He felt relief that his secret was still safe. But also annoyed at her new revelation.

"You must have seen the ogres last night or heard them at least. Yet instead of rushing to my aid you hid. You most probably saw Grimwolf too." She shook her head in disdain. "Some kind of coward. And having Black Owen's blood in your heart."

He didn't know what to say to that, so remained tight-lipped.

"Don't worry none, though. I won't say anything. Just as long as you keep your mouth shut about me," she hissed, frightened eyes returning to the approaching man.

Fieri's brother noticed them and let go of the dog. It crashed through the snow on stumpy legs, its deep but excited barks ripping through the air and echoing around them.

"I won't let your Da harm you," Jaygen whispered, feeling all at once protective over the girl beside him.

"It's not me that needs protecting," she whispered back. "It's you he'll kill."

"Jorn," Fieri greeted the dog as it bounded into her, long ears bouncing as it jumped up. Tongue already out and licking her face. "I was only gone a night."

A shadow crept over them as Fieri's brother loomed above, his wide frame seeming more imposing as he stood upon a rock, making himself appear taller.

"Da's had me out searching for you since we returned," he said, glowering at Jaygen. "Where've you been?"

"Just walking, Fin," she replied, folding her arms and matching his scowl. "What else was I supposed to do while you and Da were off having fun?"

Fin prodded a finger into Jaygen's chest. "With him?" he asked.

"It's a free land. We can wander where we like," she argued.

Jaygen looked from one to the other, not knowing what to say and wanting to be elsewhere while the bickering siblings argued. Yet he knew it would look bad if he simply walked off.

"My Da asked me to light the beacon fire," Jaygen said, pointing up the mountain. The lie came easily. It would have been something that his father wanted doing yesterday. "I asked Fieri to show me the way."

"It's a mountain," Fin snorted. "You just keep going up until there isn't any more up."

Jaygen shrugged. He had a point.

"And what's this?" Fin asked, snatching the red cloak from his sister's shoulders. "A gift from this boy?"

"No, it's…it's…" Fieri began but was struggling for an answer.

"We found it," Jaygen cut in. "Up on the slope."

Fin worked the material in his fingers before bringing it to his nose. "It's not made from any weave that I've seen before."

"It's probably made by an earth-born, before the merge," Jaygen replied, desperately wanting the cloak back but unable to think of an excuse to take it.

Fin glowered at him again before pointing down the valley. "Go," he growled, stepping aside and dismissing him. "And stay away from my sister."

Jaygen briefly glanced at the cloak and then at Fieri, before he stalked away, feeling every bit the coward that she believed he was.

He should have done something, at least said something. But he knew that it was better she thought him craven than the mythical Grimwolf. Better she felt pity for the coward than admiration for a false man trapped in a suit.

He passed a snowy mound and on impulse, kicked it. Then felt a jarring pain as his foot connected with the lump of rock beneath.

It hurt like hell as he struggled on, pretending that it hadn't happened.

At least, he resolved gloomily, his secret was safe. More than safe. She believed him to be the opposite of what he truly was. Walking away from her and her brother like a petulant child only proving the fact.

As he passed through the group of Crimlock men, he held his chin high. He may appear to be gutless to the girl, but cowardly he was not.

He met the icy stares of the fighters and the grimaces they gave him. He even went to push one of the younger ones out of the way, matching his glare and willing him to fight.

The young Crimlock boy was held back by another, possibly his father, whose face opened in a wide smile.

"You've got to be Ragna's son?" he enquired in Norse. A thick arm extending towards his and grasping it tight. "I'm Cob."

Jaygen cleared his throat, but kept the scowl upon his face.

"Erm…Well met, Cob," Jaygen said, making his voice sound deeper than it really was. "I'm Jaygen, son of Ragna."

"Son of Ragna, grandson of Bowen of the Red Path and great grandson of Black Owen himself. That's some lineage lad. I bet you've got stones of steel, aye?" Cob chuckled.

Jaygen sensed Fieri and her brother pass them, the former leaning towards his ear to laugh.

"More likely Jaygen of the yellow path," she whispered before following Fin into the tavern. Jorn barking happily behind them as he nipped at the new red cloak – his red cloak - that she was wearing.

Jaygen stared after them, frustration building within him - a response ready on his lips, but the door slammed in his face.

He was about to march inside the tavern after them. His hand was on the door when he was slapped heartily on the shoulder. When he spun around he found that the crowd and grown.

Once the news had spread of who he was, the rest of the men came closer, their steely gazes softening as they slapped him on the shoulder or shook hands with him. The younger boy who he had pushed out of his way seemed delighted to be in his presence and stared up at him in awe.

"How many men have you thrown from the Tooth?" he asked eagerly. "Bet you've killed ten score."

"I bet you could take old Stump down too," continued another, squeezing into the space beside his friend. "That loud-mouthed Axewell needs knocking down a peg or two." Others around them added similar comments and laughed with admiration as they pushed one another to shake his hand or slap him on the back.

Shaking his head, Jaygen struggled to find something to say. He wasn't used to the attention and Fieri's comment smarted. In the end he raised his arms and shrugged.

It was strange how being called a coward could sink you into the blackest of moods and how quickly you could brighten at the admiration of others. He only wished that it would be this easy to persuade Fieri how brave he could be.

Just then the tavern door swung open and his father filled the frame.

"There you are lad," Ragna said jovially. "Come inside. My brother's keen to meet you."

He held his arms up apologetically to the others as he slipped inside Black Owen's rest, his father's wide arm guiding him. He felt that he could stay outside and soak up the respect from the others for a little longer but there was only so much of himself to go around.

The tavern was full. Every seat was occupied by Vikings, meaty hands wrapped around tankards of ale as they chatted. Those that couldn't find a seat were leaning against the wall or sat at tables, steel glinting from worn scabbards and dented helmets.

Ragna guided him to a table in the corner where his mother sat between two grey-bearded men that he didn't recognise. Fieri's father, Byral, was also there, his beard wet from the ale as he laughed with his son, Fin.

Their attention was fully given to Carmelga who was on the opposite side, arm-wrestling with a young Norseman. The younger man's teeth bared in exertion, the tendons in his neck standing out as his blonde beard shook. Yet their arms were locked, neither moving one way or the other.

Jaygen glanced about for Fieri herself and found her at the bar, nursing an ale while scowling at them. She hadn't been invited to the table then.

His gaze was instantly pulled away as his father slapped a heavy hand on his shoulder.

"This is my boy, Jaygen," Ragna said, proudly.

The closer of the grey-beards stood, his hazel eyes boring into his as they came level.

"Aye," he remarked. "He's got the look of father about him." The man slapped his thick arm against his and gripped it tightly. "What do you think lad? Jaygen of the Red Path?"

"He's not as crazy as that old bastard was," Ragna offered.

"But he's as big," grey-beard said, striking his arms in a manly clap. "I'm your uncle Eric."

A sudden crash brought his attention to the table and the blonde man Carmelga had been arm-wrestling, fell face first into the solid wood.

"See," Ejan said, teasingly. "No Crimlock is stronger than a Cragg. Not even the women," she laughed.

Smiling widely Carmelga picked up a tankard of ale and drained it, foam dribbling down her chin before she wiped it with the back of her forearm. Then slammed the metal cup on the table.

"Anyone else?" she shouted. When she saw that there were no takers she sat heavily down next to the defeated Viking, patting him on his back.

"How about Jaygen?" Fin offered, raising his chin and staring down his nose. "Let's see how strong he really is."

Again, Jaygen cringed away from the attention and sank into the empty chair beside his mother. His uncle had wandered over to the bar, Ragna beside him with a brotherly arm flung over his shoulder.

"How about yourself Fin?" Carmelga asked, filling another cup from a jug and sliding it in front of Jaygen, then treating him to a conspiratorial wink.

Fin didn't reply. He grasped his own drink, stared at them with contempt before beginning a conversation with his father.

"Thanks," Jaygen whispered to Carmelga, wrapping his fingers around the ale. "You probably could beat me."

"Aye," she agreed, laughing. "But I'm not about to put my own cousin down, now am I?"

Jaygen laughed and couldn't help but catch Fieri in his sights. It was the red hair, he told himself. Such a bright colour amongst all the drab greys and browns that were in the room.

She glanced up at the wrong moment and caught him looking. His cheeks flushed for the second time that day. He tried to mask it by drinking the ale.

"I didn't see you yesterday," his mother broached, placing a hand on his arm. "And you didn't sleep in your bed last night."

"I wandered around is all," he lied. But saw his mother watching Fieri from over her tankard.

"Wandering around? So how did Grimwolf's cloak end up in that girl's arms?" Ejan asked, raising a sceptical eyebrow.

Jaygen forcefully swallowed the ale before he choked on it.

"It's not what you think," he said, keeping his voice quiet.

"No? I've seen the glances she's been giving you and the way you're looking back."

Ejan eased back in her chair so their heads were closer together. His mother's golden hair, curled into a small ponytail, skimming his nose as she turned to face him.

"I want the truth."

Jaygen clenched his teeth. She always knew when he was lying, not that he made a habit of it. Call it mother's intuition or a nose for smelling untruths.

"I went up the mountain yesterday. Peter, that is the earth-born, needed medicines which his friend had left at the top…"

"The short version," Ejan demanded, her scowl deepening.

"Fieri followed. We were attacked at the summit by mountain ogres and so I put on the suit," he explained. Then when Ejan drew a sharp intake of breath he continued. "But she didn't see me change. She thinks I hid inside the ski lodge."

"So why is she holding your cloak?"

Jaygen shrugged, feeling a little more at ease, now that his mother hadn't gone berserk.

"Avalanche."

"What!" his mother shouted.

Conversations around the table paused as more than a few heads turned their way.

"It's fine," he reassured her. "Nobody got hurt. But she was knocked unconscious and so I used the cloak to keep her warm until she awoke."

Jaygen stared at the whites of his fingernails, wishing he was somewhere else, wishing that he was at Rams Keep, grooming the horses in the stables.

"And where's the suit now?"

"Around back, hidden behind the log store," he answered and felt the irritation from his mother.

"Not the safest place, is it?" she hissed. "Take it to your room before it's found. Grimwolf maybe the key to winning this battle. If we lose, Ethea loses and we all die."

Jaygen hadn't thought of it like that. Only seeing the armour for its practical uses. For the strength it gave him, the speed and the protection.

"I'll put it away," he said, rising from the table.

Ejan was about to add something more when the tavern door swung open and more men piled into the busy room.

"Ragna?" a round Viking bellowed, his ginger beard woven in thick braids swung as he strode towards the men at the bar.

"Hethod?" Jaygen's father shouted in reply, his head towering over the other men around him.

The two men met in the middle and slapped their arms around each other.

"You're not back to dust then," Hethod remarked, joyously. "I wouldn't let myself believe it until I saw it with my own eyes."

Eric joined the pair and placed a tankard of ale in the newcomer's hands.

"I must admit, I needed to blink twice," his uncle said. "So have you come for the warring?"

"That's why the beacons were lit, so here I am," Hethod answered. "And I've brought nearly a hundred with me. All itching for a fight with the Empire."

Ragna slapped his meaty hands on Hethod's shoulder. "Our fight isn't with the Empire, it's in the north."

The ginger braids stopped swaying as Hethod absorbed his father's words.

"We're about as far north as north goes," he said. "What's north of north?"

"Hades," Ragna replied. "I'll explain more, let's get you and your men settled in. There's going to be a lot more clans arriving soon. We can do all the talking then."

Jaygen left the table and squeezed passed all the Vikings that were pushing into the cramped tavern.

He felt relief when his face found the cold air. Free from all the meaty bodies full of sweat and testosterone. All the beards, furs and steel. All the back-slapping, hand-shaking story-sharing clansmen that were getting teary-eyed over past battles and skirmishes that were long ago forgotten.

"That's him," came a voice standing beside a huddle of Norsemen. "That's Ragna's lad."

Jaygen recognised him as the youth who had held him in such high admiration, only moments before.

The men stared, looking him up and down as if not believing the words of the youth.

"Him?" asked one of them incredulously. "He's the one going to fight Stump, on the Tooth?"

Now it was Jaygen's turn not to believe the words being spoken before him. Who was he supposed to be fighting on the Tooth? He didn't remember agreeing to fight anybody.

"He hasn't even got a sword," remarked another. "He's got Ragna's height, but not the weight."

The youth jumped up and down excitedly. "He's thrown plenty from the Tooth before. Isn't that right, Cob?"

Cob was standing to one side, offering a shrug and an apologetic smile to Jaygen. It was as if they'd started a rumour that had snowballed out of control.

"See, I told you so," continued the youth. "I bet Axewell Stump won't even show up. If he does, Black Jaygen will slay him on the Tooth."

The first Norseman puffed his cheeks out and blew air threw his lips.

"I don't know," he said eyeing Jaygen up and down again. "Stump maybe missing a hand but he could kill a man with his temper alone. I'll take your bet. A silver coin that Axewell cuts him down."

The pair spat on their palms before shaking hands.

Jaygen could only stare at them, his blood running cold as the men discussed how Stump might gut him or hurl his body from the Tooth. And the Crimlock men, who had some kind of grudge against this Axewell Stump, arguing that Black Jaygen would crush him.

How was he going to get out of this?

The denial was about to leave his mouth when the tavern door opened and Fin walked out. A stern faced Fieri at his heel.

Her eyes met Jaygen's for the briefest of moments. Sharp and hard, disappointment lacing the icy blue. Her lip curled up as she brushed passed him, disgust at seeing this coward that was in her way.

"A gold coin says I'll beat this Stump," came a voice from nowhere.

For a stunned moment, Jaygen thought that he was daydreaming. That the words he'd just said were not real. But as he watched Fieri and her brother pause and slowly turn to him, a mocking smirk on Fin's face and an open mouth on hers, he realised that he was fully awake and now fully committed to besting this Axewell.

The Crimlock men shouted and hooted as they converged. The testosterone he'd left in the tavern suddenly descending on the group that were now grasping his hand and slapping his back.

His face pulled back in a rictus grin, pretending that he meant every word while his insides dissolved to tripe. What had he done? And to make matters worse, he caught Fieri marching away, long legs striding ahead of her brother.

Before he had chance to chase after her, Cob gripped him tightly in a hug.

"This has been a long time coming," he said, face grinning with delight. "That bloody Axewell Stump must have killed twenty score or more on our land.

He's a blood thirsty bastard which means I can make the odds in his favour and take more of the winnings when you butcher him, aye? Them, Fishies have been boasting for far too long now."

"Fishies?" Jaygen murmured.

"Aye, clan Seagrit. They've a whale painted on their shields. Stump is part of them."

Feeling dazed, Jaygen could do no more than nod his head, hoping that Axewell Stump would be out to sea and would never come within his range. When this was all over he would be going back to Rams Keep anyway. He'd only been here for two days and already he was sick of the north.

He made his excuses and left the two clans to quarrel over the odds of the fight while he slipped behind the tavern to fetch his armour.

He pulled the sack from under the pile of logs, threw it over his shoulder and turned to climb up the steps to his room at the back of the tavern, when Peter walked around the corner.

"There you are," the earth-born said. "I came to thank you."

Jaygen nodded a greeting as the skier sat on the logs. "Feeling any better?" Jaygen asked as he unslung his sack and hunkered down beside him.

"Yeah, you brought the insulin just in time. Any longer and I would have gone into a coma I wouldn't be waking up from."

Jaygen nodded as he stared out to sea. White waves crashing against the large icebergs that floated on the surface, groaning against each other. Foam ran smoothly over the stony beach before being pulled back out.

"You ever got yourself caught up in something you wish you hadn't?" Jaygen asked.

Peter chuckled. "Yes, like coming north to go skiing on a slope full of monsters?"

"Like that, only worse."

"You mean the gathering of all these Vikings?" Peter asked. "There's a huge battle coming and somehow you've got yourself mixed up with nowhere to run."

"No," Jaygen admitted gloomily. He had no trouble thinking about running into battle, fighting alongside his brother Norseman, his mother and father. In fact, he couldn't wait to put the suit on and begin cutting through the demons in the north.

"Because if it is, I'll go with you. I don't fancy staying around while there's a battle going on." Peter appeared hopeful, even holding onto Jaygen's sleeve.

"Never mind," Jaygen muttered as he clambered to his feet. "You should seriously think about going home though. More Vikings will be coming every day."

"I don't know if I can make it back alone. Everything is so changed and besides, I haven't got anything to return to."

"Then stay. The battle won't be around here anyway, it'll be out there," Jaygen explained, pointing out to sea. It was then that he saw the sails of several longboats weaving between the icebergs. Wide mouthed dragons as figureheads, forked tongues protruding through sharply carved teeth.

As he watched, the sails were brought in and the oars lowered into the water as they made for the harbour wall. The sounds of men grunting with the effort, being brought to him in snatches caught on the wind.

As the final sail was stored away he caught a glimpse of a huge animal painted in red.

It was a whale.

10

A Myth Among Us

Shredded clouds scattered across the darkening sky. A single star twinkling between a rare gap; cold, distant and alone – much how Jaygen felt as he blew warmth into numbing fingers.

Three days had passed since the night of the avalanche and over forty clans had descended on Craggs Head, and more were arriving every few hours. Their camp fires were spread out around the village, dotted along the valley slopes and the beach. Lanterns rocked upon the longboats that were tied along the harbour wall, roped to whatever they could get purchase on while the rest anchored offshore, filling spaces amongst the icebergs.

His father told him that there could be as many as twenty-thousand men, women and beasts in Craggs Head and he expected the number to triple in the coming days. Not that he experienced much time with Ragna as he was devoted to making council with the clan leaders and war chiefs. Attempting to negotiate peace amongst the warring clans before they killed each other. Soothing tension between the seafaring Vikings who had a natural disregard for anyone on land.

Five times his father needed to step in when clansmen wanted to settle things on the Tooth. 'Save your fighting for Hades', he had shouted, brandishing the Fist of the North for emphasis. But the longer they waited for more to arrive, the higher the tension between the clans rose. Too many battle-hardened men, too much steel and with nothing to clash it against but each other, things were getting very ugly very quickly.

They needed a common footing, a bond that would bury old rivalries, making them forget their hatred against each other - if only for the time being. Something to take their minds off petty feuds until they were across the water and fighting Hades and his demons. Only then would they truly become brothers in arms, bonded by a common enemy.

Subsequently, his mother had suggested that Grimwolf make an appearance. Something to keep the threat real and perhaps put frayed nerves at ease. Showing that they had a living myth who will fight with them. One that every Viking would instantly recognise and respect, if not experiencing a little dread.

Jaygen stretched his head to one side and then the other before snapping the wolf helm's visor shut.

It was show time.

He flexed the clawed gauntlets, resting one on the pommel of his sword. Brushing branches from his path with the other as he stepped out of the tree-line.

Snow crunched under foot as he descended the mountain. The same path he had walked along with Fieri only days before.

Looking back, he realised that he had enjoyed the time with her, right up until she called him a coward. If she could only see him now, if she knew the truth of who he really was.

He put his tongue to the roof of his mouth and made a clicking sound. It was no use thinking about ifs – she thought him a coward and that was that.

Why did he care anyway?

The girl was rude, rebellious and stubborn. She had a fixed scowl more often than not and acted as though she had a point to prove with everyone. As if being born the fairer sex meant that she was less a fighter than the men.

In truth, Jaygen saw much of his mother in Fieri. That's how he imagined she was in her youth and why his father had fallen in love with her.

"Love?" he hissed into the helm. An emotion for the bards and fools.

He pushed the red-haired girl to the back of his mind as he stepped onto an open slope, where he could be easily spotted from the closest of the campfires that spread out below.

The sounds of merry singing came to him on the back of laughter. Songs sung about battles and bravery, about hero's from long ago and the deeds that had earned them their places. He recognised some of the tunes, a number of which his father had whistled and sung around Rams Keep. Others which the bard Otholo had plucked on his lute.

Maybe after they had defeated Hades and Neptula went back to dust, they would make a song for him. But then it wouldn't be for Jaygen, it would be for the armour which he wore.

The smell of cooking meat filled his nostrils as he stalked passed the first of the camps. The firelight picking out grease on the lips of the chief as he was about to take another bite from the chicken leg. His eyes formed huge white circles around dark pupils as they found him approaching.

His hand paused beneath his grey beard and the meat fell to the ground.

"Grimwolf," he exclaimed, his voice dry.

The laughter died, followed by the singing as they all turned to where their chief was staring.

Gasps escaped mouths, nervous hands reaching for weapons as Jaygen stepped through the centre of the crowd.

The young and the experienced warriors staggered back, jaws gaping. Each pushing the other to be as far away from him as possible.

Leaving stunned silence in his wake, Jaygen prowled passed the chief, feeling the gazes of all upon his back.

He tried to stride as purposefully as possible but became too aware of himself and almost stumbled into a thin boy of his own age, who had turned suddenly and froze like a rabbit caught in flash lamp.

Jaygen shifted his own gaze upon the lad. Fixing him with the hollow stare that the snarling wolf permeated so naturally.

The boy's arm wobbled and he dropped the tankard he was holding. The metal cup making a clanging sound against his boots as it sloshed ale into the snow.

Lip trembling the boy stepped back and fell into the lap of a man who had been running a sharpening stone along his sword. He was about to growl at the younger lad when his gaze fell on Jaygen and his face went slack, the sword forgotten.

The movement stirred something in the boy and he raised his hand.

"G…G…G," he stammered, scurrying back and knocking into another clansman, who in turn tapped the shoulder of the Northman beside him.

His smile hidden from view, Jaygen stalked away hearing Grimwolf being whispered from mouth to mouth by urgent lips. Passing through the camps like the ripples from a stone, dropped into a pond.

The next fire he passed, cast the dancing shadows of three merry Vikings, jigging in time to a fiddle. Each swinging the other as they linked their elbows to spin around, the rest of their band stood in a circle clapping hands and stomping feet.

When the elderly fiddler noticed him approach, his bow screeched along the strings, leaving a painful note in the air. The dance died to nothing as the group watched him enter the circle.

The three dancers parted, two jumping back as if a mountain ogre had suddenly wanted to join the merriment, while the third stepped away into the fire, setting his boots aflame.

"It's him," the fiddler announced pointing a quivering bow, the fiddle held loose in his other hand. "It's Grimwolf."

A woman suddenly screamed, her face burning red before she fainted. The men around her lacking the motivation to catch her before she hit the ground.

Jaygen stepped over her body and paced on, heading for the huge fire on the rise. His father's fire and where all the war chiefs and the heads of the bigger clans were gathered. The tavern being too small to accommodate them all.

By the time he began to ascend the hill, the name of Grimwolf had overtaken him and instead of trudging through the noise of talking and laughter, singing and arguing, only the wind touched his ears.

The clouds briefly parted, choosing an opportunistic moment to light the valley with a full moon. As if the heavens realised that a myth walked amongst the

Northmen and wanted to add to the drama. Silver light radiated from his silver amour as if the celestial body shone a spotlight on him. Bringing the legend alive.

He felt every gaze, thousands of them and fought not to laugh. If they only knew the truth would they fear him so much?

Necks craned, men stretched over the men in front while those at the front pushed back. Everyone wanted to look, wanted to see but lacked the courage to venture closer.

The bodies before him parted like sheaves of corn to a scythe, as he ploughed through the crowd to the large circle of men surrounding a fire pit.

His uncle Eric sat beside a giant of a man with a beaded blonde beard, both stared on with open mouths. Hethod was on the other side of the fire rubbing at his eyes as if trying to wake from a dream while Byral glared on, twisting an axe in his grip. Standing behind him was Fin, his face taking on an ashen hue.

Jaygen didn't recognise the others, all probably hard men with big names and bigger reputations. He turned his head to stare at each, allowing his appearance to do the introductions for him - not that he needed any.

Grimwolf was a monster that every clan knew. The cruellest of demons to ever touch folklore. A sinister character in the stories told to children. His name a whisper, a threat, a curse and warning to any Viking caught wandering alone on a full moon.

It seemed to Jaygen that the entire north had gone still. A silent pause in time where nobody moved, stirred or even uttered a word. Where grown men were afraid to draw breath, should they elicit his attention.

Then his heart thudded widely, like a smith hammering an anvil.

Fieri shuffled from around her brother, her tall frame straightening as she hugged the red cloak, his red cloak, against her chest. Blue eyes widening in awe, an eagerness drawing her closer until Byral grasped her wrist.

She seemed to be seeing through the armour, recognising the boy beneath and glaring into his very soul.

Jaygen glanced away, afraid she would see the truth.

"You came then?" his father greeted, smiling as he poked a stick into the fire.

It caused sparks to drift up into the night and dispel the magic.

Ragna was sat on a log next to Jaygen's mother, white teeth showing though a knowing grin.

"Welcome Grimwolf," he boomed, loud enough for his voice to pass back down to the village.

Jaygen inclined his head, but said nothing.

Ragna rose from the log to shake his hand. One meaty palm slapping into his lobster gauntlet and pumping it enthusiastically.

It was a ruse they had planned earlier and it did seem to ease the tension in the crowd, although all still watched on, open mouthed.

His father released his hand to address the crowding men and women, pacing around the perimeter of the circle with his arms out wide.

"Truly the north has come together if even myths have joined our ranks," he shouted, then snapped a chubby finger at Jaygen. "Grimwolf, a name we all know, a nightmare we all fear. But still a creature of the north."

A muttering of agreement swept through the men, some nodding while most stared on, soaking up the wolf armour.

"An omen sent to us from Valhalla," he continued, raising a fist as he spoke. "Odin's champion – a Viking that we may fear no more."

Jaygen risked another glance towards Fieri. The girl now free of her father's grasp had taken another step towards him, arms proffering his cloak for him to take.

He subtly shook his head, hoping that she recognised his warning.

People had seen her with that cloak for the past few days. If she was to give it to him now, they may believe that he hadn't simply walked down from the mountains and that perhaps he was simply another man inside a suit. Not to mention that she would need to explain how she came by the cloak to her father. He doubted that simply finding it, would suffice.

Luckily she recognised his warning and checked herself, lowering her arms and carefully stepping beside her brother.

"The Sea Witch means to destroy all men and creatures of the land. Neptula will flood the world and annihilate anything that breathes the air. But we have friends," Ragna explained, his voice rising with each word. "Elora – daughter of Chaos, is fighting Neptula's forces in the south."

This news had the crowd whispering amongst themselves, but his father carried on as if expecting this.

"And yes, the Dark Army is fighting with her. If all we have left to fight evil, is more evil, then that's what we'll use."

He grasped his stick once again and thrust it into the fire, leaving it imbedded.

"We have more pressing matters in the north. Hades has set his demons to melting the great ice shelves. Making rivers where the land was frozen, turning solid ground into liquid and raising the sea level. If we don't act soon it will be too late. Once the levels reach a certain point, it will be impossible to reverse the damage."

"The ice shelves are vast," bellowed a Viking stepping out of the crowd.

He was a little older than Jaygen, with a shaved head and a single tail of beard that was beaded with a rat skull. He was short, but what he lacked in height he made up in bulk. Wide shoulders rolled as he folded his arms.

"They stretch all the way along the Arctic Circle. If these demons are melting it, then there would be millions of them. How do we fight so many?"

Nods of agreement flickered through the men.

Ragna turned to the speaker, a wicked grin forming lines along the sides of his eyes.

"We don't," he admitted.

Ragna reached over his back to grasp his war hammer. He cocked it onto a shoulder as he began pacing again, meeting everyone's eyes.

"We only need to kill Hades," he explained. "The demons will fall away once he is dust."

"Kill Hades?" rat skull asked, incredulously. "And how do we kill a god? Even the Fist of the North isn't god-created."

Ragna's grin only broadened. "You're right," he said, twisting the shaft in his hands so he could regard the huge lump of metal with Elora's hand print sunk in deep. "But he is," he finished and pointed the war hammer towards Jaygen. "Grimwolf will kill the god."

"If he truly is Grimwolf," rat skull sneered, poking an arm at him. An arm that ended with a stump. A grey flap of skin sewn over the joint where his wrists should have been.

"See for yourself, Axewell," Ragna continued, undaunted.

Jaygen swallowed the lump that had suddenly formed in his throat. He had spent the previous three days avoiding the Seagrit clan. Staying away from the longboats and the harbour while ducking away every time he saw a shield with a whale painted on it. The rumours of him fighting Axewell Stump on the Tooth, had spread throughout all the bands and clans and the odds were rising with them.

He stared at the man before him. Strong-set jaw, hair shaved to stubble and violence sparkling from dark eyes. He appeared every bit as vicious as his name.

"See him!" screeched a voice from the crowd. "I'll see this Grimwolf."

Jaygen stared but couldn't see where the voice came from. Until the men parted to allow an old lady through.

She was the oldest person that he had ever seen. Wrinkles covered her round face, deep enough to hold plates and her lids drooped over baggy eyes reducing one to a slit while totally concealing the other. Bent almost in half, she leaned against a gnarly staff that twisted to twice her height.

The old woman shuffled into the space beside Axewell, planting her staff at his feet and forcing him out of her path.

"Shannog?" Ragna laughed. "So you're still alive?"

The old woman paused long enough to regard Jaygen's father with her slit of an eye, a crinkled mouth smacking against gums as incredibly, her wrinkles deepened into troughs.

"Aye, Ragna," she replied, in a voice sounding like millstones grinding together. "Son of Bowen. I remember when your Grandpappy were little more than spit of a boy."

Ragna nodded as he set the shaft of his war hammer into the ground and leaned his chin upon the steel head.

"I remember my Da telling me stories about you," he laughed. "You were old then."

"Old as the hills," she agreed. "I was in this very spot the last time the north rallied together. Gave my council to Black Owen himself and his pig-headed war chiefs then. Not that they listened any."

"We're all ears now," Ragna chuckled, nodding towards Jaygen. "Will you agree that this man before us is real?" He raised his arms out to the crowd. "Would you all take her word on it if Shannog proves this Grimwolf to be true?"

"Aye," shouted the crowd enthusiastically. Axewell only nodding, his scowl sinking deeper.

Smacking her lips together once again, Shannog shuffled closer to Jaygen. Her narrow eye widening and pivoting in the puffy folds of her face. Glaring at the suit, she wrapped her knuckles against his chest, the hollow thuds sounding dead.

She appeared impossibly even smaller up close. Loose grey strands of hair floating above her balding pate, only reaching his waist yet when she gripped his elbow to pull him down, he felt a solid strength.

"The suit I've seen before," she informed the crowd, glaring into the eye slits. "Yet the man is new," she whispered so only Jaygen could hear.

Jaygen felt as though she could see him, as if she was penetrating the armour and revealing the boy beneath.

"The flesh is always real, but do you truly desire to be Grimwolf?" Shannog asked, raising a wire-brush of an eyebrow.

"Yes," Jaygen replied, keeping his voice low. He darted a glance at Fieri again, her face full of wonder, much like everyone else's at the gathering. "Yes," he repeated, more sure of himself.

Shannog smacked her lips together and turned to the crowd.

"It is he," she shouted, stamping her staff into the dirt for emphasis. "The wolf is amongst us, a wolf of the grimmest kind." She turned her head his way again, the fire picking out an animal bone that she wore through her ear. "Grimwolf!" And she slammed her staff down again.

The crowds followed suit and began to stamp feet or thump fists against shields in time to the rhythm.

"Grimwolf, Grimwolf, Grimwolf!"

Even Axewell was clapping a hand against his thigh. His father and mother clapped heartily and when he glanced again at Fieri he saw that she was approaching again, her red hair matching the fire, her face carrying a look he hadn't seen on her before – yet a look that he had seen on Elora when she was with Bray.

Jaygen was smiling behind the helm, fighting the urge to raise his arms and clasp his hands together in triumph. He felt like a champion, a hero, and although he basked in the unexpected glory, he acted as though he didn't care. To show emotion was to show the human side of Grimwolf. A side which shouldn't exist.

But could he share the secret with Fieri? She wouldn't think him a coward then.

"Of course," Shannog screeched, raising her staff for quiet. When the shouting and cheering tapered off she continued. "The armour comes at a price. It always has."

Jaygen didn't know what the old woman was talking about. He had known no price to wearing the suit.

"Grimwolf was created by the god of winter," she explained, poking her staff at the snow high upon the mountain. "A cold god, a harsh and lonely god - the suit is no different."

She twisted her head around like an owl tracking a mouse, her glower catching him from the one seeing eye.

"The myth is real and so too is the curse," she said, pushing Fieri back with her staff. The nobbled end digging into her chest enough to make her wince. "The suit lacks warmth, emotion, empathy. Do not be fooled - Grimwolf will fight for us but nothing more. His, is a lonely path. Any that try to get close to him, be close to him, will experience the curse."

Jaygen clenched his teeth. Was she speaking the truth?

"Should any girl," and this time her head turned to Fieri to include her, "be foolish enough to fall in love or even receive love from Grimwolf - will feel the full force of this curse. And in my experience curses are best avoided."

Fieri glanced guiltily down and shuffled back behind her father. Jaygen wanted to tell her that the old woman was wrong, that she had made up the curse, but couldn't. Maybe he would later. But then, what if the curse was real?

"Very well," Ragna boomed and raised the Fist of the North into the air. "Grimwolf is real. Any person who still doesn't believe, may give him a kiss and see if they catch the curse."

This brought a few chuckles from the crowd. "Otherwise, that's the end of the matter."

He extended the hammer once more towards him. "There is a Myth among us so it seems that even winter is on our side."

This was met with wild cheering and the crowds began to wave swords, spears and axes in the air.

It seemed to Jaygen that nothing brought men together better than an approaching battle. At least it would dampen the resolve of those clans still wanting to fight each other.

"Now down to business," Ragna continued. "Although the main body of the clans are still to arrive, we can't sit on our backsides waiting for them. We'll make up an advance party of three clans – which will be the Seagrits, as we'll be using their longboats, the Crimlocks and the Fenrays," he said nodding towards Byral who was the leader of that clan.

His father spread his arms to the crowds. "The rest of you may go back to your camps and fires. Eric will be taking charge of you so any further orders will be coming from him."

Jaygen watched the crowds begin to dissolve. Most sending cautious glances his way before departing and some even pausing to stare until they were pulled along by their clansmen.

When things had quieted down, Ragna motioned for the remaining leaders and Vikings to gather closer to the fire. When Jaygen approached, the closest of his father's men stepped aside, leaving him a gap in the tight gathering.

"Axewell, has your boat readied itself with provisions?" Ragna asked.

"Aye chief," he replied, scratching his scowl with the end of his stump. "Seagrits live on the waves, except when we're raiding of course."

This brought a few hardy laughs from his clan.

"Good," Ragna replied. "With Odin's help we'll reach the ice shelves in two days."

"Aye," Axewell's dark gaze fell on Jaygen. "And Grimwolf?"

Ragna shrugged. "He'll be coming with us. We can't very well leave the one man who can kill Hades behind, can we?"

"If, he is a man," added Byral.

Jaygen turned his head towards Fieri's father and smiled inside the helm as the older man quickly gazed in another direction.

"He's a Viking and that's all that counts," Fieri put in, coming to his defence.

There were nods of agreement at that.

"Once we've arrived at the ice shelves," Ragna continued, bringing everyone's attention back to the plans. "We'll send a scouting party ahead to range where the enemy is and mark out a route for the rest. My wife, Ejan, will lead the scouts, are there any other volunteers amongst you for the scouting party?"

"Aye," Fin said instantly, stepping from behind Byral. The father proudly slapping a hand on the shoulder of his son.

"And me," a tall man from the clan Seagrit, offered.

"I'll go," Cob yelled, obviously not wanting the Crimlocks to be outdone by a Seagrit.

Axewell raised his stump. "What about your lad, Ragna? Jaygen isn't it?"

"Aye," Ragna said, a scowl rising upon his brow. "What of it?"

"Well, if his mother can go, surely he can. Although I don't see him around. In fact, I haven't seen him since I arrived and apparently he's been itching to take me up to the Tooth."

"That so?" Ragna asked, standing straighter, slowly turning the shaft of the hammer in his meaty hands.

"Yeah," Axewell replied. "And I've a mind to take him up on the offer. But you see," and Axewell waved his stump around the camp. "Your boy is nowhere to be found. Craven is he?"

Jaygen felt a wave of heat, his fingers tightening around the grip of his sword, yet it was his father whose anger came to the fore.

"Jaygen is no less a coward than I am," he spat, slamming the Fist of the North into the ground and kicking up dirt. "I've already made it known that the only person who will be settling things up at the Tooth, will be me. Is that what you want?"

Axewell glared at Ragna, a twitch flicking at the corner of his temple. He sucked air through his teeth and then spat into the fire.

"No," he said, eyes softening as he stared at the ground.

Forcing his hand to relax, Jaygen let out the breath he'd been holding. He was sure he could win a fight against Axewell as Grimwolf, but as himself he didn't know and didn't want to find out.

"I'll go with the scouting party," Axewell continued.

"And me," Fieri offered, stepping closer to Ragna. Her father was on his feet, a refusal already upon his tight lips until Fieri set a hand on his shoulder. "I'm going. If Ejan can go, a woman of the Craggs, then so too can I."

Byral clenched his teeth, yet saw the determination in his daughter's countenance, then sat back down shaking his head in disbelief. A grin spread on Fieri's face that filled with the glow from the fire.

Jaygen was hoping that the old Viking may have persuaded his daughter to stay, but it was clear that she was her own woman in this and it would make his clan seem less brave in front of the crowd. Yet he still found himself urging Byral to act.

"Is there anyone else?" Ragna shouted. It was met with silence as the many heads at the gathering turned this way and that, searching behind them and across but nobody else wanted to volunteer. Ragna sighed, thick with disappointment.

"I'll go."

The man standing closest to Jaygen who'd slowly crept closer during the passing moments, jumped back as if suddenly remembering that the armour was actually alive.

"I'll go," Jaygen repeated, loud enough for the entire crowd to hear.

His mother folded her arms and fixed him with a glare that told him she would be having words later. His father's eyebrows disappeared into his shaggy hair. Both frustrated with the situation but neither able to refuse him in front of the gathering.

The plan was for him to only go with the advance party. To only make brief appearances and be at the forefront of the battle when it came. Volunteering for the scouting party, being up close and personal with a handful of others wasn't what his parents had planned. It would only invite suspicion should his act fail.

Jaygen wondered if he had done the right thing, the rebuke he could expect would be a harsh one. Yet as he watched Fieri's grin widen, excitement brimming as she clutched his cloak to her chest, he began to feel eager to begin this voyage north.

Then his gaze found Shannog's and a veil of doubt clouded his mood once again. He looked from the old woman, to his mother and then back to Fieri. The realisation of what he had done only now sinking in as he watched the three of them watching him. Admiration from the youngest seeing the armour, worry from his mother for the boy inside, and a curse from the elder.

He felt he couldn't take their stares any longer and so without adding any more, he turned on his heel and stalked away from the fire.

The crowds parted to let him pass, some stumbling over those behind in their haste to keep out of his way. Jaygen paid them no heed as he strode out of the busy camp and began the climb back into the mountains.

It didn't matter whether he fought before or after, whether he travelled with the advance party or fought alongside his mother in the scout party. It only mattered that he reached Hades and kill him. Everything else was simply a means to an end.

He was out of sight of the fires before something grasped his arm.

Jaygen spun, hand already reaching for his blade when he paused.

"Why did you follow me?" he asked.

Fieri stood before him, breath coming out in rapid plumes, her chest heaving with the effort to keep pace up the steep incline. He forgot how easily he moved while wearing the suit.

"I came to give you this," Fieri answered, leaning closer to him so she could throw the cloak around his shoulders.

Jaygen went rigid as she reached up on tip-toes to snap the clasps shut on the red cloth, her nose so close to his that he could count the tiny freckles on the narrow bridge.

"And to thank you for saving my life," she continued and surprised him by placing a kiss on the jaw of his wolf's helm.

Jaygen didn't know what to say. He didn't know what to feel. The kiss had been a shock and for the first time while wearing the armour, he felt exposed - helpless. Yet as he stared at Fieri, her arms held behind her back as she stared up at him expectantly, he felt elated. Was this what Bray felt when he was with Elora?

"I don't care what the others say," she admitted. "I feel safer with you. You're my protector and nothing can harm me when I'm with you."

He wanted to say something, but couldn't think of anything that wouldn't ruin the moment. But as she backed away, her gaze never leaving his, he knew that she hadn't been expecting one. Grimwolf was supposed to be quiet, was supposed to be mysterious.

Before she turned she offered him a smile, then drifted back to the camp.

Jaygen hadn't known he had been smiling until realisation caught him and his mood swiftly spiralled down into despair. She was falling for Grimwolf while believing that Jaygen was a coward.

Once Fieri was out of sight, he began the lonely climb once again, trudging through the deep snow as he wondered how the coming voyage would work and if there was any truth to Shannog's warning.

He didn't feel as though the armour was cursed. Although it went some way into explaining why he had been so frustrated while being around Elora. Maybe the suit exasperated the wearer's emotions. After all, he had found it buried in a hidden crypt within the foundations of Rams Keep. A place where the previous owner had died with heartache over losing the love of a princess.

Feeling a melancholy aura settle its familiar veil around him, he trudged up the narrow path, wanting some time alone.

His helmet brushed the low branch of a tree and when it flicked back the entire night's snow cascaded down. Fine white powder found its way inside the armour to press an icy clutch against the back of his neck.

Jaygen bunched his shoulders against the cold. Questioning whether the chilliness at his neck was a simple mishap or a warning from the god of winter.

11

The Bigger Fish

The haunting sounds of a whale cut through the ocean. A swimming giant searching for a mate or food, or simply to fill the big blue with its song. Timoshi didn't understand the dialect but was welcomed by another's company in the large expanse of water - other than the determined fish that was following.

He risked a glance back and realised to his horror that the black dot was growing bigger as it gained on him.

Struggling on, he forced his lethargic tentacles to move. His gills working hard to suck in the salty brine as his muscles bunched, writhed and kicked.

Bunch, writhe, kick. He needed to reach Neptula if nothing else.

Seven suns had crossed the above since he had escaped the daughter of Solarius. Seven days and nights endlessly crawling through stream, brook and river. Swimming against currents both in the river and estuary to reach the glorious sea. Leaving his fallen brethren behind. Martyrs to the Sea Witch's war, left in the above to rot as no skagwangle should.

Pain screamed from the wound he received from that Chaos demented whore. His ruined shoulder, blistered and cracked, slowed him to a pathetic limp. His scent leaving his body with every movement that squeezed drops of blood, leaving a trail for predators and scavengers.

Things would have been different if he still held his trident. Even a full working arm would have giving him the ability to kill his pursuer. But he was weakened by the days spent swimming. Exhausted and crippled by the wound, he'd rapidly descended the food chain. That was rules of the ocean for you. No matter the size or strength of a fish, there was always one bigger.

Bunch, writhe, kick.

The shadow of the whale sank into view. The vague outlines of a long flat body with a bulbous round head. It came into focus, its song forgotten as it sensed his coming. Timoshi hoped that the relentless dog that followed him, would decide to leave his meagre pickings and venture for the bigger fish.

Yet as Timoshi dived lower, searching for the current that would pull him further out, he saw that the dot was still chasing him. The dot becoming larger. The dark outlines of a thick dorsal fin sitting erect above a wide body. A nose shaped to a point and rows of sharp white teeth. The shark was large, even for an earth-born.

Timoshi had tangled with more than a few sharks before the merge. They were little more than a nuisance – dogs of the sea. But the shark that was pursuing him wasn't of Thea and felt no threat from a skagwangle. Only feeling a mild curiosity towards this floundering creature that might or might not be tasty, but in a vast ocean - food was food.

It was so close now that Timoshi could feel the parting eddies against his tentacles, feel the rush as it cut through the water. The reflections of sun rays that penetrated the surface as they bounced from a white belly and grey back.

Bunch, Writhe, KICK.

Parting his own mouth, Timoshi bared his teeth, screaming into the void as one of his tentacles brushed against the nose of the shark. His smooth flesh sliding over harsh rough skin.

Bunch, WRITHE – KICK!

The shark pushed harder as it closed in for the kill. Its great mouth opening, rows of triangular teeth placed around a deep black opening. It would swallow him hole.

Timoshi pushed on. Knuckles popping, arms aching – chest heaving. Neptula must know.

BUNCH, WRITHE – KICK KICK KICK!

His body suddenly lurched as he passed over a shelf, a deep trough opening out on the seabed. He felt a tooth graze against a tentacle – felt the pain as it snagged.

Then all at once there was an explosion of movement.

Dizziness overwhelmed his senses as he was shoved, spun and dragged. His tentacles flying out in all directions in a maelstrom of bubbles and blood. Pain screaming from every part of his body, sinuses crushed under the pressure.

When the world stopped spinning, Timoshi kicked away from the cloud of blood. Red blood, not green.

The shark was writhing in the jaws of a trench eel. The mouth that had tried to devour him working up and down in a silent scream as it was dragged deeper. The dog had drastically dropped from the top of the food chain and was most likely puzzled as to why.

The eels mouth closed tighter until the shark's bones cracked and it its thrashing body became limp.

There was always a bigger fish.

Timoshi slowed the pace of his gills as he watched the eel work its way back into the hole beneath the shelf, pulling its prize with it. Now the worlds had merged, Earth was experiencing creatures that hadn't been in these waters for tens of thousands of years.

He gave a final salute to the eel and began to swim away. There were still bigger monsters that swam the depths than a trench eel. And now that he bled from the end of a ruined tentacle, as well as from gaining a gash in another limb, he would be open prey.

Pushing once more for the surface, he continued his journey, hoping that no other sharks would track him. He doubted he would survive another attack.

Green clouds of blood pooled around him, filtering the sun's rays as he neared the surface. His life fluid rushing from his body as he worked it harder.

Heat from the above touched his face as he neared, the salt stinging his wounds. It was critical that he reached his god. The Chaos whore must pay for what she did to him.

Thoughts of revenge filled his mind, the pain goading the images of curling his tentacles around Elora's throat and slowly constricting her wind pipe. Making her watch while he killed her mate – maybe by the trident or fed alive to snapping cray fish.

The grin that had crept upon his narrow mouth vanished when he sensed another creature rising from the deep.

It was directly below him. A vast mammoth of a shape, bigger even than the trench eel and coming at some speed.

Timoshi had no fight left in him. No energy to swim away, barely enough to even feel sorry for himself.

On land, if you were killed or simply died, you usually became dust. Left to rot in the ground. But in the seas and oceans you were always food. If you were not eaten in the attack that killed you, if you somehow lived long enough to simply die of age - your body would sink to the bottom and become food for the crabs and crustaceans. A perfect circle of life. Live, eat – die, get eaten.

Shifting his body to face his attacker, Timoshi bared his teeth. At least he would meet his death with the dignity of a skagwangle and not a coward.

The huge creature pivoted on long fins, turning to come level with him. A long beaked head gliding inches from his own, followed by a narrow serpentine body.

Bubbles of laughter escaped Timoshi as he raised his webbed hand to brush against the scales of the water dragon. He wouldn't be given over to food just yet.

Putting any final energy into kicking his limbs, Timoshi reached around the water dragon's neck and locked his tentacles around the thick muscle.

It was tame and didn't struggle as he mounted her.

"Take me to the jewel," he commanded to the scaly beast. "Take me home."

His words were cast as thoughts picked up by the water dragon as she changed direction.

Once his tentacles were locked in place, Timoshi relaxed the rest of his body, fatigue burning through every muscle and fibre. He would need sustenance soon, but first his god awaited him.

Calming his heaving chest, he became a simple passenger on the noble creature's back. Enjoying the rush of water as it cut through the sea at frightening speed. The body working up and down like a snake, long webbed feet kicking the brine behind.

It ascended towards the above, stretching into a more streamline shape before breaking the surface and continuing into the air.

The momentum carried them high above the water. White waves crashing about them as the sea dragon spread out silver blue wings, catching the sky beneath the fine membrane and glided.

When the momentum slipped away and they came back down, the dragon tucked its wings tight into its body and dived beneath the waves. Slipping so smoothly it didn't disturb the water.

Powerful webbed feet propelled them on, cutting through the sea with the ease of a sword fish. Another thrust of the legs and they shot into the above once again, gliding over the shimmering surface. Drops of water falling from the sleek body.

Timoshi drifted in and out of consciousness. Barely aware as they flew, dived, sprang and soared. Dipping into the brine and out into the above. It was only when the sun began to fall over the horizon that he realised they were almost there. The coral flute of the jewel protruding out of the sea like a crooked finger. Neptula's tower rising like a beacon in the new world.

The dragon climbed steeply into the air, banked to one side then hurtled into the sea in a vertical dive.

Once beneath the waves they swept closer to the jewel, following the living rock down to the seabed where an army of skagwangles patrolled. Hundreds of thousands of soldiers protecting the queen, the god that resided within the porous walls of the jewel.

There were other water dragons idly swimming around a leviathan who slept on the seabed. Its body disappearing out of view as it lounged in the soft silty floor.

They halted beside the entrance and two shell-armoured guards helped him from the gliding beast.

"Take me to Neptula," Timoshi ordered, bubbles laced with green blood spilling from his mouth with each word.

He was vaguely aware of the dragon swimming away as he was pulled into the dark opening, much the same shape as the shark's jaws that had tried to devour him. He hoped that when he was swallowed by this mouth, he wouldn't meet with the same conclusion. The Sea Witch could be fickle and he didn't know how she would react to the news.

The spiralling corridor was bursting with life. Small clown fish and sea horses floundering around the bright red anemones; yellow grasses floating above angel fish, popping clams revealing golden pearls and even a rare speckled monk ray, which was fighting for space with a velvet starfish.

Timoshi dragged his injured limb behind him, the other creatures taking an interest in the blood that began to drift to the floor. He could almost laugh. The last time he had been in the jewel was when he was leaving to present the message to the daughter of Chaos.

Flanked by his brethren he had felt proud, swimming out with polished trident in hand, determination in his heart.

How things had changed. Damaged, ripped, torn and missing his companions – his pride had sunk with the mission. Suddenly the corridor seemed less alive, less colourful. Every eye turning to him with hunger. Would he become food before the sun sets in the above?

The spiralling corridor came to a large circular chamber, the walls shining with all the colours of mother of pearl. It was tall, the upper half reaching out of the water and forming the tower he had seen while riding the dragon.

Sitting on a coral thrown, her silver skin shining from the sun's last rays passing through holes in the upper part of the chamber, was Neptula.

"Timoshi?" she offered lazily, the spines on her head raising as she stretched the membrane in between.

Letting go of the guards that had escorted him, Timoshi drifted further into the room, feeling every bit like a limp crab entering the cave of a trench eel.

He became aware of Neptula's thick tentacles that were spread out, reaching around the walls and flowing over the throne. A shoal of tiny crumb fish nibbling at her skin as they cleaned and preened her.

He formerly bowed his head, the movement sending a pulse of pain from his injured shoulder.

"My Queen, my Goddess," he offered, attempting to put authority into his voice but only sounding choked. "Elora, the daughter of Solarius has refused the treaty."

Raising his head, he noticed Neptula's gills begin to work harder, like dark crescents pumping from the side of her head. Her spines shook violently for a moment before flattening against her scalp.

"What?" she screamed. The voice high and shrill like a siren. "Elora refuses my offer? As a demigod, she had a right to be among the small gods."

Neptula narrowed her black eyes to slits and stared up at the above. "She will only live long enough to regret that decision."

The Sea Witch appeared to calm, although Timoshi sensed anger and witnessed the violence in her dark dead stare. And so too did the crumb fish who had suddenly made themselves scarce.

"She killed my brothers," he continued and held up the damaged arm. "She did this to me before giving me a message to give to you."

Neptula leaned closer, her tentacles coiling and uncoiling like a nest of sea serpents. Wrapping around the legs of the throne, curling under the holes in the wall and squeezing around her trident.

"And the message is?" she hissed, bubbles filtering through her sharp teeth.

"That she is coming for you. She said that wherever there is darkness there is Chaos."

Timoshi cringed away from the goddess. Yet as he drifted back, he met the solid embrace of Neptula's limbs as they wrapped around his waist and his own tentacles. Sliding and weaving until he was fully trapped.

The grip was punishing. Tightening until he could feel the blood pushing to his head, crushing his already damaged body as if attempting to wring another answer from him.

She pulled him towards her face. Her gaping mouth, which could easily enclose his head, snapped shut a hair's width from his chin.

"Chaos? Darkness?" she demanded. "The land-dwelling demon throws my offer back in my face and promises to kill me?"

Timoshi's eyes bulged, the pressure of all that blood in his head making him dizzy. Light in the chamber began to dim, or was that him?

He felt his back straining, then twisting - a sudden painful crack from inside; then felt nothing.

She released him and his numb body didn't feel his own. The chamber seeming to shift as he began to float on his side, his limbs no longer responding. Had she broken his spine?

"No matter," she whispered, her gaze falling on a hole in the above. The faint twinkling of the first star hovering in the darkening sky. "I have friends that also play within the darkness. And another who has blended in with the Vikings in the north. A spy that tells me of their plans to kill Hades. Elora is a fool for believing that I rule only the seas."

Timoshi helplessly floated to the surface, his flaccid tentacles drifting uncontrollably in all directions. Strangely, he felt no pain as he bobbed and turned at the mercy of the waves so he now faced down and watched his queen from above.

"Make ready the leviathans," she demanded and the guards by the entrance turned and swam away.

"I've a war to begin, a new world to make," she said to herself. Then as if she suddenly remembered she wasn't alone, looked up. A playful smile curling her cruel lip.

"Timoshi," she sang, almost lovingly as she grasped him with her rubbery limbs and pulled him back down. "It appears you are well and truly broken."

She spun him so his face was inches from her own. He tried to speak but had lost the power of his mouth. He was simply a passenger in his own body.

"A broken sea creature has only one use," she explained teasingly. "It truly is a cruel circle of life under the waves."

Timoshi didn't fight or resist as she sank her teeth into his neck. He could only watch in horror as the chamber filled with a green cloud. Terror of realising that he was being eaten alive. The pain filling his world as his sight dimmed, the chamber shrinking to darkness.

There was always a bigger fish – all the way up to Neptula.

12

Elven Traditions

Bray smiled as he watched Elora slip the ring onto her thumb. Part of a pair that Zilabeth had created in her workshop. Spending over a month in the Shadowlands while only two days had past at Rams Keep. He wore the other, an Elven tradition for those that were to be bonded together as man and wife.

He glanced at his own thumb ring, rubbing the spinning outer loop which sat above the base of the thicker band. Marvelling at the intricate design and the details which the master metalsmith had created.

The delicate leaves of ivy were forged from goblin silver, overlapping the elven scrollwork to words which weaved around the band of gold. The spinning loop which he was rolling back and forth was carved from one of Grycul's scales and was imbued with charm runes, cast and bound by Thatch and Thud.

"It's beautiful," Elora remarked, holding it out so it caught the flaming sky above. Her gorgeous violet eyes soaking up her wedding gift. "Thank you," she said to Zilabeth as she pulled her into a hug.

They were standing beside the dragon forge. Bray had enticed her to the plateau, inventing a reason that she must inspect the new fort they were building in the Shadowlands. It wasn't a complete lie. There were things that needed to be looked at but a good enough excuse to bring her to Zilabeth's workshop to present her with the rings.

"You're welcome," Zilabeth chuckled, her face flushing. "But Teaselberry helped. And I couldn't have done it without Grendel providing the gold and Thatch and Thud to make the runes work."

Elora grasped each of them, her excitement and happiness forming tears as she lifted Teaselberry off the floor, the wood troll's feet kicking in the air.

When she lowered her back to the dusty ground, she examined the ring once again, slowly rotating the outer loop.

"What does the writing say?" she asked.

"It's elven," Bray answered, reaching an arm over her shoulders and placing his thumb against hers, the metals clinking together. "Words to an elven song that dates back to the first of the elves. They say '"Today will pass and tomorrow may die, yet our love will outlive the eternal sigh.'"

"The eternal sigh?" Elora smiled in wonder, narrowing her gaze on the swirling text as if attempting to decipher the words herself.

Bray kissed the top of her head as he pulled her into an embrace. "It's the end of days. The eternal sigh is when life itself lets go a final breath and all that has gone before shall be forgotten."

"Apart from our love?" she suggested, gazing up.

"Apart from our love."

He kissed her again, then became aware of the others watching them. Zilabeth and Teaselberry grinning like proud parents while Thatch and Thud stared off into the building site, appearing awkward at the emotion on display.

"They're perfect," she said. "And the runes?"

"I'll show you," he replied, turning to Zilabeth who nodded.

"They work, we've already tested them," the metalsmith answered, making a shooing motion with her arms. "Stand as far away as you like, they'll work from anywhere."

"Anywhere?" Elora repeated, her eyebrows knitting together below her blonde lock of hair.

Bray paced to the other end of the plateau, leaving Elora and the group to watch on in anticipation.

"Hope this works," he muttered to himself as he curled his index finger over the dragon scale loop and spun it.

The ring rotated, the runes becoming a blur as the scale made a whispering sound, scraping against the metal beneath.

He spun it again and when the loop picked up speed the runes began to glow red, each symbol lighting the once next to it. Once the outer ring was completely lit the inner band began to radiate with a green light that spiralled along the elven lettering.

An excited squeal escaped Elora as she bounced up and down on the spot, holding her ring up.

"It's spinning by itself," she cried, enthusiastically.

Bray smiled as he spun his ring again, the green and red luminosity on his thumb, brightening as the whispers born of the scraping sound began to form words.

He brought it closer to his ear and indicated for Elora to do the same.

"I don't understand it," she admitted, concentrating on the ring.

"The elven words have come alive with the charm," Thatch explained. "Today will pass and tomorrow may die…"

"Yet our love will outlive the eternal sigh," Thud finished, holding a chubby hand over his chest.

Bray allowed the poem to repeat itself another cycle before he stopped the ring spinning with a finger.

"Now you try," he suggested.

Her face beaming brighter than a cliff beacon, Elora held up her hand and spun her thumb ring.

Instantly Bray's begun to spin by itself, glowing red and green as the elven words whispered from the charmed ring.

Elora was laughing now, spinning the ring faster as she came running across the plateau to jump into his waiting arms.

"I love them," she said, planting kisses all over his face and neck. "They're perfect. More than perfect."

Bray set her down and put an arm around her.

"Technically, in elven law we are now husband and wife," he explained. "We don't need a fancy ceremony or church."

"Really?" she said, sounding a little crestfallen. "No wedding?"

"Nope," he replied teasingly. He knew she wanted a ceremony in which she could invite her mother and friends. "But then, I'm only half elf and you're a demigod so…" He shrugged and watched the brightness return to her face. "You can have what you want."

"So another ring?" Zilabeth asked as she fished a piece of wire from one of the many pockets of her utility belt and created a small hoop. She placed it over the wedding finger of Elora's hand and twisted the ends together to form a circle. "Is that comfortable?" she asked, tugging it over the knuckle joint.

Elora slid the wire ring up and down her finger. "Yeah, that fits perfectly."

"Good," Zilabeth replied, pulling the wire from Elora's hand and placing it back in her utility belt. "Now I've got the size it won't take long to make a simple gold band. Unless you want something special?"

"No, a gold band it perfect," Elora replied, lifting Bray's hand up so the metalsmith could place a wire over his wedding finger. "Is that alright?"

"More than alright. It's perfect," Bray said, copying Elora's own words. "You're perfect."

He couldn't remember ever feeling so happy, so complete. It was as if the entire world and everything in it was an incredible pattern of events – all leading up to this precise moment.

He felt his thumb ring begin to spin and when he looked down he saw that the runes had begun to glow again, the elven words whispering as Elora squeezed his hand. Her finger spinning her own ring.

"I'll have them ready before the day is out," Zilabeth said as she began to walk back to the cave entrance of her workshop.

"No need to rush," Elora shouted after her. "We don't plan to marry until after the war."

And with those words Bray's heart came tumbling back down to the harsh reality. Crushing the perfect moment where he had momentarily escaped the cruel situation.

"What's wrong?" Elora asked him, her features pinching into concern.

"Nothing," he lied, steering her back the way they had come. "It's just that I'm worried something is going to happen. That we're not going to get the happy ending we want."

Interlacing her fingers within his own, Elora leaned into his arm and held the back of his hand to her cheek. "We will get our happy ending," she assured him.

Bray nodded, but couldn't feel the confidence of his bride to be. He had spent almost his entire adult life fighting. Usually against the odds without ever feeling true fear. None for himself anyway. But ever since falling in love with Elora, it seemed that the hold over fear was slipping through his grasp. His desire to keep her safe was an unbearable weight around his neck. A chain that he couldn't remove until the war was over and his steel slid away for good.

They walked through sliding hangar door of the workshop, passing from the hot dusty land into the cold winter of Rams Keep. Their horses were tied up outside, Daisy snickering as she watched them approach.

"Do you know what's funny?" Elora asked as she untied her horse and climbed into the saddle. "I don't even know your second name. Is it an exotic elven name or am I to be, Mrs Elf boy?" she laughed.

Placing a foot in the stirrup, Bray hauled himself up onto his horse and gently tapped his heel into the mare's flanks.

"Bogsquelch," he informed her. "A good strong elven name. Mrs Elora Bogsquelch."

Bray kept his face straight for as long as possible, but when he watched Elora's expression go from shock to disappointment and then struggle to hide it beneath a fixed smile, he gave in.

The corners of her mouth curled up as she realised he was teasing. She slapped his arm playfully. "No, what is it really?"

Bray shrugged. "I don't have one, not a proper name."

"Everybody has a second name," Elora stated, guiding Daisy around the cobbled streets of the Keep and saluting to a platoon of Dark Army soldiers who were marching passed.

"Not me, I was an orphan," he explained, staring ahead. "I was left on the steps of a church to the Blessed Mother. And orphans in the Empire inherited the name of the place they were born in. So, my second name is Rona."

He sensed a quietness settle over Elora as she nudged her horse closer and placed a hand over his.

Offering her a reassuring smile he continued. "My father was a soldier, a Shade. He was stationed in Roseland when he met my mother. An Elf by the name of Liania. She had come to the Empire to study and learn our culture, aiming to be a diplomat of some kind. The details don't matter, what I learned about them were only rumours that I managed to pick up once I grew old enough to care."

"Why did they leave you?" Elora asked, voice thick with concern.

Again Bray shrugged. "The rumour goes that my father was killed in a brawl shortly after I was conceived and my mother couldn't return to her people with a bastard child. Especially a half-breed."

"So, she simply left you?"

"It's no big deal," Bray explained, nodding a greeting to the guards at the portcullis who raised the huge steel spikes to allow them beneath. "There were plenty of orphans in Rona, I was never alone."

"Didn't you ever try to track your mother down?"

"Thought about it once or twice when I was younger. Before I joined the Shades, but by then, Liania had returned to her people."

"To the elves?"

"Yeah. They don't mix well with humans. They trade and sometimes form short alliances if a common enemy raises its head, but most of the time the two races stay away from each other. There are very few elves living in the Empire."

"And Liania's people? Where are they?"

"Way out west, across the ocean which Earth called the Atlantic. Somewhere in the vast states of what was America."

"Oh," Elora replied and Bray felt her mood sink as the conversation progressed.

"But if I had been brought up differently, we may never have met," he said, putting a cheery edge on his words.

"True," she admitted, that rare gorgeous smile returning. "And we wouldn't be getting married."

Bray nodded, grinning himself. "And I wouldn't be about to beat you back to the inn," he added, kicking his horse into a canter, now that they were free of the Keep.

"Hey," Elora laughed from behind as she shouted Daisy into a gallop.

He only half-heartedly pushed his mare on, allowing his bride-to-be gain level, both horses nostrils flaring with the effort. Startling birds from the trees, hooves thumping along the meandering track, scattering snow and clumps of frozen mud.

They were both laughing as they slowed to a trot at the inn and warmed the horses down, steam rising from hot flanks as they circled the well.

"So who are you going to have as best man?" Elora asked, violet eyes sparkling from the exercise.

The question caught Bray off guard. "I don't know," he admitted as he climbed from his mount and walked her to the stables. Elora followed, patting Daisy gently on the neck.

As a Shaigun, Bray didn't have friends, not really. During his training he counted Flek and the twins as such. They were close during the trials to become a Shaigun, helping each other struggle through the pain and tasks to reach their goals. But not now. Not since they had organised the joining of the worlds, not since they had killed hundreds of thousands of innocents and upset the balance. And not since they had attempted to kill Elora - and himself for that matter.

"Why the sad face?" Elora asked as they entered the stables and began to unbuckle the saddle girths.

Bray attempted to slip on an easy smile, but it felt fake; probably looked fake too. Instead he continued to remove the saddle and placed it on a stand. Then reached for the bridle when he paused.

"It's a bad idea seeking parley with Flek," he advised, turning to Elora. "Especially if Quantala and Quantico are with him. They'll more likely kill you on sight."

Elora sighed as she began to brush Daisy. The mare snickering with the attention.

"I know," she admitted softly, not meeting his gaze.

"And from what Thatch and Thud have told us, Flek has the same orbs as Dethtil had. The same machines that will trap you should you turn to smoke."

"I know."

"Not to mention the tens of thousands of imperial guards he'll have stationed in the palace and surrounding Rona."

"I know."

Bray inhaled deeply, the musky smell of horse and sweat filling his senses as he calmed his rising temper.

"You're still going to go, though?" he asked, already knowing the answer.

Elora placed the brush away and folded her arms around his waist. Leaning into him and resting her head against his chest.

"I have too," she said. "My Dark Army is too thinly stretched. Half the body is already north awaiting Ragna, the other half is split. Most are on their way to the outer edges ready to defend the landmasses against Neptula, leaving the rest here to defend the Keep should it come under attack from Dethtil. If Neptula decides to begin attacking the lands we will need every soldier, bulworg and grumpkin to defend it. And that's the ones that haven't deserted already. I've been having reports of rogue bands leaving every day.""

She glanced up into his eyes and he recognised a worry in hers that he hadn't noticed before.

"I don't have the time or the resources to fight against the Empire should it throw all its might against us."

Bray knew she was right. If it was possible to form a truce between them and the Empire, it would make things a little easier, even if it was only until they had defeated Neptula. But he knew Flek, at least he thought he did.

"If you offer peace they'll think you weak and will attack all the more," he informed her, attempting one final persuasion. Yet he knew her mind was made up.

"Probably, but at least I would have tried. I would have given the lives of the men that will fall beneath our blades a chance."

Bray didn't know how else to stop her. No words would steer her away from what she believed was the right thing to do. Instead he placed a kiss on her head as they emerged from the stables and walked arm in arm towards the inn. Although he sensed that his sullen mood had now passed on to her.

"Norgie," he said.

"I don't see him," Elora remarked, glancing about.

"No," Bray chuckled. "You asked who I would have as a best man. I've known Norgie the longest. He's been a good friend in the past, still is."

"Great choice," Elora agreed as she pushed open the door and stepped into the common room.

Otholo was sat by himself at a table, plucking a waltzing tune from his lute. The fire crackling behind him adding its own melody. When the bard noticed them he smiled, his expert fingers never faulting from the arpeggios he was playing as he turned the music into the wedding march.

"I hear you'll be needing a wedding singer," he said cheekily.

"Yeah," Bray replied as he closed the door behind them. "Although a good bard is hard to come by."

"My friend Ben can play a note or two," Elora offered, chuckling as Otholo grimaced while mimicking a knife stabbing into his heart.

When he began to play once again, Elora approached. "Otholo, would you do us the greatest honour of playing at our wedding?"

Smiling to himself, the bard stopped playing and reached for the glass of wine on the table. After taking a delicate sip he placed it down and studied his fingernails.

"Oh, I don't know. I am in high demand at the moment. The Golden Flute of Goseland, the onetime Songbird to King…"

"If you don't, I'll have your fingers broken," Elora teased.

Otholo paused, mocking a shocked expression. "I suppose I can stretch myself to perform at your wedding. It's not every day you get to play in front of a demigod."

"Great, that's settled then," Elora said, treating the bard to a rib crushing hug.

"Very good, but let us hope you'll be fettled up in fine splendour on the day and not," he wrinkled his nose. "Covered in red dust and smelling of sweaty horse."

Elora chuckled as she planted a kiss on his cheek and then another on Bray's. "Since you so delicately put it, I'm going for a bath."

"Maybe I'll join you," Bray offered, leading her across the room to the narrow staircase. "I can always scrub your back."

"Not until we're married," Elora laughed, placing a hand against his chest as they paused outside the bathroom. "I will remain innocent until I'm Mrs Elf-boy."

"It was worth a try," Bray admitted, placing a kiss on her lips.

She gave him a wink and closed the bathroom door behind him, leaving him standing in the corridor.

Sighing, he turned and paced into their bed chamber and flung himself on the four-poster bed. Placing his hands behind his head as he lay there, listening to Elora singing to herself.

He had never loved somebody the way he loved Elora. And couldn't believe how incredibly lucky he was to feel the same affection returned. He only hoped beyond hope that somehow, against all the odds, they would defeat Hades, Volcaneous, Flek, the twins and Neptula. That they would win the war and see peace settle over Ethea. And above all – see Elora walk down the aisle to where he would be waiting for her – where they would be wed and where they would begin the rest of their lives together.

He glanced at his hand and spun the thumb ring.

It instantly glowed as the familiar elven words began to sing.

Elora slipped into the tepid water, her voice briefly rising a note as she adjusted to the cold.

Norgie had poured the bath hours ago and it was now room temperature, which in the winter with icicles hanging from the windowsill outside, was freezing.

Closing her eyes, she changed her song to the tune for the element of fire and felt the heat of the water begin to rise.

Within moments steam was rising from the bath and she sunk into the hot water, allowing her aches to be washed away.

Suddenly and without warning, her new thumb ring began to spin. The runes glowing beneath the surface.

She lifted it out and the elven whispers filled the room.

Smiling, she spun the ring herself, knowing that Bray was probably lying across the bed, worrying about her.

Elora held the ring up to the lamp light, the intricate etching and scrollwork seeming incredibly detailed and expertly created. Zilabeth had done a fine job in making them.

Her smile widening, she began to scrub with soap made from beeswax and honey. Taking up a song that reminded her of a time on the Molly with Nat. Of how he used to sing to her as the boat coasted along at a gentle speed along the canals of Gloucestershire and Somerset. Lazy hours spent watching the world go by as she rocked with the swaying motions, her feet dangling in the cool water.

Sadly, both the barge and her uncle were buried, but the memories were alive.

Closing her eyes, she leaned back against the tall basin, listening to her own voice as it echoed the words taught to her years ago. She was partly through the second verse of the Minuan rhyme, when a light flittered across her lids.

When she gazed around the bathroom she was unable to find its source. The room was still, although condensation had built up over the window and hugged the mirror on the wall.

Elora was beginning to think she imagined the flickering light when another bright flash darted across her vision.

It zipped around a stool at frightening speed before changing direction and shooting along the far wall. Yellow green and white colours sparkled from the tiny phenomenon as it hovered in place for a moment as if deciding where to whizz to next.

Elora thought it might be a kind of bug, like a firefly, yet it moved so quickly. Leaving a trail of fine golden sparks, like the spitting flashes from a fireworks sparkler.

She kept still, not wanting to frighten the small creature as it zipped closer.

It hovered above the bath, the outline of a minute fairy flashing as it flapped glowing wings. Too fast for Elora to take in the details, yet she caught the image of a white sparkling cherub creature, no larger than her smallest fingernail. It was fairy size to a fairy and would fit in Prince Dylap's hand. It was a sprite of some kind.

It circled around Elora's bare knee which poked above the water, her hand holding the soap that rested upon it.

The sprite circled a few more times before landing upon the back of her hand, so light Elora couldn't feel it.

Folding its sparkling wings behind its back, it leaned closer to the soap, now moving slow enough to reveal a childlike face, full of mischief.

It was a girl sprite, Elora guessed, watching mesmerised as she stuck her tongue out and experimentally licked the beeswax.

She licked again and then smiled. Her colour brightening from a greenish yellow to an eye watering white. The sprite seeming satisfied with its find, she swiped at the soap with her hand, gathering up a tiny amount and instantly sprang into the air.

"Hello," Elora said, unable to contain her excitement. This was the first time she had seen a sprite. A sugar sprite, her soul memories told her. It was attracted to the honey in the soap.

On hearing her words, the sprite startled and zipped away, crashing into a candle stick on the mantle in its haste, causing it to rock.

"I mean you no harm," Elora offered, feeling disappointed that she had scared the little creature.

The sprite raced around the room, bouncing off the walls and crashing into objects leaving a sparkling trail in the air and green lines in Elora's vision as she tried to keep up with it.

"Please," she coaxed, holding the soap out. "You can take what you like."

She didn't know whether the sprite could understand her or not, but the creature halted in the air, the light hovering inches from the mirror so it appeared that there was two of them. Then when it began to creep back towards her, she realised that there was indeed two of them. The newcomer buzzing with less enthusiasm while the original sprite was whizzing around, approaching Elora and then rushing back for the other.

When the second one landed on her knee she saw that the newcomer appeared older and more tired. Although it still held a child's mischievous innocence on a chubby face. Its wings a duller shade of gold and yellow as it delicately lowered its head to the soap. Its partner excitedly encouraging it.

After tasting the soap, the duller sprite suddenly brightened, its lethargic wings beginning to rapidly beat the air as it rose once again above the bath.

Elora couldn't be sure, but she thought she could hear the pair of them laughing in a high pitch squeal before the two of them began to shoot around the room.

"Incredible," Elora remarked as she watched them dance and weave between each other. The two sparkling dots moving with such speed and dexterity that she couldn't tell which was which.

Then without warning they spun once more around the room before speeding towards her. They halted within inch of her nose and appeared to examine her.

Elora needed to squint through the brightness as she witnessed them talk to one another, yet the only sound she could hear was high pitch squeaking.

They seemed to come to some agreement, both hovering closer and placing a kiss on the end of her nose. Elora having to go cross eyed to watch them, yet still couldn't feel their touch.

Once they had kissed her they sparkled before zipping back around the room and vanished into the mirror. A single golden ripple of light spreading from where they disappeared until that too vanished.

Elora doubted she would ever get used to experiencing such things. Ethea was full of the strange and magical. A world which she wished to explore. But she could only do so once all the battles had been fought and when all the warring was over. She only hoped she would be alive to enjoy it.

After she climbed out of the bath and dried herself, she made her way to her bed chamber, ready to tell Bray about the sugar sprites. But as she pushed the door open she found that he was fast asleep. Arms tucked behind his head as his chest gently rose and fell.

It was a rare peaceful sight. A perfect sight, spoiled only by his light snoring.

Sighing to herself, Elora gently climbed onto the bed and lay beside him. Closing her eyes and thought about all the magical places they would go to together, once this was all over.

13

Invisible Chains

Flek awoke with a start, the empty glass in his hand spilling the remaining drops of wine onto the marble floor. Splattering like tears of blood before it was lapped up by the dog that he'd been forced to endure while his betrothed stayed in the palace.

Sitting up, he stretched the stiffness from his neck and gazed about the throne room. He had fallen asleep in the chair again, a thick hangover thumping inside his head as he worked spit around a parched mouth.

"More wine," he croaked, holding out the glass to be filled.

The man servant hurriedly grasped the crystal in both hands before scurrying away to the decanter.

"And somebody please remove the dog before I throw it from the balcony."

He glanced down at the tiny ball of fluff, feeling the urge to boot it across the room. It gazed back at him as it cocked a leg against the throne and urinated. Showing what it thought of his loathsome commands.

Something had awoken him. He remembered having a bad dream about being a toy that was thrown from one annoying child to another. The faces of which belonged to Neptula, Elora and the twins. Each pulling and tugging at him as if he was a favourite doll they were all fighting for, yet didn't seem to care if he was torn apart. He was scared stiff in the nightmare, the fear still lingering as he rubbed the grit from his eyes. It had been the dragon that had startled him awake. A dark shadow passing into the dream world and its scream which brought him to reality.

Thankfully the only beast around was the infernal dog. He wondered if the Princess of Paqueet would take offence if he had the mutt killed.

Most likely, he guessed. And it had taken weeks of careful bargaining with the King of Paqueet to agree to the marriage. The union of the Emperor with one of its largest country's daughters. Together the Empire would grow in strength.

He saw it as a sacrifice for the greater good. Surrendering his life for that of his people. Uniting with the Royal family that would secure the future for his lands. At least that was what he should be thinking. And not that he was forced, in order to quell a rebellion by the other kings that made up the Empire. The scheming figureheads of most nations wanting to remove him. The very links that formed the chain that he wore around his neck. An invisible chain, a metaphorical chain, but one that would strangle him should things go awry.

Some days, he felt that invisible chain tightening, the icy grip of Neptula twisting one end while Elora twisted the other. And now the Princess of Paqueet wanted to put her chubby manicured mitts on it too. Yet what could he do, he was only the Emperor?

The problem with the Princess would be easily solved. He only need sire a son by her, then he could have her dealt with. Poison, hidden in her food, the Blessed Mother knew how she loved her food. And that rat of a dog would be buried with her.

He thought being Emperor would be easy, but he had more worries as the most powerful man on Ethea, than he ever had as the Voice.

Snatching the proffered wine, he drank deeply, glowering at the dog at his feet as if his entire trouble were caused by the retched thing.

"Not a dog person, then," Hashim snickered.

The Shadojak treated him to a sneer, the only attack he could do as he stared down from the wall. Stretching against the manacles that bound him, his wrist and ankles anchored into the wall.

The dog suddenly began to bark at the tall man on display. High-pitched yaps that penetrated Flek's skull.

They had found Hashim a few days ago, hiding in the city while attempting to raise a militia to kill him. The fool had almost succeeded if it hadn't been for a spy that had infiltrated his confidences.

Now he was nothing more than an ornament. A living display piece, to warn others when they visited, that treason was dealt with severely. He would be hanged in the morning.

Flek gazed up at the tall dark Shadojak, his spear safely locked in a glass cabinet beside him. Ready to be thrust into his heart and given to another.

"Shut up," Drifid growled, stepping forward and driving a fist into Hashim's belly with enough force to fold him over, yet the restraints prevented him from moving.

Flek swallowed another mouthful of wine, attempting to wash his worries away. How Hashim had survived after falling from the airship, he would never know. The memory of him being dragged over the edge before he had a chance to shoot him, flickered across his mind. He had felt worry at the time, an annoyance at not being able to confirm his death. Yet it had seemed close to impossible for any of them to survive that slaughter. But then, Shadojak's were tenacious bastards if nothing else.

"Calm yourself, Drifid," Flek ordered, his words sounding less dry now that he had wet his lips. "You're a Shadojak yourself, so act like one."

Drifid nodded back, his pinched face showing the petulant boy that he was. Maybe it had been a mistake giving the former Shaigun a soul blade. But he had attacked his former master, Sibiet and personally dragged him into the palace. Throwing him at the feet of the Emperor and the twins and swearing allegiance to them. Something which none of the other Shaiguns had done. Not that it mattered – they were all dead now. It was the only way to be sure that they wouldn't lead the Shades against him.

Drifid was a different breed of Shaigun and he had earned the right to be his personal bodyguard.

"Of course, your Excellency," Drifid replied, treating Hashim to a sneer of his own, that pinched face of his was built for sneering.

Flek glanced at the other prisoner attached to the opposite wall, his head hanging so low his swollen face was hidden. Unlike the dark-skinned Shadojak, this former balancer was truly, a broken man.

Sibiet's chest heaved up and down, the broken ribs and bruises causing the movement to be juddery, like a damaged toy that no longer moved correctly. His filthy turban was partly unwound, the strip of cloth touching the floor and his robes bore the dark brown stains of old blood.

It was hard to think that at one time, not so long ago, Flek had feared both men that now adorned his walls. It was strange how things turned out.

He pulled his gaze away and felt the sudden urge to be sick.

Swallowing down the nausea with another mouthful of wine, he rose on unsteady legs and approached the balcony for fresh air. The sight of Sibiet and the smell he permeated, did nothing for his hangover.

Breathing in the fresh air, Flek surveyed the grounds below. The foundations and the main building of the palace fared better than most of Rona. The merge crushing the capital city of the Empire with the Earthen city of Rome. Soapstone and timber mixing with brick and concrete.

The airship was now anchored from the remaining tower that survived the merge. Not that he used it much. He had a niggling fear that Grycul would suddenly appear out of the sky and burn the ship while he was on it, thousands of feet up.

He shuddered at the thought, something which he did more frequently each day. If he wasn't jumping at a random shadow in the shape of a dragon, he was scrambling away from screwed up bed covers which had tried to strangle him in his sleep or cut his skin from his bones like a grumpkin. And anything that made a tapping-tak noise forced him to leap in the air and cringe his legs away from the takwiches that he invented in his head.

An ear splitting screech suddenly pierced the sky and he momentarily glanced the vast shadow of Grycul as it skimmed over the grounds below. Rubbing his eyes, he drained the last of the wine from his glass and looked again, but the shadow had gone.

He exhaled – just the lingering memories of the nightmare. Flek scraped the stubble of his chin, he was becoming a nervous wreck.

Beginning to feel vulnerable standing outside on the balcony, he turned to wander back into the relative safety of the throne room, when he noticed a figure lounging against the outer wall. Her arms were folded, an easy grin on her face as if she was enjoying the evening sun.

"Have I caught you at a bad time?" Elora asked.

Flek's glass shattered against the floor as his bowels turned to water.

Elora slipped from the wall as Drifid came rushing out of the throne room, his soul blade glimmering green in the sunlight. Boots scuffing as he spun, his face a mask of shock as he registered who she was.

Although the petulant Shaigun had taken the position of Shadojak, he neglected to use the memories contained within his sword.

His nose crunched below Elora's fist and Drifid flopped to the floor, his blade sliding out of reach and stopping when it hit the balcony wall.

She noticed that the blade had been the former Supreme's before he was butchered by Flek and the twins.

Sliding her toe beneath it, she flicked the sword into the air and caught it by the hilt before levelling it at Flek.

The Emperor pulled a gun out from inside his tunic and raised it at her.

With a simple flick of her wrist, she turned the barrel away and pushed the point of the sword into the fleshy part of Flek's hand.

He yelped, dropping the gun to the floor. Elora kicked it over the edge and watched as it spun out of view.

"Please," Flek begged. Slowly stepping over his bodyguard.

Grycul chose that moment to screech her disapproval as she swept low over the rooftops of Rona, leaving flags whipping out in her wake. The Emperor screamed in fright. His legs buckled and he went sprawling onto the marble floor and began to crawl away.

Elora fought the urge to laugh as she followed him, taking careful yet purposeful strides. The biggest bullies always made the worse victims.

As she stepped over Drifid, she retrieved an object from within her cloak and dropped it onto his unconscious body. From the corner of her vision she watched it hastily scurry into the Shadojak's hood. She left the takwich to do its job while she entered the large oval chamber.

She glanced around the room, noticing that a man servant had thrown open large doors in his haste to raise the alarm. His shouts echoing in the corridor.

She could expect company any second.

The last time she had been in the throne room, she had knelt before the previous Emperor. Swearing to rid the worlds of Grycul. It had changed a lot since then. Now the perfectly carved stonework was filled with patches of plaster and the occasional brick in a futile attempt at keeping its original shape. Oil paintings and fabrics had been hung in places to hide other irreparable damage.

It was what she had expected. A rushed, botched job as Flek acted at being an Emperor, instead of fixing things properly. What she hadn't expected was the two former Shadojaks, hanging by chains from the wall.

She was as surprised to see Hashim and Sibiet as they were to see her. The former watching her with dark eyes, while the latter hung limp from his manacles, most likely unconscious.

"I never thought I'd see you again," she said to Hashim.

"Nor I, you - daughter of Chaos," his deep voice sounding cold as if laced with a hatred he was struggling to control.

"I am what I am," she replied, flatly. "But I am glad to see you alive. Sibiet too."

Hashim snorted disdainfully, his fingers flexing but was unable to curl them into fists. Flek had been cautious with this one, Elora thought.

"Guards!" the Emperor suddenly screamed, attempting to slide away from her as she turned to him.

He pulled himself away, an angry dog yapping as it bounced up and down on his chest. Teeth bared as it barked.

Raising an eyebrow, Elora glared at the fluffy bundle and it ceased yapping. Then cautiously backed away, rolled onto its back and showed its belly.

Giving the dog a playful stroke, she inclined her head towards Flek. "I must admit, I don't like what you've done with the place," she said, leaning closer until her face was inches from his. "And you reek of alcohol."

Flek's skull struck the base of the throne as he cringed away. Elora felt disgust at seeing the cowardice of the man who ran the Empire. "You can get off the floor, I'm not here to kill you," she informed him, although it would be so easy for her to slip the sword she held into his heaving chest. The blade would part his ribs as if he was made from straw.

Flek hastily scrambled back and climbed onto the throne, anxious eyes darting to the open doors. Expecting help to arrive at any moment.

Elora casually approached them, taking a candlestick from a side stand and jamming it between the handles.

It wasn't great, but it should hold long enough for her to talk with Flek.

"What do you want with me? What are you going to do?" Flek demanded, his voice rising an octave.

She placed the tip of the Supreme's blade between Flek's feet and leaned against the pommel, easy hands resting on the hand-guard and showing the Emperor that she had control over him.

"I'm not going to do anything. Yet. But my dragon…" she let her words trail off as Grycul's raging scream cut across the palace roofs. "May tire of circling above and descend into Rona."

With a quivering lip, Flek glanced to the balcony. "You wouldn't?"

Elora smiled. "I'm the daughter of Chaos, remember. Although that is not why I'm here."

Features subtly softening, Flek gulped, his Adam's apple bobbing as he curled a finger into his collar. "Whatever you want, you can have, just don't hurt my people," he whimpered.

Elora gripped the pommel of the sword with finger and thumb and idly spun the blade. "I may be my father's daughter, but I'm no monster," she said, wondering if Flek truly wanted to save his people or was only acting the dutiful Emperor to mask the fears for his own life.

"I want peace," she informed him.

"Peace?" Flek repeated, his eyebrows furrowing.

Elora slowly nodded. "For now anyway. The precious god you follow is only using you. Neptula wishes to flood the world and everything in it. Including you and the Empire."

Flek's scowl deepened. "But she was the one who gave me the Empire."

"Yeah, she used you. Used you to bring the worlds together and then kept you in place while she, and the other small gods, make Ethea their own."

"If that was so, then why put me on the throne?"

"Because it would placate the people while she manoeuvred her other pieces into place. And she knew you would keep me out of her way."

"Why?" he asked, raising his hands.

"Because I'm the only one who can stop her."

"But…surely I would know if she planned to attack Ethea. And as strong as Neptula is, she doesn't have the power to flood the entire planet."

"Have you eyes in the oceans? Do you know what is happening at the top of the world where the great ice shelves are? Do you even know where Neptula is and if there are skagwangles even now, swimming up the river systems and streams ready to attack?"

Elora raised the sword and slammed in into the marble floor, rending a crack that splintered along the polished stone.

"No, you don't," she answered for him. "Because all of your efforts have been concentrated on me."

"My people wouldn't want peace with you," Flek admitted after a moment's contemplation. "They wouldn't stand for it, not with the Queen of Darkness. Not after you merged the worlds and bound the people to unimaginable suffering."

Elora had to concede to that. After all, it was her hand on Zalibut's machine and by her hand she had merged the worlds.

"Then give me a ceasefire. Long enough for me to defeat Neptula and save Ethea from a watery death." She breathed a heavy sigh. "Then you and your Empire can have your war."

She nodded towards the Shadojaks bound to the wall. "Although, I see what you do to your loyal subjects."

The doors suddenly rattled and were shoved inwards, the silver candlestick bending with the force.

"Open up!" came the booming voice of Quantala. Or was that Quantico. Elora couldn't tell the difference, the twins sounded so alike.

Drifid chose that moment to stumble into the room, his hand running along the wall for support. Confusion warped his face as he stared at the rattling doors. They cracked under the force of shoulders; the noise setting the dog to yapping again.

Flek's eager gaze switched from Drifid, to the doors and back to the sword in Elora's hand. Most probably wondering if the twins would break through in time to rescue him.

"If I were you I'd become smoke and leave while you still can," Flek warned her, a cocky grin now finding his mouth as the balance began to swing his way.

"You forget, oh glorious leader of the Empire. I have your spell binder and caster," she said. "They told me of the smoke capturing orbs you have scattered around the palace. Dethtil tried to use the same mechanism against me. He failed, by the way."

"Oh," was all the Emperor replied to that.

There was another vicious attack upon the doors then the candlestick fractured and broke apart in several pieces. The twins burst in. Both swinging arms and pointing pistols at her. They were flanked on both sides by imperial guards who spread out along the wall, each with a rifle.

Realising that her odds of leaving alive had drastically dropped to almost none, Elora spun behind the throne and slipped the blade of the Supreme's sword under Flek's chin. With her other hand she drew her own pistol and placed it against his temple.

"Stay where you are or the Emperor will be dead twice over," she informed the gathering men before her.

Flek's arms shot in the air, calling for calm while attempting to ease the pressure from the sword biting into his flesh.

As the guards slowly continued to fan around Elora, she had no choice but to pull Flek from the throne and keep him between her and the others. Easing back towards the balcony while the twins crept closer.

"You can't escape," Quantala growled, the barrel of his pistol shifting position as he searched for a clean shot.

"Surrender now and we will make it quick," continued his brother, slipping closer and attempting to find an angle for his gun that wouldn't cut through her shield.

"Do you really expect me to yield?" Elora asked as she felt sunlight on her bare neck, the fresh air teasing her hair.

"No, not really," Quantico answered with a shrug. "I just thought it would be rude not to offer. We're probably going to kill you anyway."

When Flek's feet stumbled passed the threshold to the balcony, and there was little chance of the others getting around her, Elora paused.

"I tell you what," Quantala offered. "Give us back our heavenly leader," he said without bothering to hide the sarcasm. "And we'll give you a few seconds head-start."

Elora switched her gaze from brother to brother, weighing her options and deciding that they would no more give her a few seconds than they would drop their own weapons.

Behind the pair, she noticed that the takwich who had taken Drifid's body, take a rifle from one of the guards and was pointing it at their backs. Her gaze locked with his and she subtly shook her head, no.

"Not happening," she informed Quantala. "I'll tell you what I'll do. Unlock Hashim and Sibiets's chains and I'll give you your Emperor back."

The twins laughed. "Do you think we're idiots?" Quantico asked. "You've got nowhere to go. All we need do is wait."

Elora chuckled to herself. "Yes, I think you are idiots. And I can go through the last door, taking Flek with me." She pressed the barrel of her gun deeper into her hostage's temple, until he squealed with pain. "Death isn't new to me. I don't know about him though. Shall we find out?"

"No!" Flek yelped, his arms flapping about before him. "Please, just do as she asked. Let the traitorous Shadojaks go."

The twins looked to each other, shaking their heads in unison before turning to Drifid and tossed him a set of keys.

The takwich caught them and immediately began to unlock the shackles that bound Hashim and his former master. The tall black Shadojak having to hook Sibiet's shoulder over his own as he half carried and half dragged the broken man. As he passed Drifid the former Shaigun handed him his spear.

"Get behind me," Elora ordered and hoped that Hashim wouldn't run her through with his soul weapon.

"I trust you know what you are doing?" Hashim hissed into her ear when he dragged Sibiet onto the balcony.

"Of course I do," she whispered. "In a kind of 'making it up as I go along' kind of way."

Quantala took a step towards them, gun still raised as he beckoned Flek from her with an open hand. "Now it's your turn. Hand us back our Emperor."

"Hand him back and we will die," Hashim whispered. "At least kill him first. Let his judgement be a lesson to the rest."

Elora brought her mouth closer to Flek's quivering cheek. "When Neptula strikes, she won't care whether she attacks my people or yours. She will try to kill us all," she hissed. "I am the only one who can stop her. You know that, so when the time comes, either join me or stay out of my way."

"Fine," Flek agreed, his voice coming out dry and choked. "I'll do as you ask."

A shadow suddenly descended over the balcony and Elora caught the reflection of a large red object rising behind them. The sound of cloth being snapped taut against the wind and the unmistakable clank and thud of a heavy machine gun being cocked and loaded.

"Bray?" the twins asked together, their mouths open in shock.

Elora spared a quick glance behind her and watched as the large airship steadied itself against the side of the palace. The long oak beams of the hull grazing the soapstone walls. Her grinning boyfriend swinging the huge barrel of a fifty calibre anti-aircraft gun on the guards inside the throne room. Captain brindle was at his side with a platoon of men, all levelling rifles.

"Drop your weapons and I'll think about not sending you back to dust," Bray offered. "Oh, and Grycul is getting a little impatient – not to mention hungry."

There was a loud clatter of metal against marble as every man in the throne room threw down their guns.

"Climb aboard," Elora ordered Hashim.

When she was satisfied that the Shadojaks were safely on the airship, she gripped tightly to Flek, holding him close to her chest as she leaned in. "After all this is over, I will come back for you," she promised, then shoved him roughly forwards.

Flek stumbled over his own feet and fell into the twins who were none too gentle in catching him.

Elora treated them to a theatrical bow before springing aboard the airship and into the arms of Bray.

"Let's go. I think the Emperor has gotten the message."

Bray signalled for the airship's pilot to take them skyward. The man, held at gun point by Pudding, began to spin the helm and the craft rose.

As they left the throne room beneath them, Elora watched as the twins sprang onto the balcony with the imperial guards, weapons now recovered as they began to fire.

Bullets struck the ship's underbelly, but were not powerful enough to penetrate the thick wood.

Captain Brindle leaned out over the side and pulled the pin of a flash grenade. The harmless device dropped amongst the twin's feet before it exploded. Smothering the crowd in a bright flash that sent them careering back inside.

When they were high above the city safely out of rifle range, Elora turned to Bray and handed him the soul reaver she had taken from Drifid.

"This was the Supreme's," Bray said as he grasped the hilt and hefted the green blade.

Elora nodded. "And now it's yours. I guess you are now officially a Shadojak."

Bray stared at the sword, his face expressionless as he approached the gunnel. For a moment, Elora thought he might throw it over the side but instead he opened his smuggler's pouch and drew out his old sword. The shape similar to the new one.

"Before you do that Bray," Hashim warned as he came closer, his tall frame leaning against his taller spear. "You have some explaining to do."

"I think we all have some explaining to do," Elora agreed as she joined Bray and stared down at the city that was quickly disappearing below a white sea of cloud. "Like how you're not dead. I thought I was the last of the Shadojaks."

The dark skinned warrior offered her a sad smile. "Flek and the twins almost killed me when they attacked the Supreme. Those bastard traitors tricked us all into coming aboard this very vessel. The three of them had guns and murdered us in cold blood. When Yaul-tis-munjib was shot, he grabbed me before falling overboard," Hashim pointed his spear at the spot by the hull where the attack had happened. "And as I fell I spread my cloak as wide as I could, attempting to slow my descent."

"That's incredible," Bray stated, agreeing with Elora's own thoughts.

"The ground would still have killed me, yet the drag slowed me and I landed in the river."

"Still incredible," Elora repeated.

Hashim sighed, his huge nostrils flaring as his dark gaze soaked her in. "Is what they say true? Was the joining of the worlds by your hands, Elora?"

"Yes," she answered. "I destroyed Zalibut's machine and broke the balance. I am to blame."

"And you now rule the Dark Army?"

Elora nodded. "I wasn't lying when I said I was the daughter of Chaos."

"But it's not what you think," Bray intervened, coming to Elora's defence. "She, we both, were tricked into merging the worlds by Flek. And he himself was used by Neptula. She is planning to flood the world."

"So I heard," Hashim said, sounding unconvinced.

"Blasphemy," Sibiet grunted, spitting onto the deck between his feet.

The old Shadojak was sat on the floor, back resting against the wall as he struggled to wrap the tattered turban around his head.

"Calm yourself, Sibiet," Hashim warned. "Whatever the girl is now, she rescued us. And it seems she has set herself the mission of freeing Ethea of Neptula's hold."

Elora crouched beside Sibiet, attempting to help him fasten his turban, until he slapped her hands away.

"Don't touch me," he snapped. "You stole my sword, you turned my Shaigun against me. You, broke the worlds."

"No," Elora argued, yet kept her voice soft as she stared into his copper eyes. "Drifid was never fit to be Shaigun. But the rest is true."

"After I climbed from the river," continued Hashim. "I was in a bad way. Winded and with my shoulder dislocated. I made my way back to the garrison to warn the others. But by then the worlds had merged and everything was in utter chaos. In the confusion, I met up with Sibiet and realising that we would be killed if found, we went to ground."

"Then you began to raise an army against Flek?" Elora asked, filling in the details.

Hashim nodded. "Only there was a rat amongst us. Quantala and Quantico, with an entire battalion of

Shades cornered us in Rona and…" he shrugged. "They arrested Sibiet and I before butchering the rest."

"Slaughtered," Sibiet mumbled, his stare trailing off into the distance.

More lives that Elora could count as her fault. Yet the numbers that had already tallied since the merge, since the day she first sung the Eversong even, were too great to make a difference. But still she felt the pain of realising that they died because of her actions.

A dark shadow crossed in front of the sun as Grycul swept above them.

"By the blessed mother," Hashim exclaimed, bringing his spear about.

Elora touched his arm. "It's alright. She's here to escort us home, to Rams Keep."

Bray uncoiled a length of rope and tied a large loop at one end. "Hope this works," he said as he took a step towards the gunnel and threw the loop out into the air.

"It will work," Elora reassured him as Grycul caught the rope in her sharp talons.

She helped Bray secure the other end of the rope to the mast and told the others to hold onto something.

When she was sure everyone was secure, she sent an image of the Shadowlands to the dragon.

Grycul suddenly banked to one side and screeched. A moment later and the airship was tugged in the same direction. The entire vessel listing over as a tear ripped open in the sky and they passed from cold blue to warm red.

A soldier, not having gripped tight enough to the rigging, slipped down the foredeck and was almost cast over the edge. It was only Bray's quick actions, as he whipped his arm out to grasp him by a strap, that prevented his body dropping the thousands of feet to the dry cracked land below.

Elora projected a second message to Grycul and the dragon let go of the rope.

The airship suddenly righted itself, the huge sausage-shaped balloon momentarily morphing into a fat maggot as the ship swayed.

"It worked," Bray laughed as he wrapped an arm around her.

She teasingly elbowed him in the ribs. "I told you it would. And here is the Necrolosis."

The large ship of bones came closer, the green sea of souls which it floated upon gently stroking the airship as it pulled alongside.

"Extraordinary," Hashim exclaimed, admiring the gruesome ship, although Sibiet seemed less than pleased.

They had travelled to Rona through the Shadowlands on the Necrolosis earlier in the day. The entire trip from Rams Keep seeming to take days although only an hour had passed in Ethea.

When the two vessels came close enough, Zionbuss leapt across the small gap, his bare feet slamming hard against the oak boards of the airship.

"Not bad," the demon informed her as he glanced about the ship. The horns that grew from his head almost touching the balloon that kept them afloat. "Not bad at all, but it isn't to my taste," he continued, tapping his long nails against the brass finishing that banded around the polished oak mast.

"No," Elora laughed, nodding towards the Necrolosis and the skeletal crew that stared back from empty sockets. "Your tastes are a little more gruesome.

But you did tell me that things would be easier if you had two ships."

"So I did, my Queen," Zionbuss replied.

"Queen?" Hashim asked and Elora noticed his feet slowly shift apart, his weight balancing on his back foot.

"Like I told you before," she admitted, holding her palms up. "I am what I am."

Elora caught the subtle movement as Bray slipped his new sword between them. "She's still a Shadojak."

"No," Sibiet spat, struggling to rise on shaky legs. "She isn't."

Elora looked from Zionbuss, to Bray, his arm still wrapped around her waist and then to Sibiet.

"I've sworn to protect the world - that hasn't changed," she explained. "I will kill Neptula and remove the new Emperor. And I will help those that need it, if it is in my power."

"But you rule the Dark Army," Hashim argued, the leaf-shaped blade of his spear catching the red glow of the Shadowlands upon its green edge.

"I shall not deny it. But I cannot save Ethea without it."

She watched Hashim study her. The words she had spoken being played over in his mind as he judged her. Then she looked once more upon Sibiet. His battered and bruised face making him seem older, more delicate.

Elora slowly approached him and gently lay her hand upon his shaking arm.

"Join me?" she asked. "Both of you. Two Shadojaks would be a great asset. Only until we defeat Neptula and free the world. Ethea needs you. I need you."

She expected Sibiet to flinch from her touch, but he only moved to hide his face.

"I am no longer a Shadojak," he breathed. "You beat me in battle and took my blade."

Zionbuss stepped beside her, the large scimitar he had tucked into his belt, now held in his hands.

"I couldn't get on with it," he grumbled as he reversed the grip and held it out to the broken man. "I prefer to use my hands."

Sibiet grasped the hilt of his old sword. The soul blade seeming to suit him more than it did the demon. As if the large curved blade was back where it should be.

She couldn't be sure, but Elora thought the Shadojak stood a little taller. His chin no longer resting against his chest as he rubbed a thumb along the blade's edge. Then his copper stare fixed firmly upon hers.

"Very well," he said, tucking his sword into his belt. "But only until we defeat Neptula."

Elora nodded. "Agreed. Only until the Sea Witch is dead."

14

The Bet

The longboats creaked as they rocked lazily on the water. Shields depicting the emblems of many clans hanging over the sides, catching the rhythmic reflections from the sun bouncing off the water. Now laden with supplies and men, they were ready to set sail. The advance party was already aboard the three ships, wrapped in heavy furs against the weather as they waited for the tide to turn. Ragna paced back and forth along the deck of the largest vessel, his thick arms waving about as he organised them, his booming voice echoing out along the sea and rebounding against tall icebergs.

Jaygen had already stowed the wolf armour in his father's cabin, where it wouldn't be discovered and was on his way back to gather more supplies when he found Peter at the water's edge.

The Earth-born was lying on a slab of rock at the base of the harbour wall. Hands either side of the ledge while he held his face beneath the water. Bubbles breaking above his head as if he was talking to the fish.

"What are you doing?" Jaygen asked, tapping him on the side of the leg.

Peter yanked his head from the sea, his wet hair swishing back and flicking him with water. His face was bright red from the cold, small beads of ice sliding from his cheeks and chin.

"It's supposed to be rejuvenating," Peter explained through chattering teeth.

He crawled back from the edge and stood, holding the harbour wall for balance.

"And is it?"

Peter rubbed his hands together, breathing warmth back into his fingers. "It certainly wakes you up. I can't say I feel any younger though." He drew the zip of his ski jacket up as far as it would go and pulled the thick hood over his head. "So are you leaving today?" he asked, nodding towards the longboats.

"Yeah. It's not a long voyage, but I'll be glad when we reach land again."

"You don't like the water?" Peter asked as stared out at the ships.

Jaygen followed his gaze and watched as a shield that hadn't been hung over the side properly, fell into the sea making a galumph sound. It floated for a moment before sinking beneath the surface. The Viking that had absently knocked it from its perch staring after it and shaking his head.

"I don't mind the water," Jaygen answered. "It's what's beneath it that worries me."

"Oh," Peter said, glancing out over the peninsular. "And what's beneath it?"

"Neptula."

Jaygen put a hand on the boy's shoulder and squeezed. "I wouldn't go putting your face in the sea again, you don't know what could be down there. And besides, we'll all be gone soon. Maybe it's time that you headed back to where you came from. There will be nothing here for you."

Peter grinned. "No, I'll be coming with you."

Jaygen stared at the Earth-born, the skier seeming so out of place amongst the people of the north. "You don't want to go where we're going."

"I do. It's going home that I don't want. Well, to the place that I used to call home. It's not there anymore. Just a mess of twisted buildings and strange people. I have no family and you found the remains of my only friend on the mountain. My only friend apart from you, of course."

"But we're going to war," Jaygen argued, attempting to talk sense into the boy. "Battles, fighting, blood and death. The kind of war where even the hardest of us may not return."

"Yes, I know what a war is," Peter admitted, eyes rolling inside his deep hood. "But you forget that my time on this world is limited anyway. Even without the war. I'm diabetic, remember? The insulin you recovered for me will only last a few more weeks."

"You can find a healer. Thea didn't have the doctors or scientists that your world had, but it had alchemists and sorcerers. Warlocks even."

It was Peter's turn to place a hand upon Jaygen's shoulder, although he stood a foot shorter.

"I'm coming," he said, grinning. "I've already asked your father. Ragna isn't it? 'We'll have you if you want to fight. Any man that can lift steel, is welcome.'"

"But…"

"They were his words, not mine."

Jaygen sighed. "Yeah, sounds like something he'd say."

"I want to help. I might not be any good fighting in a battle, but I can help with the wounded or suchlike."

Jaygen wanted to say more but was interrupted by Fin as he came jogging towards them. He got a feeling that whatever he wanted, it wasn't good.

"Finally found you," he blasted, sounding out of breath.

"What is it?" Jaygen asked.

"Fieri," Fin answered as he glared at Peter, as if the Earth-born shouldn't be here at all, let alone standing before them.

"What about her?" Jaygen asked, a knot working in his stomach.

"She wants you to come quick, it's urgent."

The knot suddenly tightened. "What is it, is she hurt?"

Fin bit his lower lip and shook his head. "Just come with me. Alone."

Jaygen told Peter that he would see him later and then followed Fin as he led him at a run, away from the village.

A hundred different scenes panned through Jaygen's mind as he ran. Fieri being ravaged by a mountain ogre, or that she had fallen and broken her leg or arm – or back. That she had being attacked by different clansmen and was butchered. That she had suddenly found out who he really was and wanted to personally tell him that she thought him a coward for not saying so before. A lot of scenarios, a great deal of scenes with her injured or himself being told that she hated him, despised him. He followed Fin blindly as they climbed the mountain path and forced themselves through broken ferns, not realising where he was until he pushed through a group of men and onto the Tooth.

"Bout time you showed up," a heavy-set Viking chuckled from the furthest end of the rock. It was Axewell. His wide body silhouetted against the grey sky behind; back to the sheer drop, wind racing up the mountain teasing at his tail of a beard and setting the rat skull swinging like a pendulum.

Jaygen glanced around the semicircle of men who had gathered around the Tooth, but couldn't see Fieri anywhere.

"I told you I could bring him," Fin boasted. "The fool has got a thing for my sister, he didn't take much persuading."

Axewell laughed as he ran a finger along the blade of a bearded axe that was strapped to his stump. "Doesn't matter how, he's here now and so we can settle things."

The gathering men muttered in agreement as they closed in, Fin giving Jaygen a hard shove which sent him sprawling onto the protruding rock.

"What?" he blurted out as he realised he had been played a fool. He tried to go back the way he had come but the path was blocked by large men bearing heavy shields. Jaygen caught a glimpse of a shorter Viking on the edge of the group, his apologetic expression showing through as he shrugged.

"Sorry lad," Cob offered. "But a bet is a bet."

"You can take him, Black Jaygen," shouted another familiar voice, a fist pounding a shield. "Jaygen, Jaygen, Jaygen…" chanted the Crimlock youth.

"We will see," Axewell said as he took a practice swing of the axe.

It made a whipping sound as it cut through the air, seeming to Jaygen as deadly as its intent.

He suddenly became aware of the shear drop either side of him, and the very real situation that he found himself in.

Raising his hands to placate the baying crowd, he tried to be heard. "My father said there was to be no fighting on the Tooth."

"Don't you dare try and get out of this," said another Viking. Jaygen recognised him as the man who bet against him days before. "I've got a silver coin says you're going to be gutted."

"Or thrown off the rock," piped in another.

"He doesn't even have a sword," snapped a burly man, shaking his head in disappointment.

"Give him yours then," Axewell snapped, sounding impatient.

"No. How am I going to get it back when he's smashed to bits at the bottom of the mountain."

"I'm not fighting," Jaygen shouted above the excited crowd.

"Oh, but you are – Black Jaygen," Axewell growled, spitting his name out as if it tasted bad on his tongue.

"I'll fight you after the war is won, there's no honour lost if you wait until then," Jaygen pleaded, hoping that the Seagrit would see sense.

"Honour? I don't give a rat's arse about honour, boy. But I have a name to live up to and I'm not having a whelp like you weakening it."

Jaygen pulled his gaze away from Axewell and made to push through the gathering Vikings, but they were a solid wall. Some even linking shields to prevent him from leaving. Fin's sneer gloating above all others. His relish for blood adding a demented sparkle to his eyes.

Wind snapped at Jaygen's hair and pulled his cloak. Flinging specks of ice into his face that had drifted down the mountain. It seemed that even the elements were against him.

"There's only one way out of this boy," Axewell informed him, twisting the arm that had the axe strapped to it. "And that's through me."

"What's going on?" came a female voice as somebody pushed through from the back.

There were times that Jaygen wished that his father was elsewhere. Or that his mother wouldn't fuss him so much. But this wasn't one of them. At this moment, he would give anything to have his parents barge through and put a stop to the fight.

He breathed a sigh as the speaker squeezed to the front, expecting Ejan to step onto the Tooth. Yet the fates had sent him the last person he wanted here.

"What is going on?" Fieri demanded as she pushed a shield aside. The bearer shrugging innocently as he stood back. "Ragna said no fighting."

"That he did," Axewell confirmed. "But the great protector of the north isn't here. And his coward son, has been boasting that he's going to knock me from the Tooth. I'm here to give him that chance."

"More like you'll be flinging him from the Tooth and facing Ragna's wrath," Fieri snapped, hands on hips.

"See that boys?" Axewell shouted, lifting the axe towards Fieri. "The coward even needs a wench to come to his rescue."

"What have you done?" Fieri whispered to Jaygen. Her words barely audible above the annoyed crowd, who were begging for blood.

Fin stepped closer and put an arm around his sister. "Leave him, Fieri. The coward deserves what's coming."

She pushed him away and drew her own sword. Jaw muscles clenching tight as she dropped the point to the rock.

"There will be no fighting here today," she shouted. "Unless you want to fight me, Stump."

Jaygen felt the heat rise to his cheeks. Shame burning him from the inside as he felt every bit the coward he was branded. 'Black-Jaygen'. It wouldn't be long before he was being called Yellow. The coward son of one of the hardest names in the north.

"I've no dispute with you, Fieri," Axewell chuckled. "Though you've probably more fight in you than that craven fool."

"I'll fight," Jaygen growled. His words catching the ears of Fieri as she squared up to Axewell. She turned to him, the first words of an argument forming on her lips, but he shook his head. He knew she wouldn't take no for an answer, proving that she was braver than he was and would more than likely get herself killed.

"Speak up boy," Axewell demanded. "Maybe I was wrong and you may die today a Viking."

Jaygen stretched his neck one way, the tendons clicking as he turned it the other. He may not be in the wolf suit, but a piece of Grimwolf must be in him. After all, it was only armour.

"May I borrow your sword?" he asked, Fieri.

She held it out for him to take, shaking her head as he grasped the hilt. "You've got nothing to prove, Jaygen. Fight him and you'll only get yourself killed."

Breathing in the cold air and filling his lungs, Jaygen stood straighter, consoling himself that she would no longer think him a coward. "Sometimes the only answer left is steel," he whispered, wondering where he had heard those words before. He met Fieri's gaze and wondered if this was the last time he would speak with her. Wondered if she would kiss him before they began. Wondered if she would shed a tear if he fell from the Tooth.

Still shaking her head, she treated Axewell to a cold glare before turning on her heel and barged through the shields. Jaygen hoped she would have at least stayed to watch, but it seemed she had better things to do than observe his death.

"Let's get this done," Jaygen snarled as he took a practice swing of Fieri's sword. It was smaller, narrower and should have been lighter than his own blade. Yet it felt like a lead weight in his cold hands. The armour lent him strength as well as speed and he had never fought without wearing it. Maybe he would never wear it again.

Axewell grinned, his bearded axe appearing razor sharp as he cut it across the air between them, making a whacking sound. In his other hand he held a long dagger. Jaygen didn't see where that had come from. Or if it had been there the entire time.

"Time to die, son of Ragna."

Axewell ground his foot into the rock, a low guttural scream rising in strength and volume as he leaned forwards. Spit flying from his mouth, eyes alive with violence. "Odin!" The name wrenched from his chest as he sprang.

Jaygen barely had time to yank Fieri's sword up before it clattered against the swinging axe. The blow sending a painful shockwave through his arm. The impact knocking him back into the wall of watching men.

The rim of a shield jarred into his shoulder as he was flung back onto the Tooth. Staggering over Axewell's foot as the momentum carried him towards the edge.

Jaygen arched his back and dug his heels into the slippery rock, his toes creeping over the sheer drop as he caught his balance. The hundreds of fern trees below seeming impossibly small and far away, stretching towards him like sharp hungry teeth. With a grunt he flung back his arms and by luck caught Axewell a blow to the jaw with the hilt of the sword.

The Seagrit had intended to push him off the ledge and the blow had stunned him long enough for Jaygen to slide away from the drop. Stepping cautiously away as if the wind might suddenly reach out and snatch him from the rock.

Axewell, soon regained his balance. His long tail of a beard swinging from side to side as he feigned an attack low, before coming in high. Axe arcing down at an impossible speed.

Sparks flew from the ground, the impact leaving a gauge in the granite as the Viking spun for another lunge.

Jaygen had side-stepped the first swing but wasn't ready for the next.

The bearded blade whipped across his vision, the grey blur of steel momentarily catching as it hooked beneath his cloak and tore through his furs.

The men gathered, suddenly cheered or shouted in disappointment. Complaints mixed with excited praise as they watched on with eagerness.

Gasping with panic, Jaygen patted himself down, expecting to feel hot blood running down his chest, but it appeared that the axe had only cut through his clothing and not the flesh beneath. So far, luck was holding out on him, but he knew it wouldn't last for much longer. Axewell held most of the advantages. An older seasoned fighter, the weapons best suited for close combat and the desire to kill.

Encouraging the shouts, Axewell raised his axe into the air, opening both arms out to the crowd as if the glory was already his. Hungry eyes seeking out Jaygen as he lowered his axe towards him.

The thought of the man wanting to slay him, suddenly spurred Jaygen into action. He might not have the experience of fighting out of the armour. He might not have his huge sword or the speed or strength. But he did have his height. If he could only keep Axewell at sword's length, work him until exhaustion, he might be able to finish him. Rage would tire a man quicker than anything else, his Da used to say. He only hoped it was true.

Axewell approached for another swipe. Grunting with the effort as he attempted to chop into Jaygen's legs.

Steel scraped against steel as Jaygen blocked the axe and then caught the dagger on the back swing. He sunk low and knocked his shoulder into the Seagrit, clashing meat against meat, the height winning out against the bulk as Axewell staggered back.

Now the initial attack had elapsed, Jaygen got a feel for how Axewell fought. His foot work was sloppy, his strikes and lunges inaccurate and his defence was totally open. The man fought with brute strength alone. Using savage attack after savage attack.

Jaygen gradually circled his way around Axewell. Blocking an upper cut, counter attacking a lunge and almost succeeded in tripping the Viking up. Axewell's anger rising as his attacks became more vicious, yet becoming more blind. Some of the strikes were so apparent that Jaygen only need duck or lean out of range, throwing the other off balance.

"Bloody, Die!" Axewell growled between breaths and blows. His scowl deepening with the effort and concentration needed to keep up the onslaught. "Die, Die, Die!"

Jaygen slowed his breathing, relaxed into the rhythm and watched as the strength of Axewell's blows weakened. His face contorted in rage, began to crease with worry.

Taking control, Jaygen used his foot work to slip further around him, edging the older man towards the drop. Catching, parrying and dodging each cut and blow. Jabbing with the borrowed sword when he saw the openings, the crowd's shouts rising in tempo as they demanded blood and then erupting with cheer as he swiped at Axewell's dagger and sent it spinning from the rock.

Amongst the slamming of shields and the gleeful whoops and shouts he spotted a lone figure, standing out because she remained still, her face showing none of the excitement of the others.

Fieri had returned to watch after all.

With this onlooker, Jaygen felt a surge of pride. He would show her he wasn't the coward she thought he was.

Axewell's next attack was a last desperate effort at gaining some ground back, struggling to gain a strong foothold as his heels scraped off the rock and met only sky. His axe came in from the side, his hand grasping his forearm to add force to the blow, a scream breaking through gritted teeth.

Jaygen stepped into the attack, slipping the point of his sword down the bearded steel, the scrape of metal against metal torturing his ears as he cut through the leather bands which bound the axe to the stump.

The axe head spun away. The dull grey weapon clattering into the rock before slipping off the edge to follow Axewell's dagger. And to be closely followed by Axewell himself.

The fervent whoops and cheers suddenly quieted as the crowd of men stepped closer, eagerly anticipating the Viking's demise. The silence unnerved Jaygen as he glowered down at the man he was about to kill.

Tired, broken and shamed, the man he once feared met his eyes; resignation coating a sadness to his demeanour. The surprise at being the one about to die no longer present. His tail of a beard seeming pathetic, the rat's skull beaded into it, sharing the wearer's misery.

Feeling the weight of those watching, Jaygen placed the tip of Fieri's sword against the man's chest and resolved himself to do the grisly task.

It wasn't as if he had never killed a man before. Grimwolf had slaughtered hundreds of the Dark

Army's creatures. But the person before him was one of his own. A Viking.

He met Axewell's sad gaze, gripped the hilt of the sword tighter, the muscles in his arms tensing, the fatigue of the fight beginning to sink into him now that the adrenalin was ebbing away. Axewell wouldn't have thought twice about killing him if things had turned out the other way around.

"What in Odin's name!" Ragna bellowed as he roughly shoved men out of his way. Two of them reeling precariously close to the drops either side as they made way for his huge frame. A dropped shield bounced from the rock and rolled over the edge, screaming in protest as it crashed against the rocks on the way down.

Jaygen lowered his sword as he confronted his father. The triumph of the fight evaporating beneath the dark glower he was being given.

"I said there was to be no fighting," Ragna boomed, the Fist of the North appearing huge and brutal in his massive hands. "The only one to fight on the Tooth would be me." He slammed the hilt of the war hammer into the rock, hard enough to dislodge some snow. Jaygen felt the anger permeating from his father and for a moment he thought he might get shoved from the Tooth in his wrath. "Is there anyone here man enough to do that? No?" Ragna's glare left Jaygen to spread throughout the crowd. "Any of you?" His answer was silence as the men around him suddenly glanced shamefully at the ground. "Then I suggest you make your way to the boats. We're leaving for a bloody war, in case any of you have forgotten."

The crowd backed away, heads hung low and avoiding eye contact as they scurried away. Jaygen lowered Fieri's sword, readying himself for his father's angry rebuke, when he felt the ground at his feet shift.

It suddenly dropped an inch, a crack opening along a jagged line from the point where Ragna's shaft had struck the ground.

Instinctively he stepped over the crack as the protruding end lurched, the tip of the Tooth tilting down as it dropped, yet he was now safely on the solid ledge - feeling the presence of his father as he gripped him by the shoulder.

Axewell, his body too tired to react to the tragic dilemma, began to fall away with the broken rock, slipping almost as if it was in slow-motion. Arms flailing, both hand and stump as he sought for a purchase that wasn't there.

Jaygen stretched out but the body had already teetered out of reach, the vast drop looming beneath, ready to receive any offerings. Axewell's gaze went skyward, eyes becoming large circles, mouth open ready to scream.

"Odi…"

Jaygen's fingers found the tail of beard as it flicked up. He closed his hand into a fist, the hair sliding through his grasp until they halted at the rat skull. The sudden stop yanked the body straight, cutting the final salute off as he pulled Axewell onto solid ground.

The sound of heavy rock crushing against and bouncing off the mountain echoed around them, followed by the snapping of branches and smashing wood from far below.

Between himself and his father, they dragged the weaker bodied man from the Tooth and dropped him in the snow.

"Get cleaned up, get your men ready and get into your bloody boat," Ragna growled at the shivering figure at his feet. "You lot," he pointed the hammer at the dispersing crowd. "Help him down and see him to his clan."

The men gathered around Axewell and helped him to his feet.

Jaygen attempted to creep away, expecting his father's wrath to turn on him but came face to face with Fieri.

Strands of her hair brushed against his cheek. They were stood so close, her blue stare giving him a strange feeling in his belly. He fumbled and almost dropped the sword he had borrowed as he offered it to her, hilt first.

"Thank you," he said as she took it from him. Her fingers fleetingly touching his as she bit her bottom lip.

"You're welcome," Fieri replied, a redness tingeing her cheeks, which Jaygen didn't think had anything to do with the cold. He wanted to say something else, to stretch that moment out but his father chose that instant to slam a heavy hand down on his shoulder.

"Come with me," Ragna ordered, his glare briefly catching Fieri. "Alone."

She offered him a weak smile, yet said nothing as she followed her brother down the snow trodden path after the others.

When they were alone, Jaygen's father slipped the Fist of the North over his shoulder, holding it like a milk maid's yoke with hands resting on the shaft, fat fingers dangling. The fury that he had held only minutes before, slipping away to be replaced with concern. "That was stupid," Ragna muttered, shaking his head.

"Yeah, but I was forced," Jaygen replied, raising his hand in defence. "I didn't want to fight. Truly I didn't. But…"

"No, not the fight," his father explained, blowing air through pursed lips. "Letting Axewell bloody Stump, live. That was stupid."

The statement caught Jaygen off-guard and it was a moment before he realised what his father had said.

"There comes a time when a man has to fight. When the only answer left is steel." Ragna rolled his eyes as he stared into the grey clouds above. "Odin knows, I've had my fair share of them. And mercy, for those that deserve it can be a grand thing. But I don't trust Axewell. He's a spiteful man who holds a grudge."

Jaygen hadn't thought of it like that, yet even then – could he have really killed him?

"I'll keep a close eye on him and I think you ought to do the same." Ragna twirled a finger in the air, making small circles. "A lot of things can happen in a battle, a lot of confusion with a lot of sharpened steel. Just watch your back, is all I'm saying."

"I will," Jaygen replied, wanting the talk to finish.

"And no more fighting, not unless you're Grimwolf. Understand?" Jaygen nodded. And his father's smile split his shaggy beard. "Good," he said. "And thank Odin that it was me that had found you up here. I'd hate to think what would have happened if your mother had stumbled upon it. I dare say Ejan would have thrown the pair of you from the Tooth."

Jaygen inwardly cringed at the mention of his mother. She had a tongue sharper than a soul reaver. "You won't tell her, will you?" he asked, anxiously.

Ragna chuckled as he shook his head. "Do you think I'm crazy. I'd rather face a horde of rampaging ram beetles." He nodded towards Craggs Head below them. "We better get going, we've still things to do before we set sail this afternoon."

They descended together, Jaygen feeling luckier that his mother hadn't found out about the fight on the Tooth, than him actually beating Axewell.

Chapter 15

Sirens

"What were you bloody thinking?" Ejan screamed at him. Loud enough for the entire ship to hear, her rage only amplified by the small confines of the Captain's quarters. Jaygen forced himself to keep still, his gaze firmly locked on his feet as he fought the urge to cringe away from his mother. How had she found out?

"Don't answer that. It's quite clear that you hadn't being thinking at all!" Ejan continued, prodding him painfully in the chest with each word. "Because if you had been thinking, you would have realised that if you died up at the Tooth, our chance of destroying Hades would have been lost. And the fate of Ethea would have been lost to Neptula. Not to mention I would have lost you."

"But I didn't lose," Jaygen argued, briefly glancing into his mother's face as he spoke, then back at his feet as she narrowed her eyes. She was a good foot shorter than he was, she may as well have been taller than the mast and rigging for how small she made him feel.

"Selfish - that's what you are. Selfish. Risking the lives of people all over the world so you could show off to that girl, to Fieri."

Jaygen shook his head. "It wasn't like that. I was tricked into fighting. I didn't want to, really I didn't, but…there comes a time when a man has to fight…"

"That something stupid that your Da might say," his mother snapped. He couldn't deny it; those were exactly the words his father used. "If you've any sense left in you, you will climb into that armour of yours and not take it off until this war has finished."

Jaygen wanted nothing more than to leave the tiny cabin and feel the fresh sea air on his face, to experience the colossal icebergs the longboats was forced to weave between, and if she was out on deck, spend a little time with Fieri.

"I'll put it on when we reach land," he resolved, attempting to placate his mother. It would be no good arguing with her while her temper was up. Yet while her rages were fierce, they were short-lived. She wouldn't be angry with him for long.

"Yes, you will," she affirmed. "And you won't step a foot upon deck until we get there." Placing her hands on her hips she stepped away. "And you can wipe that shocked expression from your face too. It's your own fault that you must stay hidden. If you hadn't volunteered yourself to go with the scouting party, we wouldn't need to fake your sea-sickness."

Jaygen rubbed the stubble on his chin. Of course, he couldn't go out on deck as himself and then suddenly emerge later as Grimwolf. It would be only too simple to work out who Grimwolf was. And with the longboat being thick with bodies, there were a lot of eyes around. The mythical wolf-man was supposed to be meeting them there.

"So how will this work?" he asked.

"You're Da came up with the solution. You're to hide in here, like I said - feigning sea-sickness, and when we're close enough to land, Raggy will call a halt and anchor overnight. Then under the cover of darkness you will row ashore and meet us when we land the following morning."

"That's an awful idea," Jaygen complained as he sat heavily on the narrow bunk. "There must be another way." The thought of rowing on the open sea, no matter how short the distance, worried him. Not to mention that there may be skagwangles or sharks beneath the waves.

His mother shrugged. "It's the only plan we have. And it will serve as an excuse to keep you out of the way while Grimwolf is about camp." She crossed the cabin in two short strides and opened the door wide enough for her to slip out. "Unless you can come up with a better plan." She glanced about the cramped chamber. "You'll have two days stuck in here to think about it."

Then she was gone, closing the door behind her.

"Two days?" he gasped, as he flopped back on the cot and stared up into the dusty rafters. Two entire days stuck in this dingy dark hole. It wasn't fair. He desperately strived for another idea, a better one which would see him walking up on deck, but failed to find anything. He couldn't one minute, be rowing amongst the other Vikings, and then disappear and come back as Grimwolf. His secret would be out.

He placed his hands beneath his head, resigned to the fact that he was going nowhere. Maybe he could simply sleep for the entire journey. At the least he would be fresh for fighting when they arrived. Closing his eyes, he attempted to shut the thoughts out and concentrate only on the rising and falling of the boat as it rocked with the waves. The creak of the planking and mast as they groaned under the pressure. The grunting of men as they rowed, an old Viking tune being carried by a few to help them keep a rhythm. Seagulls honking with complaint as the vessel cut through the water, scaring the fish into the blue depths.

After a while he felt himself slipping into sleep. Drifting into a peaceful slumber.

Night had fallen when he was awoken. His father crashed through the door, slamming it closed again and stumbled to light a lamp, which swayed with the harsh motion of the boat. When the amber glow lit him up, Jaygen saw that his father was drenched. His hair, furs, boots, were all glistening wet.

"What is it?" he asked, as he dropped an arm below the cot, reaching for the bundle of rags that covered his armour.

"Rain," Ragna replied, wiping water from his face, drips running down his thick beard. "There seems to be as much wet stuff above the boat as there is below."

"A storm?"

"Oh aye, it's a storm. But this far north it should be snow – or even sleet. Not rain and it most definitely shouldn't be warm."

Jaygen rose from the bed, but his father patted him back down. "Nothing we can do yet. This is the work of Hades. He's making a good start of melting the ice shelves. We need to reach him before he turns it all to water."

The door suddenly flung open once again and his mother entered the room, Ragna having to press himself into the corner to give her space.

"There's more icebergs," she hissed, wringing her hair on the floor as she grasped an oilskin cloak from a hook and threw it around herself. "Too many for this time of year. I think the large land hugging bergs are breaking away to follow the current."

"If the current goes south," Jaygen offered, "they'll melt soon enough and the main body when it follows will sail safely through."

"You say that like it's a good thing," Ejan remarked, shaking water from her head. "The ice melts and the sea water will rise."

Ragna took a second oilskin cloak and threw it over his body, although it did little more than cover his shoulders and part of his back. "Your Earth-born friend isn't taking this voyage to well either."

"Peter?"

His father nodded. "The lad's had his head over the side since we left. He's gonna bring up his inners if he carries on."

Ejan chuckled. "So you're not the only person experiencing sea-sickness."

Jaygen was about to suggest that Peter could share the chamber, but remembered that he could no more reveal himself to him, than any other. "Keep an eye on him will you. I don't think he has any friends other than me."

"He'll be fine," reassured his father. "Just so long as we reach land before he coughs his lungs up."

Jaygen watched as his parents left the room, closing the door and shutting the storm outside. The lantern still swinging and making strange shadows with the movement. He was beginning to feel a little nauseous himself. He lay back on the cot and placed the pillow over his face.

At some point during the storm, he must have slipped back into sleep for when his mother crept into the room again, daylight streamed in behind her so he could only make out her outline.

"What's it like out there today?" he asked, rubbing grit from his eyes.

"Damp," Fieri replied.

Jaygen sat straight, suddenly becoming aware that he was partially naked beneath the blanket. He pulled the coarse furs up but not before Fieri had an eye-full of his stomach and bare chest. When she noticed that he had caught her, she guiltily looked away.

"Are you feeling any better?" she asked, sitting herself on the edge of the cot, having to push her sword out of the way.

"Erm…yeah," Jaygen replied, then remembered the ruse his mother had told him to endure. "I mean, no – not really. I don't travel in boats too well."

"Neither does your friend, Peter – is it?"

Jaygen nodded. "My Da, said he was sick."

"Like nobody I've ever seen," she chuckled. "All anybody has seen of him is his legs and back as he heaves over the side. And when he is face up, it's a pale green. His head has been inches from the brine since we left the harbour."

"And I suppose that storm didn't help," Jaygen smiled. "So why have you come to see me?"

Fieri glanced at the door as if expecting somebody to intrude where she herself shouldn't be. "I'm just checking on a friend. Your Da said you were ill and when I asked your mother she told me to take my interest elsewhere."

"She can be a little over protective, but her heart's in the right place."

"Or she doesn't want her boy messing with the likes of me," Fieri suggested, sliding a little closer so one of her hands pressed against his leg, her voice gaining a husky quality. "As I may lead him astray." She raised a red eyebrow and leaned closer. Jaygen felt his heart quicken as her nose almost brushed his. A strange squeezing sensation fluttered inside his stomach.

Then she paused, a playful grin curling her lips. "It's a good job we're only friends," she laughed, pulling away from him. "I only came to check on you. You know, half the ship is talking about what you did up at the Tooth. Black Jaygen; it's a name that's being said by most of them. I only wish that you were in the scouting party with me." Jaygen noticed her cheeks flush as she glanced away. "Now I know that you can handle a sword, I might feel safer with you there."

Jaygen clenched his teeth to halt the words that were about to spill from him. "My Ma will be with you. And Grimwolf."

"Grimwolf," Fieri repeated, pronouncing the syllables slowly. "He can fight, but he doesn't say much."

Jaygen couldn't argue with the fact - if only she knew the truth. He wanted to say more, his gaze falling once more to her lips, but Fieri began to rise from the cot and her foot struck the rag-covered armour, hidden beneath.

"What's that," she asked, as she reached an arm below the feather mattress.

Panic rocked through Jaygen as he sat bolt upright, an arm reaching for hers to prevent her from reaching further. But his action only added to her curiosity. Her smooth features creasing into a frown as she pulled away from him.

No.

She was about to learn the secret. It could ruin everything. Frustration drove Jaygen to shuffle further along the bed, his mind racing for something to distract her, hoping that his parents would walk in and stop her from finding out the truth.

Then before he realised what he was doing, his hands rose to her face, gently brushing the soft cheeks as he turned her head towards him and crashed his mouth against hers.

Jaygen half expected Fieri to thump him in the side of the head, even flinching when her arm swung about, yet her hand reached over his shoulder to pull him closer, her body pressing tight against his.

Fieri's scent filled him, the pleasant taste of cherries from her tongue as she explored his mouth, the salt in her hair and warmth from her face. Should he have his eyes closed? She did, hidden beneath deep lids as she curled her fingers through his hair. Closing his own, he attempted to kiss her back and hoped he was doing it right. This was his first ever passionate kiss and he hoped he didn't fumble it. Yet the longer they were locked the more he felt it was right. More than right. It sent shock waves through him, heat - a dizzying mix of appreciation and something stronger. Something powerful that he didn't have a word for, unless it was - love.

The door creaked loudly as it swung open and his mother stepped into the room. Feeling flustered, he almost leapt from the mattress as he put a gap between himself and Fieri, who he noticed had gone a shade redder.

Ejan didn't say anything. She didn't need to, for her face said it all.

Fieri slowly rose from the bed and crossed the room, having to come within an inch of his mother before slipping through the door. She cast a final glance towards him, a satisfied smile lighting her beautiful face. Then she was gone.

When the door closed, his mother placed her hands on her hips, shaking her head in disappointment.

"Don't say it," Jaygen pleaded as he pulled the sheets up around him.

"What?" Ejan snapped, "You didn't have a choice this time? Is it a case of, 'sometimes a man has to kiss'."

Jaygen could have said that he did it to prevent Fieri from finding the armour, that he didn't have a choice but to distract her. Yet he chose not to. "I like her. A lot," he admitted and felt a little pride at saying it to himself as well as his mother.

"Well, good for you. Just remember that we're in a war. That no matter how you feel about a person it may not stop them from getting hurt or killed."

Jaygen couldn't think about that. "You and Da got together during the raids."

"Yep," his mother replied with a sigh, conceding to his argument as she came to sit beside him. "We did. It's a lot harder fighting in a battle, keeping one eye on the enemy while trying to watch your lover. It isn't easy."

"But possible."

"And what if Shannog's words are true. What if the armour is cursed?"

Jaygen didn't believe it was. It was pure coincidence that the original Grimwolf died of a broken heart. "The curse is only words spread by that old witch. They're not true."

"Really? Can you afford to take that risk? The god of winter created the suit – the curse was made to force Grimwolf to serve him and not his heart."

"I've never felt the presence of the god of winter," Jaygen replied. "And I've been wearing the suit for a few months."

"I don't know, maybe you were too far south. But now you're back in the north, the god may have a stronger grasp over you."

"We'll see."

"Aye," Ejan sighed. "We will. In the meantime, keep away from that girl. Only trouble will come of it."

Jaygen remained quiet, the thoughts of Fieri filling his mind and he didn't trust himself to reveal his feelings – especially not to his mother who seemed to hold a dislike for her. That is if he could work out what his feelings were.

The night had been long and sleep had eluded him. The memory of that kiss and the exciting emotions that it rode upon, chased away any thoughts of slumber. Adding to that the movements of his mother and father as they crashed in and out of the cabin, made sure he was awake. Jaygen wondered where on the boat, Fieri was. If she had found sleep herself, tucked up tight into one of the corners, or was she rowing, or huddled up close to the other men on the cramped vessel. The last thought brought a pang of jealousy with it. He felt the tension in his fist and willed himself to relax. It wasn't as if Fieri was his, and even if another claimed her, she was her own ruler and no man would tell her who she should be with.

Jaygen watched the dawn creep along the gap below the door. Stretching towards him in a rocking motion with the sea. The creak of timber as it swayed, the slapping of oars in the surf and the spray of water as it slapped the hull. He was desperate to be out of the cabin. But he consoled himself that today would be the day that they would reach land. He only need wait until dusk and hoped that his parent's plan would work.

"Raise oars!" Shouted his father, his voice booming on the other side of the door. "Drop anchor." There came a clatter of wood as men lifted the oars from the sea and a loud splash as the anchor was loosed – the heavy chains rattling as it sank into the depths.

"I don't like it," Jaygen heard his mother say. "It's too quiet."

"These shores are cursed," he heard a Viking yell. "Look over there, upon the rocks – Sirens!"

Jaygen wished he could see. He strode across the cabin and opened the door wide enough to peer out.

Every man and woman were on their feet, gazes fixed on the black rocks ahead and the sweeping bluff that came down from looming cliffs. They were still a quarter mile from shore but Jaygen could make out the shapes of creatures sitting atop rocks that lay either side of a lagoon entrance.

They were dark, slick with water as the waves crashed against them, spraying foaming water over their naked torsos. Long dank hair hanging low, momentarily catching a breeze to show glimpses of scaly flesh. They stared at them through lidless eyes, smiling warmly while beckoning them closer with slender arms. An involuntary shudder shook through Jaygen. These were creatures of the sea, beasts that were under the command of Neptula.

"It's a trap," Ragna suggested. "They knew we were coming."

"How?" Ejan asked, staring at the rocks. "Nobody knows we were coming. Not even Neptula could have predicted our intentions."

"That sea hag is cleverer than you think," Jaygen's father replied. "But we've still got to go through them. And I don't like sitting out here like a blind goose in an archery contest. We need to carve a path to the lagoon before the main body arrive."

"It shouldn't even be a lagoon," an elderly Viking offered, his weathered face screwed tight as he swung an arm at the land ahead. "This should have been buried beneath ice and snow. Even in the summer, only the upper portion of the cliffs would be visible."

Jaygen's father shook his head. "So, Hades and his demons have managed to melt a good portion of the ice shelves already. Sirens or no Sirens – we're going through." Then raising his arm, he signalled for the anchor to be raised once again and signalled for the men to place oars back in the water. "Easy does it," he instructed. "And if you've any spare cloth, jamb it into your ears."

The longboat began to skulk forward, the people aboard tense as they heaved the long oars in and out of the sea, the huge vessel lurching over the tidal waves which also drove them towards the rocks. The dark creatures enticing them closer, sharp teeth shining through crescent grins, like a cat toying with a mouse.

"When you think you can strike them, let your bow sing," Ragna whispered to his wife. Ejan slowly nodded as she slipped her bow from her back and knocked an arrow from her quiver.

Jaygen had seen his mother use the bow at home and knew she had a remarkable ability with the weapon. But he guessed that the sirens were far out of range and the shot would be made harder by the coastal breeze and the motion of the ship. So, he was surprised when she pulled the string back, her fingers brushing her ear, arm locked out and steady.

The bow hummed as the arrow was released.

He followed the shaft as it rose in a graceful arc, flying too high and to far right to be on target. Yet as he watched, mesmerised by the flight, he realised that his mother had been aiming into the wind, and as the shaft began its descent, it swung back.

The arrow struck one of the sirens in the chest. The metal head thumping through ribs and meat with enough force to knock the beast from its perch. A single choked wail escaped her as she fell into the foaming waves below.

A cheer went up from the Vikings in the boat, the men's spirits rising. Even Jaygen gave his mother an appraising whistle from inside the cabin, yet Ejan paid them no heed as she knocked another arrow and aimed at the second siren. But the remaining creature slipped lower from her perch and before Ejan could take aim, had submerged into the brine. Resurfacing long enough to grimace at the approaching vessel, a hissing snarl escaping her.

This was met with another cheer from the men aboard the longboat, although it was short-lived.

When the siren opened her mouth, her shriek pierced the sky. Ripples cut through the surface, spreading away from the screaming creature to engulf the longboat. An immense pain suddenly exploded in Jaygen's head and he fell to his knees, his palms pressed flat over his ears.

The shriek cut through his entire body. Intense vibrations that shook to the very core of his bones and skull. He rolled onto his side, curled up in a foetal position as he watched the entire crew fall about, their own hands clutching their heads – oars and weapons forgotten. His father had somehow managed to roll his body over his mothers. Large arms attempting to protect her, although the siren's wail penetrated through every fibre and Ejan's face was contorted in pain.

Jaygen's entire world reduced to violent vibrations. He watched on through half-lidded eyes as tentacles curled over the gunnel and skagwangles began to slide over the rail. Wet bodies flopped onto the deck, dark eyes and evil grins spread on ugly faces as they clutched nets and tridents. Stalking amongst the writhing Vikings who were left defenceless in their torture. They would slaughter the Northmen with an evil ease and there was nothing anybody could do.

Yet Jaygen had to do something.

Struggling onto his back, he squirmed away from the door, kicking his legs out to slam it shut. He closed his eyes against the shaking world as he shuffled towards the cot – pain in his head so immense that he feared falling unconscious at any moment.

When his shoulder struck the wall, he reached beneath the mattress and felt for the bundle of rags and the armour hidden beneath. With a shaking hand, he curled his fingers around the wolf helm and slid it closer to his painful head. He struggled to undo the tooth shaped clasp, his arms beginning to spasm uncontrollably. But when the face mask sprung open, he edged his head into the helm and snapped it closed.

The siren's scream instantly dulled to a whine. Still painful but not debilitating. He found the strength to rise and flip the cot over to grasp the rest of the armour. He slammed the feet into the greaves, and locked the fur carved thigh guards into place. The waist, stomach and breastplate interlocked and swivelled around his torso allowing him to slip his hands through the arms and shoulder plates; flexing his fingers inside the lobster gauntlets shaped like claws.

When the suit was complete the scream reduced to an annoying buzz. The whisper of the steel as he drew his sword grated the buzz to nothing.

The cabin door splintered beneath his shoulder as he rammed through the opening. His blade leading the way as he leapt upon the closest skagwangle. Its trident poised above Ragna and his mother, ready to drive through the writhing pair.

Jaygen caught the weapon with his own, the force knocking the skagwangle off balance. Its tentacles flowing around the wet deck as it righted itself. A narrow slit of a mouth partially opened in surprise before Jaygen's swung his claws across its throat.

Green blood sprayed up through clutching fingers, spattering the deck and men before the creature stumbled back and fell from the boat. The vicious attack he had dealt attracted the attention of the other skagwangles on board. Several of the closer ones approached him at speed, nets swinging low and tridents held aloft.

Jaygen ducked the first flung net and launched himself into the sea-beasts. He hacked left, his sword catching an arm below the elbow and severing the limb before bringing the blade back and taking the head off another. Tridents were thrust into his torso, the points striking the god-created metal before harmlessly sliding off. Jaygen swiped them away with his arm, his upper body swinging to one side before he swung back – driving both fist and blade through his attackers. Hack, punch, thrust. Drive, chop, stamp.

He suddenly felt a tentacle wrap around his wrist and momentarily hold his arm on the backswing. Jaygen closed his own hands on the snake-like appendage, coiling it around his arm before he wrenched the skagwangle off balance and using his heavy feet, pivoted on the spot and flung the creature into the mast. It bent double around the thick shaft of wood – its spine snapping before it crumpled to the deck.

More skagwangles climbed over the gunnel and began to squirm towards him, long tentacles coiling and uncoiling as they closed in.

Jaygen couldn't take them all by himself – there were too many of them and the Vikings were paralysed with pain and couldn't help.

Searching for a plan, his gaze fell on the siren in the water. The tide had brought the small flotilla of boats closer to her. If only he could use his mother's bow, he could kill her quite easily from this distance. But her bow, along with her arrows were tangled amongst her writhing body and that of his father. He doubted, with all the skagwangles that were approaching, that he would have had a chance to aim the weapon in the first place.

The longboat suddenly jolted as the vessel beside it bumped against the hull. Oars on both vessels splintering as the heavy crafts jostled against each other at the mercy of the waves. The third boat was on the further side, its stern scraping against the rock and cracking timber with each wave that spewed it further inland.

Jaygen saw his chance.

He swung his sword about, striking the approaching skagwangles from his path and not caring whether he had cut them open or not. His red cloak billowed behind him as he bounded across the deck, jumping fallen Vikings and vaulting the oarsmen benches onto the gunnel – and leapt across onto the second boat. Landing into a roll he avoided a thrusting trident, then sprang back onto his feet. Ramming a shoulder into a surprised skagwangle and taking him with him as he drove across the boat placing a foot onto the back of a large man in furs who was curled on the floor, and jumped onto the third vessel.

He landed hard, flinging the skagwangle from his shoulder before sprinting for the stern.

The wood splintered with another forceful crack as the stern smashed against rock and water began to pour in. But there was nothing Jaygen could do about that and his focus was at the other end of the boat.

Not bothering to duck the next blow, he allowed the trident to harmlessly slide from his armour as he powered his legs on – bowling the attacker over as he made for the hull. Springing onto the prow, he gripped his sword in both hands and launched himself overboard.

The siren stared up, mouth forming a large circle – teeth glistening as white as the surf as Jaygen fell upon her. His blade cracking the top of her skull with enough force to part her head to the jaw. His feet met the solid pebbles of the beach below the water. The tide battering against his knees, threatening to knock him over, but he held fast.

The siren's scream that had rendered the Northmen useless, cut off sharper than the steel which split her face. Dark eyes crossed as they inspected the blade, green blood pouring from her mouth as she attempted to utter another word, but only a choked gargle escaped.

Feeling disgust, Jaygen wrenched the sword free and the siren sunk into the foaming waves, bobbing below the surface before floating face down. Hair spreading out in all directions like a macabre veil.

He watched as the body began to sink and drift away from him, as if the siren attempted to flee his blade – yet there was no fleeing death once it had been dealt out. Although Odin, soon spat his father from the Halls of Valhalla.

Jaygen shook the thoughts from his mind as he suddenly realised that he was under attack. He barely had chance to gather his breath before he was overwhelmed with skagwangles.

Several of Neptula's beasts slammed against him at once, joining the force of the tide as they brought him to his knees. Instantly he felt his arm being wrenched out as a tentacle encircled it, squeezing with enough force to break an arm if it wasn't in the suit. His other arm was twisted the other way, his sword still gripped tight in a gauntleted fist, but he couldn't get a decent swing on it. He was overwhelmed by the slippery beasts that rose from the water, adding weight against the onslaught.

More appendages coiled about his waist, ankles, chest and neck. He could feel the muscles squirming and bunching, small suckers attempting to find purchase on the god-created armour as they latched on. His head was held still as he was forced lower into the water, each cold tide washing over his body. The skagwangle that stood before him continued to jab his trident at his face, attempting to thrust one of the three-pronged spikes through the eye holes in his helm. Jaygen twisted his head the best he could, using the wolf's nose to block the attacks, although he knew it wouldn't be long before the skagwangle got lucky.

Small triangular teeth clenched together, black eyes narrowed, gills fluttered as the creature continued to jab, each thrust getting closer to the mark; it would happen soon.

Suddenly the skagwangle's head imploded. Green gore fountained from the mush that had once been his skull, now replaced with a grey block of metal; Elora's hand print etched an inch deep.

The steel lump of the Fist of the North tilted forwards as Ragna lifted it from the mutilated beast, strings of ichor sticking to the grey metal.

Jaygen let out a strained breath as his arms and throat were released. His captors now bounding over him to meet the wave of Vikings that were charging towards them. A mass of screaming men in furs, swords and axes raised, maces, spears being swung as they clashed against skagwangles.

Ragna kicked the lifeless body over and offered Jaygen his hand. Jaygen grasped it and was pulled stiffly to his feet.

"You did well," his father laughed, green blood speckling his grin, "but we can't let you be having all the fun by yourself."

He turned and sprang after the closest sea creature, the Fist swinging a mighty arc above the waves, skimming water as the hammer connected with the back of a fleeing skagwangle. Ragna stepped closer and re-cocked his weapon onto his shoulder but the beast had already succumbed to the first blow.

About him, Jaygen watched as the Northmen cut through the sea creatures. The ferocious attack, the screams, the brutal violence. The surf was running with a greener colour; the foam being churned up by the many legs and bodies that thrashed about the water. He caught a fleeting glance of his mother amongst the melee, her short sword slick with blood. Fieri was beside her brother, both hacking the tentacles from a thrashing skagwangle before Axewell Stump moved in and chopped into the back of its cranium. Another large Viking had skewered a sea beast through the face, its body suddenly going rigid before the shaft was retrieved and the carcass dropped limp to the water.

Jaygen was about to join the fight when he realised it was over. Any skagwangles that hadn't fled were now floating, mutilated and broken upon the waves. Rising and falling with the flow.

When there was nothing else to fight, the Vikings paused and looked about at each other. Grins splitting beards as they began to cheer. Ragna thrust his war hammer into the air and yelled, "Odin!" and the men and women about him joined in the salute to the Norse God.

After the cry had run out and the echoes faded, Jaygen noticed that all eyes had turned to him. Faces, covered in blood or running with sweat and salt water, hardened warriors staring as they heaved in great breaths. Then as one they raised their weapons once again and cheered.

"Grimwolf, Grimwolf, Grimwolf!"

Jaygen witnessed awe, excitement, admiration from the warriors before him. Even Axewell was shouting his name with a new-found respect. He could have stood there in the cold surf and soaked it all up, could have remained the centre of attention for a little while longer, yet knew that Grimwolf - the Grimwolf from legend – wasn't to be the object of adoration. He was to be feared.

Still smiling beneath the helm, Jaygen slid his sword back into his scabbard and paced out of the water, putting his back to the men as he climbed the pebbly beach. He got as far as the cliff face before somebody grasped him by the elbow.

"You did well," Ejan offered, turning him around so he faced back out to sea. "Killing that damn siren before the skags slaughtered us." She flicked her hair back and wrung the salt water from the braid she was growing.

Jaygen stared at the floundering longboats as the men set to dragging them ashore. His father was amongst them, dragging a boat single-handed while shouting orders at the others. "Sometimes a man must fight," he said, shrugging. "So what excuse are you going to use for me being here? And why Jaygen wasn't fighting."

His mother smiled. "Your Da's going to send a boat back to warn the main body of the attack. Jaygen will be going back with them."

Jaygen nodded. That made sense, but it didn't make him feel any better. It still somehow made him look like a coward.

"I don't know how, but Neptula knew we were coming," Ejan continued, her face a mask of worry.

"You mean a spy?" Jaygen asked. He didn't believe that any of the Vikings would turn against each other. He watched them struggle with the boats and knew that however much the clans despised each other, they were all Norseman and would remain loyal against the common enemy. Then his gaze fell on a lone man, smaller and weaker than the rest who had crawled from the waves and now sat on a rock, poking at the floating body of a skagwangle with a stick. A perturbed look on his pale face. What was Peter doing?

"Perhaps. Just keep an eye out," his mother warned. "If the Sea Witch is in contact with Hades, he'll know we're coming."

"I will," he said, glaring up at the dark cliffs, gleaming wet in the sun. "I'll have a hunt around, see if I can find a way over."

"Good idea, the scout party will be ready to move once we're dry," Ejan said, then smiled at him warmly. "I'm proud of you, me and your Da both."

"Da?"

The voice came from behind a rock only feet away, startling Ejan into pulling her sword free from its scabbard. Jaygen kept his blade sheathed. He recognised the voice.

"Da?" Fieri repeated as she came around, her blue gaze locking with his. Her notched eyebrow drawing dangerously close to the other.

Ejan held up her arm, not yet putting her sword away. "Go back to the others girl, you're not needed here."

Fieri ignored Ejan's request and came before Jaygen, placing her hands on her hips as she tipped her face this way and that, attempting to see inside the helm. He noticed that the shock of going into the water and the cold wind brought a rosiness to her cheeks that brought back the memories of that kiss the day before.

"Jaygen?" she asked.

"Did you not hear me girl? Do as I ask and go back to the others. You know not what you're meddling with."

Ejan grasped Fieri's sleeve and attempted to spin her around and propel her down the beach, when Jaygen placed his gauntlet over her forearm.

"It's no use, Ma. She knows," he said. He stared at both sets of eyes as they glared at him. Both blue, both angry, yet felt the love they both portrayed.

What happens now?

16

Rising Tide

Flek pinched the bridge of his nose, attempting and failing to ebb the pain that throbbed inside his head. The dog yapping at his feet adding to the agony, sharp barks stabbing into his brain as it competed with Quantala's words.

"Get this thing out of my sight," Flek snapped as he aimed a kick at the annoying creature. It skittered away from the throne and into the arms of a serving girl who bowed low before leaving the chamber. Thankfully his wife-to-be was visiting family to the south of the country. She searched for excuses to be away from him and he was only too willing to allow her to go. He sensed that she hated him as much as her wretched dog did.

"Now tell me again, what's happening at the coast," he ordered, sitting back more comfortably now the irritation had gone.

"Not just the coast, the Sea Witch is attacking up rivers and along waterways," Quantala explained, slamming a fist into his palm. "Skagwangles have been snatching people who were foolish enough to venture close to the banks and there have been several reports of water dragons flying further inland, using lakes and locks for landing."

"And some of the water supplies have been fouled," Quantico continued. "More than a few wells have been poisoned. Including one right here in Rona. And the naval fleet has sustained heavy losses."

"How heavy?" Fleck asked, not wanting to hear the answer.

"Every galley, warship and trading vessel is at the bottom of the sea. Leviathans lay waste to the ships while sharks and skagwangles drowned and ate the crews."

These were the exact words that Flek had been dreading. Elora was right; Neptula had waged war on the Empire. Then maybe her other warning was equally as true. Is the world to be flooded?

"So, the Queen of Darkness was telling us the truth?" Quantico exclaimed, shaking his head.

"Yes," Flek yelled, "the bloody God of bloody Chaos was bloody right!" The outburst was childlike and had only cranked the intensity of his headache further up the pain scale.

He tapped his metal hand against the arm of the throne and made a ringing sound. The god-created weapon had been a gift from Neptula, a token of trust she'd said, as she manoeuvred him onto the Empire's throne. Irritation flowed through him as he realised he had been used. He flicked out the inch-long blades along his steel fingernails and raked them across the air.

"Bitch!" he screamed in frustration. Then as he felt the stares of both twins and Drifid upon him, he attempted to quiet his nerves. She may have given him the Empire as a means to her own ends, but he was more devious than she gave him credit for.

"I want every shade battalion to move in along the coasts," he ordered, snapping his fingers as he spoke. "The imperial guards patrolling out along the rivers and the people to be told not to go near any of it…"

"They'll be thinly stretched," Quantala offered. "It may give any rebels in the Empire a chance to raise a militia against us."

"Then put a curfew on the people," Flek growled, "must I think of everything?"

Quantala sighed heavily. "They won't like that."

"They don't like anything. It's for their own good. Execute anyone who opposes the order and you'll soon get them bending to our will."

"And Elora?" Drifid asked. "Are we to halt our attempts at capturing her and the Dark Army?"

Flek didn't forget the promise he had made on the balcony on her last visit. That he would stay out of her way and allow her full-rein to kill Neptula. He brushed the scab on his neck that had come from the blade she had held against his throat, and wondered how far Dethtil was away from Rams Keep. And if the revered Warlock was anywhere close to tackling the fairy protection that surrounded it.

"No," Flek answered, rubbing his chin. "She is to be killed on sight."

Drifid raised his eyebrows. "Maybe it would be wise to allow her to come to our aid…"

"I said no," Flek snapped. "Our only chance at destroying the Queen of Darkness will be when her back is exposed to us. While she's busy fighting Neptula and her forces. And I won't let that chance pass." He glared at the former Shaigun. The man given the title of Shadojak and the sword that went with it, only to lose it days ago, when Elora had so easily taken it from him. Flek saw the confusion in his pinched face and smiled. "I'm not such a fool as to allow us the use of the Dark Army – it may be that, which chases the sea creatures back into the sea where they belong. So, this is what you are going to do."

Flek leaned back and smiled as an idea came to him. "Drifid, send a message to Elora, warn her that we are under attack from Neptula and that I will keep my promise if she will come to our aid."

"But…" Quantala interjected, until Flek held up a hand to quiet him.

"I want you three to personally convey my orders to all the commanders in the Empire. Tell them to cease attacking the Dark Army and allow them free movement, let the God of Chaos use her own forces. However," he leaned closer to the men before him, "should a chance arise, should say, Elora be in a weakened position or have her back to us," he curled his steel fingers into a fist, "kill her."

"I like it," Quantico said, his grin matching that of his brother's.

Captain Furghan scratched at his greying beard as he glared out of the crooked tower he and Fosse were occupying. The crumbling structure leaned out over the Thames River at an acute angle. Thick trees which had merged with brick and steel supporting the weight, preventing it from toppling into the murky water.

"Do you think they'll come again?" Fosse asked, his imperial helmet sat askew on his head. The uniforms they were wearing were a strange mixture of British Army camouflage with imperial steel breastplates buckled over the top. It was the Empire's attempt at merging the armies together without forming two groups. Forcing the Earth-borns and Etheans to work as one to protect the new world, Ethea.

"They've come with every tide for the last few days – I don't see why they wouldn't continue," Furghan replied, wishing that he had better words to reassure the lad.

Fosse had needed to do a lot of growing up since Earth went to pot last year. After the lights went out and his trawler sank, taking Fosse's father down with it. The boy had experienced a world of hurt with the Dark Army and then almost died when Earth merged with Thea. It was a wonder the teenager hadn't gone mad. Or had he? It was Fosse's idea to join the imperial guard and become part of the new Empire. And Furghan recognised the glint of revenge in his eyes as he sought a way to avenge his father's death – which he blamed on the daughter of Chaos and the Dark Army which she ruled. Hell, Furghan reckoned he had gone mad himself. Was that the reason he had volunteered to go with him, to sign his life over to the Empire and become an imperial guard? Or had he done it out of guilt? After all, Fosse senior had died on his boat. Even though there wasn't much he could have done with a kraken the size of several lighthouses, bearing down on his tiny vessel.

Fosse slapped his army-issue rifle. "Gonna kill me a skagwangle this time," he said, attempting to sound fierce. Although Furghan saw through his bravado. Nobody could remain brave after witnessing other men being killed around them.

"Right you are," Furghan replied as he made a silent prayer that the Dark Army, or Neptula's sea creatures, would leave them alone. Hadn't they both done enough between them to ruin the worlds?

A head poked around the twisted door frame. "Skagwangles and water dragons spotted at Tilbury," the platoon officer informed them. "They'll be on us soon. Remain vigil."

"Aye, Sir," Furghan and Fosse said together, Fosse even attempting a salute that went unnoticed. The officer had bigger worries on his mind.

"You might just get your chance at bagging a skagwangle," Furghan told Fosse, forcing a grin on his face. "But mind you don't do anything stupid and get yourself shot. They may only have bows and arrows but them skags are bloody good at using them."

Fosse shook off the warning and cocked his rifle. Furghan mimicked him and trained the weapon out of the slanting window as he waited for the tide of violence to arrive.

He witnessed other guards in the building across the river. Platoons of men taking positions in the fallen towers or hiding in the rubble of warehouses and docks which were now no more than rusting girders and torn sheeting. Some had partially fallen in the Thames as the river claimed more of the man-made structures each day. Further up the fast flowing waterway, Tower Bridge remained impossibly intact. Men hurrying along the wide structure and taking up positions facing down the river. Snipers were poking long barrels out of the tower windows and large gunners were situated on the ramparts above.

It was some sight, Furghan had to admit. Who'd have thought that one day he would be taking part in a battle in London. He felt an overwhelming pride at seeing the old bridge still in use – a heritage going back to a world that didn't exist anymore. A history of kings and queens stretching over hundreds of years to his own queen. Queen Elizabeth who still ruled over them, but was herself ruled by the new Emperor. He couldn't guess where she was now, probably in some safe castle or tower, miles away from the battle. He couldn't blame her. If given the choice, that was exactly where he would be.

The first shots of gunfire rippled along the river from Tower Bridge, snapping him out of his musings. The heavy guns were opening up, bursts of fire erupting as they aimed down the stretch of water and out of sight.

Fosse shifted his position to get a better look. Leaning out of the window as he enthusiastically brought his rifle about. "I can't see them," he complained.

Furghan gripped him by the back plate and yanked him inside the room. They both fell to the sloping floor as arrows suddenly clattered against the frame where they had just been.

"Damn it lad!" he snapped, his eyes going wide as shadows flew passed the window. Large water dragons slipped into view with skagwangles riding atop of them, ugly black bow strings being pulled back, ready to take another shot.

He watched the slender beasts cut through the sky, skimming above the water as more creatures burst from beneath the waves. The closest dragon screamed as bullets tore into its dark blue flesh. Green blood mixing with the water droplets that fell from its back, along with the rider who suddenly lurched off, a large hole opening in his head. Both beast and rider plunged into the Thames below, spewing up large white sprays before being swallowed by the river.

On the far bank a dragon collided with a pile of bricks, the soldiers hiding on the other side beginning to rain bullets into the stunned creature. It bucked and writhed in pain as it succumbed to the attack. Men screaming as they cut it down. Then before it toppled over another dragon landed heavily. Scattering bricks and men as its rider fired arrow after arrow at the soldiers. The skagwangle triumphantly raised his bow as the men turned to flee, but not before the dragon caught an unfortunate soldier between its sharp teeth. The unfortunate man screamed as he was lifted off the ground. Slamming futile punches into the dragon who began to shake him like a rag doll, before hurling him to the ground. The soldier's screams were cut short as his body disappeared beneath the huge webbed talons of the beast, which were more fin, than foot.

Furghan gazed away, the contents of his breakfast threatening to come up. Yet no matter where he looked, the other scenes were no better.

Tower Bridge was being attacked by several other dragons. The beasts flying beneath and over the structure, swinging about and curling back as they circled the men atop it. Sniper fire cracked through the air, smoke billowed from the hot guns that rattled volley after volley but for every skagwangle and dragon they brought down, another two took their place.

They were being attacked from every direction.

Furghan edged to the window once again and poked the barrel of his rifle over the ledge. He aimed down the telescopic sight, trained a water dragon into the crosshairs and fired a burst of three rounds – like he had been trained to do when he joined the guard last month.

The bullets missed.

"Bugger," he hissed as he ducked beneath the window as the rider of the dragon he had fired at, swept around and came back.

The entire building rocked as the huge creature slammed into it. Masonry crumbling beneath sharp talons as it found purchase. Its sleek head darting into the room and snapping at them.

Scrambling away from the thrashing beak, Furghan kicked out, his foot connecting with the immense jaw, but doing nothing more than enraging the beast. Arrows skittered through the gap between the dragon's neck and window frame. Long black shafts that thudded into the plaster walls and carpeted floor. If he had the time, Furghan might have contemplated that before the Earth merged into chaos, this building would have been a busy hive of office blocks. Floors of staff sat at desks answering calls to strangers, exchanging talk at the coffee machine or copier, living mundane but safe lives. Not being moments away from being eaten by a dragon that came out of the sea. Being shot at by a vengeful creature that was part man and part octopus and not striving to survive in a world where magic was more accessible than electricity.

- Damn, he missed his trawler.

"Captain..." Fosse, screamed as he pushed the barrel of his gun into the gaping mouth of the dragon and fired.

The head jerked rapidly, chunks of flesh and bone being torn away as he emptied the full magazine of bullets in one long burst. When the rifle stopped firing, Fosse collapsed back, landing beside Furghan on the floor. Together they watched as the beast's neck slumped to the carpet, before the weight of its dead body pulled the ruined head out of the window and snatching it from sight.

They heard it splash into the river below but neither of them had the desire to look. Furghan placed a hand on Fosse's knee as he struggled to stand. "You killed a dragon as well as a skag," he said, trying to catch his breath. "Your father would be proud."

Fosse only nodded as he pulled himself up, taking a spare magazine from a pouch to place into the rifle.

"Well done, soldier," shouted the officer as he poked his head back into the room. "Keep it up. We'll make decent imperial guards out of you yet."

Fosse shrugged as he returned to the window, the hole now bigger as the frame and the surrounding bricks had been torn out when the dragon fell. He took up a firing position, his rifle pulled tight into his shoulder as he aimed down the sight and then paused.

"What is it?" Furghan asked as he watched the boy's complexion suddenly pale.

"It's the kraken," he said, his voice trembling. "The same one that sunk the boat, that killed my dad."

"It can't be," Furghan retorted, trying to convince himself. How would something so large fit in the Thames? Yet when he craned his head out of the window, he felt his bowels loosen. Wriggling along the river, its bloated body scraping mud up along either bank was the same beast that had sunk his trawler.

"Leviathan!" came a scream from across the other side of the river, at the same time as the officer burst into their room, having to hold onto an overturned desk for balance.

"Concentrate your fire on the leviathan," he ordered, pointing a shaking hand at the colossal creature.

"It's a kraken," Fosse snapped, an eagerness prompting him back into a firing position.

"No, it's a leviathan," the officer argued as if Fosse had said something stupid.

Fosse, pressed his cheek into the stock and stared down the sight. "Kraken," he hissed.

"I don't bloody care what it is," Furghan growled. "How in god's name are we to kill it?" Yet his question was wasted as the officer had trudged from the room to see to the rest of the platoon, scattered throughout the building. Instead, he joined Fosse at the window and watched the wriggling beast come closer.

It was so immense that the rear trunk of its body blotted out London's skyline, while its thick tentacles reached hundreds of meters from its squid-like head, thrashing about the broken docks and land, like meat-filled tube trains. Flattening trees and curling about buildings before pulling them into the Thames. Entire structures that once reached high into the sky, falling beneath the power of the kraken. Killing men, snuffing them out as if they had no more substance than ants. For that's what it felt like to Furghan. They were tiny worthless insects compared to this gigantic beast.

Furghan watched in horror as a fat tentacle squeezed between two fallen buildings and into what once was a warehouse on the docks. In one simple flick, it lifted the roof and crushed the entire structure flat. The shouts and screams of the men inside smothered in an instant.

Making a silent prayer for the second time that evening, Furghan gripped Fosse's arm and pulled him back. "Time to go," he ordered.

"No," Fosse spat through gritted teeth. "You go if you want, but I'm staying."

"You'll only get yourself killed, there's no stopping that," Furghan argued, attempting to make the boy see reason. But Fosse shrugged him off and returned to the window. "Damn it!" Furghan yelled. Realising that he was going from silent prayers to damning things in a matter of breaths. "Bugger it."

Placing himself beside Fosse, Furghan pulled his rifle back into his shoulder and trained the barrel on the approaching death. He didn't aim down the sight, he had no need to. As long as the weapon was pointed in the general direction of the kraken, the bullets would hit some part of it.

"It's going for the bridge," Fosse explained, waiting for the creature to come a little closer. "It'll tear it down as if it's made from paper."

"Over my dead body," Furghan spat, feeling his blood heat up at the thought of this un-earthly beast stealing away his heritage. Crushing the history which was once part of a great nation.

His finger squeezed the trigger and his rifle jerked in his hands. The entire magazine emptying in seconds and sending thirty bullets thudding into the kraken's gaping mouth. Furghan's heart sank as he realised that they had no effect on the beast. Even the big guns on the bridge did little more than annoy the creature as it squirmed closer, the trunk of its body flattening everything along both banks.

Furghan knew that when it came to them, the building they were occupying wouldn't stand a chance. It would be crushed and he and Fosse along with it. With the feeling of impending doom laying solidly in his heart, he changed the magazine and re-cocked his rifle, feeding another bullet into the chamber. Hoping that the officer would order a retreat from the structure.

Water washed up river as the kraken dragged itself along, wide tentacles slapping the surface ahead as they snaked passed the window and momentarily blocked out the world. Furghan braced himself against the far wall as the entire building shook. White ceiling tiles raining down with plaster and brick. Strip lighting shattered against the floor as the structure violently lurched into the beast. The steel frame of the wall grazing against thick rubbery flesh and shedding masonry. If he chose to, he could reach out and touch the very monster that sunk his ship and killed Fosse's dad.

The noise was deafening as the world fell around them, even if the officer ordered the retreat, Furghan doubted that the building would remain stable long enough for them to run. Steel screamed, timber snapped and groaned, and glass splintered everywhere. The floor suddenly dropped and Furghan struggled to hold onto the wall as he watched Fosse slide down the vertical drop to the floor below. Then the wall he was holding onto crumbled and fell away, taken him with it as he followed Fosse down.

Pain exploded in his chest as he struck a broken table. "Fosse?" he yelled through the dust and debris that surrounded them, his words coming out choked from being winded.

"Over here," replied the boy, as he crawled into a gap where daylight seeped through. Fighting the urge to fight his way out of the claustrophobic space, Furghan scurried over the broken room and damaged furniture, squeezing alongside his partner.

The kraken was driving its body along the building, attempting to bring it down but the Thean trees which it had merged with, gave enough support to prevent the place from toppling into the river. It rammed its head in frustration against the structure but miraculously, it held.

"We won't last much longer," Furghan yelled as the screams of their comrades above added emphasis to his words. The rubbery flesh pushed up tighter as it drove on, the grey wrinkly skin giving way to the delicate membrane of the large eye as it came level with the gap. Larger than a dump truck, the socket scraped along the hole and forced it wider.

Both he and Fosse yelped as the huge orb rotated the horizontal goat-like pupil to focus on them. Furghan's blood suddenly ran cold as he stared into the same bronze-coloured eye he witnessed all those days ago, on the North Sea.

He stepped back and rammed the barrel of his rifle into the inky blackness of the pupil, leaning his entire bodyweight against it as it pushed through the wet membrane. Then squeezed the trigger.

Green blood poured over his arms as the eye began to fall apart. Gore and wet ichor slopped out of the hole he was making as the kraken attempted to wriggle away.

From outside came a thunderous scream. It sounded like the trumpet of an elephant only much, much louder. And with a violent judder the creature broke free from the building, blood gushing from the damaged eye as it began to back up, slamming its thick appendages in pain and anger.

A cheer went up from the other side of the river as the kraken withdrew, struggling to worm its way back the way it had come.

The strength left Furghan's legs and he fell to the floor, his entire body soaked in green goo. His arms dropped into this lap as he leaned back against an upturned chair, his aching ears picking out the beast as it trumpeted in complaint.

Fosse slumped down beside him, his pale face spotted with the same green blood that covered the room. They glanced at each other and began to laugh. A loud, belly-aching laugh that made Furghan weep. It was strange what some men found funny when their lives were on the brink of being snuffed out.

The officer chose that moment to shout down from the floor above. "They're retreating," he informed them, shaking his head in wonderment at the laughter that both Furghan and Fosse tried to quell. "Well done, I guess you found a weak spot."

When he regained his composure Furghan stared up at his commanding officer. "Aye sir, but they'll be back with tomorrow's tide."

"Yes, soldier, you're probably right. And they'll have reinforcements. Each wave is stronger than the last. I only wish there was an easier way of killing the leviathans. It's so big that our guns barely graze it."

"I've an idea about that," Furghan offered, a plan beginning to form in his mind. "Are the dams up river still functioning?"

17

Volcaneus

Elora plucked a feather from the crow. The bird squawked in complaint as it jabbed its beak at her. But she was quicker, snatching her hand free from the cage before the beast of Dethtil inflicted any damage. She held the feather up to the fiery sky of the Shadowlands and watched the rainbow mix of colours reflect from the black fibres – like the surface of oil under sunlight.

They were inside the cave entrance to Zilabeth's workshop. Captain Brindle and Smudge were sat at the other end of the workbench while the Shadojaks, Sibiet and Hashim occupied the other.

"Do you think he senses us?" Elora asked, as she sat down, the caged bird glaring at her through the bars. "The Warlock, I mean. Does he know where his crow is? Is he watching us through its beady little eyes?"

"I expect so," Bray offered as he sat beside her, taking the feather from her and slowly spinning it between finger and thumb. "It's a part of him. Maybe we should just kill it."

Zilabeth lifted her head from beneath the bonnet of the Spitfire she was working on. The impressive world war two fighter plane was almost finished and ready to test.

"That might not be a good idea," she suggested, as she raised her goggles from her face and turned off the acetylene torch she had been welding with. "The sorcery imbued in the bird won't die with the crow. It will return to its master. Keeping it alive will ensure the magic trapped within its body will remain. Rendering him that little bit weaker."

From the other side of the Spitfire's bonnet, Teaselberry raised her head and nodded enthusiastically, agreeing with Zilabeth.

"So we wait until Dethtil arrives and breaks down the fairy barrier," Elora asked as she dropped a blanket over the cage to surround the crow in darkness. "He could be here any day now."

Bray put an arm around her shoulders and hugged her tight. "Don't worry about it. We'll be ready."

"And this beauty is almost ready for flight," Zilabeth offered, tapping the side of the fighter plane. "And I must admit, I'm feeling excited at the prospect of flying her." Teaselberry nodded enthusiastically and saluted. Elora found it amusing that the wood troll had taken to wearing flying goggles ever since Smudge had returned with the Spitfire.

Smudge himself chuckled as Teaselberry's grin widened her pug-like face. "Captain Brindle has supplied us with the fifty calibre guns which I've installed into the wings," he explained, pointing at the barrels protruding from the slender craft. "She'll have as much presence as your dragon in the sky."

"Dragons, flying metal birds, magic crows – it's madness is what it is," Sibiet grumbled, as he adjusted the turban on his head, the swollen black lumps around his face now faded to a mottled green. Elora waited for the next inevitable word.

"Blaspheme!"

"It is," agreed Elora, feeling more than a little irritated at the Shadojak's attitude. "But in case you've forgotten it is the gods themselves who we are now battling against. Call it blasphemy all you want but I'm going to use what tools and what weapons we have in bringing peace to Ethea. And you," she jabbed a finger at Sibiet whose dark complexion had turned a shade of red, "will play the role in which you are given. You're a balancer, a judge, a Shadojak. And if I need you to be blasphemous – then that is what you'll be."

She didn't know where the anger had come from, but by the time she had finished speaking, she was ready for Sibiet to draw his sword, even feeling a thrill at the prospect of fighting him. But swallowed the emotions down. They belonged to that other her and although she felt more in control of the daughter of Chaos, she didn't allow her full rein.

Thankfully, Sibiet calmed himself and splayed his fingers on the bench, his copper gaze cooling as he regarded her. "And what is my role, Elora. What will you have me do?"

Elora had been waiting for an opportune time to ask him. The job she had in mind for the pair of Shadojaks wasn't one they would relish. Sibiet especially, yet she couldn't find a reason not to tell them now.

"Neptula has begun attacking Ragna and his force of Vikings in the Arctic. Somehow she knows of their mission to kill Hades and has attempted to hinder them along the coast," Elora explained, meeting each of the Shadojak's gazes. "I've sent a huge contingent of the Dark Army north to aid them but I feel they will need more. I wish for you both to join them in cutting through Hades' demons and help destroy Hades."

"Working with the Dark Army?" Sibiet growled, his temper rising once again.

Elora nodded. "Working with, alongside and joining the very darkness which our order has sworn against, for the past few thousands of years. It is the only way we will defeat them. Weakest is already there. He's meeting up with Ragna, Ejan and Grimwolf. But they will welcome any help from us."

"And what of you?" Hashim asked, his slender fingers grasping his spear which was perpetually in his hands. "Will you not come with us to lead your father's army?"

Elora shook her head. "They are my army, not my father's. But no, Dethtil may attack the Keep at any moment and with the threat from Neptula, I must use whatever I have left to defend the waterways."

"Not to mention, Volcaneus," Bray offered. "Smoke from his volcanoes have been spotted in the Antarctic. The heat is already melting the ice and snow and flooding the oceans with fresh water."

"The only trouble is, the Shadowlands don't stretch as far as the Antarctic," Elora explained, grasping Brays hand. "So I will be going there alone." She felt Bray's grip tighten around her own and knew he hated the thought of it. She also hated the prospect of being away from Bray, but there was nothing they could do. Besides, she would have Grycul with her and Volcaneus was a lonely god; he had no army.

"And Drifid's message?" Sibiet asked, his lips curling in disgust at saying her former Shaigun's name.

The message was delivered that morning by a scrawharpy. A small piece of parchment tied to the bird's leg with hasty words scribbled in ink.

"The takwich which has taken Drifid's body has warned that Neptula has begun her attack against the

Empire. Her forces, which include an army of skagwangles, water dragons and everything else the seas and oceans has to throw at us - including leviathans - have begun a campaign against the mainland."

"And the traitor Flek has asked for your help?" Hashim asked.

"He has," Bray answered. "He has called a ceasefire between the Empire and the Dark Army. But Drifid also warned that Flek has orders, that if the chance of killing Elora arises, it shall be taken."

Sibiet shook his head, the vein at the side of his temple throbbing with anger. "Treacherous bastard," he spat.

"I agree with you," Bray said, "although our duty is still towards the Empire and its people. That is why I will be leading a force against this onslaught. We will not expose Elora to the threat."

"And now that Bray has a soul reaver," Elora added, stroking her fiancée's arm, "he'll be able to harvest memories from the sea creatures and find out where Neptula is lurking."

"But if Elora goes alone, she will be exposed to Volcaneus," Hashim remarked, solemnly.

"We, all of us will be exposed to threats," Elora replied, hearing the sorrow in her voice. She hated putting anybody in danger. "My own should be no less than anyone else's. And there is still a chance that The Green Man will come to our aid. Although, I have yet to see proof that he even exists."

"He exists," Zilabeth informed her as she came to join them, lifting her welding goggles from her face.

"But he's a god of the spring. He'll come soon enough, we're on the cusp of the seasons changing."

"I hope you're right," Elora said, treating the inventor to a sad smile. "There's already too much at stake."

She rose from the table and began to pace away from the group, frustration rising as she began to walk around the fighter plane. "I can't afford to wait any longer. I'll leave for the Antarctic as soon as I'm satisfied that the Keep is ready for Dethtil's attack."

"We have it under control," Captain Brindle reassured her. "The fortifications of the walls and portcullis have been finished. We have GPMG's mounted on every turret and armed guards surrounding the perimeter. We have also made contingency plans, should the walls fail the keep." Captain Brindle rose from the table and nodded towards the huge hangar doors that were the porthole between Rams Keep and the Shadowlands. "An evacuation strategy has been set up – all soldiers, Earth-born, Thean or Dark, have been drilled in how to retreat with the civilian population, through here and then the porthole shall be sealed."

"Very good, Captain," Elora praised Brindle. "Then there is little more I can do here." She motioned for Bray to follow her and said goodbye to the rest of the group. "I'll see you all when I return," she said. Then lead Bray away as they linked arms and strode between the machines and dismantled vehicles to the end of the plateau.

"I don't…" Bray began once they were alone, but Elora placed a finger to his lips to silence him.

"We've been through this already," she said, pulling his arm around her shoulder and clutching it tight. "I need you to fight the sea creatures and to seek out where Neptula is hiding. Once I've dealt with Volcaneus, she will be next on my list. And with her death, I will free Ethea."

"But what if Volcaneus succeeds? What if he," Bray glanced away, pain forcing his words through a strained jaw, "kills you?"

Elora knew the risks. Volcaneus was a full god, not merely a demigod like herself. And although he worked alone, he had the strength to push and grow volcanoes anywhere in the world. A being with that strength wasn't to be taken lightly.

"I won't let him."

She offered Bray a reassuring smile as she turned his face to hers. "There's too much at stake should I fail." The moss-green eyes that stared back were sparkling with anxiety. "And Death himself couldn't stop me from marrying you."

"No truer words were ever said," Bray whispered, treating her to a false smile. "If you die it will kill me."

"Then I won't get myself killed."

She put her hands either side of his face and stood on her toes to reach his lips. "I'll be back soon enough. Just mind you don't get yourself injured." Then she kissed him, tasting the remnants of honey. "I want my Elf boy back in one piece."

"It's a deal," he said and kissed her more passionately. When they pulled apart she noticed that his smile wasn't as false as before, although still some way from meeting his eyes.

Grycul cut through the dusty landscape, her shadow skimming over the dry cracked plains of the

Shadowlands. Elora lay in the saddle, lying flat against the slender neck with her face pressed into the scales. The tears she had shed at leaving Bray had dried to her cheeks as she pushed all concepts of failure from her mind. She would be coming back. The thought of not seeing him again would be a burden that may get her killed. Instead she stared at the way ahead. Watching the black jagged mountains appear on the horizon and grow steadily closer. Tempting that other her to come forward and guide her actions, her emotions and will. Yet that darker Elora, the one they called the Queen of Darkness, had grown closer to her since the worlds had joined and now lay teetering beneath the surface. The daughter of Chaos was as easy to slip into, as putting her hand into a well worn glove. Even the dragon sensed her change. Grycul's mind being more inclined to the more destructive part of her, purred with pleasure and seemed to gain more speed.

"Faster," Elora ordered eagerly. The thrill of the hunt heightening her senses as she anticipated the kill. The dragon responded, tucking her form into a more slimline shape as they flew as far south as the Shadowlands allowed.

A wall of fire formed the barrier where her father's creation ended. The very fabric of red dust and molten rock bending in a way that made her feel dizzy, looking at it. A kaleidoscope of red and black shapes fizzling into one another as if fighting for the same space.

Elora dug her heels into Grycul's flanks and the dragon folded her wings tight to her body as they dived through the strange phenomenon. Feeling a sludgy tug of heat attempt to gain a hold on them before they broke through.

Cold air struck Elora's body as they appeared on the other side. Grey clouds above a dark ocean meeting her gaze as Grycul screamed at the fresh sky. The transition from a hot dry climate to a freezing wet one was unpleasant as both she and her dragon fought to climb above the dull vapour.

Grycul screeched once more as they levelled high above the clouds, the air becoming dry once again yet the moisture which had clung to the dragon's scales had turned to ice, even though the sun glistened off it. Elora concentrated on keeping her body warm. Folding her cloak tightly around herself as she considered the fight ahead, the thought sending pulses of heat through her veins.

Having fire in your blood had its advantages, she mused as she willed Grycul to fly faster. She only wished that Volcaneus didn't possess one of the devices that prevented her from becoming smoke.

Up ahead the clouds began to dissipate until only the clear blue sky reflected from the calm waters below. Was Neptula down there? No, Elora guessed. The Sea Witch would be in the northern hemisphere, throwing her armies against the Empire and the Vikings in the Arctic. She had underestimated Elora, not believing that she would attempt to stop Volcaneus from spreading his vents from the ocean floor and melting the polar ice. Elora only wished that she too didn't underestimate the god, yet doubt wouldn't win this battle.

"Get out of my head," she screamed, pushing the negative emotion aside. Doubt belonged to that other her, the lesser, weaker girl who put love above lust – who put honour above chaos. There was no room for her here.

Up ahead she noticed a single column of black smoke rising from an outcrop of ice. The thick white cliffs of glaciers protruding out of the ocean to form the coast of the Antarctic.

"There," she spoke to Grycul, "head for the smoke. That's where our prey will be." And prey is what he was, thought Elora. Nothing could defeat the Daughter of Chaos.

Grycul felt the excitement and plummeted to the water's surface, gliding above the white foaming waves as they tore towards the sheets of ice.

Dark water gave way to the solid white mass of the land, Grycul's imposing shadow spreading out in an elongated shape as the low sun stretched the form to that more akin to the grumpkin. It sprang forwards and shot away as it projected over the sharp lumps and ice formations that littered the untouched landscape; scaring a pair of polar bears who bounded away from the large flying beast, unused to feeling a threat from something bigger than themselves.

Ahead, the column of smoke spiralled from the pristine scenery, blotting the white barren land and marking where a volcano had pushed up from Ethea's crust. As they grew nearer the wide circular vent began to take shape. Reaching up into the sky, taller than most mountains it spewed molten rock. It made a thunderous rumble as magma bubbled and spat in its filling basin. Spewing glowing liquid from the land's open wound as it ran down the sides to form a river of red, snaking along the ice. Either side of the lava, the ice instantly became steam; forming warm clouds that rose as grey vapour before becoming rain. Elora watched a bus-sized clump of ice, that was probably hundreds of years old, suddenly melt and form a large puddle. Joining other bodies of water as it flowed into a widening stream which was rapidly becoming a river itself.

Elora steered Grycul above the volcano, flying through the smoke and heat to find the god who had created it. Yet she felt he wasn't there. There was nothing living other than the bubbling pot of the world's life-blood below them; spitting huge clumps of liquid rock in an attempt at striking them.

Feeling her frustration rising, Elora broke from the smoke and rose higher into the forming clouds. Volcaneus was elsewhere, if he was even here at all.

They circled the area, scanning the barren ground until Grycul's keen eyes spotted a mountain in the distance - a single grey blot that barely rose from the horizon. She had no proof that the god of volcanos was there, but where else would they search in a place that appeared the same in all directions?

It didn't take them long to cover the ground. The mountain beginning to take shape as they drew nearer. Snow dusting of its peak to flutter down to the snow below. The other her may have called it beautiful, in a poignant if not lonely way. She, however, thought it was how she saw it. Cold, boring and as good a place as any to do battle. With plenty of room to spread Chaos.

When they reached the peak, Grycul completed a circle around the white cap before spiralling down. Searching out anything of interest in the grey rock, but saw nothing. Elora was about to look for somewhere else to search when movement caught her eye.

Below them, a lone figure clad in dark robes raised its head to regard them. Its face hidden beneath a hood as it watched them loom closer. It didn't seem panicked; it didn't show any signs that it felt anything more than a mild interest before slowly walking away.

"No, you don't," Elora screamed as she turned Grycul into a vertical dive, heading straight for the robed figure. It had to be Volcaneus. Yet before they reached him, the god had sauntered into a narrow cave, disappearing from view.

Irritated, Elora gripped tightly to Grycul as she struck the ground, the impact shaking loose rocks from the mountain and dislodging snow.

"Come on out and show yourself, Volcaneus," Elora bellowed into the cave. Her echo bounced around the landscape, breaking away until it became nothing. "Volcaneous!"

Grycul padded closer to the mouth of the cave and craned her head inside, but the crack was barely wide enough to fit in more than the tip of her nose.

Projecting her wishes to the dragon's mind, Elora ordered the beast to fill the cave with fire.

Grycul's flanks suddenly filled out as she screamed into the crack, spewing forth white flames that crackled as it scorched the rock and filled the cave.

Nothing living could have survived that, Elora surmised as she jumped from Grycul's back. Even immortals would have wilted under the god-created fire. Yet Volcaneus was the god of Volcanos. Most probably he was at home with the heat.

Elora slipped the soul reaver from the smuggler's pouch and crept closer to the cave entrance. Placing her hand against the blackened rock she stared into the darkness beyond. He wasn't coming out, so she needed to go in. She gave Grycul a nod, telling the beast to remain here, and felt the dragon's own frustration at being left by her master.

"If I get killed, tear the mountain apart to reach him," Elora ordered, stroking the dragon's chin, "and make it a painful end."

She turned to face the entrance and leading with her blade, squeezed inside the cave.

Shuffling deeper into the body of the rock, she left behind the world of snow, feeling the warmth that Grycul had supplied with her breath, seeping away. She had expected the guts of the mountain to be black but light filtered down from a crack high up in the cave ceiling. A single ray of daylight that pierced the gloom to reveal a widening chamber. An old tree root system clung to the walls, the ancient wood frozen in thick limbs as they formed a leafless tree that had at one time grown from the rock itself. It was funny how life found the strangest of places to strive to grow. Now it was as lifeless as the grainy matter it was anchored too.

She slouched out of the narrow tunnel and gripped her sword in both hands. Levelling it at the robed figure who stood with his back to her, a foot taller with red hands pressed against the wall as he began to chant.

The words which he was reciting were as old as the world itself. An ancient language like the words which made up the Eversong – a language spoken by the gods. And as Elora listened to his deep dulcet tones, she noticed that the veins in his hands pulsed with each syllable, a glowing light that passed from his red flesh into the rock where it passed deeper into the mountain.

"Volcaneus?" Elora probed, stepping closer to the god.

The figure continued to chant, yet inclined its head and Elora saw the outline of a red chin and a mottled cheek. "By the order of the Shadojak, yield," she ordered.

She thought it strange that she would give him the opportunity to yield. What did she care for how the other her liked to do things? Yet she didn't feel as irritated as she guessed she should. Maybe she was becoming more like the other Elora than she wanted.

The figure paused his chanting and began to make other strange sounds and it took a moment for Elora to realise that he was chuckling.

"Spawn of Chaos," he said as he slowly turned to face her, "a Shadojak?"

He reached for the edges of his hood and slipped it from his head. Red mottled skin covered his slender face and scalp. Eyes as crimson as her own stared back at her. A hooked nose curled over thin lips which twisted into a sad smile. "Yield?" he asked.

Elora didn't know whether he offered her the same chance she gave him or was simply questioning her reasoning for giving him the opportunity. She guessed at the latter. "Maybe the term is a little redundant," she said, shrugging her shoulders, "It's just a formality. I'm still going to kill you."

Volcaneus calmly placed his hands together, palm to palm as if in prayer. "I see you have your father's sword. Tell me, is it true that you killed Solarius?"

"Yes," she answered, seeing no point in denying it.

"And you think me as easy to Kill?"

Again, Elora shrugged, her father hadn't been easy to kill. The only consoling thought was that it had been the weaker Elora who had wielded the blade that had ended her father. Had it been herself she may have found the experience easier.

"You know, Solarius and I had worked together at times," Volcaneus volunteered. "He had a real passion for fire and ash, much like myself in that regard - although he seemed to enjoy the pain and suffering it brought others. I on the other hand, saw only the beauty of rendering the landscape clean. Returning the ground to a more purer form."

"And Neptula?" Elora demanded, "Why are you working with the Sea Witch? All she wants is to flood the world and make Ethea an entire ocean."

Volcaneus tuned his hands so they were palms up, fingers forming bowls, or, as Elora realised, imaginary volcanos. "I remember a time when the world had been beneath the waves. A clean sterile planet where I vented the world's blood from the ocean bed and shaped the crusts and plateaus that would one day become vast landmasses," he said, smiling as he spoke as if the memory evoked a more happier time. "I care not one speck of dust for Neptula herself, but the thought of wiping the slate clean, starting again with the world is one that I find most pleasing."

"And all those lives you will have lost? All those innocents who never asked for any of this?" Elora demanded, not understanding why she suddenly felt compassion for others where she only wanted destruction before. Unless she was getting precious about the chaos which would be spread by another's hand.

"Life will always find a way," he replied, then indicated the dead tree which had grown from the rock.

"And it will return to the lands. Once the lands have been reborn."

"But why side with Neptula? Why not simply do these things yourself?"

Volcaneus shook his head. "There is no reason, other than Neptula asked. I care not for life, yet I also care nothing for death. I'm only a conduit for the world's blood and the flowing rock which must be vented."

Elora steadied her thumping heart as she rested the tip of her blade on the ground. A show that she wouldn't attack the god. "Then I ask you to reconsider. Stop this madness. Cease the melting of the Antarctic ice."

"I cannot," Volcaneus replied. "I have given my word to Neptula."

Elora's anger had been steadily rising as she watched the passive calmness settle over the god. His features settling into a serene state as he pressed his hands once again to the rock.

"Then you leave me no choice," she snapped, irritation driving her anger as she brought her blade up and launched herself at the god.

The sword passed harmlessly through Volcaneus. His form becoming smoke and flowing over the sharp metal to reform once the blade struck rock.

"You waste your time, daughter of Chaos," the god informed her, "I will not fight you, nor will I give you the opportunity to kill me."

Elora screamed in frustration as she swiped her blade through him, yet the sword passed through smoke again. Cut after cut, blow following blow, Elora used every fibre of strength she could muster but her opponent offered no more substance than the smoke that she knew only too well was impossible to hurt. Unless…

Becoming smoke herself, Elora smouldered into a fury. Twisting herself into a heat filled emotion and threw herself upon the god. She felt herself clashing against him, sensing the hot embers which were a part of her attempting to devour his flesh. Yet when he became smoke she could do no more harm as she had before. Even less so.

The blackness which was his very essence, coalesced as it merged between and over her, curling and hooking, dragging and balling as it tugged parts of her away. And before she had chance to fully reform he had imbued a portion of her into the very rock of the mountain.

Pain engulfed her as she became flesh once again. Fire erupted in her arm as she reformed, the limb was encased within the rock. Her arm ending at the elbow, the unseen portion merging into the cold solid matter.

In a wave of panic, she attempted to tear her arm free. The sharp agony which tortured her being as she did so, brought tears to her eyes. She had the full crushing weight of the mountain pressing down on her.

"I did warn you," Volcaneus said, thumb and finger stroking his chin as he watched her struggle. "Now you will witness the birth of a new vent. You will be part of the beauty that will wipe this landscape clean."

Although tortured with pain, Elora curled her fingers into a fist and punched the god in the face.

He began to chuckle as her hand passed through smoke once again, the movement sending a heightened jolt of pain through her arm.

"You can turn to smoke and escape your prison," Volcaneus suggested, speaking the very thing Elora was about to do. "Although your arm is forever locked in the rock. You will re-materialise without it. Now if you'll excuse me, I've a volcano to build."

Feeling her pulse quicken as her heart hammered inside her chest, Elora blinked the tears from her eyes. She reached out and grasped Volcaneus by the arm.

"Please," she pleaded, feeling every bit the weaker her which she now knew had taken over. The daughter of Chaos shrinking away as if the mere thought of being trapped would kill her. "Don't do this. You can kill me but end your pact with Neptula. The world doesn't deserve it."

She felt a pang of hope as Volcaneus frowned. His brow creased up as he considered her words.

"I am sorry, but I gave my word. I will not go back on it," he said, then simply stepped into the rock itself, leaving her alone.

"Please!" Elora shouted, the sudden movement causing another wave of pain. "If I kill her will you stop? If I Kill Neptula will you end this madness?" Her words were met with silence. She guessed that wherever Volcaneus was now, he was too deep into the mountain for him to hear her. But then a deep rumble reached her ears through the solid matter, to echo around the cave.

"The deal will end with Neptula's life, should you somehow escape and manage to kill her."

"I will kill her," Elora shouted, yet didn't know how she would escape without losing an arm. "Can you hear me? I will kill her!" But there was no reply.

Fighting against the pain, Elora leaned back, placing her head to the rock as she attempted to link minds with Grycul. She instantly felt the dragon's presence as she raked at the rock. The huge talons scouring channels into the icy surface yet not penetrating enough to do any real damage. Elora projected calmness to Grycul, it wouldn't do any good her getting worked up into a frenzy. She guessed that if she needed to, the dragon could melt a path through the cave with her white fire, but it would take time, perhaps a few days and by then the entire mountain would have become a volcano.

-Think! Elora goaded herself. How was she going to get out of this predicament?

The pain in her arm had subsided to a dull ache. Pins and needles fizzled from her elbow down to her fingertips. She knew that the nerves in her muscles and skin were growing numb with the lack of oxygen.

Staring at the join, she could see where her flesh met rock, her arm joining with the cave wall where no two materials should collide. This is what must have happened to some of the people when the worlds merged together. How awful it must have been. At least she had the opportunity to reduce to smoke and live, albeit with the loss of her arm as she reformed. But she didn't want to lose her arm – she was attached to it. Along with her father's sword which she guessed was still attached to her fingers somewhere inside the dense rock.

After a few moments of futile thinking her mind drifted to Bray. Would he still love her if she was missing a limb? She guessed he would. His love for her went beyond that of the physical being. She felt a fool for even considering it. Yet fighting Neptula would be a great deal harder with only one arm. And if she lost her soul reaver, she would need to gain another.

Suddenly her thumb ring began to spin, the green band turning above the elven words and the runes began to glow. She spun her ring some more to create the whispering song that sang of the love that would outlive the eternal sigh. Somewhere in the world, most probably at the coast or river, Bray was about to do battle with the sea creatures which Neptula was sending against the mainland. She hoped he would be safe, she prayed that he wouldn't get hurt.

She stared at her buried arm. Calming her own nerves as she prepared to let it go. Attempting to reason with herself that her life and that of the people of Ethea was more important. If Bray was with her, he would tell her to turn to smoke. At least she had Volcaneus's word that if she killed Neptula, he would halt his mission at melting the polar ice. The world still had a chance of surviving.

She brushed a thumb beneath the joint she would lose. Working herself up to do the grisly task ahead. 'If you've made your mind up to do a task – you just had to act it out'. She was sure she had heard those words before, although it was little comfort now.

She blinked the tears from her eyes and glanced at her thumb ring, wishing that it would give her the strength she needed.

When the glow of the runes dulled once again, she noticed that the light in the room had shifted as the sun moved around the mountain. The beam of light now beginning to fall on the dead tree that grew out of the rock. Revealing warped and cracked wood which at some point in the distant past had be a living organism.

If she didn't escape from this cave before Volcaneus pushed molten magma through it, she would be experiencing the same fate as the tree.

Then as the light beam rose she was sure she caught movement further up, where the skeletal branches brushed the ceiling. She heard it groan as if attempting to stretch towards the light. The wood bending itself to gather more of the ultra violet which was precious to all living things. Was the tree still alive?

There came a sudden flurry of rustling as the top portion of the trunk moved. Two small holes appearing above a round knot. Below which a gap yawned open. It was a mouth.

As she gazed at the strange tree, a face began to appear in the folds and cracks of the very wood it was made from. The shadows of small leaves fluttered into eyebrows and thick hair, the dark knot shifted and protruded as if becoming a nose and the rim of the gap thickened into cracked lips. The dark eyes glared at her before softening to a milky white and the mouth formed a smile.

"You must be Elora," the tree said, its voice sounding as old as time itself. Each word full of splintered groans.

Elora's smile matched that of the rooted being before her. "And you must be The Green Man."

The tree inclined its head in a slow nod, branches of hair snapping as he made the motion. "Winter has begun in this part of the world, the sun will set permanently," he groaned as he reached a knobbly finger into an ear and withdrew a frozen worm that had long ago died in there. He held it up to the light for inspection before putting it into his mouth, crushing the dead insect between square teeth.

"Crunchy," he informed her.

18

Leviathan's End

Bray parried the trident and stepped into his attacker, driving an elbow into his bare stomach and bowling the skagwangle onto its back. Tentacles writhed in the air as the creature attempted to scramble up, but before it had chance, Bray placed a foot on its slippery abdomen and drove his blade through its chest.

The god-created steel bit into the green heart, silencing its final beat and harvesting the skagwangles memories. The soul licked up the reaver before the single flame was absorbed into the sword. This was the eleventh soul he had taken that morning, each kill along the Thames had given him an insight into how these skagwangles moved and attacked, each memory revealing their weaknesses and their plans.

A shadow passed above. Instinctively Bray ducked and rolled before a large water dragon struck the concrete river bank, rendering a vicious crack where he had just been. He spun away from the sharp talons and dodged the arrows that had been loosed from the rider sat atop the flying beast. He was ready to swipe the legs from under the dragon, when rifle fire erupted from the other side of the Thames.

Bullets struck the glistening scales, ripping through flesh as the creature screamed. Bray wasted no time in driving his blade into its heart, before pulling back and allowing the huge mass of sea flesh to fall to the ground. The rider had already succumbed to his wounds, a large bullet hole leaking blood from its forehead while a larger hole engulfed the back of the cranium.

He waved a thanks to the imperial guards on the other side of the river, who had been firing from a wreck of a warehouse. But his attention was soon snatched away as the fighting further up river suddenly intensified. A large leviathan had lodged itself between two crumbling buildings as it reached out towards Tower Bridge. Flying around the bridge were many water dragons, their riders raining arrows down upon the soldiers on the historic structure.

Bray knew that arrows and tridents were no match against rifles and heavy guns, yet the imperial guards were heavily outnumbered and the colossal wriggling beast would flatten the entire bridge once its wide appendages were close enough. Then Neptula would gain access further into the city.

He turned to the contingent of soldiers he'd brought with him through the Shadowlands: an entire battalion of the Dark Army, and signalled for them to advance on the bridge. The bulworgs, grimbles and men ran in violent glee. Raising sharpened steel, rifles clubs and claws as they clambered over the battle strewn ground. Bray ran to his bike and swung a leg over the machine before kicking it into life.

The engine roared as he wound the throttle back, the wheel spinning dirt and loose stones behind as it propelled him further up river. The steam bike was a wonder of engineering. As were the many other vehicles that Zilabeth had brought back to life. They numbered well into the hundreds. Adapted trucks and four-wheel drive cars were spread out around the coasts of Britain. Being driven by trained men and grumpkins, they were an awesome asset that covered the ground quicker than any horse. The cleverness and ingenuity Zilabeth had shown in building them was only marginally outweighed by the new machine she had adapted.

Furghan was mesmerised by the sight before him. As was Fosse who had forgotten the empty rifle in his hands; his finger still pressing uselessly upon the trigger. From the crumbling building, they watched as the Dark Army cut through the sea creatures. Giant vicious dogs and trolls, clashing against the water dragons and skags, men, dwarfs and ugly beings with baggie skin, brutally clattering against ranks of Neptula's forces. And commanding them was a single man that had ridden in on a motorbike. How that was even possible when every other machine in the entire world had died along with electricity months ago, Furghan couldn't say.

"I thought the daughter of Chaos and the Dark Army were our enemies," Fosse questioned, finally realising that his rifle had run out of bullets and began to change the magazine.

"Aye," Furghan agreed, "they are. Elora was the one who merged the worlds together and killed the old Emperor."

Fosse scratched his head, his gaze not once veering away from the battle below. "Then why are they helping us?"

Furghan shrugged. "Neptula wants to flood the world – I guess that would include drowning the Empire and the Dark Army both." He watched as one of the large dogs leapt upon the back of a passing water dragon and sunk its fangs into the rider. A troll-like creature below, with tusks sprouting from the corners of its mouth, reached out and bore the dragon to the ground where it repeatedly battered at its head with a wooden club. He felt disgusted at the sight of all those hideous beings attacking with such violence, yet felt equally glad that he wasn't on the receiving end. The Dark Army was indeed gruesomely dark. "Remember," Furghan warned, "if the daughter of Chaos shows up, you're to shoot on sight."

"If she shows up I'll let her kill the leviathan first," Fosse huffed. "I don't see any way we're going to prevent it from ripping down Tower Bridge this time."

"No," Furghan grinned as he scratched his beard. "But the overgrown bugger won't be going back out to sea."

"How's that?"

"About now the guards should have closed off the dam up river, so when the tide goes out the Thames will drain quicker than the kraken can retreat."

Fosse's brows creased up. "But wouldn't that trap it here?" he asked pointing out of the window. "Where it can do more damage."

"It'll trap the bitch here alright. But without the support of the water, a beast of that size will choke under its own weight. It isn't meant to survive out in the open air."

"And what will happen if your plan doesn't work?"

"It will."

"But if it doesn't?"

Furghan glared at the boy. It was hard enough to convince himself that it would work, but he'd be buggered if he couldn't make at least one person believe in him. "It will."

"We'll soon find out," Fosse said, as he pointed at the river.

The water line had drastically begun to drop. The concrete docks and banks revealing thick green sludge and mud which hadn't seen the light of day for years. The water dragons and skagwangles had begun their retreat with the tide as it began to flow back out to sea. But the kraken couldn't.

"It's working," Furghan said excitedly as the beast struggled in the mud, unable to wriggle back and only succeeding in wedging himself further into the mire.

Fuelled by panic the huge sea creature attempted to raise its squid-like head as it screamed into the sky. Tentacles smashing back down into the black stream that the Thames had become. And with no water there to buoy its gigantic body, it sagged under its own weight. The eye closest to them, rolling around in fright as it began to understand its own plight.

The retreating skagwangles realised what was happening and began to return to the beast, steering their water dragons as they circled above, giving it protection as it thrashed in the sinking mud. The Dark Army took the opportunity presented and launched an attack on the kraken.

The closer of the imperial guards began a volley of fire, shooting the beast in its flanks as swords and axes rained blow after blow on the leviathan.

"Take the skags out," Furghan commanded as he brought the sight of his rifle to his eyes and took aim. But the water dragons were too swift and training the creatures into the cross hairs, long enough to make the shot, proved difficult.

Beside him, Fosse fired several times but hadn't managed to hit anything.

"What's that noise?" he suddenly asked, cocking his head to the side.

Furghan pulled the rifle from his face and strained to hear beyond the sounds of battle. He couldn't hear anything other than the screams and shouts at first, but then he picked up a droning sound. Like the whirring of an old plane.

Through the clouds a black spot appeared and rapidly grew larger.

"Impossible," he heard himself say as he watched a plane drop from the sky to sweep between the towers of Tower Bridge.

"It's…it's…it's…" Fosse spluttered excitedly.

"A Spitfire!" Furghan finished, feeling every bit as shocked as Fosse appeared.

They both leaned out of the window frame as the fighter plane banked along the curve of the river, bright flashes opening-up from the wings as it fired at the water dragons.

The circling beasts scattered as the plane flew above the leviathan, two lines of bullets ripping and tearing chunks of flesh from the squid-like body as it made the pass.

Skagwangles were fighting to control the dragons they were riding. Turning them towards the new attack and firing arrows but the Spitfire was too swift and the only shaft that struck the fuselage snapped on impact.

Fosse whooped with joy, his face wide open with delight as the fighter plane suddenly rose high above the London skyline, sharply banked around and descended once again to make another pass.

Furghan could have nipped himself to ensure that he wasn't in the middle of a crazy dream. The scene before him was surreal – a Spitfire in a dog-fight above Tower Bridge, fighting against dragons and giant sea creatures. This was something to tell his grandchildren, if he ever had any.

The heavy machine guns that fired from the sleek craft, cut into the leviathan once again, snagging a water dragon in the same attack. It came low enough for him to get a good view of the cockpit and he was surprised to see a woman pilot, hair billowing out behind flying goggles. And sat directly behind her, face pushed up to the glass window was what he could only describe as a troll. Its pug-like face squashed tight to the glass with a thick tongue poking between a wide grin.

"The Dark Army is all kinds of crazy," Fosse commented, witnessing the same view of the cockpit.

Furghan nodded. "I'm just glad we're not fighting them."

On the third pass the water dragons fled. The fighter plane chasing them back down the muddy Thames to follow the tide back out to sea.

A cheer went up from the Dark Army and the imperial guards alike, and as one they pushed onto the dying kraken. Men and monsters wading through the mud or dropping planks to cover the gap between river bank and beast as they climbed onto the struggling giant.

Like a nest of ants covering a fallen fruit, they scrambled around the thrashing mass of meat.

Fosse climbed out onto the ledge and began to lower himself down. "Come on," he shouted as he dropped to the thick tree that had merged with the bricks below. "I'm not missing out on this."

Furghan was about to call the lad back when he paused. He had to admit, Fosse had a point. Spitfires and dragons, swords and monsters with Tower Bridge as the back drop. This was something special, like a monumental point in history which will be talked about for generations - and he wanted to be a part of it.

"Wait up," he shouted after Fosse as he slung his rifle over his back and began to climb out of the building.

Bray leapt across the planking that the imperials had laid between the bank and the leviathan. The wood bouncing with each foot fall but he allowed his momentum to carry him on as he jumped the final few steps onto the rubbery flesh of the creature. His sword was already drawn as he pushed through the throng of men who were hard at work: shooting, striking, slashing and battering the beast. Dark green puss oozed from a thousand different wounds, running slick down the skin and making a slippery mess.

The tentacles raised sluggishly, the strength leaving the creature as its head sunk lower into the mire. Bray scaled towards the top as it trumpeted a frightened scream, the movement throwing a few of the soldiers from its body but many more joined the melee.

Sliding to a stop midway between the leviathan's eyes, Bray drove his blade into the creature's flesh. The soul reaver slicing easily through the skin until it stopped at the hilt. Then using both hands to grip below the pommel, Bray began to work his sword up and down in a sawing motion; hacking a long gash open and revealing the surface of the white skull beneath.

Blood bubbled to the surface. The hot green liquid steaming as it spilled around him, bathing his boots in viscous fluid. Yet as he raised his sword to strike through the thick porous bone, the gap closed again, the rubbery skin squeezing back together.

A young imperial guard saw what he was attempting and scrambled to help. He yanked a spear from where it had been left, imbedded in the creatures wobbling flesh and thrust it into the wound Bray had created. His face grimaced with the effort as he wedged it in deep and pulled it down, levering the gash wide open again. To his aid came another imperial guard. This one of senior years with a large greying beard.

"On three, Fosse," he shouted above the noise. "One…Two…Three!"

And as the pair of guards revealed the skull once again, Bray reversed his grip on his sword and slammed it as hard as he could through the thick cranium.

Bone splintered to either side of the god-created steel, the tortured metal screeching as it punctured through and bit deep into the beast's brain.

Instantly the leviathan went rigid. Its tentacles stretching out in a sudden rictus jolt, throwing men and soldiers from its body. Then all at once the tentacles dropped.

The thick appendages slammed into the mud and banks, a couple of them bouncing once or twice before settling and the entire beast sagged then went still.

Bray pulled his sword from the leviathan's skull and searched for something to wipe the blood from the blade. He caught the pair of imperial guards regarding him with curious fascination.

"Thanks for your help," Bray said, offering the older man his hand.

The bearded guard shook it firmly. "No, it is us that should be thanking you. If you hadn't have come when you did – especially with your Spitfire, the kraken would have pulled down Tower Bridge."

Bray raised an eyebrow. "Kraken?"

"He means the leviathan," the younger soldier corrected.

"Aye, leviathan. This damned creature was what sunk my boat."

"And killed my father."

Bray stared at the unlikely duo. The pair of them seeming out of place wearing imperial uniform mixed up with British Army fatigues. "How do you know that it was this leviathan that did those things?" he asked.

The older soldier's mouth dropped open. "There are more of them?"

"Neptula had sixteen. The remaining fifteen could be anywhere in the world."

"That's not good," he stated, staring back down the sludge filled Thames as if expecting another colossus beast to come up.

Unable to find anything to wipe his blade, that wasn't covered with green gore or blood, Bray said farewell and began to make his way to the river bank when the bearded one grasped his arm.

"What are we supposed to do with this?" he asked, waving his arm over the giant carcass.

Bray shrugged. "There isn't much you can do. The beast is well and truly stuck. I'm surprised the river dropped so rapidly, though. You'd have thought the leviathan would have retreated with the tide."

The younger soldier, Fosse, slapped the other on the shoulder, jolting the older man. "No, it was the Captain's idea to dam the river as the tide began to turn and let the run-off wash away quicker than the thing could wriggle."

"Then it is I who have you to thank for trapping it," Bray stated.

"Keep your thanks," the bearded soldier said, shaking the gesture off. "But I don't think it'll be the last we'll see of the sea creatures." He eyed a passing grimble suspiciously and his fingers found the trigger of his rifle. The large ogre wiped blood from one of its tusks before wedging a finger up a nostril and began to root around as if he suspected there was treasure in his nose.

"You're, probably right," Bray agreed, thinking it might be best that he withdrew the Dark Army before tensions rose between the different factions and they began to fight each other. "In the meantime, I'll be chasing them along the coast."

"And what of your Queen? What of this Elora that had murdered the old Emperor and clashed the worlds together?"

Bray halted a passing grumpkin and steered him towards a gathering group of bulworgs, grimbles and other Dark soldiers. "Tell them to pull back to the bridge, we're moving out," he ordered.

The bearded man wrinkled his nose in disgust at the grumpkin, who limped away, holding parts of his face together as he began to gather the troops around.

"Don't believe all you hear," Bray informed the imperial soldiers as he put his back to them. "Elora didn't kill anyone that didn't deserve it. And she will be the one who will save the Empire."

He ambled along the bouncing plank and made his way to his bike, wiping his sword on a rag that he had picked up from the ground. After slipping the blade into his smuggler's pouch he climbed on the bike and kicked it to life.

The Dark Army had now formed into ranks and had begun to march west, towards the coast. In the distance, he heard the Rolls Royce engine of the Spitfire whirring as it made manoeuvres in the sky. The plane had done well. A great asset that he was sure would help when they began their assault against Neptula herself. And with all the memories he was harvesting he had a good idea where she was.

Casting his gaze over the scene, Bray observed the giant sea beast, its body bigger than the buildings around it. Appearing like a mud soaked lump that had been dropped into the once bustling city. The lifeless body sagging into the green sludge that now coated everything, including the imperial guards as they paced around the beast, arguing on how to go about removing it.

Death was an ugly business, Bray thought as he rode away. Even the biggest of creatures couldn't escape it. The great corpse made a hideous sight, dead tentacles splayed in all directions, the wreck of its trunk now a mass of meat with men crawling over it and its remaining eye already going glassy.

He steered his bike along the crumbling bank, weaving between the detritus of buildings, trees and bodies that littered the pathway. He only hoped that Elora was already back at the Keep. Death always seemed to dance close to her and she had a knack of stepping on its toes.

Elora heard the scream from Grycul and felt the frustration the dragon permeated as she thrashed against the rock outside the mountain. Elora projected a calmness to her before she did damage to herself or collapse the cave system. That thought worried her almost as much as the arm that she could no longer feel as it merged with the rock. It was as if she no longer had it. Any feelings ending below the elbow where it met the cave wall.

"I remember when this tree was a sapling," The Green Man offered, his voice sounding aged and full of cracks and groans like the old wood itself. "Such a tiny seed, carried in the mouth of a gull." The milky eyes rolled to the dimming crack in the cave roof. "It was dropped from above and landed here. Spending the next few hundred years frozen above a smudge of dirt." The Green Man shook his fingers and a tiny seed rolled onto the palm of his knobbly hand. "A simple seed like this one," he explained as he slowly stretched out a branch-like arm, the movement making snapping noises that echoed around the confined chamber. He rolled the seed onto the end of a gnarly finger and pressed it into Elora's trapped arm, indenting the skin at the point it met the rock. "But what power such a small little pod has. So much strength and influence held tight inside the little seed."

He applied pressure to the little pip and pushed it into the rock, his index finger growing as it fed the seed deeper into the rock. When he pulled his hand back, the finger had stretched over a foot in length.

The leaves and twigs that made up his hair, rustled as he sank back. The aged face forming a warm smile amongst the knots and crags of his face. "Given time, life will grow almost everywhere, even through the hardest of materials."

Elora, didn't see how something so small could help her. She had hoped the god would have produced a sword or would have had the strength to smash the rock itself.

"We don't have much time," she said. "Volcaneus has already begun turning this mountain into a volcano."

The thick bushes above The Green Man's eyes drew together. "I know, I sense him. Such a lonely existence, but don't you fret, Elora. The seed is already growing; do you feel her? Can you sense the coming of life, the strength and the power?"

Elora had to admit she felt nothing. Yet that could have been because her arm below the elbow was totally numb.

"No," she admitted.

The Green Man smiled. "Patience. Even the rare Alabaster tree, which the Farrosian fairies have made a palace from, started life as a little pip. Like the forest itself."

"Where Prince Dylap is from?"

The ancient tree nodded, the warm smile returning to his lips. "Prince Dylap, a good friend to the forest."

"You know him?" Elora asked, wondering where the little fairy was now.

"I know all," The Green Man replied, raising his hands once again. "Every whisper in the woods, every word that is said, all who touch nature and all that breaths. For I am life."

"Then why didn't you help before?" Elora demanded, attempting to keep the anger from her voice but failing. "You could have stopped the worlds merging."

The Green Man slowly shook his head. "No. Mankind caused the rift in the first place and man merged the worlds back into one. Such short lives, yet so violent. War destruction, death – they are close friends with man. Nature doesn't get involved with such matters. Nature exists to grow and exists to be. I have no kinship with man."

"But you could have prevented all those deaths when the worlds collided," Elora argued. "All that suffering, all that pain."

"Suffering and pain has a part in nature," The Green Man replied. His smile vanishing as he leaned closer to her, seeming to fill the cave as his presence loomed darker, mightier than the frail old tree that he seemed to be only moments before. "Do you not think I feel it every time a tree is chopped. Sense the loss of a friend when an oak is felled, butchered or hacked? Do I not suffer the loss when an entire forest is burned and cleared?" His being filled the cave, his branches suddenly thickening, tortured wood groaning in protest. "Do you not think I choke when man spills chemicals onto the earth, when he fills the air with poisons?"

He was so close, his face directly in front of hers, that Elora could see directly into his gaping mouth, heard the wooden teeth scraping against each other as he spoke and smell the rotten mulch from within.

"Nature would thrive so much better with man removed from this world," he continued. "And given enough time, man will destroy itself and solve my problems for me."

Elora cringed away from the wrath that The Green Man was imposing on her. It was as if he saw her as the very epitome of mankind, along with all its faults. She thought he might kill her, crush her against the very rock she wanted to escape from. His mouth yawned wider as if he would swallow her head, and she caught a glimpse of the skeletal remains of a tiny mammal at the back of his throat – was she to share the same fate?

"Man has been my nemesis since they first broke from the apes, to rape nature to torture my kin. Mankind is my enemy!"

Elora closed her eyes, fear shaking through her and bringing fresh pain from her arm. The jolt forcing a moan through clenched teeth.

"Agh, the tiny seed has begun its journey through life's cycle," The Green Man offered, his voice returning to the old caring being he was before his angry tirade. And when Elora opened her eyes she saw that he had returned to his side of the cave, the warm smile returned to his mouth. The transformation from the raging creature he was only seconds ago making her feel as if she had somehow imagined it. She might have dwelt on that more if it wasn't for the sudden pain that exploded in her buried arm.

A loud groan emitted from the rock and a crack appeared above and below her trapped limb.

"Almost there," The Green Man informed her excitedly.

The cracks widened, the entire cave wall shaking violently as pale green shoots erupted, spraying chippings of rock onto the ground.

The shoots thickened into roots, sprouting leaves as the tendrils coiled in on itself to widen the cracks further.

Elora's arm felt that it was being squeezed between vices, before the pressure abruptly disappeared and she fell to the floor.

For a few shocking moments, she thought her arm had been crushed to the point it had popped off, but as she glanced down, relief flooded her as she saw her arm - fingers still grasping her sword. Pain throbbed through her limb, flames suddenly licking up the wounds, healing the cuts and scratches inflicted by the ordeal.

"Time to go," The Green Man suggested, pointing towards the cave exit. "Once life is in progress, only death will halt it. And I'm not one for death."

Elora felt the tremors shaking the very mountain she was in. The roots still thickening as branches sprang out of the rock.

"You're not coming?" she asked as she slipped her blade away and attempted to get to her feet.

"Not in this form, I am rooted," he replied. "But I will meet you at Rams Keep. We've plenty of things to discuss."

Wondering how The Green Man would be able to travel all that way, she clambered along the shaking cave and squeezed herself through the narrowing walls.

Snow fell around her as her head emerged from the darkness. She needed to use both hands to pull herself free from the mountain as the cave entrance began to close. Rock slamming against rock and sealing it off.

Grycul screamed in pleasure as she came bounding up the slope, almost knocking Elora off her feet as she rubbed her large head against her body.

"We better go before the mountain starts spitting lava," Elora suggested as she climbed upon the dragon's neck and slid into the saddle.

Grycul bunched her legs before springing into the clouds. Her vast wings beating the air as she ascended in the darkening night.

Fatigue consumed Elora as she lay over the saddle horn. She had come to kill Volcaneus but was almost killed herself. At least she had his word that if she somehow defeated Neptula, he would halt his melting of the polar ice.

Red light suddenly brightened behind her and when she cast a glance over her shoulder she saw that the hot magma had erupted from the mountain. Steam was filling the sky as the snow all around it evaporated, followed by the ice below.

Elora knew that they hadn't much time. Ethea's oceans were already beginning to fill with water. It wouldn't be long before the sea levels began to rise and the land masses would begin to shrink.

Before they reached the Shadowlands, the darkness had consumed the night sky. Stars filled the heavens and the wavering veil of the Southern Lights cast its green spiritual show from above. It was beautiful yet as they left it behind to engulf the hot dry lands of her father's creation, Elora felt relief. There was a sad loneliness to the polar regions. A melancholy mood that could only be enjoyed by the lonely, such as Volcaneus.

She let her eyes drift shut, sleep finally catching up with her as she put all her trust into Grycul to take them home.

19

Meeting the Enemy

Snow became more scarce the further north the small group trekked. The once frozen and barren landscape becoming awash with streams and rivers that hadn't see running water for centuries. More than once the party had needed to double-back and find other means for crossing rivers that had become too wide. And it wasn't only the ground that was saturated with liquid. Thick clouds hovered above. Darker than grave soil they loomed into the distance, curtains of grey rain strafing with the battering wind; slamming against them and reaching skin beneath furs and oilskin cloaks. Up ahead, smoke curled skywards from thousands of different locations. Unhindered by the deluge, the black swirling columns fanned out, choking the sun and blanketing the world in a dreary twilight haze.

Jaygen's mother brushed water from her hair before pointing at the smoke. "That's where they'll be," she said as they crested a small rise to reveal a damp peat plain. It had been frozen for years and had lain hidden beneath layers of snow. Now it was open to the elements, running with water and would be as solid as soggy porridge.

Axewell Stump stepped precariously out into the sludge and his foot sank to his knee. "We're not crossing that," he complained, another Viking pulling him back onto the crest. His foot made a galumph sound as he pulled it from the mud.

"What about those rocks?" Fieri asked, nodding towards an outcrop of boulders that lay scattered around the base of a hill.

"I don't know," Axewell admitted, rubbing the tail of his beard. "We'd be high enough for Hades' forces to spot us."

"No," Jaygen offered, forcing his voice to be the deep throaty whisper of Grimwolf. "They wouldn't be expecting us."

"Well, they damn well knew that we came across the sea," Axewell argued, although Jaygen noticed that he didn't direct his voice at him. "There is a spy. How else would Neptula have known to send sirens and skags?"

"Doesn't matter," Ejan intervened, pulling the hood of her cloak over her head. "In a short while there will be an entire army of Northmen marching towards them. They'll feel the ground shake and hear our songs before they see us."

Jaygen rested his fist on the wolf's head pommel of his sword as he stared at the thickening smoke. Then without saying a word, began to stride towards the outcrop of rocks. He didn't look behind him to know that the others would follow. He instinctively knew they would. Over the past couple of days Grimwolf had become a kind of beacon. A leader who the others followed like sheep followed the shepherd. Maybe it was because they thought him a kind of god or a mythical Viking at least. Whatever the reasoning, they still flocked to him like lost lambs. Although Fieri stayed at his heel for quite different reasons.

It had been hard persuading the girl to keep quiet when she was desperate to tell her brother his secret. And it was even harder persuading his mother to let

Fieri come with the scouting party. In the end, his mother had conceded – she had no other choice – and Fieri had sworn to Odin himself that she would keep his secret to the grave.

Fieri skipped ahead of him now. Her lithe form making light work of the tough terrain as she danced from a rock onto the boulders. Every now and again she would pause to give him a smile or wink before leaping ahead. Jaygen found it hard not to watch her and more often than not, found that he was smiling beneath the mask.

"I don't know if I trust that girl," his mother said as she strode beside him. Eyes narrowed at Fieri's back.

"She won't tell anyone," he whispered, making sure no others were in earshot.

"It's not just the secret," Ejan admitted. "What if Shannog's warning is true and that suit of yours is cursed. Grimwolf is forbidden to love."

"It isn't," he hissed, feeling annoyed at the reminder. "If we listened to Shannog long enough, she would have cursed everything."

"Is that what the girl said?"

"No," Jaygen lied. It was, in fact, the very words which Fieri had said when she attempted to steal another kiss from him the previous night. He had held her back and mentioned that he was worried, should the curse be proven true. Once this war was won he would bury the armour in the volt he'd found it in back at Rams Keep. If the suit was cursed, then the curse would be buried along with Grimwolf.

His mother seemed unconvinced but didn't broach the subject anymore. Instead she paced ahead, notching an arrow as she overtook Fieri; treating the younger girl to a glare as she passed. Jaygen was thankful that Ejan was concentrating on the distant smoke and didn't catch the face which Fieri had pulled behind her back. He hoped the fighting would begin soon so the pair wouldn't be fighting each other.

The rocky outcrop rounded the hill, the boulders becoming thick slabs of wet stone before dropping into a large ravine. Water ran deeply in the dip, churning and frothing as it made its way out to sea. Beyond that, lay a land of snow stretching out to the horizon. A single track of footsteps snaked through the otherwise pristine landscape. Then where the footsteps ended, the white blanket abruptly stopped and a thick wall of blackness spread out in the distance.

"There," Ejan pointed as she drew the scouting party closer. "Over the next rise."

Jaygen joined her and stared at the direction she was indicating. "I don't see…" then he saw it and words failed him.

Fin clambered upon the next rock to gain a higher view, his face pinched in confusion. "I don't see anything, Only a blackened land."

As he finished speaking, the blackness suddenly began to glow red, like the smouldering of burning coal. Long tendrils snaked from the dark phenomenon into the snow, instantly turning it to steam.

"It's them," Ejan offered, spreading her bow out to include the land before her.

"Who?" Fieri asked.

Jaygen sighed as he slipped his sword from his scabbard as his mother continued. "Hades and his demons, the fire itself."

He watched Fieri's face as the astonishment dissolved into shock. "That's them? But there's got to be millions of them. Hundreds of millions."

The blackness spread towards them. A multitude of beings made from glowing embers and glistening oil, flames licking at their very flesh as they ambled through the snow, turning it to water. They were loosely human in shape, although some had extra limbs and varied greatly in size. Jaygen even spotted one such creature with two heads sprouting from the same shoulder. Glowing eyes searching the ground as it spat globs of fire from its mouth. The greasy flames struck the white blanket. Melting holes and creating slush.

"Hideous," Fin remarked, shaking his head in disgust. "It's as if Hades couldn't care how they looked when he created them."

"He doesn't," Ejan offered, putting an arrow to her bow and drawing the string. "He wanted numbers enough to melt the north, not for them to appear pretty."

She let go of the arrow and it arced gracefully into the sky before thudding into the closest of the black creatures, striking it in the thigh. The shaft suddenly erupted in flames, the heat consuming it in moments and reducing it to ash.

If it felt pain, the demon didn't show it. Its attention never leaving the snow as it proceeded to melt the ground.

"Did it even know it had been hit?" Fieri asked.

"Maybe," Ejan replied, "yet it wouldn't care. Its sole reason for living is to burn, not to fight."

"We'll soon see about that," Fieri growled as she drew her sword and began to climb down the boulder, until Ejan grasped her by the cloak and hauled her back onto the rock.

"We came here to find them. Not to engage the enemy. Not until we bring the rest of the army with us." Ejan hissed. "If it hasn't escaped your notice, there are only seven of us."

Fieri shrugged out of Ejan's grip, her face a mask of petulant anger. "This is only a small portion of the entire force," she explained, thrusting her sword in the direction of the flaming blackness. "Even if we had every man woman and child the north can supply, we wouldn't make more than a dent in this."

A lone figure suddenly dropped from the higher rock and landed beside the group. Startling those that hadn't already drawn weapons, while the others hastily brought their blades or bows about.

"We only need to slice through them to reach the god," the figure said as he removed the hood to reveal the face beneath.

Jaygen was shocked to see a copper stare gazing back.

"Sibiet?" Ejan whispered, as she fell to one knee and bowed.

The southern Shadojak nodded, hands tapping lightly on the hilt of his huge scimitar. "And I've brought friends enough to cut a mighty wedge."

Jaygen suddenly felt movement to his side as Weakest padded beside him, rubbing his lupine form up against his body. Mouth pulled back in a rictus grin and displaying long canines. Jaygen, stroked his head.

"What is this?" Axewell demanded, swinging his axe between Sibiet and then Weakest.

"Friends," Ejan offered as she lowered her bow.

"Friends?" Axewell continued, mouth going wide. "A Shadojak and a bloody bulworg."

Jaygen loomed over the Viking as he glared at him. "Friends," he snarled, and smiled as he watched Axewell's Adam's apple bob. Yet his smile was hidden from the Seagrit.

"Hashim is with Ragna," Sibiet explained, defusing the situation. "Along with half of Elora's Dark Army. Might I suggest we make good time in returning to them so we can begin our attack?" He glared at the small group, briefly nodding towards Jaygen before his gaze settled on Axewell. "Grumpkins and grimbles don't mix too well with Vikings."

The colour drained from Axewell's face and Jaygen needed to bite the inside of his cheek to stop himself from laughing. He never thought he would be glad to see Sibiet again, but the thought of having him and the Dark Army with them sparked a thread of hope.

"I thought you were dead," Ejan said as she began to lead the group away.

"So it seems," Sibiet explained, "that everyone did. The usurper Flek murdered the league of Shadojaks. His mistake was leaving myself and Hashim alive." Jaygen noticed that his aged hand gripped tightly to the pommel of his sword. "A mistake that will see him and those blasphemous twins, dead."

The camp was in utter disarray. Tents had been pitched along the beach, and against the longboats which had been dragged ashore. Several fires were dotted around, smoke rising into the night as men huddled close; holding hands out to the flames while discussing the coming battle. Other forms loitered at the edges, dark eyes gleaming in the firelight. Grimbles glaring at the Vikings, grumpkins sharpening knives while bulworgs snapped and snarled. It made the Northmen edgy and Jaygen noticed that they kept swords to hand, or axes in easy reach.

They ambled across the pebbles, his mother guiding them up the bluff to a natural path that wound between the cliffs to an outcrop that sat above the beach. A crowd of men gathered in the clearing. They stood aside to allow them through, casting uneasy glances his way, fear of the myth written plain for all to see.

He kept his gaze ahead as he stepped into the circle which had formed at its centre. Ragna paced around the fire pit, the Fist of the North stretched over his shoulder with his hands resting on either end, thick fingers dangling. He smiled as they entered, treating Ejan to a wink before regarding the newcomers.

Jaygen recognised the excitement building in his father. His grin splitting his ragged beard as he glared at the crowds of Vikings around him, the spitting flames brightening dark faces. At the base of the fire lay the burning remains of a demon. The blackened corpse curling in on itself with the heat.

"They don't die easily," Ragna bellowed, so all could hear. "These spawns of Hades have only two weaknesses. Remove the head, it will drop, although it will carry on burning, and the heart. The heart pumps the flames around their oil blackened bodies. Skewer that and the beasts will fall."

Jaygen's gaze fell on another body which had been dragged into the circle of men. It lay on its back, slack face staring up at the stars with lifeless orbs. Its mouth hung open to reveal teeth sharpened to points. He guessed it would be almost as tall as himself when it was alive, with wide shoulders and thick arms.

"This is what Hashim and his men had captured earlier," Ragna clarified, nodding towards a taller man who held a spear which was of a height with himself. A green leaf-shaped blade sat atop the shaft – god-created, Jaygen thought, a soul blade. He nodded in return, light reflecting from his bald pate.

"I harvested this one's soul," Hashim explained to the crowd, pointing his spear at the corpse. "Its memories speak of burning, of devouring and flooding the world. It is a creature of few emotions. Feeding on the hate and torment which its god, Hades, is feeding them. They know we are here and are expecting an attack. And although only lightly armed, they have the numbers and do not fight with fear of death."

A murmur spread throughout the men, heads turning to one another as they spoke in hushed and worried voices.

Jaygen couldn't blame them. A foe that fought without fear of death was a formidable one. He was beginning to feel a rising dread at the prospect and he had a god-created suit of armour to protect himself. He glanced to Fieri who was stood between her brother and father, her blue eyes seeking him out and offering him a knowing smile.

-Damn, he found her beautiful. He only hoped she wouldn't come to any harm.

Ragna stepped closer to the fire, gathering everyone's attention as he slammed his hammer into the ground.

"We are Vikings!" he bellowed, quieting the crowds. "With steel in our hands, fire in our bellies and Odin at our side – we fear nothing." He raised the war hammer into the night and shouted a salute to the Northern god. "Odin!"

Men around the fire sprung to their feet, raising weapons and pointing them into the sky as they all competed to be the loudest. "Odin!"

Jaygen found that his own sword was in his hands and joining that of his brother Vikings, his god's name ringing from his lips.

When the men had quieted once again, Ragna lowered the Fist, his face becoming uncharacteristically solemn.

"Yet one of us is a traitor," he continued. "One of our own has warned the enemy of our coming. A spy has been in communication with Neptula and is to blame for the lives lost in the crossing. An entire long boat, with all hands lies at the bottom of the sea."

The crowd remained silent, although many glanced around. Anger and worry adding to the unease which settled around them as clansmen eyed each other suspiciously.

Fin suddenly stepped forward, his grimace turning on Ragna.

"It is the Earth-born," he suggested, thumping his fist into his palm. "Peter who is a friend with your son."

The crowd suddenly erupted in anger, rage-filled faces darting around the camp amongst nods of agreement.

"He has been spotted near the water's edge many times, sinking his face into the sea. And he is not a Viking."

Jaygen's fingers curled into fists. Was this true? Had he been tricked by Peter? He cast his mind back to the day before they left Craggs Head. Before he fought on the Tooth against Axewell Stump - he had warned Peter not to put his face beneath the waves as he didn't know what was down there. Was the Earth-born tricking him all this time? Was he a traitor?

Ragna raised his hands for calm.

"Let him speak for himself. Where is this Peter?" he asked.

On the periphery of the crowd, men parted to allow a lone figure wander into the circle. Bewilderment fixed on Peter's face as he was roughly shoved forwards. His hands still clutching a turnip, a knife imbedded into the vegetable as he was caught in the act of cooking.

"See," Fin snapped, pointing at the object in Peter's hands, "he plans to poison us."

Ragna rested a hand on Fin's shoulder. "Easy lad, you can't prove that."

"No?" Fin shouted, pulling away from Ragna's grasp. "I say we let the gods decide. Justice by blade."

A roar went up from the gathering. Vikings were always eager for blood.

"Justice by blade?" Ragna argued. "The Earth-born has never held a sword in his life. It wouldn't be fair."

Jaygen knew that his father was right. Justice by blade meant that Peter would need to fight Fin. The accuser defeating the accused. The guilty party would be whoever lost – which usually ended in death.

"They'll be no fighting," Ragna continued louder so that everyone could hear. "Anyone who disagrees with this will deal with me."

"And let the traitor go?" Fin yelled, his face contorted in contempt. "How are you to lead us to battle when you won't make this judgement."

Jaygen watched as his father stretched out to his full height, the muscles in his neck clicking as he moved his head from left to right. "You'll do as I say, boy," Ragna growled, cocking the war hammer onto his shoulder.

At that Fin's father came to join his son. "I say we have justice," Byral demanded. "Let the gods decide."

The cheer went up from the crowd once again, men leaning closer in anticipation of a fight. Peter stood in stunned silence, not understanding anything that was being said in Norse, but realising that a lot of anger was directed at him.

"I'll back the accuser," shouted another Viking from out of the circle. "And me," said another, offering to fight in the accuser's place.

Fin held up his hand as he drew his sword. "No, I will meet out justice myself," he said as he paced around Peter, sizing him up as a grin crept upon his face.

Peter flinched from the noise as the crowd erupted in a loud raucous. His frightened eyes now finding Fin's blade and beginning to understand that he might receive the pointy end into his guts.

Jaygen approached the arguing men and lay his hand on Peter's shoulder. The moment he did so the crowd fell silent. The sound of the turnip falling from the Earth-born's hand and hitting the ground, filled the void.

"I, will stand for the accused," Jaygen growled, drawing out the final word and grounding it down in his throat. He turned his gaze towards Fin and felt satisfaction as the shorter man stumbled back a pace.

"But…" Fin began, attempting to regain his composure but failing.

"Maybe you should let the volunteers stand in your place," Byral whispered to his son.

Jaygen slowly turned and faced the other men surrounding the circle. "Will anyone stand for the accuser now?" he shouted. His only answer was the wind as it cut across the land, fanning the flames.

When it became clear that nobody would be fighting, Ragna slammed his hammer into the dirt. "Let that be the end of it, then," he said.

"But he's still a spy," Fin argued, although Jaygen noticed that his fury had diminished to a whimpering annoyance. Darting flurried glances his way.

"Even if it is true, which I doubt," Ragna snapped, "then what else has he got to report? We're here now and at dawn we fight." He glared at the men surrounding the fire. "And dawn comes quickly this far north, so I suggest you take what rest you can. Sharpen your steel and prepare for battle. Tomorrow you will live like Northmen and if needs be, will die like a Viking."

His words echoed around the still night before men raised swords and axes, or thumped fists against shields. All proving that they were braver than the man standing next to them. Jaygen wondered, if in their own private thoughts, they truly wished for battle.

Ragna turned to his brother. "Eric, round up the war chiefs and clan leaders. We've got plans to discuss."

Nodding, Eric wandered off to find the men he wanted amongst the departing crowd. The group that remained at the fire was small. His mother, Byral, Fieri and Peter who had picked up his turnip and began to brush off the dirt. Until Ragna gripped him hard around the elbow and pulled him close to his face.

"Tell me true, boy," he growled through clenched teeth, speaking in English. "Are you a spy?"

The turnip fell to the ground for the second time. "Spy?" Peter whimpered, eyebrows disappearing into his hairline. "No, I'm here to help. I'm not good at fighting but I can help with cooking or…your son Jaygen knows I'm not a spy. Tell them," he said, turning his frightened face towards Jaygen.

Jaygen's eyes widened.

"Quiet you fool," Ragna snapped, shaking the boy. "How do you know who Grimwolf is?"

Peter tried to pull away from Ragna's grasp, but Jaygen's father's grip only tightened.

"I saw him hide the armour under the stack of logs, back at Craggs Head."

The memory of that day suddenly flashed through Jaygen's mind. It was the same day he had returned with Fieri after the avalanche. Although he hadn't realised that Peter had seen him hide the suit.

Ragna turned his gaze on him and Jaygen gave him a nod to confirm Peter's story.

"Right," his father said, easing his grip on the boy, "yet that knowledge may be equally as dangerous as you being a spy."

"I'm not a spy, and Jaygen's secret is safe with me. I won't tell a soul," Peter stated, beginning to fold his arms until Weakest stalked by him and made the boy flinch away.

"We will see," Ragna said. "But for tomorrow, I cannot leave you here."

"Then I'll go with you. Give me a sword and I'll fight alongside your son…alongside Grimwolf."

A grin split Ragna's beard. "That will put you up front and centre of the vanguard."

He gazed at Jaygen who gave a subtle shrug. He didn't like the thought of Peter being amid the danger, but then again, he didn't truly trust the boy. If he was a spy, then being in the heart of the battle would prove him either one way or the other.

"I suggest you don't leave Grimwolf's side until the battle," Ragna continued as others began to arrive at the fire. "There is a lot of sharpened steel out there and in the dark, you don't really know who's sticking who."

Peter gulped as he stepped away and came to stand by Jaygen.

"Thank you," he whispered.

"I wouldn't go thanking me just yet," Jaygen replied in a hushed voice so the others wouldn't hear him speaking English. "Battles are no places for somebody in your condition."

"You mean my diabetes? I lost my pack in the crossing. I ran out of insulin this morning. I'm a gonna in the next few days anyway. I may as well be of some help. As little as that might be."

Jaygen wanted to say more, but by then the war chiefs and clan leaders had arrived and were waiting for Ragna to speak.

His father cleared the ground at his feet and took an arrow from his wife's quiver. He sank to his haunches and drew a line in the dirt.

"The attack will take place on the flat plain where the scout party came into contact with Hades' forces," he explained, pointing the arrow at the line. "We will form up in three divisions. Byral will advance from the left while Eric will push in from the right. You're to push as hard and as fast into the enemy as you can, keeping parallel to each other. It's depth we need."

"Aye, Chief," they both agreed.

"On the outer edges of your flanks, you will both have battalions of Dark forces, softening the attacks from the demons. They will lend a hand and replenish numbers when needed. But if you can, leave them to carry on pushing through." Using the arrow, he scratched two more lines to the outer edges of the first, making a H shape in the dirt.

"I'll be leading the front line, pushing hard at the centre," he continued and scraped a deep channel through the middle of the H. "It'll be vicious and brutal. We aim to penetrate through to the heart of Hades' armies where we will hopefully find Hades himself." He drew a small circle in the upper portion of the drawing.

"They won't turn and run," Axewell commented, leaning over the crudely drawn diagram. "And with their numbers they will eventually overrun us."

"That is why we keep pushing," Ragna continued. "The two flanks remain locked to our outer edges, protecting the main attack group from being attacked from the side while we thrust on like a spear cutting through a savage beast. And at its tip we will have the sharpest and deadliest point." Ragna slapped Jaygen on the shoulder, jarring his teeth inside the suit. "And at his side will be Weakest, myself and any volunteers who think they're vicious enough to fight through." Ragna raised his arm and drove the arrow through the circle which represented Hades. "And I don't want volunteers who are going for the glory or for honour. I want some real nasty bastards who don't mind getting bloody."

Axewell glanced at the map, then at the smouldering body of the demon in the fire, before spitting into the flames. "I'll go," he offered.

"Me too," Fieri volunteered, her brother holding her back.

"It's no place for a woman," Fin argued as Fieri yanked her arm free.

For once, Jaygen agreed with him. Although he saw the anguish and hurt in her face.

Ragna puffed his cheeks out and blew air through pursed lips. "Your brother's right," he said.

"Like hell he is," Ejan snapped. "I'll be right up there at the front. If she wants in, let her."

Ragna turned on his wife, about to refuse her when she glared at him; eyes narrowing to deadly slits.

Ragna's face creased up in pain, then he sighed. "So be it," he said, grudgingly.

Fieri glanced at Ejan and gave her a nod. Jaygen's mother nodded back - an understanding uniting the pair of women against the men which would protect them.

"That goes for me too," Carmelga added, pushing between Axewell and Eric. "And you can keep your mouth shut, Da." she snapped as Jaygen's uncle flexed his hands out in frustration. "My axe is as good as any." She slapped the double-headed weapon against her hands and stared her father down. In the end, he realised that he wasn't going to persuade her otherwise so hunkered back down, muttering curses under his breath.

"And you can count both Hashim and myself in there," Sibiet declared. "Hades will fall just as easily under our soul reavers as he will beneath Grimwolf's blade."

"Good," Ragna confirmed, his grin returning. "Spread the word through the clans for any more. Once we begin cutting we'll need reinforcements should one of us fall. Now get some rest yourselves. I want us formed up before dawn."

Jaygen stepped aside to allow the others to leave. Watching Fin begin arguing with Fieri and Byral, yet it seemed the red-haired girl wouldn't back down. The same conversation was being had between his mother and father. Yet he knew who would win that.

"So what was all that about?" Peter asked as he glanced down at the arrow sticking up from the mud.

Jaygen had forgotten that his father had placed Peter right at the front with them. He wouldn't last five minutes out there. Or was that Ragna's plan. Did he believe him to be a spy? Sometimes a man must fight. Sometimes a man must die, even if it was simply a means to an end. Ridding the campaign of traitor and a problem in one fell swoop. He glanced at the burning corpse of the demon. Empty gaze staring up and wondered if tomorrow would bring a similar end to Peter. Or to himself or the lands and countries that made up the world.

"Nothing much," he muttered to the Earth-born. "But, if I were you I'd try and scavenge some armour or at least a shield."

Peter clenched his teeth and straightened up. "I'll see if Carmelga can find me something. She's the only other person who has been kind to me."

Jaygen left him in the capable hands of his cousin while he climbed the rest of the path to the top of the cliff. Out of the firelight and away from the stares and glares of the Vikings, and away from the corpses. It wasn't long before he heard the light footsteps of another, following him out into the darkness.

"I didn't think we would ever get to spend a moment alone," Fieri said as she grasped his gauntleted hand and pulled him into the crevice between two large rocks. "Your mother has eyes like an eagle. Always watching us."

She stood up on her the tips of her toes and kissed the end of the wolf's helm. Closing her eyes as she lay her lips against the steel nose.

Jaygen was smiling as he reached up and unclasped the face mask, swinging the nose and snarling teeth open to reveal his face.

"There you are," Fieri grinned, and crushed her mouth against his.

Heat filled Jaygen's belly as his hands drifted down to her waist, her arms wrapping around his lower back to pull him against her. He could feel her heart hammering through the god-created torso, and his own which thumped to a faster beat. His senses filling with her, the dizzying mix of excitement and lust, desiring more from this girl who he knew felt the same way about him.

Then his thoughts skipped to the coming battle.

"What's wrong?" she asked, her notched eyebrow raising. She stepped away from him, brushing fingers through her red hair.

"Nothing," he grumbled. "Well something, but…"

"I'm worried too," she admitted. "I don't want you getting hurt tomorrow. And I've my brother and father to think about. Whatever happens, at least we'll be together." She came closer and rested her head against his chest.

"And what of the curse?" Jaygen reminded her. "Shannog said…"

"Shannog's an old crone who has wrinkled into an ancient prune. She's all runes and fire smoke. The curse isn't true. Does being with me feel wrong to you?"

"No, it feels," he placed his arms over her, careful not to let the weight of his armour dig into her shoulders, "like we are supposed to be together."

"It feels real," she agreed, tapping her knuckles against his back plate. "Solid, something physical which we can touch. It's not just runes and smoke."

Jaygen kissed the top of her head, the tinges of relief stroking away his worry. Fieri was right. How could something that felt this good be cursed.

"When the battle's over I'm burying the suit. Curse or no, Grimwolf will be no more." Jaygen sighed as he rested his cheek against her fiery hair, feeling the warmth radiating from her. This was what his father felt when he held his mother, this was what Bray felt when he put his arms around Elora. This was love. "We've just a simple battle to win, that's all."

"That's all," Fieri repeated. "Now how about another kiss from the big bad Grimwolf."

20

Spear Point

Dawn was no more than a grey smudge on a lead horizon. Rain thundered down from a slate sky, thumping against amour, helmets and shields. It ran in fat rivulets down mail and steel before adding to the quagmire which was rising ankle-deep as they waited for the rest of the division to form up.

Jaygen watched the men around him. Hardened warriors, staring into the gloom and the smouldering beings at the other side of the gurgling gully. Steam rising in twisting clouds that stretched into the distance. The creatures themselves were as black as their intent. Thick red veins pulsing with fire as they glowered at them. Wide muscles contracting as they gripped rocks, branches and clubs. The crude weapons either found or torn from the earth, were still deadly held in the hands of the demons.

"There's so many of them," Peter remarked, as he huddled behind his battered shield. The small round lump of wood had seen better days but was the only one Carmelga could find for the Earth-born. He gripped the bent short sword he'd spent the last few hours attempting to hone an edge to.

Fear was creeping over Jaygen. It was wringing his guts as they waited for the others to get into position. So, he guessed it would be a whole lot worse for Peter. "They have the numbers," he informed him, "but not the steel or the skill to use it."

Jaygen watched the monsters that lay before them and hoped that his words were true.

"But, they're like a solid wall of burning coal," Peter complained. "A wall that stretches out of sight. Surely we don't mean to fight them all."

"If needs be, boy," Sibiet cut in as he gave a practice swing of his curved scimitar. "Yet our aim is to penetrate as deep as we can into the bastards."

"How deep?" Peter whispered, his eyes growing wide.

Sibiet grinned, "All the way to the centre, where we will meet with Hades himself."

"Oh," Peter replied and gave Jaygen a weary look. Jaygen had no words of comfort to offer the boy and so shrugged. It is what it is.

"I've squared off against bigger numbers before," Ragna admitted, his tall frame silhouetted in the dawn light as he leaned against his hammer.

"I remember," Ejan said, as she loosened the arrows in her quiver, her bow barely visible in the dull light. "We faced into the entire Dark Army in the Shadowlands. And now the same beasts are fighting with us. How things change."

Weakest growled as he sank between Jaygen and Peter. His huge body dwarfing the Earth-born.

"Still," Peter whispered, "there's so many." He ran trembling fingers through his hair, the wet greasy strands sticking out at all angles.

Jaygen thought him the bravest soul here. The Earth-born being the only person to have never held a sword before. And now he must fight amongst people who he didn't know, strangers that called him a traitor from a world so much different from his own.

"Whatever happens," Fieri murmured into Peter's ear, "today you will live like a Viking."

"Or die like one," Fin offered, treating them to a furtive glare.

Ragna leaned in close to the shivering boy, "Spy or no, you try your damn hardest to stick the pointy end of that bent blade of yours into a demon, and you'll be a Viking to me." He lifted his shaggy head to the sky, now fractionally a lighter shade of grey. "It's time."

Jaygen slipped his sword free, apprehension playing out along his nerves as he did so. This was it. He summoned all the courage he could muster, gritting his teeth behind the mask and shoving all other thoughts aside. If he was to become the spear point to drive a wedge into the smouldering beasts, he needed to focus on being a lethal, brutal killing machine. A cold slayer, a predator – he needed to become Grimwolf.

He watched his mother notch an arrow into her bow. An oil-soaked rag wrapped around the tip. His father cupped his hands around it while Carmelga struck a match and put the flame to it. The fire sizzled and hissed in the rain as Ejan raised her bow and fired the arrow into the dawn. Jaygen watched it fly high before being snatched by the wind and gutting out. But it burned long enough for the signal to have been given.

The sound of a war horn, blasted from the far right, quickly followed by a blast from the left.

Ragna turned to him and laid a thick hand atop his shoulder, "Proud of you son," he whispered so only he could here, then thumping the wolf chest hard enough to knock him back a step said, "Now be the vicious wolf that I know you are and cut me a bloody path to Hades!"

Jaygen gave his father a not to gentle slap across his belly and paced out in front of the line. As he passed his mother, he subtly inclined his head; trying hard not to see the worry that creased her brow or the fear she showed for her son as she bit her lip. Fieri too, portrayed an apprehensive look. He put his back to all of them as he strode across the gully, the fast-flowing water crashing against his calves, striving to unbalance him. Splashes erupted behind him as the vanguard followed. His heart thumping hammer blows against his chest while he climbed up the gully bank to confront the mass of smouldering bodies that lay between him and Hades.

The wall of demons glared back. Red glowing embers of coal casting hatred from tens of thousands of misshapen bodies. Smoke escaping from evil grins, jagged teeth formed from black mineral as they goaded him on.

Jaygen glanced to the periphery of his vision and noticed the far flanking ranks crossing the water, thousands of men, women and beasts, both Viking and Dark Army trudging against death. They were greatly outnumbered; their entire divisions would be swallowed by the vast superior numbers of Hades' forces. They all knew it and accepted it. Ethea depended on the outcome of this battle. An entire world's destiny lay in the outcome of this fight. They only needed to survive long enough to kill the God of the Underworld.

Breathing deeply, Jaygen raised his sword. The god-created steel shining brightly in the dull rain and let his gaze fall on the multitude of death before him.

"Odin!" he bellowed, the salute echoed behind him before being taken up by the flanking ranks, until the name of the Viking god was thundering through the heavens themselves.

He broke into a jog, blade held out to the side, sensing the ground shake as thousands of heavily armoured men began to run with him. Mud sloshing up his legs, rain pounding against his armour as he broke into a charge. Sword raising as he closed the distance between himself and the wall of charcoal beasts – between the men of the north and oblivion.

Water struck his face as he brought his blade to the fore, driving the tip into the chest of a demon.

Steel punctured through the coal-crusted ribcage and pierced the heart. The creature's mouth gaping wide and spewing molten blood in a silent scream. Jaygen drove his shoulder into the beast and sprung on, pushing deeper into the foe. Slamming his gauntleted fist into the head of another and feeling the smouldering skull crush beneath.

Screams erupted all about him as his fellow Norsemen ploughed into the demons. The boom of clashing steel and of the weight of flesh hammering into the burning creatures. He was vaguely aware of blows landing on himself. The pathetic taps and scrapes of the demons as they fought back – wooden clubs and branches, fists or misshapen feet, slamming into his armour but doing nothing to halt his onslaught.

Drive, slice – push, kick. A severed head spun over the others, red flames leaking from the stump of neck before he decapitated another. Elbows digging into faces, distorted grimaces baring teeth, fists falling short, limbs following. Bodies pushing back, feet stomping.

Jaygen ducked beneath the swing of an approaching beast. The creature had four arms and sharpened stakes held in each. He hugged an arm around its mutilated midriff and hoisted it clear from the ground as he ran on; leaning into the momentum and using the extra weight of his opponent to forge a path.

The many limbed beast screamed as it struck him from above, below and to the back, attempting to find a weakness where there was none. Jaygen was screaming himself as he launched into the air, his knees driving into the faces of those in front before landing hard; crushing the chest of the beast he carried.

He spared a glance back and witnessed his father's hammer making twin fountains of flaming blood as it crushed the head of a blackened body. Sibiet, spinning through another and severing its torso in half. His mother jabbing her short sword into a chest while Carmelga yanked her axe free from a shoulder. It was violence on a mass scale. Ugly brutal and fierce. Men were screaming battle cries, steel torturing against bodies, blood, mud and fire mixing into a chorus of death as they strove to widen the path.

Suddenly, Jaygen's world span. A strange 'pah' sound escaped his lips as he found himself lying on his back, demons shouting as they landed blow after blow upon him. Sludge gripped his cloak as he attempted to rise from the ground. Mud squeezing through fingers as he strived to push himself up, but the sheer weight of creatures held him in place. One piling on top of another. His head was twisted in the grip of thick hands as it was repeatedly thumped into the mire. Once, twice – Jaygen felt the armour sinking, rain hitting his mask and finding the eye slits. It ran down his face and into his mouth to join the growl that was shaking his chest.

Pain adding strength to his struggle, Jaygen rolled onto his front and gathered his feet beneath him. The pressure of ten score of beasts clambering onto his back, sinking him further into the mud.

He closed his eyes, clenched his teeth and using the god-created power that was in the armour, bunched his legs together and drove upwards.

Several bodies flew into the air. Arms, legs and torsos tangling as they landed in heaps to be crushed by the Vikings that poured into the gap he had created.

"No time for lying around," Ragna shouted. Mud clumping to his beard to mix with the blood and the rain. "We need to push further."

Jaygen looked at the progress they had already made and was disheartened. They'd only come a hundred feet. All that effort and they had barely made a pin-prick in the smouldering army.

Anger was beginning to build up inside him, Jaygen used the fresh emotion to press on. Grinding his foot into the mud he crouched, raised his sword, and launched himself into the multitude of black beasts.

"Don't look back," he told himself, over and over again, as his steel cut into the smouldering darkness before him. Like a farmer reaping his field, or the Grim Reaper himself, carving himself souls.

His sword severed, sliced and skewered. Killing and spreading death before him. Making a path of corpses to scramble across. Better to walk on the fallen than sink in the mud, he thought as he removed the head from another demon. He kicked the body over and stepped over it, driving ever on. "Don't look back," he reminded himself. Repeating the words until they became a mantra, spoken in time with his lunges, his actions as he tore on.

It didn't feel like he was striking flesh. His blade cutting through a thick crust before finding a soft meat which spewed molten blood. He felt the heat the beasts permeated as he bounded on. Trusting that the rest followed close behind.

Losing count of how many he had slain, Jaygen smashed his fist into an approaching figure. Making a crushed mess of its face before the limp body fell to be replaced by another. He caught this one with his sword, the tip finding little resistance in the black material they were created from and slipped between grating ribs to puncture the heart.

As the body fell he heard a scream from behind.

"Ma?" he shouted as he spun.

It wasn't his mother that had screamed but Axewell, his arm erupting in flames. A demon having sunk its teeth into the flesh below his stump. He frantically thrashed at the beast, smashing the rim of his shield into its head, yet it wouldn't release the hold.

Jaygen was debating whether to rush back to him when Weakest pounced upon the demons back. The force knocking the pair to the ground where Carmelga clambered over the top and dropped her axe through the black crusted neck, severing the head.

Worry still wrenching his heart, Jaygen searched desperately for his mother but couldn't see her in the melee. The battle was a mass of confusion. Screaming, shouting, clashing and fighting. Fast, furious actions of violence and a lot of flashing steel amidst the mud and gore.

Then his eyes caught a flash of red and he recognised Fieri, her body obscured by the filth as she drove her sword into the back of a wide monster. The tip of her blade poking out from the chest momentarily before she withdrew it and allowed the body to fall. Behind it had been Ejan, her arms raised in defence and her sword sticking up from the stomach of the corpse.

He watched his mother retrieve her sword and the women exchanged a mutual nod before they began attacking afresh. Chests heaving as they fought on.

Hashim spun into his line of sight. His tall spear was a blur as it struck a beast in its eye before he yanked it free and swiped the legs from another. His dark glare caught Jaygen and he pointed on.

"Force a path to those boulders," he shouted. "We need to rest and regroup."

Jaygen set his gaze on the boulders and drove on. Hacking, dodging and slicing. Cutting, piercing and lopping the heads from the beasts as he strived to reach the higher ground.

The black crusty flesh parted beneath his steel as he bore through the wall of bodies. Digging deep for the strength the armour provided, pushing his body on. His muscles aching with fatigue, with pain – teetering on the edge of exhaustion. Crunch, thwack, squelch...and then he hit rock. He'd made it.

Scrambling up the boulders he gained the flat top and began to swing his sword into the black beings that were perched there. Two hands gripping his blade, he cut through them, cutting them down and sending what was left spinning over the edge. Moments later he was joined by Sibiet and Hashim, the Shadojaks didn't even seem out of breath. Then his father clambered up the rocks, flames dancing in his beard from the gore that had spattered against him. He put them out and raised the Fist of the North into the air.

"Push them back and hold this position," he growled, his voice gone hoarse from all the shouting.

Jaygen scanned into the chaos he had left in his wake. Searching once again for his mother and Fieri. He found the pair working together as they cut down a lone beast that had broken through the outer flanks. It didn't last long under the duel blades of the women, before it fell lifeless into the mud.

The path he had created began to widen as more and more Vikings pushed up from the rear, driving the smouldering army back where the outer flanks crushed them. Screaming bodies climbing up the gully a good way behind. They had come a great distance. A long grey muddy line cutting through the darkness that surrounded them. A thickening line made from mud, blood and bodies. Both demons and Northmen.

"That's it," Ragna bellowed, "keep the bastards out."

With the flanks holding the army of the underworld back, Ejan and Fieri came to join them on the flat rock which was beginning to become overcrowded.

Axewell clambered up, aided by Fin, his damaged arm swollen and red. Carmelga dragged Peter up, who against all odds, was still alive. Although he had lost his sword and helmet and clung to his shield as if it was a barrier between this world and death. Which, Jaygen thought, it probably was.

"Form a baseline at the foot of the rocks," his father growled, spit flying from clenched teeth as he swung the hammer about. "They'll concentrate their efforts there."

"Concentrate?" Fin asked, dropping Axewell at his feet. "They're practically on top of each other as it is. We can't fight through that."

Jaygen stared ahead, dread crawling up his neck as he soaked up the masses in front. What they had just fought through was a drastically watered-down version of what lay before them.

It was no longer a wall of smouldering bodies, but a sea. A black sea of death that spread all the way back to a shallow hill in the distance. A lone figure standing atop.

"That's him," Ejan remarked, holding a hand in front of her face to shield her eyes from the rain. "That's Hades."

Jaygen's sight wasn't as good as his mother's but he guessed she was right. The tall imposing shadow could be no other than the God of the Underworld. Standing in a dominating view to command his army. Wind playing with the tails of his cloak as he glowered at them. Horns sprouting from the top of his head as he held aloft a thick staff.

"There's our prize," Ragna shouted, slamming the shaft of his hammer into the rock. "There is our glory."

Fin snorted. "And what about the millions of charcoal bodies between?" he asked, shaking his head.

"More glory," Fieri hissed.

"Damn right," Ragna repeated and treated the red-haired girl to a wink.

"Madness," Axewell, exclaimed, resting his sweaty brow against the rim of his shield as he rubbed the injury on his handless arm. The skull tied to the end of his beard no more than a lump of mud.

"You want to stay here?" Ragna asked, cocking his head and grinning. A wickedness glinting in his hazel eyes. "You've made it this far, Stump. And you've cut some of the nasties down, so you've earned the right."

Axewell sucked air through his teeth before groggily rising to his feet. "Nah," he said glancing at his arm and twisting the double blades strapped to the end. "I'll keep fighting until I've lost my axe. And then probably carry on anyway."

"That's right," Ragna agreed, slapping the stocky man on the back. "Because you're a Viking. We all are."

The few around the rock nodded or slapped their fists against their amour and Weakest stalked onto the edge of the rock and growled into the land before them. His snarl carrying over the silent demons to echo around the hill which Hades occupied.

"I hate to break your self-righteous back slapping," Sibiet put in as he stretched his blade out to point into the foreground. "But if I'm not mistaken, those smoking piles of stones over there, are forges."

Jaygen searched the area the Shadojak was pointing and found hundreds of small mounds of stones, dark smoke rising from the top while a red glow radiated from within.

"Forges?" Ragna asked, "Why would they have forges?"

"Why else," Hashim offered, leaning on his spear, "but to create metal. These lands are full of iron ore."

"You mean they're making swords," Fin snapped, his knuckles turning white.

Hashim shrugged. "Swords are maybe a little too advanced for them. And the metal would be an inferior iron. But they'll be crafting blades or jagged tools for cutting and gutting."

"And even iron can be sharpened to a lethal edge," Sibiet added.

Jaygen narrowed his eyes and observed that there were indeed weapons being passed around Hades' forces. Long flat pieces of metal, the morning light catching the jagged edges as the burning beasts took practice swings before advancing on them.

"May Odin have pity on us," Axewell grunted, speaking the words that everyone else was thinking.

"Pity?" Ragna growled, twisting his war hammer in his grip as he stood tall, looming over the rest of them. "Odin doesn't want to give us pity. He gave you me, in case you have bloody well forgotten. And I for one will slam the entire army of blackened coal-freaks, flat beneath the Fist before I will take anyone's pity."

Jaygen's mother slipped an arm around her husband's waist and tugged at his beard. "You ready to shed another one of your five bellies, Raggy?"

Ragna smiled down at Ejan and planted a kiss on her lips. "We'll be back at the Keep before spring comes and you can feed me back up. Either that or we'll be in Valhalla, drinking the place dry."

"It's suicide. You won't get ten paces into that without being cut down." Fin complained as he glared out at the sea of demons. "Come on, Fieri. Let's find Da and leave these fools to their glory."

He made to take her hand but she flinched away from it. Instead moving to stand beside Jaygen.

"I will share in their glory, Fin. You go if you want," Fieri suggested, and Jaygen felt her fingers as they interlaced within his. Her calloused hand locking into his gauntlet. "We won't think any less of you."

If anybody had missed the fact that Fieri had taken his hand in hers, they didn't fail to see her leaning into him and resting her head against his shoulder.

"Madness," Fin hissed, leaving Jaygen to determine whether he meant the situation or the fact that his sister was showing affection to a mythical killer. Yet he didn't leave.

Ragna nodded, satisfied that his men were now committed. He embraced Ejan once more before turning to Jaygen.

"When you're ready then," he said, slapping him on the back. "Aim for the hill and that bastard atop it. Don't stop until you reach him."

"We'll try to keep up," Hashim said, offering him a smile, "Unless we die of course."

Jaygen gave the group a final glance, feeling his mother gently squeeze his shoulder as Fieri lay a kiss against his jaw. What he would give to be able to snap the visor open to taste her for one final time. Yet the odds were stacked incredibly high against them. And they all knew it.

Sighing deeply, Jaygen stepped away from them and nodded towards Weakest. The bulworg nodded back, coming to stand beside him as he faced out to the hill in the distance.

"Odin!" Carmelga shouted as she raised her axe and the others took up the salute, screaming from the tops of their lungs as Jaygen leapt from the rock.

He came down, both hands gripping his sword to slam it into the closest beast. The blade cutting through its head and imbedding into the sternum. He wrenched it out as a shadow passed above and Weakest landed on another. His weight taking the black creature and the other behind it, down. Jaygen didn't waste any time jumping into the gap Weakest had created, dipping his shoulder low to drive into the stomach of another body, running him as far as he could until he collided with several more of Hades' soldiers.

Something struck his upper arm, clanging dully against the god-created armour. And when he turned Jaygen saw the flat jagged blade swinging in for a second blow.

He parried the swing, slipping his own sword over and under the weapon, striking the demon's hand and sending his blade spinning into the air. He was about to finish the creature when another jumped in his place. Forcing Jaygen to duck and arch his body away from the second attack.

Driving his knee into the face of one, he slammed his fist into the neck of the other; vaulting over the pair to carry on his momentum as he pushed for the hill. The sounds of clashing steel behind him letting him know that the Vikings were following.

The monsters came on like a tide of burning coal; smouldering arms and legs swinging blow after blow as teeth sought purchase upon his armour. He felt the heat of the attack through the metal, scorching his own skin as he blocked, parried and punched his way on.

His blade swiped vicious arcs to his front, slicing heads, limbs and grins from the multitude of blows that lunged his way. The weight of them pressing in so tight that even they hadn't the room to duck or dodge his attack. It felt like wading through black treacle. Jaygen kept his gaze up, focusing on the hill and Hades that stood upon it. Ever watching – patient even, as if he knew their effort was futile and stayed only for his own amusement.

Jaygen wanted to feel his blade cut through the God of the Underworld – could even sense it in his vision as he sank his sword to the wolf's head hilt. But he had work to do. An entire field to plough through, a smouldering crop to reap.

Teeth locked tightly, he growled as he fought on. Red eyes, glowing mouths, nails, coal, death. His sword danced between, separating limbs from bodies, removing heads from necks, yet with each one that fell another took its place.

-Head up, focus on the hill. He goaded himself. Nobody could forge this path but himself. The north depended on it – Ethea depended on it.

Steel sparked as he carved a screaming beast open, the blow so brutal that it cut the demon in half. And as its torso fell it wrapped strong arms around his legs, squeezing them tight and preventing him from advancing further.

Jaygen almost lost his balance as he struggled to stay upright. The butchered creature that was holding him was swiftly joined by others, turning his struggle into an impossibility.

Reversing his grip on his sword he drove it down into the back of his attacker, yet as it squirmed he missed its heart and its grip grew tighter.

In a blur of movement, the tide poured over him. Seeing the opportunity in their foe being pinned, they didn't waste any time in engulfing him.

Jaygen felt his arms being pulled wide, many hands gripping his armour and twisting it around. His other arm being pulled in the opposite direction as he writhed around, attempting to free himself, but couldn't find the room to manoeuvre his blade.

Weakest leapt to his rescue. Leaping upon the backs of those in front. Yet as the weight of the army swept over them, the bulworg was overwhelmed with smouldering bodies as they gripped, bit and pulled him into the mud.

"No!" Jaygen screamed, as he watched his friend being crushed beneath the horde of bodies, their glowing smiles hissing with rain as it cascaded down.

He watched helplessly as more and more forms closed in and his own legs buckled. The ground slamming against his face as cold mud sloshed across his mask to seep into the eye slits.

His body was locked in place. He had no movement in any of his limbs. The blackness piling on top as the god-created metal groaned beneath the mass above. It was like being buried alive.

Through the mud, he watched a Viking spring into the melee. Fin's sword darting in and out, piercing crusty chests in an attempt at rescuing him, yet as the numbers rose, he was soon overrun. His sword parried by a demon baring a jagged length of iron. The two metals clashed, Fin knocking his opponent's blow skyward but he didn't notice another beast slip beneath him, a crooked blade poised ready to strike.

"Fin!" Jaygen shouted, yet his words went unheard as he watched the crude weapon slide between Fin's ribs.

Fieri's brother went rigid, his eyes going wide as he glanced down at the length of iron been dragged from his chest. His own blood running down the blade.

Shock was written in his face as he fell to his knees and slowly toppled over. The demon who had stabbed him, stepping over his body as he charged out of view.

Jaygen clenched his teeth as he watched the light leave Fin. His expression now slack, blood slipping from one side of his mouth. Had Fieri seen him fall, was she still alive?

The sound of battle filled his world as he was pounced upon. More bodies adding to those already holding him. He couldn't move an inch, could barely breath. He thought he heard his mother shouting, his father raging orders and others screaming in pain. A large grimble bounded into his line of sight. The huge troll pounding at a demon's head as others bit into him. His clothes, now no more than torn rags were aflame as he grunted on. Head butting all that came into range, stabbing with the tusks that protruded from his snarling mouth.

The grimble killed three before succumbing to the flames. He fell beside the lump of bodies that had buried Weakest. Huge fists relaxing as his soul left his body.

Without being able to do anything but stare through the visor, Jaygen realised that their efforts were for nothing. Hades and his forces were too powerful. Even for the great army of Northmen that had banded together in an attempt to defeat him.

Jaygen felt numb, his entire being filling with an icy chill that stole his strength. He was sinking further into the mud, the sounds of the battle beginning to fade as either the Vikings were being pushed further back or that his helmet was beginning to submerge into the sludge.

Feeling his life ebb away, his world closing in; a darkness narrowing his image until his last sight was of a tiny green shoot.

The minuscule plant having impossibly sprouted from the very muck he was being buried in. Pale green leaves unfurling on a narrow stem to reveal a cone-shaped flower. It appeared so delicate amongst the ravaging of battle.

His life ending while another, smaller life fought to grow. Maybe that's how it worked. As one life passed, another takes its place. Maybe there was only a finite amount of souls that could exist at any one time on Ethea. Maybe this entire battleground would be a field of plants by the end of the day.

That is of course, until Neptula drowns the planet.

21

The Last Fight

Norgie set a tray of breakfast at the inn's long table. Elora's stomach clenched as the smell of bacon and sausages hit her nose, yet she lacked the desire to eat. The worry of what was happening in the north chasing away any hunger. She knew the attack was underway, but as thick clouds had moved over the battle, her scraw-harpies had yet to relay images of the outcome. She didn't know whether Ragna and the Vikings had reached Hades or even if he was still alive. The God of the Underworld was strong and she had seen through her flying eyes-in-the-sky, how large his army was. She hated the not knowing.

Gurple brought a pot of coffee from the kitchen and she helped herself to a mug, grasping the cup in both hands as she blew steam from the surface.

"It's so quiet around here," Athena remarked, filling a plate from the tray and pushing it towards her.

"That's because anyone who is sensible has already taken refuge in the Keep," Elora replied. "Where you should be, mother."

Elora still hadn't gotten used to the fact that she had a mother.

It was true. The inn was eerily quiet. The only people remaining in the old building were Norgie and Gurple. The others had taken up residence within the protection of Rams Keep. The threat of Dethtil and the garrison of soldiers now under his command, was too great to leave people in the inn.

"I'll leave here when you do, Elora," Athena replied. "I've lost you before and I'm not about to do it again."

The coffee was bitter, but it gave her a strong hit of caffeine as she sought to turn the conversation to a different topic which didn't have an equally bitter taste. Yet she struggled to find anything to say. Her life over the past few months had been harsh at best. And unless she had some good news from the north, it wouldn't be getting better any time soon.

Her gaze followed Bray as he entered the room. He threw a log on the fire before joining them at the table.

"Why didn't you wake me sooner?" she snapped at him and immediately regretted using such a hard tone. If he took offence, he didn't show it as he placed a kiss on her cheek and sat beside her.

"You were tired," he explained, combing his fingers through his scruffy black hair. "That flight back from the Antarctic drained you – along with whatever Volcaneus did." He grasped her hand and squeezed it.

Elora forced a smile as she leaned into him. "I'm sorry, it's just that time is something we don't have."

Bray chuckled dryly. "You sound like Diagus."

"Yeah? Now I know what kind of stresses he was under. Did he ever know any peace?"

Bray's laugh was more genuine this time. "I think he had a day or two where nothing much happened. Not that he would have known what do with it."

Elora finished her drink and placed the cup on the table. She prodded the bacon with her fork but knew she couldn't eat. "I've got to face Neptula," she said. "Today."

"I'll be going with you," Bray replied, absently stroking the back of her hand with his thumb.

"No," Elora replied. "You said it yourself, Neptula is in a coral palace, in the middle of the ocean. You won't be able to get there. And Grycul will fight better with only me on her back."

"I'll fly the Spitfire," he responded as if he had already come up with the scheme in anticipation of her words. "If the soul memories I harvested were correct, the Sea Witch will have a host of water dragons patrolling the sky above the Jewel."

"But you won't keep up," she argued, apprehension building at the thought of him flying into danger.

"I won't need to. Not if I pass through the Shadowlands in Grycul's wake. Like we did with the airship."

Elora realised that Bray had worked it all out. That was perhaps why he had let her sleep so long. That, and she was dog-tired from the long flight home.

"Will you two stop bickering," Athena insisted. "You're talking as if you won't be coming back, when I know that you both will."

Elora stared at her mother, wishing she shared her confidence.

"Neptula is the last fight. The final battle to save the world," Athena informed her, while taking both her's and Bray's hands in her own. "I believe Ethea will cease to be without you in it."

"I doubt that. The world will keep on turning even if, I...we, come back. Or even if Neptula succeeds and the small gods return," Elora said, conceding to the fact that Bray was going with her. Whether she liked it or not.

Athena narrowed her eyes. "You will be coming back. I swear by Minu. And you will be having that wedding."

"Here here," Norgie agreed, as he came in from the kitchen, Gurple in tow. "And I've got my best man speech all worked out and everything."

Elora sighed. "Yeah, I seem to be fighting any old god lately. It doesn't matter if I've got to fight some more to secure my wedding."

"There's only one," Bray said, planting a kiss on the crown of her head. "Neptula."

"The last fight."

"The last fight," he repeated.

She squeezed his arm and felt a spark of hope warm her heart. She would feel better if she knew where The Green Man was. The god of nature hadn't been seen when she returned. And she wondered if that was because of the fact that spring had yet to arrive at Rams Keep.

Suddenly something hit the inn's window and bounced off the leaded glass. They all turned their gaze to the sound as something else struck.

Elora rose from the table and crossed the common room. She was at the window when another object tapped against it.

"I think it's a stone or seed," she informed them as she inspected the small brown object that came to rest upon the windowsill. She wondered who was throwing them or why.

With Bray by her side they left the inn and covered the short distance to the outside of the window, yet didn't find anybody.

"Strange," Bray remarked as he picked up the tiny stone and rubbed it between finger and thumb. "It's a seed alright. But from what? There's nothing here close enough to grow."

"Except that sapling," Elora suggested, pointing towards a thin tree on the edge of the courtyard. Only a few years old, its spindly trunk was barely thicker than her wrist yet it had already begun to sprout buds from fine branches.

As they stepped closer the sapling's upper branches began to wave against the breeze and group together as if forming an arm. Thin, almost skeletal fingers pointing towards the lake.

"Look," Bray said, and nodded over to the great willow that grew beside the icy water.

The willow had prematurely thickened out. Thick fluffy pussy willow bobbing to an unheard rhythm as it beckoned them closer.

"It's him," Elora said, her heart suddenly lifting. "It's The Green Man."

They walked briskly to the lake, covering the short distance quickly. And with the inn being almost deserted their footsteps echoed eerily around them.

When they came close to the willow, its thick veil of branches parted to reveal the silver trunk. The Green Man's face appearing at its centre; large eyes forming from holes in the bark while his mouth spread from a widening crack, into a smile. The soft fluffy pussy willow formed eyebrows and a shapely goatee beard that made him appear a lot younger than the ancient god she had met in the Arctic.

"Finally," he said, the word rumbling from inside the wood, making deep knocking sounds. "I've been waiting patiently since yesterday. And although this is a nice spot to wait and grow, there isn't much time."

"Sorry," Elora apologised. "I was expecting you in person or, you know – to maybe appear at the inn or something."

The Green Man shook his head and the entire tree shook with him. The pussy falling like fat snowflakes.

"It doesn't work like that. I don't have the freedom to wander like the mammals, or crawl like the insects. I'm rooted."

Elora felt foolish for not realising it sooner. The Green Man was nature himself and not an animal.

"Yet my roots run deep and are spread throughout the world."

"So you have seen what is happening in the north?" Bray asked, using the same words Elora was about to speak.

"I sense there is a lot of death surrounding Hades. Always burning, killing, destroying."

"And my friends?" Elora asked, desperate for some news. "Are the Vikings winning the battle?"

Dread filled her heart as she watched the thick eyebrows descend into a frown. "Their's was an impossible task, Elora. They struggle against unbearable numbers – against an unimaginable force. Hades is a strong god."

Elora blinked the tears from her lashes and forced the images of her friends dying in the cold, out of her mind. "Please, is there nothing you can do?"

"My children, my seedlings. They are emerging from the mud that has been frozen for such a long time. They see, they tell me what is happening and it is most unnerving."

"Tell us," Elora asked, kneeling at the foot of the willow, placing her hands to the rough bark. "Will they help?"

"They wish to, they strived to, yet they lack the strength. Like your falling comrades, they perish in the mud."

"Please, is there anything that can be done?"

"Water, they have plenty - food locked in the mud are nutrients enough but they lack sunlight."

"Sunlight?" Bray asked, shaking his head. "How are we to get sunlight?"

"A dark problem, without light," The Green Man admitted, sap rolling from the corner of his eye.

"If we clear the surface of the mud, if daylight can reach the seedlings below – will it be enough?"

The god of nature stared at her, one of the thicker branches forming an arm; the hand at its end scratching his chin. Or the nobble of wood that resembled one.

"Maybe. Water, food and sun, that's all they'll need. Yet I don't see how you can perform such a task."

"Scraw-harpies," Elora replied. "There must be hundreds of them circling above the battleground."

"But you said they can't fly through the thick rain clouds. The water would make them too heavy."

Elora gripped his arms as she pulled herself up. "Too heavy to fly, but all they need do is land. Then they can scratch through the mud."

Before she even clarified the possibility of the plan working with The Green Man, she closed her eyes and sent her thoughts to the birds in the north. Pressing the urgency of her commands into her father's former eyes in the sky. It will work, it has to.

Through her mind, she could see the slate grey clouds below her. A blanket of flowing darkness that covered the land. She linked with the others of her kind as they soared in place or circled around the area they knew their brother soldiers were fighting.

Dive – she willed them. Dive now and save your brethren. Save the world.

A dizzying sense of vertigo rushed through her as she experienced through the bird, the sudden drop. Wings tucked tightly to the feathered body as they descended through the rain cloud. The cold air fighting against them as they pushed, blindly down. Trusting in her command.

"Elora?" Bray probed, his strong arms holding her up as she came back into herself.

She gripped his shirt to prevent herself from toppling. "It is done," she said. "The scraw-harpies are falling to the battleground."

"Then we will see if it works," The Green Man said. Then his gaze fell on the tree-line beyond the lake. His scowl deepening. "But for now, might I suggest you find somewhere to find protection."

Instinctively Elora drew her gun, as did Bray. "What is it?"

"I can't decide. You humans all look the same to me. Yet I sense a great number of men heading this way."

Fear forced Elora to release the safety catch on her pistol as a crow broke from a nearby tree and glided towards them. Squawking into the sky, it landed on Nat's gravestone. Regarding them with an intelligence that didn't belong to a normal bird.

"Dethtil," Elora stated as she scanned the air for the rest of the warlock's flock – no not a flock, a murder of crows. Her gaze fell upon imperial guards as they began to emerge from the tree-line.

"We've got to warn the others," Bray snapped, taking Elora by the arm and guiding her from the tree.

From the edge of her vision, the willow moved in a blur as a long branch flicked out and knocked the bird from the gravestone, sending it into the lake and leaving a single black feather to spin to the earth.

"Go now," The Green Man ordered, "I'll hold them back the best I can. But you must seek the end of this war."

Gunfire erupted from the guards as they advanced. Smoke rising from barrels as bullets hit the ground around them.

"Run!" Bray shouted as they fled the lake.

By the time they had reached the courtyard, Norgie and her mother had emerged from the inn to see what the noise was.

"Get down," Elora bellowed as she grasped her mother around the waist and pulled her back inside the inn. Followed by Norgie and Bray.

"What's happening?" Athena demanded as the windows began to explode. Glass raining down around them. Gurple who had been sat at the table, suddenly leapt down and scurried underneath. A thick sausage dangling between his teeth.

"Dethtil has dissolved the fairy protection and has brought a garrison of imperial guards across the barrier," Elora explained. "We've got to get to the Keep."

Another barrage of gunfire erupted. The sound of bullets pinging into the brickwork and thudding along the wall.

"Come on," Elora growled as she picked Gurple up and rushed through the inn to the back door.

She kicked it open and hurried across the rear courtyard to the stables. Then placing Gurple down she swiftly went inside and retrieved the two horses.

"There's no time to saddle up," she shouted as she hoisted Gurple onto Daisy's back. His little paws gripped onto her mane as Elora climbed on behind. "Give me your hand," she ordered her mother. Athena reluctantly offered it up and was pulled onto the mare, sliding her legs behind Elora. Bray and Norgie climbed onto the other horse.

Trusting that her mother and Gurple wouldn't fall off, she dug her heels into Daisy's flanks and spurred the mare into a gallop.

Hooves struck the cobbled yard as they dashed across open ground. Bullets whizzing passed them, striking the stone floor.

"Yah!" Elora shouted, willing more speed from Daisy. The horse's nostrils widening with the effort as she lowered her head and pressed on.

The pathway ahead broke through the tree-line, tall oaks to either side with men quickly jumping into the gap. Rifles raised as they took aim.

Elora slipped her pistol from her thigh holster and fired off two rounds in quick succession; both bullets tearing into the shiny breastplate of the closest soldier. The polished metal split as his body propelled backwards, blood spraying from the damaged armour.

Before he hit the ground, Daisy had trampled over him, knocking the other aside as they raced by. The nose of Bray's horse close enough to catch Daisy's tail.

Elora worried that the remaining guards would shoot them in the back. But as she glanced over her shoulder, she watched as the oaks seemed to come alive; wide branches becoming animated as they wrapped around the soldiers and crushed them.

"Thank you," Elora shouted into the forest, hoping that somewhere The Green Man would hear her.

They galloped along the narrow path at a frightening speed. Athena squeezing Elora's waist so tight she found it hard to breathe, while Gurple bounced in front of her. His small furry body jolting with each thundering bound. But mercifully they didn't meet any more soldiers along the way.

As they raced towards the tall gate, Elora fired her pistol into the air to get the gatekeeper's attention. From the rotund silhouette atop the ramparts, she recognised who it was.

"Pudding!" she bellowed, fighting to stay atop her horse. "Close the gate. We're under attack."

Pudding didn't move at first. Shock making his face turn slack as he watched them approach. Then in a bustle of movement, he picked up the alarm signal and began to shake the bell as if he was throttling the life from it.

"Drop the portcullis!" he shouted down to the pair of grimbles that where in the wheelhouse, and the thick spikes of the gate began to lower. "Stand to! Stand to!" Pudding screamed, his face turning red as he dropped the bell and cocked the bolt of the huge machine gun that was secured to the turret. By the time Elora and Bray had ridden beneath the tower, there were more than a dozen soldiers joining Pudding above the rampart.

Before the steel spikes of the heavy gate locked into the ground, Elora caught the sight of thousands of armed men emerging from the surrounding tree-line.

Now safely behind the Keep walls, Elora reined her horse in; turning Daisy about so they faced the gate tower. Captain Brindle was running up the stone steps to join Pudding on the wall.

"Easy," he shouted, raising his arms to his men. "Nobody fires until I give the signal." He glared out into the open ground beyond the perimeter; scowl deepening as the ground began to shake.

Elora climbed from her horse and threw the reins to Norgie, who had already dismounted from Bray's mare.

"Spread word through the Keep," she ordered, offering her mother a sad smile. "Tell them we're under attack and that everyone is to evacuate into the Shadowlands. They know the procedure."

Norgie nodded that he understood. "I'll see every man woman and child through there personally," he replied and led Daisy away.

Trusting Norgie to do as she asked, she and Bray made their way to the top of the gate tower, taking the steps two at a time.

"How many?" Elora demanded as they joined Captain Brindle.

Leaning against the old stone, she surveyed the men marching towards them. Row upon row of neat ranks. Large square formations that came to a halt a hundred paces from the wall, circling the entire Keep.

Brindle cleared his throat. "I wouldn't like to give a specific number," he said, "but at a guess, it's in the tens of thousands." The ground rumbled with the weight of men marching together.

"I think the whole garrison has turned up to the party, Sir," Pudding offered, both hands resting upon his machine gun.

"And then some," Bray added, exchanging a worrying look with Elora.

She watched as crows flew over the army of men. Cawing into the cold air before they came together. Flying around each other at a dizzying speed. Forming a maelstrom of black feathers, a blur of movement until the birds merged into a single figure.

"Dethtil," Elora whispered, removing her hands from the stonework as she involuntary stepped back, slipping her soul reaver from the smuggler's pouch.

The approaching man stepped out in front of his men. Long hair brushing his shoulders, a cocky smirk playing upon full red lips.

"Elora," he chuckled, pausing at the foot of the tower, head craned up as he gazed at her, his naked torso glistening from the winter sun. "This is no way to greet your husband-to-be."

Bray tensed as if he was about to leap from the ramparts, until Elora steadied him by placing an arm around his stomach.

"You're no husband of mine and never will be," she shouted down, wanting to tear that smirk from his face. "I'd sooner marry a grumpkin."

This brought a laugh from the men around her, but she saw the anger clenched into Dethtil's fists and his smirk dissolving into a snarl.

"You will be mine, daughter of Solarius," he yelled, voice sounding petulant as he lost himself to anger. "Even if I must break through your pathetic defences and kill every single man, woman and child you hold under your protection. I will toast their blood with our wedding vows."

"Never," Bray growled, drawing his pistol and firing a single shot at the warlock. Yet Dethtil dispersed into a murder of crows, only solidifying into his human form once the bullet had passed. He was about to fire again until Elora pushed his gun down.

"You won't hit him," she warned. "Save your bullets for something that they can kill."

The warlock raised his eyebrows and drew down his lips in a sad expression. "You will learn to obey me, Elora," he said, lifting a bare arm into the air. "I'll give you one last chance to save your precious people before I break down these walls and destroy everything you have sworn to protect."

Elora witnessed the eagerness of the attacking army. Tens of thousands of men, armed with rifles and steel; formed up to do as ordered and only waiting for the signal. She felt the excitement building in Dethtil. The long-awaited dream of becoming a god at his fingertips, and the wife he would make of the girl that would make it possible. She sensed the overwhelming odds of everything that stood against her. If she wanted to, she could end it now. She could sacrifice herself in order to let her people live. A life of servitude for those she loved. It would be the easy choice, perhaps the right choice. Yet no matter if Dethtil let her people go. Neptula would still drown the rest of the world.

Bray's fingers interlaced with her own and she held tight to them, sensing the warmth and the love that radiated from him.

Movement from beyond the army, caught her eye. The subtle shifting of the tree canopy, the naked limbs moving against the wind. The deep knocking of wood, the rumbling and grating as the trees twisted and bent into different positions.

Elora let her gaze fall back to the Warlock, his arm still poised in the air, ready to give the command to attack.

"You came to me seeking immortality," Elora announced, glowering at the man who would steal Bray away from her. "Yet all you will receive is death."

Dethtil's face contorted into a sad smile as he placed his fingers together. "So be it, Elora. But in time you will regret your actions, Not I."

His arm dropped and as one, the army began to move.

Riflemen, dropped to one knee as they adopted firing positions; hundreds of long barrels raised up towards the ramparts. Other soldiers advancing, marching in step as they raised pikes and swords, sharpened steel glinting from the approaching blanket of men. There was so many, and much more stepping out from the tree-line, shining armour and polished boots, the Empire's finest.

"Guards," Captain Brindle shouted, raising his own rifle. "On my command, open fire."

He turned to Elora, ready for her permission to carry out the order. Yet she wasn't ready. How could she give the order that would instantly see men die? Most of them were only following orders themselves. As were her own soldiers.

She watched the Empire advance, several flags jostling in the wind, bright suns emblazoned on scarlet cloth. The imperial elite that would slaughter her own people.

Elora swallowed down the guilt and gave Brindle a curt nod. This was Dethtil's work, along with Flek's. The true blame lies with them. As indeed it did with Neptula – and she would see the Sea Witch die for forcing her hand in killing others.

The Captain turned to his men. "Fire!" he shouted, and explosions from many rifles filled the battlements. The rapid bursts of bullets spat from Pudding's machine gun, his own face pulled back into a snarl as he aimed down the crosspiece, his finger held tight against the trigger.

Elora stared at Dethtil, their eyes locking onto each other as she felt hate radiating from every fibre of her being. She didn't flinch when bullets began to thud into the stonework around her. Broken masonry flying chips and chunks all about her. Bray attempted to drag her out of harm's way but she was going nowhere. She wanted to stay. She wanted to fight and was desperate to kill the warlock.

"Elora we must leave," Bray implored as he tugged at her arm. "We can't do anything here. We must defeat Neptula before Volcaneus creates more volcanoes."

"I can't simply leave the Keep to defend itself," she argued, wanting to scream in frustration as one of the bulworgs on the rampart was shot in his chest. His limp body fell heavily from the battlements to slam into the ground below.

Dethtil gloated, his arms spreading wide as he stalked closer; body blurring into black feathers as bullets harmlessly passed through him.

"Elora," Bray persisted, still attempting to pull her away. "Our last fight is with Neptula, not here."

"He's right," Captain Brindle agreed, as he deftly changed the magazine on his rifle. "Go now, before they breach the wall. My men will hold them back long enough to evacuate the Keep, then we'll follow."

Elora doubted their chances, once the warlock had gained entry. And since he had the power to destroy the fairy protection that surrounded the Keep, he would find the outer wall a simple task.

Forcing her legs to take her away from the rampart, she gave Brindle a brief hug. "Please don't take any risks, once they've breached the wall, retreat."

The Captain nodded that he understood, although Elora got the impression that he would stay there until the bitter end.

Dropping down the steps, Elora climbed upon Bray's horse and wrapped her arms around her fiancé's waist. "Let's get this done," she said, and held on tight as the large mare broke into a gallop as it thundered through the winding streets of the Keep.

People were running from buildings. The majority of the men and women ran towards the outer wall to aid in the defence, while the elderly and new mothers made their way to Zilabeth's workshop, carrying babies or young children. Elora recognised the scared faces of most of them, had known them for the last few months, spent time with them, shared food and the occasional laugh. She saw Ben scrambling after Slater. The newly trained defender, clumsily grasping his rifle while he attempted to fasten the chin strap of his helmet. His girlfriend gazing after him as she held their son, her eyes brimming with tears as they parted. It was enough to bring tears to Elora's own. She blinked them away as they pushed on.

She gripped tighter to Bray as the horse jumped a low wall into a cobbled courtyard, scraping up the old stone as they thundered towards the huge workshop.

Zilabeth and Teaselberry met them outside and took the reins from Bray.

"Dethtil?" the inventor asked, glaring back the way they had come.

Elora nodded, "He's here, along with half the Empire. The Keep is under siege." She watched the wood troll's ears flare up in distress and gently lay her hand against the top of her head. "It'll be alright," she reassured them as a steady flow of people shuffled through the large doors. "They won't harm you in the Shadowlands."

She grasped Zilabeth's hand and led them through the busy workshop to the sliding doors that opened up into the other world.

"Once everyone is through I want you to seal the door," Elora said, pausing to ensure that the descendant of Zalibut understood. "The Empire won't follow you into the Shadowlands, but Dethtil will."

"I hope he tries," Zilabeth remarked, pointing to the floor in front of the sliding door. "I've found a way to capture the warlock."

Elora only noticed the silver netting as it was pointed out to her. It stretched the length of the door with a fine rope tied to each corner.

"Is it a trap?" she asked.

"It's still a prototype," Zilabeth admitted, touching her finger to her bottom lip. "Yet I see no reason why it shouldn't work."

Elora embraced the inventor in a tight hug. "I've full faith in you," she said. "But if all else fails, you must escape into the Shadowlands." Zilabeth nodded. "Bray and I will be flying directly to Neptula."

"And I'll need to borrow the Spitfire," Bray put in. "And as much ammunition as she will carry."

Zilabeth turned to Teaselberry and raised an eyebrow. "Tease, get the old bird fired up," she said, as they made their way through the large sliding door, careful not to snag the silver netting on their boots. "I'll need to give Bray a crash course in flying."

Teaselberry's tongue flopped from her mouth as she scurried away, kicking up dust in her haste to reach the plane which was parked on the flats of the plateau. The sleek wings and fuselage, polished to a high shine as if on display.

"I'll be gentle with her," Bray continued, realising how much pride Zilabeth had put into that machine.

"She is a thing of beauty," Zilabeth added, sliding a hand down the slender nose cone. "But she is also a tool of war. She can take a hammering."

Teaselberry had primed the pump and lay her hand against the propeller, awaiting the command to fire her up.

"Climb up," Zilabeth instructed, and Bray pulled himself into the cockpit. Elora waited until he was strapped in before touching his hand.

"I'll meet you in the sky," she said, then turned to give Teaselberry a hug. She would leave Bray to have his brief lesson in flying the Spitfire, while she sought her dragon.

22

The Jewel

Grycul cut through the dusty sky. Her long shadow that trailed across the cracked barren ground was joined by that of the spitfire's. Glancing to her side, Elora watched Bray fly the fighter plane, its curved wing inches from them. Steam billowing from the rows of pipes that protruded from the V-twelve engine. He turned to face her, smiling through the eighty-year-old glass that covered the cockpit. She returned the smile, praying to Minu, or the Blessed Mother – or to any god that was listening, that they would defeat Neptula and end the world's suffering. To settle down and be properly together with the man she loved. Was that too much to ask?

Thoughts of Rams Keep crept into her mind, aided by the anxious feelings of their mission. She hoped everyone had made it to safety. Then her reflections drifted towards the north and her friends who were being cut down in the mud. What if The Green Man was unable to help? What if her scraw-harpies were too late to free the seedlings? What if Jaygen, Ejan and Ragna were already dead?

It was doing her no good, dwelling on such things. She needed to put her trust in the powers-that-be and concentrate all her powers on the battle ahead. The last fight. It wouldn't be long before they would be passing through into Ethea, somewhere out in the great ocean.

Up ahead, floating above the horizon was a dark smudge. As they flew it grew until Elora recognised what it was and she began to smile. It was the Necrolosis.

The gruesome vessel was already at full sail, leaning hard into the wind as it ploughed through the green sea of souls that kept the craft in the air. It was travelling in the same direction they were going, its deck full of Dark soldiers, grimbles and grumpkins.

Elora steered Grycul alongside the Necrolosis while Bray flew along the other.

"What are you doing?" she shouted to the Captain, whose large hands were gripping the wheel, his pointed teeth displayed in a grin.

"I'll be coming with you, my Queen," Zionbuss answered, bowing his head. "The Necrolosis, my crew and I, have been far from battle and now that the last is upon us, we want to be a part of it."

"But can your ship still fly in Thea? I thought you were bound to the Shadowlands," Elora shouted above the noise of the sails snapping tight.

Zionbuss shrugged his huge bare shoulders, the swirling scrollwork that was tattooed upon his skin blurring. "Maybe," he acknowledged, his grin spreading wider. "Maybe not, yet I've spent far too long trapped here. Oblivion awaits us all and I would rather meet it head on than wait an eternity for it."

Elora couldn't argue with that and she felt relief for having him with her when she met Neptula.

"Then let us hope that you don't fall into the ocean once we pass through the barrier," Elora bellowed, "I doubt your ship would float on real water."

Zionbuss stuck out his bottom lip, mocking offence. "She's the finest galley in all the worlds," he laughed tapping the skeletal wheel.

Elora grinned with him, although she really did doubt that the vessel would stay afloat if the sea of souls suddenly evaporated.

The demon faced forwards and pointed ahead. "Either way, we're about to find out."

There was no sign or indication that this was the place that they should pass through the barrier between worlds, other than Elora felt that it was right. This was confirmed by Grycul who ascended above the Necrolosis and as gentle as she could, grasped the crow's nest of the ship with one talon. Her other she touched the top of the spitfire's fuselage, applying just enough pressure to keep contact.

Elora braced herself, gripping tighter with her knees and wrapped her arms as far around the dragon's neck as she could.

Then with a cry, Grycul dipped her head and they flew through the barrier. Breaking out into cold fresh air and the shimmering blue ocean stretching far below in all directions.

Worried, she glanced at the Necrolosis, yet the gruesome ship stayed aloft. Zionbuss, leaning out over the wheel, laughing menacingly. Below the ship, Bray swung the spitfire clear of the vessel before rising to fly level with her, giving her a wink through the cockpit window.

At least they made it this far, Elora mused, hoping it was an omen of things to come. Although she got the distinct impression that disaster was awaiting them. Neptula wasn't expecting their arrival, but that didn't mean that the Sea Witch wasn't protected. The task ahead wasn't going to be easy.

On the flat horizon, rising from the water was a tall structure. From this distance, it appeared to be nothing more than a finger-shaped rock, reaching up into the sky. Yet as they neared, the Jewel took more shape. The outlines of skagwangles roaming its pinnacle while the dark shapes of water dragons glided above. It didn't seem like a lot but Elora knew that below the surface was an endless number of teeth, claws and tentacles that were loyal to Neptula.

The guards on the Jewel became more animated when they realised that a threat had arrived. Sharp-nosed fish also followed them from below. Bursting out of the water, long sword-shaped noses allowing them to keep pace as they swam and leapt above the surface before diving back under; leaving white foaming waves in their wake. Other fish and creatures of the vast ocean accompanied them. The dorsal fins of sharks cut through the brine, racing ahead like a thousand sharp blades slicing open the sea. And in between them and the Jewel, the water was a foaming white miasma of thrashing movement. Becoming more excited the closer they got. Elora knew that if any of them fell into the water, they would be instantly torn apart.

The soldiers aboard the Necrolosis stared down from the gunnel and rigging, sharing nervous glances as they watched the enemy below. Even Zionbuss gripped tighter to the bony rail as he observed the creatures beneath him. God-created or not, the demon wouldn't survive long if he fell.

Elora watched as he signalled to his crew and they brought large wooden chests and barrels to the side of the ship, before lifting them on to the gunnel itself.

When Zionbuss noticed she was watching him he smiled. "Present from the Dark Army," he shouted before ordering his crew to open the lids and tip the contents into the sea.

Thousands of takwiches plummeted from the casks and barrels. Legs and pincers snapping together as they splashed into the big blue and instantly sank beneath the surface.

"I know you said you would never order the use of takwiches," Zionbuss yelled. "But this was my choice and I humbly request my Queen's forgiveness."

Elora watched the sharks and swordfish below as they suddenly halted their chase and began to struggle under the waves. She couldn't see what was happening yet knew that they were under attack from the takwiches.

"Will it work?" she asked, feeling a glimmer of hope as a hammerhead shark lifted its bar shaped head out of the water and sunk its teeth into the great white beside it.

"It appears so, my Queen," Zionbuss replied.

"Then I forgive you," Elora shouted, although her voice was drowned out by the rising noise of the vicious attack that was happening below. It would aid them greatly to have a few fish turn against Neptula. She was beginning to regret not using them at the Keep. Yet the real threat was from the water dragons which had begun to fly towards them. Rows of large gliding beasts with skagwangles riding upon them, drawn bows in hand.

Grycul screamed as they approached, spreading her large wings out as she ascended above and spat a ball of fire at the leading dragon.

The white sphere of heat hit the creature directly in the head, spitting flames on the rider behind. They both writhed in agony as they tumbled into the sea. Instantly they were ripped apart by the hungry creatures, green blood clouding the waves. Elora barely had time to register the gruesome ending of the pair before Grycul banked higher and came around to spit flames at another.

The spitfire roared as Bray flew through the middle of the ranks of water dragons. Tipping the craft on its side to avoid collision as bullets tore into Neptula's flying army.

A heartbeat later a cannon boomed from the Necrolosis, belching flames as the large ball crunched through one dragon and into the one flying behind. The tangle of limbs crumpling together as they plummeted below.

The soldiers aboard the vessel aimed rifles and were firing at will. Their superior firepower working well against the onslaught.

Grycul lurched to the side, avoiding a spear that had been flung at her. The shaft grazed her neck and narrowly missed Elora's face. She drew her gun and fired twice into her attacker. Then held tightly on to Grycul as she banked around, swooping below another water dragon and raised her gun to fire into the water beast's belly. It screeched in pain, flinging its rider off as it careered blindly into another dragon.

Two neat rows of bullets tapped along the surface of the water, the rapid pattern only broken as Bray's rounds found meaty targets. The fighter plane's engine thundering under his controls as he skimmed above the water before rising once again to make another pass.

Skagwangles roared, dragons screamed and the cannon boomed. The fight was becoming more vicious as the two forces came together. Zionbuss shouted orders, his crew firing arrows into the air, hitting the enemy while receiving black jagged arrows in return. The skagwangles being more manoeuvrable and able to fire from above as well as below. Yet the vanguard of Neptula's army was soon becoming weak as their numbers reduced to only a few.

Elora felt her confidence rise with each water dragon that they successfully dispatched, yet when her gaze fell upon the Jewel again, her heart sank.

There were more rows of water dragons heading their way. Many, many, more rows. They swarmed over and around the jutting Jewel, darkening the sky as they grew closer. A flying army that moved as one, diving, dipping and gliding. They would be on them in moments.

Guiding Grycul to fly alongside the Necrolosis, Elora attracted Zionbuss's attention and pointed at the looming mass. "Climb higher," she shouted. "They have the numbers but will struggle to reach us."

Zionbuss bowed to her and then bellowed at his crew.

Elora circled the ship as it rose, flying through the sea of souls. A chill ran through her, forcing an involuntary shiver as the souls pulled at her like a thickening fog. Tortured faces and spectral limbs brushing against her in their eternal torment.

After she passed through the other side, she made a mental note to stay clear of it in the future.

Steam chugged from the whirring engine of the spitfire as it slowed to keep pace with them, Bray's firm face fixed on the coming onslaught. He slid the cockpit window open, eyes narrowing against the wind.

"I'll make a path through the middle of them," he yelled above the noise. "Follow close behind until we reach the Jewel."

"No," Elora shouted back. It would be a suicide mission for Bray. If his plane hit a dragon, it would be pulverised, and if he survived the crash, he would only end up in the water. "I'll fly over the army and drop in from above. They can't hurt me while I'm smoke."

Bray clenched his teeth. "You cannot fight Neptula alone. Not in her environment – she's too strong."

"She's strong," Elora agreed. "But I am my father's daughter. Chaos will defeat her."

Bray was about to protest when Grycul screamed and spat a fireball ahead. Smoke trailed the firing projectile as it struck a skagwangle that was about to fire an arrow at them. The flaming ball engulfed the creature, knocking him from his steed and into the sea.

"It'll work," she shouted at Bray before he spoke. "You and Zionbuss provide a distraction."

She saw the anguish on his face and the anger in his moss-green eyes. But he didn't attempt to argue. "I love you," she mouthed and then turned away. She needed full concentration if she was to pull this off.

The fighter plane's engine increased its pace as Bray pushed it on, his twin guns bursting to life as he fired at the approaching dragons. Elora lay flat against Grycul's neck, leaning into her attack. She placed her gun into her holster and retrieved her soul reaver. Pointing the blade at the wave of flying sea beasts as they raced into a head-on collision.

Droplets glistened from the water dragon's nose, head and wings. Like its rider, its mouth was pulled back in a rictus grin, sharp teeth shining white beneath rubbery flesh. Eyes narrowed and gleaming with violence.

The instant before impact, Elora and Grycul flashed through the barrier into the Shadowlands. The fresh sea air instantly giving way to dry arid dust.

She leaned back, visualising her intentions to the dragon beneath her. Then pressed forwards as the dragon responded. Rising up to a near vertical climb as they headed for the fiery ceiling of the god-created world.

Elora guessed that they had travelled the distance needed, before they broke through the barrier once again. The flaming ceiling giving way to bright blue as they emerged onto an Ethean sky.

Still climbing, she glanced behind her and witnessed the Jewel directly below. The narrow finger of rock appearing tiny amidst the tumultuous foam of the sea as it slapped against it. The dot of a solitary being stood motionless at its centre. Staring out at the battle.

Neptula.

Elora lay her hand to Grycul's side. "It is time," she exclaimed.

The dragon gave a final beat of her wings before tucking them into her side. Her body slowing as gravity reached its grasp around, spinning the pair of them slowly until they began to descend.

Headfirst they plummeted. The dive accelerating until Elora was forced to close her eyes against the wind that whistled through her hair.

The Jewel rushed up to meet them. The finger of rock reaching out, surrounded by the thick cloud of water dragons that were still unaware of their approach.

"Stay with Bray," Elora ordered her dragon. Although the words were snatched away in the fall, her command still penetrated Grycul's mind.

In the final moment before impact, Elora threw her arms wide and allowed the airstream to tear her away. She reduced to smoke as Grycul swept beneath the water dragons and out to join Bray and Zionbuss.

Elora trusted that the three of them would hold out long enough for her to do the grisly task ahead.

Waves battered against the Jewel, white foam crashing over the porous walls, washing over the flat bed that sat atop the sliver of rock. Elora hit the ground as the water receded over the edge, becoming solid once again; her blade held before her.

Neptula stared out to sea and was unaware of her approach. The robed figure was hidden beneath her hood, the soaked material hanging low to the coral rock.

Elora approached silently, the tip of her sword inches from the Sea Witch's back. With a single thrust, she could end the war. With a flick of her wrist she would save the world. Yet she had a code to abide by. She must offer the sea god a chance to yield – a chance to kneel before her justice was met out. Even though Neptula would die whether she yielded or not.

Taking another step closer, Elora gripped her sword with two hands, pulling it back, bunching her muscles in anticipation of driving her steel through Neptula's heart.

In the distance, she heard the spitfire's engine roaring as Bray banked around a line of water dragons. The twin guns spitting flames as he rapidly shot bullets into the beasts. Grycul following close behind. Twice the size of her seafaring cousins, she viciously cut, bit and slashed her way through the ranks.

Breaking her gaze away, Elora concentrated once again on her foe. Yield? Did the Sea Witch offer the worlds a chance to yield before she planned on merging them together, before she slaughtered thousands - millions of innocents? Did she offer anything to those she planned to drown? No. She would see all land-dwelling creatures: man, animal and plant, die. Neptula didn't deserve the opportunity to yield.

Closing her lids, she allowed the other her to come forward. The daughter of Chaos wouldn't think twice before slaughtering Neptula. Wouldn't give a damn about any code or oath sworn as a Shadojak.

Feeling a thrill of excitement rush through her, Elora licked her lips. She tightened her grip on her sword, stepped into the robed figure before her and drove the blade through Neptula's back.

She felt the tip cut through flesh and scrape against the ribs before puncturing through the other side.

The body before her snapped rigid and arched back, the hood falling as the Sea Witch screamed. Azure spines sticking erect from her scalp, the fine membrane between, shaking as it pulled tight. It lasted only seconds before the body relaxed, the head flopping forwards and the scream tapering off to a watery rattle.

Elora slid her soul reaver free and let the carcass fall. The creature she had killed flopped against the rocks. A wave crashing against the Jewel washed over the ridge and under the beast's head, rocking it gently as if the ocean caressed its former god. Neptula stared out to sea, her mouth slack as it filled with water.

Slick green blood ran down Elora's blade, dripping from the tip and into a shallow rockpool. Tiny crabs scurrying along its bottom, sensing a feed somewhere. Everything in the sea was food for something else.

Was it done? Was the war won? Was it that easy?

An unease crept up Elora's spine. The other her now dissolving and allowing her to take control, although they were far less different than they had ever been. She placed her foot against Neptula's body and rolled her over so she now faced her executioner.

"No," Elora gasped. It wasn't Neptula. It was a strange hybrid of skagwangle and the being that the Sea Witch was. The realisation of her mistake was only confirmed by laughter, coming from behind.

When she turned, Elora saw a tall, robed creature standing beside an empty hollow; steps circling down into the rock itself. Another wave crashed against the Jewel spraying a fine mist across the top.

"You will find that I won't die as easily as my daughter," Neptula chuckled, showing rows of tiny triangular teeth.

"Daughter?" Elora asked, feeling a sudden pang of guilt for slaying the girl in cold blood. Did she deserve it?

"Yes, my daughter," Neptula confirmed, taking a step down into the hollow. "But don't worry. We sea creatures don't think of our kin as lovingly as you humans do. I've mothered thousands more." She took another step, grin spreading wider as she curled a webbed finger, beckoning her closer. "If you look over your shoulder now, you may see another of my children as she crushes your lover."

Panic wrenched Elora's head around as she sought out Bray. The spitfire was sweeping in low, skimming above the sea and avoiding the rush of water dragons. She thought he was making light work of Neptula's forces, yet as she watched, a thick tentacle reached up from beneath the surface.

It was a leviathan.

"Bray!" Elora screamed as she helplessly observed her fiancé. He steered the plane around the tentacle which could crush it like paper. But when another darted from the frothing white waves she realised that Bray couldn't avoid them all.

In a desperate attempt at reaching a safe altitude, Bray pulled the spitfire into a steep climb, yet his actions were too late.

Horror tore through every cell in Elora's body as she knew that he would collide with the solid mass of the leviathan. Steam raced over the sleek craft, its flaps rising at a right angle to the tail wings as a tentacle raked down the under belly of the plane, tearing a large gorge along its fuselage.

She breathed a sigh of relief when Bray cleared the air, climbing out of reach. Although she knew the damage had been done. Flames fell from the tank on the plane. Liquid fire rippling out of the hole in the barrels beneath. Bray wouldn't be flying for much longer.

"Your mate does appear ravishing, don't you think? I hope my army saves some tasty morsels for myself. Once I've finished with you."

Elora returned her attention to the Sea Witch. Anger, hatred, frustration welling up from her core – venting itself in the grip around her sword, in her muscles as she tensed; ready to hurl herself at Neptula.

"I'm not such a fool as to fight you out in the open, Elora. I know the true power of Chaos."

Before the Sea Witch descended another step, Elora reduced herself to smoke and flowed across the space between them, aiming to cut her off before she disappeared below. Yet as she flowed through the fine sea mist, an icy chill seeped into her being. The world that as smoke she witnessed from a million different angles suddenly blurred and she found it impossible to travel further.

Neptula was laughing once again as Elora reformed, a clammy cold setting deep inside her bones.

"Smoke doesn't pass through water as well as you might like," the Sea Witch explained as she slowly shifted down the steps, pendulum hips swaying like the rolling waves of the ocean. "Join me below, daughter of Chaos. There, at least, we will meet as equals."

Gasping for breath, Elora stared after the figure, the spines on her head fluttering as she disappeared.

She spared a glance at Bray. The spitfire was struggling to stay in the air. The engine beginning to splutter and cough plumes of smoke.

"I love you," she whispered in his direction, spinning her thumb ring before she turned away. Resolved to finishing the war.

Flames began to course through her veins as she descended the steps into the hollow of the Jewel. It was time to finish this.

23

Hades

Surrounded by darkness, Jaygen forced air into his chest. The pressure from the weight of demons pinning him down, blocked out the world whilst grinding him into the mud. They had failed. The entire north had marched to their own destruction, forcing battle against an overwhelming force. Defeated. And soon the world would perish. Every man, woman and child would drown because they couldn't kill Hades.

Jaygen attempted to move, but didn't have control over his fingers. He could wiggle his toes inside his boots and lick the sweat from his lips, but nothing else. His mind wandered to his mother, to his father and Fieri. Were they dead already? Like Fin only moments before, were they slain and now waiting for him to join them in Valhalla? Was he to be the last to die, the cursed suit giving him enough protection for a slow death?

Panic began to sink into his being as he fought to breath. Suffocating, as air was denied, ebbing away until he began to see white dots fizzle at the edge of the darkness. He didn't know whether his eyes were open or closed, the flashing stars were all he could see. His mind drifted to happier times. Riding his horse through the forest at Rams Keep, exploring the dungeons beneath the ruins – that kiss with Fieri.

Something suddenly poked him in the shoulder. It scraped along his back-plate, grazing like a knobbly stick rubbing down a tree. He felt it bend and twist, snaking beneath his abdomen and hook around. Was this the end? Had the demons found a way to fasten a rope around his midriff and were about to pull him apart?

Yet the snaking feeling was joined by others. Long tendrils that fed around his suit, weaving over and between his legs, his arms and thickening as they progressed. Maybe he would be crushed, then. Hades having summoned demon snakes to twist him into nothing.

His entire body suddenly jerked and a pinprick of light broke through his visor. It widened as he felt himself dragged up, movement returned to his head. Shaking more mud from the visor, he sucked in the fresh air, wrenching his arm free and swinging it before he could focus on what he was swinging it at.

His gauntlet met a solid lump. The crunch of bones breaking beneath his fist as he cocked it back for another blow. They would kill him eventually, but if he had movement, he would take as many of the beasts down as he could.

Hooking a finger into his mask, he pulled the rest of the clotted mud from his face and glared about him, expecting to see a solid mass of demons with dead Vikings at their feet.

Instead, he watched scraw-harpies fall from the sky. Hitting the ground and beginning to scrape into the wet earth. Hundreds of the large birds, ignoring Hades' army as they tore at the mud.

Jaygen was about to cut through the rope that bound him when he realised that it was a thick vine, rippling with leaves as it uncurled its grip from him. Then, twisting into the air, it rose higher than the surrounding demons, thickening as it swirled around like a cobra and darting at the closest being.

The green vine weaved around the demon's neck several times before pulling tight.

One of his comrades struck the plant with a jagged blade of metal, slicing it in two, and the choking creature fell into the mire. Yet before his body sunk to the ground, another vine broke from the mud. Followed by more.

Strands of winding stems erupted all about them. Stretching passed the scraw-harpies that had been digging them out. Pale green shoots reaching skywards before seeking out the black oily beasts. Wrapping themselves around limbs and necks, holding them tight before dragging them to the floor.

Jaygen didn't know how it happened or why the plants came alive, but he felt grateful. They may be the turning point of the entire battle.

With his other arm now free, Jaygen raised his sword and began to cut a path to Fin. Hacking through demons and lopping the heads from others. Yet before he even reached Fieri's brother, he could tell that the boy was dead. As was a lot of Vikings that lay about the ground.

He cast his gaze about the destruction in search for others. A thick vine, wrapped around a demon, suddenly yanked him bodily into the air to reveal Ragna. The large Viking now free, managed to pull himself up and began to swing the Fist of the North.

A growl to his side brought Jaygen's attention to a pile of charcoal beasts that were punching and kicking someone beneath them. In a single bound he reached them and began to swing his blade. He sunk the steel into the skull of the closest, then wrenched it free in a spray of molten blood before thrusting into the back of another.

The growl grew louder until the rest of the coal-crusted bodies were shoved from beneath and Weakest rose, striking out with his lethal claws.

Demons fell around them, either by their own hands or by being entwined amongst the growing number of vines and taken away. When a space began to clear, Jaygen got a better grasp of the situation. The strange plants that had come to their rescue, were busy attacking Hades' army, leaving the humans alone. And the more the scraw-harpies dug into the mud, the more came forward. Yet he knew it still wouldn't be enough. There were still far too may demons and they would overpower them by sheer weight of numbers. The black mass of smouldering beings stretched into the distance in almost all directions.

Jaygen also realised that they were still a long run from Hades himself. And the god was swinging his large staff, forcing more demons into existence. The dark shapes rising from the ground at his feet. Crawling from the mud as he touched the tip of his staff to each, giving them life.

"Hades!" Jaygen bellowed, his voice reaching as far as the mound from which the God of the Underworld stood. Hades paused, his glowing eyes turning his way, his expression unreadable beneath a thick visor.

About him, flaming creatures writhed in the mud, wrestling with the vines as they curled about them. The men of the north taking advantage and bringing about swift ends on the end of sharpened steel. The noise was deafening. Screams, shouts, wails – roars of triumph, screeches of pain and the clash of weapons against weapons, or metal against bone and flesh.

Free from the bodies that had brought him down, Weakest prowled beside him, rubbing his matted fur against his greaves. His narrowed gaze staring at the mound ahead.

"It's up to us," Jaygen said to the bulworg, realising that nobody was mobile enough to push through the throng. The mass of bodies, demons and plant life, rolled and twisted in a field of chaos. He rested a hand upon Weakest's head. "Let's finish this."

Clenching his teeth, Jaygen broke into a run, reversing his grip on his sword to give him more stability. He charged through the tightly packed crowd. Using shoulder, elbow and fist to carve a path.

Weakest danced beside him, his four legs and nimble agility making easy work as he weaved between or leapt above the masses.

"Move," Jaygen screamed in frustration as a blackened beast fell into his way. He punched it in its smouldering mouth, the claws of his gauntlets crunching through the jaw and sending several crooked teeth spinning into the air. Arms flailed as the beast went down, crushed beneath his feet and the wave of men charging behind. The ground shaking with the weight of thousands of feet, stamping in the same direction.

Jaygen kept his head up, gaze locked on his target and urged every fibre of his being into getting there. The armour supplying him with the means to keep moving. Like oxen pulling a plough, he cut through the field, dividing men, plants and mud, demon's limbs and torsos.

Ahead, Weakest snarled at a large two-headed beast that had cut a vine in two. It swung a thick shard of metal around its body, bellowing into the throng with twin mouths. It watched the bulworg approach, grinning while it began arcing the jagged blade towards him.

Keeping the momentum flowing, Jaygen sidestepped around a broken body and flicked his wrist. His sword skimming between his elbow and one of the demon's grotesque heads.

Steel sliced through coal-crusted flesh, the stump spewing flaming lava as the body swayed back. Its other head opening a gaping mouth, showing a shocked expression as Weakest launched from the ground and sunk huge claws into its skull.

As he landed, he immediately sprung once again, driving into another black demon. Jaygen barely had time to register that a large sharpened stake was lowed towards him before his instincts took over and his free arm came up to batter the thick shaft of wood aside. His god-created metal absorbing the impact as his feet crunched down upon the fallen demon's chest.

Progress was slow and tiresome, but with the strange snake-like vines aiding them, they were gaining ground. He couldn't spare a glance to see if the Vikings were following. He only trusted that he and the bulworg would make it to the mound.

Somehow the vines had sensed what route they were taking and seemed to concentrate on spreading out in that direction. Curling around waists and necks, twisting about abdomens and limbs, the plants yanked the oily beings from the ground or flung them aside.

The heavy hordes before them parting like corn in a field

The realisation that the mound was coming closer spurred Jaygen on. The thrill of the chase, the blood thumping through his ears to be lost amongst the screams of the raging battle, his only song. They were closing in on Hades.

Then he misplaced his footing, his toe catching in the tangled limbs of a demon and he stumbled over. Falling to the mud once again, his gaze going skyward as a blur of muddy fur rushed below him and Weakest caught his fall.

Using his strong neck muscles, the bulworg levered Jaygen onto his own back.

Jostling up and down, he fought to keep balance, but it was clear that the bulworg meant for him to ride him like a horse. The pair of them covering the ground with more speed as they bounded along the path the plants were creating.

Flicking his sword expertly around his wrist, Jaygen lowered the tip of his sword forwards as he leaned into the charge - nothing could stop them now.

The tide of bodies parted before them; men, demons, vines – flesh, coal and plant, divided to allow them swift passage across the tumultuous ground.

Jaygen pushed all thoughts aside. His mother, father, Fieri; there was no room for them as he concentrated on the figure ahead. Hades had his full attention. The balance of Ethea and everything in it, lay in this one battle.

At the base of hill was a wall of demons, glowing embers staring from empty eye sockets, flames glistening along jagged strips of metal they held before them - slashing at the vines as they attempted to squeeze though. Yet these coal and oil golems seemed cleverer than their brethren that festooned the battlefield. They fought the whipping plants with more accuracy. With a higher sense of ability. Above them the god himself. His own crimson stare radiating from behind the thin slit in his visor. Hades lowered his staff and slammed it into the mud, spewing sodden earth. Dark flames spat from the floor itself. Fire sprouting from vents created in the mire to torch the god's attackers.

Smoke curled from the charred stems of the vines, blackening the vegetation along with any humans that came too close. Demons caught fire, yet it didn't hinder them at all as they fought on; bodies feeding the flames as the entire field began to burn.

Weakest suddenly yelped as his paws set down upon the charred remains of a plant that had curled around a golem. The yelp grew into a fierce growl as his pace suddenly picked up and the bulworg jumped.

Jaygen leaned with the movement. Rising from Weakest's back as the momentum carried them above the wall of armed demons.

As they began to fall, he leapt from the bulworg and landed heavily before Hades, shrinking into a crouch ready to thrust his sword up into the chest of the god.

Yet, as quick as the suit allowed him to be, Jaygen's lunge seemed slow compared to the shaft that Hades wielded. The long staff parrying his sword with ease before he slammed the butt of it into Jaygen's shoulder. The force strong enough to knock him onto his back.

Hades raised an iron-clad foot to slam down and grind into his wolf's helm. Jaygen had only enough time to register what was about to happen, the swiftness of the god was far faster than his own body. The hilt of his sword caught against his chest armour as he attempted to block the attack. He wouldn't bring it up in time. Yet as he fumbled, it was Weakest who came to his aid. The huge bulworg slamming into the god. Lethal claws scraping down the amour as his teeth sought flesh to sink into.

The impact pushed Hades back a step, but his amour was impenetrable. The god caught his balance, righted himself and then reached beneath Weakest's muzzle, squeezing his windpipe.

The bulworg thrashed, all paws scratching the iron-clad man as he pushed away from him, but Hades held on. Shaking the bulworg as if he was nothing more than a rag doll.

"No!" Jaygen screamed, his lungs burning as he rose from the ground and threw himself against the god. Wrapping an arm around his waist while sliding his blade along the belly plate, seeking a weakness in the armour.

The two metals squealed as the god-created steel scrapped along the thick iron, pushing Hades back another step.

The impact had been strong enough for the god to release Weakest, and the bulworg fell. His head bouncing from the ground, tongue flopping from the slack mouth, lids shut; blood dribbling from his ears.

Hatred blazed as Jaygen drove his fist into the god's abdomen. Once, twice – screaming profanities as he rained blow after blow, yet Hades seemed to soak up the impacts, his armour barely jolting, the dull thuds sounding pathetic.

"Die," Jaygen spat between clenched teeth, blood rushing through his ears; booming in time with his hammering heart. Reversing his grip on his sword, he thrust the hilt up under the god's chin. Metal meeting metal once again and knocking Hades' head back. The move should have killed a man but did little more than irritate the god.

All at once, a tremendous clang exploded at the side of Jaygen's temple and he was flung to the ground.

His vision blurred as he tried to sit up. The world through the eye slits was murky, a ringing sound filling his head as he shook the dizziness from his mind. He'd been struck on the side of the head by Hades, his weapon still vibrating with the impact.

As Hades stepped closer to deliver another blow, Jaygen raised his sword to deflect the attack. It was then that he realised his blade lay in the mud by his feet. Out of reach.

Hades swung the staff high, thick gauntleted fingers tightening around the strange weapon before he brought it crashing down.

Jaygen locked his forearms together and the staff cracked into them. The armour absorbing the shock as much as the god-created material could take. Yet the blow was strong enough to lift him from the ground and hurtle his body into the wall of golems that were approaching from below.

Gripping with many flaming limbs the demons picked him up and hurled him back. His tortured body landing beside Weakest as Hades approached for another strike.

The god walked with ease, his staff swinging playfully as he circled him. "You're no god," he informed him, voice dry and raspy. "You wouldn't attempt to kill me if you were."

His arm unexpectedly shot out and his staff struck Jaygen in the chest, knocking him onto his back and driving his breath from his lungs.

"No - only man is foolish enough."

Another blow, this one so fast that Jaygen only knew it had happened when fresh pain brought tears to his eyes, a fist-shaped dent concaving his shoulder plate. He turned his head in time to watch Hades' foot connect with his stomach and flip him over, so he was staring up at the god, struggling to gasp air through his battered body.

Rain gushed down the iron armour, running in thick rivulets to drip from the tips of the square chin and V-shaped visor. Twin crimson lights glowing menacingly from beneath the helmet. They appeared to brighten as he raised his staff, gripping it two-handed.

"The time of man has passed," Hades continued, flicking a catch on the staff and releasing a long blade from the bottom of the shaft. Flames rippled along the shining steel that Jaygen knew would puncture his armour as if it was tin. "Now is the time of the small gods."

Jaygen was defenceless as he lay there watching his own death unfold. The staff went up, the blade hovering above his face as he focused on the water that dripped from the lethal tip. Tears that should have been shed from his mother, his father and possibly from Fieri. Tears the world should cry as it realised it was soon to be given over to Neptula.

"Sorry," Jaygen croaked through his broken lips as he sensed Hades tense and the staff slam down.

"Odin!"

Suddenly Hades was knocked from view. His head torn ferociously back by the Fist of the North.

The mighty war hammer connected powerfully with the god's helm. Ragna followed the god as he reeled backwards, cocking the Fist onto his shoulder before swinging it again.

Jaygen struggled to lift himself up onto his elbows as Hades deflected the second blow, ready to drive his staff into his father. Yet as Ragna attempted to leap out of the way, an arrow slipped through the eye-slit in the god's visor.

Screaming in pain, his hands rising up to his face, Hades stumbled back and fell over Weakest's body. He crashed to his knees, his body jolting, flaming blood leaking from the crack in his visor, gushing over thick fingers.

Ragna didn't waste any time in dashing forwards, a war cry ripping from his throat as he swung the hammer with all his might. The steel head whistled through the air before thumping into the god's chest, knocking him onto his back.

"Stay down," Ragna screamed, his face locked in a demented grin as he worked the hammer hard, striking the grey armour, again and again.

Ejan slipped an arm beneath Jaygen and hoisted him into a sitting position. "Finish him," she hissed, sliding his sword from the mud and placing it in his hands. "Do it before he heals."

Jaygen was still struggling to suck more than a phantom of air into his lungs as he stumbled into a kneeling position. His gaze falling on Hades as the god gripped the shaft of the arrow and yanked it from his face. Flaming drops of blood spat as the arrow head came away, a single red stare locking with his father, hatred burning bright.

His body screaming in protest, Jaygen rose on unsteady legs. The fizzling dots still surrounding his vision before he shook them from his head. He leaned towards Hades, the god having regained control and slammed a fist into his father's ribs.

Ragna received the blow, only wincing as he twisted the shaft of the hammer, teeth gritted through his beard.

The steel head struck Hades across his helm, tipping the horned device back. Jaygen saw his opening and putting everything into his swing, arced his sword at the neck plate.

His blade bit deep into the iron, sparks flying as he opened a long gash and put the god on his back, head bouncing from the mud.

Before the armoured body came to a stop, Jaygen leapt upon his chest, straddling the god as he raised his sword and drove it down into the flaming visor. The blade entering through the eye slit, steel scraping against iron as it bit into the meat beneath.

He felt it slide through flesh before striking the back of the helm, Hades' arms locking out rigid, fingers shaking as they flexed. Then with a final gasp, the god fell still.

Rain spattered the grey iron helm, sizzling as it touched the flames that burned from inside, yet as he watched, the flames dulled before hissing out. The red glow dimming to nothing.

Tears – Jaygen thought as he leaned against the hilt of his sword. The wolf's head carved into the handle grinning back at him. They cry for anybody these days.

"You did it," Ragna wheezed as he lay a heavy hand upon his shoulder, his other hand holding his side where the god had struck him. "You killed Hades."

Jaygen glanced at the carnage around him. Everything had gone quiet. The burning golems and demons had fallen, becoming smouldering piles of coal and ash. The vines had ceased weaving through the ranks and had become still. And the Northmen stared at each other, puzzled expressions written on many faces.

"We, did it," Jaygen replied, as his mother helped him rise from Hades' body, his sword sticking up at a right-angle from the dead god's helm. He let go of his mother and hunkered down beside Weakest, raising the bulworg's face to his own.

The beast's tongue slowly drew inside his mouth as he took a slow laboured breath.

"You're alive," Jaygen stated, now smiling behind his mask. Weakest blew air through his nose in reply.

Leaving him to come around, Jaygen gave the bulworg a pat on his flank before surveying the carnage they had caused.

The threat now gone, the Vikings began to approach. Some limping, a couple helping the injured and Carmelga dragging her axe in a limp arm, but smiling through a blood-spattered face. Even Peter, his wooden shield now no more than a battered lump of wood, came to the aid of a Northman who had lost an arm. But many more lay still, face down in the mud, covered in ash and dust. The dead lay scattered along the path he had carved, snaking all the way back to the main body, half a mile away.

Panic began to spread through his being, Jaygen hungrily scanned the battleground, searching for that red hair. Surely it would stand out amidst all the mud and muck. Yet he failed to find it anywhere. Then as Carmelga stepped closer, she revealed Fieri. The girl was stumbling in the mid-ground between the hill and the outcrop of rocks. She appeared unhurt.

Jaygen's breath caught in his chest. Amongst all that horror, all that destruction, chaos and carnage, he witnessed beauty. When she noticed him, she smiled, the notched eyebrow rising as the sun broke through the dark clouds to brighten her face. Behind her a vivid rainbow arced across the land, the gorgeous colours piercing the greys of the sky to offer its prize over the fallen.

Jaygen had never before felt so complete. Even with the carnage before them, the death and mutilation, he found something that had been missing in his life. Something which he had sought in another. Yet only now coming to realise that what he felt before was a wilting flower compared to this.

Now the battle was won he could take off the armour. Reveal the man beneath and marry the girl that had stolen his heart. He would gladly trade the suit, the myth and the curse for Fieri - for love.

Behind him his father raised the Fist of the North, his face creased in pain, yet a grin breaking through.

"Odin!" he yelled, his salute to the God of the North echoing around them until every Viking in the field raised their own weapons towards the sky and repeated the name.

Glory – it was exactly how the bards sung about it in the songs from long ago. A victorious heart was a proud one, but Jaygen would give it all up gladly to have Fieri.

The cheering didn't die down as the group came together. There was much back slapping and chest thumping, tears and laughter. So much merriment amongst the dead and dying that it seemed like the world's biggest irony. But Jaygen found he couldn't pull his smile away, not even as he ambled over the dead, stepping over his fallen brethren to meet Fieri.

A young Viking suddenly stumbled amidst the cheering, falling into a bowman. His laughter piercing above everyone else's as the loosed arrow flew high in the sky. Then as people watched it, they cheered once again. Jaygen chuckled himself as he watched the shaft fly harmlessly up into the wind. It may even be the last arrow he'd ever see get fired on a battlefield. At least he hoped it was. The time had come to leave the suit behind. Bury Grimwolf and everything that came with the name. The god of winter could keep him.

Still chuckling he watched the clumsy arrow reach its zenith and begin to arc down, the tip glinting in the rainbow as it fell through all the colours of the spectrum. Then his laughter faltered.

"No," he whispered, willing the arrow to stop, to halt in mid-air, to change direction - to vanish from existence.

"Fieri!" he screamed, yet he already knew he was too late.

The arrow came down, its arc so graceful as it slipped into Fieri's chest.

Time came to a dramatic halt. Sound ceased to be. Jaygen's vision focusing on that one being.

Fieri, the smile vanishing, the crease deepening upon her brow as a tiny bead of blood seeped from the corner of her lips to run down her chin. Her lids fluttered closed and she toppled.

Time began once again as Jaygen bounded across the battleground. Rushing this time in the opposite direction as he had before, yet with an equal terror in his heart.

Men stood gaping at him as he shoved them aside in his race to reach her. He shouldered them out of the way, punched or slapped them from his path.

"Fieri?" he growled as he slid to a stop. Pushing passed another as he reached down to his love. "Fieri?" his voice now a whisper as he touched her cheek, his steel gauntlet seeming wrong next to her delicate skin.

He was too late.

Tears ran down the side of his face, hidden beneath the wolf's helm. Grasping her hand, he gently pulled her up into an embrace, the arrow scraping along his chest as he lifted her into his arms. Her empty gaze staring straight through him without seeing. Glowering into his soul accusingly – blaming him for falling in love, for setting the curse of winter upon her and claiming her life.

Her head flopped to the side as he stalked away and he raised his elbow so it fell into his shoulder; long red hair swinging in time to his gait.

Crossing the battlefield in silence, he carried her through the staring Vikings and across the rushing stream. Passed the rocks they had scouted upon the day before and headed in the direction of the beach.

The twin funeral pyre was complete. Jaygen placed Fieri's body gently upon the stack of logs, crossing her arms over the still body and gently laying her sword into cold hands. Her eyes were now closed and she seemed at peace, the arrow removed and the wound cleaned so not a speck of blood or mud appeared on her. Hauntingly beautiful, she appeared asleep.

Byral had joined him earlier as he cut down the sparse trees and found enough wood to burn. The pair of them had worked in silence, each wrapped up in their own thoughts as they built the piers; one for Fieri and the other for Fin. And amongst his own loss he found enough pity for the elder Viking, for he had lost both his son and daughter that day.

Stepping back, he gave Byral the room for him to kiss his daughter goodbye. Tears cascading down his matted beard. Once he was done he straightened up, grasped the burning torch and put it to the base of the pyre.

Fanned by the wind which crested the cliffs, the flames caught the dry kindling, swiftly spreading beneath the stacks. Smoke rose between the logs, offering a veil over the dead as their earthly bodies were consumed.

Byral came to stand beside Jaygen, the pair of them staring as the fire began to devour the bodies before them. Black smoke curling into the night sky to dwindle with the stars.

In a way, Jaygen consoled himself, these two were luckier than the rest of the Northmen who had fallen in battle. There were too many to build pyres for, as trees were rare. Instead, using the remains of the golems and demons, the survivors simply set fire to the entire field. Burning their dead in the biggest pyre in history. He didn't know the exact amount of lives lost that day, but

Jaygen wouldn't be surprised if the number was closer to the tens of thousands than not.

"I'm sorry," Byral finally spoke as the remains of his kin were swallowed by the flames. Jaygen didn't know if he was speaking to him or his dead children. Not knowing how to reply, he simply lay his hand on the older man's shoulder.

"I've made plenty of mistakes," he continued, pausing between words, choking on emotion as he talked to his dead children. "But bringing you here wasn't the biggest, not by far."

"This was not your fault," Jaygen soothed, attempting to console him. "Neptula is to blame."

But deep down, Jaygen blamed himself. The fault lay with him. It was he that had fallen in love with Fieri, he who had scoffed in the face of the curse, even after the warnings Shannog had given.

"Neptula is the cause, but it was I that made the mistake," Byral enforced, wiping his nose with his sleeve. "Yesterday, back at the beach camp. The Earth-born was accused of being a spy, of warning the Sea Witch of our coming. If she hadn't known we were closing in on Hades, maybe we could have killed him easier and with a lot less death."

"No, Peter was not the spy," Jaygen replied, "we have yet to find that traitor."

Taking a lumbering breath, Byral raised his chin, eyes sparkling in the firelight. "I know it wasn't him," he admitted, drawing his sword and throwing it on the ground.

Shaking his head, the old Viking sank to the snow before Jaygen, hair falling over his face. "It was me. I warned Neptula. I'm the spy."

The words hit Jaygen harder than a battering ram. "You?"

Sniffing, the huge Viking gazed up, arms held out to either side. "You see, I am to blame. I was approached by a skagwangle, days before Ragna returned to Craggs head. They offered me and my kin safe passage to a new land, a way to survive the tides that would drown the world. All I need do was warn her of any gathering forces. Send word of any attempts of attacks in the north."

Ice chilled through Jaygen's blood. A shiver racked his body as he drew his sword. The steel whispering against the scabbard offering the only solution.

"Regrets, I have plenty," Byral continued, unflinching from the sword that now hovered above his head. "Had I known we had a chance of killing Hades, I wouldn't have taken the offer. But regrets aren't worth anything. I cast my lot and now I pay the price. I've paid it three times over. For Fin, for Fieri and for myself."

"No," Jaygen spat. "You paid it thousands of times over. With every life that was lost on the journey here." Yet Fieri's death was Jaygen's to keep. That regret was his and he wouldn't let Byral take that from him.

"True," Byral admitted, shame lowering his head once again. "The lives of the fallen lay at my feet. I am the traitor and will die as such. Odin will not find a place for me in Valhalla. I will not die a Viking's death, like my children." A single sob escaped him before he straightened. "Kill me now, Grimwolf. I don't deserve to live."

Fire from the pyres reflected along Jaygen's blade, dancing along the sharp steel inches from Byral's scalp.

It drew his attention away from the traitor beneath him and out to the starry night.

Slowly he crept away from the kneeling man, leaving him to the tears that racked his heaving body. Leaving him alone in the cold and with the dead.

When he was clear of the cliff top, away from prying eyes, Jaygen re-sheathed his sword and strode purposefully into the night. He knew what his next mission was, knew what Grimwolf was – and he knew what he must do.

24

The Bad Guys

Pudding put his weight on the GPMG which he had set against the stone turrets. His trigger finger working on rapid bursts from the heavy machine gun as the belt of empty cases fed out from the working chamber. He focused through the bead at the end of the barrel, working it along the rows of charging men. Bullets striking polished armour, helmets and flesh. Bodies dropping to the cold ground to be trampled over by those behind and many more emerging through the tree-line.

He had never seen so many men. There were thousands of them. Surrounding the Keep, closing into the walls and hammering at the gate. The noise was a deafening crescendo of gunfire, explosions and screams of rage and pain. From along the battlements, others were firing into the charging masses. Stone cracking and crumbling in places where the returning bullets struck the wall. White flashes and smoke filled the air, grimbles grimacing as they threw down rocks, bulworgs snarling, eager to feed upon the enemy, grumpkins hobbled along the battlements, shouting orders while holding their faces together, hungry eyes searching for their next skins to wear.

"Marilyn Monroe, Marilyn Monroe..." Pudding chanted. The length of time coinciding with the bursts he was releasing from the gun. A way to keep a rapid rhythm without overheating and warping the barrel. "Marilyn Monroe, Marilyn Monroe..." A shiver ran through him as he fought the urge not to dwell about his dark companions. "Marilyn M…"

A flock of crows veered up in front of his vision. Sharp beaks and talons suddenly flying into his face, scratching nipping and biting. Feathers filling his view as they screeched.

He let go of his gun to swat at them, yet as fast as his hand was, he didn't make contact, with a single bird.

"Pudding, keep firing!" Captain Brindle ordered as he came to his aid. Raising his rifle, he slammed the butt into the crows, but they evaded him and flew down the rampart and into the wheelhouse. "It's the warlock," Brindle snapped urgently, "he's going to raise the portcullis." Slapping the closest bulworg on the back, he pointed in the direction the birds had flown. "Get after him," he shouted.

Snarling as it leapt from the battlements, the large dog-beast dashed after his quarry, followed by two grimbles and a grumpkin.

"You," he growled, slamming a hand on Pudding's shoulder. "Keep cutting them down."

Training his eye through the bead once again, Pudding squeezed the trigger. "Marilyn Monroe, Marilyn Monroe..."

A new noise erupted from the open ground. The cracks and groans of wood, knocking together in a deep rumble as the forest canopy swayed against the wind. Pudding trained his gun on the forest, expecting giants to wander out into the open.

Then suddenly the forest itself came alive. Thick branches reaching out and impossibly grasping men, crushing, impaling and tossing them aside. The back ranks of imperial guards staring about in horror as the mighty oaks began to swing thick limbs. Scattering them apart as if they were tin soldiers. Hundreds more emerged from the forest, sprinting into the safety of the open ground, leaving behind the tortured screams of their comrades that remained within the mass of trees. Hidden from view beneath the thrashing canopy, being pulverised by the animated wood.

But still the Empire came.

An explosion shook the wall. The deep rumble that followed sank into his very chest as the chain links of the portcullis, suddenly went slack. The links rattling through the wheelhouse, now unburdened from the heavy gate.

Men flooded through the opening. The pace of the crowd suddenly picking up as they charged.

"The Keep's been breached!" Brindle bellowed, slapping Pudding on his arm. "Fall back!"

Pulling the GPMG from the wall, Pudding followed the Captain as they pelted down the steps and into the courtyard.

It was chaos.

The large area was a thrashing throng of men and beasts, blades and guns. Clashing of steel, flashes of muzzles, snapping teeth and ripping claws. Shouts, screams and snarls.

Pudding reached the bottom of the steps and lost his footing. His boot finding a slick pool of blood and he slipped onto his back. The soldier the blood had leaked from attempted to crawl away from a bulworg who suddenly pounced on his back, pinning him down into the cobbles before sinking teeth into his neck. Bones crunched and the man went limp.

Above the carnage, leaning out from upper window were the two wizards. Thatch was waving his arms around the air in slow concentric circles, flames glowing from both palms. Thud scowled down at the battle, muttering strange words under his breath. Then all at once, the flames from Thatch's palms leapt into the air and a large serpent began to weave its way down to the battling soldiers.

Gaping mouth opened wide, fire spitting from every tooth and scale, black smoke curling from narrowed eyes - it wrapped itself around a guard. The man inside the armour shrieked as the snaked curled its body tighter, crushing the body within. Seconds later and the flaming serpent left the smouldering corpse on the floor before floating after another victim. The wizards watching from the window, still waving their arms and speaking in that strange language.

Swallowing down bile, Pudding struggled to his feet, hugging the heavy machine gun as he stumbled around the edge of the courtyard.

Ahead, a grumpkin viciously twisted the head of an enemy. Pulling it back by his blonde curls so he could insert his knife beneath the scalp. His thick tongue darting between broken lips as it concentrated on making fine work of its new clothes. Beyond him, two large grimbles were swinging huge mallets. Large teeth jutting from their boar-like heads as they pulverised an enemy soldier. The two mallets coming together, crushing the man's chest and forcing a strange whistling sound from his blooded mouth.

Pudding winced at the sight and dragged his gaze away, fighting the urge to throw up. Sweat plastered his hair to his head as he pushed between a pair of men locked together, sword scraping up along a spent rifle, faces spitting curses at each other as they sought to gain vantage over the other. He felt cold with terror, finding it hard to keep his eyes open to the horror. Even harder as he realised that the enemy was wearing a similar uniform to himself; British Army fatigues below the polished armour. These men that they fought against could easily have been friends in another life.

Someone grabbed him from behind and shoved him into a narrow gap between two buildings.

"Move it, Pudding," Brindle shouted into his face. The Captain gave him another shove before turning on the crowds that were flooding into Rams Keep, and began to fire.

A burley soldier with a rifle identical to Brindle, poked his head into the narrow passage and adopted a kneeling position. The Captain fired two rounds into his forehead, the holes appearing within an inch of each other.

Pudding watched his body slip to the ground, eyes open in shock, lips pulled tight as if the soldier refused to accept the outcome of the fight. Pudding tried not to look beyond the body, at the carnage that was being inflicted in the courtyard. At the violence that Elora's army was fighting with; the rage of the bulworg, the brutality of the grimbles and the disgusting habits of the grumpkins. These creatures that were his brothers.

"Fall back," Brindle ordered him as he nodded down the passage. "We need to get everyone into the Shadowlands."

His weapon clattering down one wall, Pudding began to run away from the gate, exiting the narrow gap and into another cobbled courtyard. His breath coming out in short gasps.

As the Captain passed him, he grabbed his arm.

"Sir, are we the bad guys?" he asked, his eyes being drawn to a dwarf in boiled leather, his axe swinging around to take the legs from the first of the enemy that were swooping through the Keep.

Brindle brought his rifle up and shot the soldier. His bullet hitting his chest and knocking him back. A dwarf who was about to swing his axe at his legs, treated Brindle to a hostile glare, as if he somehow he'd cheated him out of some fun. He watched the little man run after the next, axe raised and full of violence.

"No," he answered, turning his attention to Pudding. The overweight soldier's face was beetroot red and he was breathing erratically. It was easy to see how we were the bad guys, especially when we were killing the very soldiers we used to work alongside. But he couldn't tell Barker that. "Listen, Pudding. If we let them win, if Elora fails - the entire world will drown. Do you understand?"

Pudding slowly nodded, his expression resolving into determination. "Sir."

"Now get your arse to the workshop and make sure…" Brindle began, but his words were cut short as his body was flung up in the air.

His world spun – blue sky, grey stone, blue, grey.

The wind was knocked from him as his slammed into the cobbles, his jaw jarring against his rifle. He glanced up in time to watch Pudding disappear down a flight of stairs that would lead him to the other side of the Keep. When he checked, what had thrown him, he saw a foot, swinging for his head.

Rolling out of the way, he scrambled to his feet and brought his gun up, levelling it at the half naked man before him.

"Dethtil," he hissed, the name leaving his lips as he squeezed the trigger.

A burst of three rounds spat from the barrel, yet the bullets passed harmlessly through the flock of birds the warlock had become without grazing a feather.

The magical being reformed into his human state in time to snatch the rifle from Brindle's grasp and toss it over his shoulder. The action was so swift that he only registered what had happened as his gun clattered against a far wall.

Brindle swallowed his fear as glared at the warlock, wondering if death was upon him.

"Where's Elora?" Dethtil demanded, his delicate hands twisting Brindle's shirt as he pulled him closer. "Where's my wife?"

Brindle stared into those dark eyes, his own reflection staring back though the black pools of madness. He gripped the thin bare shoulders, attempting to find purchase, seeking a way to fight the powerful creature. Yet he seemed made from marble. Instead, his fingers found the warlock's curling locks.

"She's having her nails painted," he offered, and yanked the youthful looking head to the side. Yet the effect only seemed to enrage Dethtil.

"Liar," the warlock replied, obviously unused to sarcasm, then drove his fist into Brindle's chest. It was like being slammed in the gut by a sledgehammer.

Brindle doubled over, bringing his arms protectively over his belly and saw that he had wrenched a fist full of locks free. The pain far outweighed the prize in his hand but it still made him smile. But that left his lips as a foot connected with his thigh, spinning him onto his back and he crashed onto the cobbles once again.

Dethtil loomed over him. His boot coming to rest heavily upon his chest. "Where is my Wife?" he repeated, applying enough pressure to Brindle's chest to crush the air from his lungs. "Where is she?" With every word, he pressed a little more until Brindle heard, then felt a rib crack.

"She, she's…" Brindle winced, his tortured lungs unable to form proper syllables as he struggled to breath. "doing…" The pain was excruciating.

"Where?" the warlock demanded, leaning down, pressing his face close to Brindle's, close enough to touch, to bite, to almost kiss.

"She's shopping for dresses," Brindle growled, and as Dethtil's brows drew together, he slipped his pistol from his holster and placed it to the warlock's temple. "For her marriage to Bray." Then he pulled the trigger.

"Fool!" Dethtil screamed. The sound morphing into a shriek as he transformed into his crow form, feeling the air spin around the bullet that lightly brushed his feathers. He witnessed the human on the ground, from many different pairs of eyes as they flocked around him. Saw his hand-cannon jerk, the plume of smoke, the defiance in his glare. Fool. But he was of no consequence. His insignificant life wasn't worth a thought. A pathetic grain of sand that soon passes through the hourglass of life. Not like his own. The eternal life of a warlock and soon-to-be god.

Once he had found Elora, his wife-to-be, she would bind his body to a god's and he would be truly immortal.

The many wings beat the air beneath them and he flocked to the eaves of the closest roof. The human already forgotten as he surveyed the Keep below. In this form, he perceived the world from hundreds of different angles. The information coalescing, gathering into one core thought which was at the centre of the crows.

The fighting was fierce. The Empire fighting against the weaker Dark Army. Even with the grimbles, the bulworg and grumpkins. Elora's loyal servants will be crushed by the sheer number of imperial guards that flooded Rams Keep. Not even The Green Man had much influence once the Empire had infiltrated the walls. Not that it would have made a difference in the grand scheme of things. Once he had Elora, he would abandon the Empire as well. Neptula will drown the lot anyway. And he would be a god.

From his perch, he watched the scene beneath. The women and the younger children running in one direction, the men the other. Dethtil would have assumed his wife-to-be, would be in the thick of the fighting. Yet she was nowhere to be seen. Unless she was helping with the evacuation. Yes, that was it.

He also sensed that the lost bird, the crow that had been captured by the dragon, was close. It called to him, drawing him in the same direction the weaker humans were fleeing in. Maybe Elora already had a piece of him with her. Did she think she could do him harm with that particular bird? If she did, she was greatly mistaken.

Dropping from the eaves, he swooped down and flew through the battle. Gliding over and between the clashing throng as he weaved his way towards the other side of the Keep. It didn't take long to cross the rebuilt ruins. The chaos which was happening below merely providing a background noise as he searched out his other.

Children cried in their mother's arms as they were led down a stone courtyard and into a large building below a tower. It had wide sliding doors, soldiers standing either side, ushering people through.

Pathetic.

Dethtil flew above one of the men, materialising in his human form to slam a fist down into his head.

He dropped like a discarded doll as his partner brought up his long cannon. The few children and women that were about, ran around him and through the wide doors. Panic forcing strange grimaces and expressions on their faces.

Becoming black feathers, Dethtil swept over the small lumps of metal and flew into the soldier's face. Beaks biting, talons scratching as he attacked the man, dragging him to the ground. When he went down, holding his hands up to protect his head, Dethtil returned to being a man. He snatched the cannon and using it like a club, struck the man on the back of his neck. He felt the spine fracture through the impact and the body went still.

What a pathetically weak creature the human was.

Dropping the weapon on the fallen soldier, he placed his hands behind his back and strode purposefully into the large building.

It was a warehouse or workshop of sorts. Cranks, tools, winches and benches were pushed to the walls and corners. The people who were inside, hurried to a large sliding door at the back. Runes glowing around the frame.

"Elora?" Dethtil shouted.

Those that hadn't seen him enter, turned.

Panic, herding them together in their haste to be away from him. Except for a taller human. Strange goggles pushed up onto the top of her head and a belt with many pockets and pouches buckled around her waist. Her long leather coat brushed the ground as she paced towards him. A small cage held in her hand. When Dethtil looked at what was inside, his temper spiked.

"Stay where you are, warlock," the woman warned, lifting and placing a strange device that spat a blue flame. Pipes fed from the back of the long object, snaking down to a cylindrical tank.

Zilabeth held the welding torch to the caged bird. The iron in the bars instantly glowing red with the heat. She glanced up at the semi-naked man that had strode into the workshop. Noting how young he appeared, although if you were powerful enough to appear how you wanted, why choose to be old. Yet as youthful as he looked, she knew he was frighteningly dangerous.

But she was ready for him. Had anticipated this confrontation and was prepared to spring the trap. All she needed to do, was guide him above the hidden net that lay only a few steps from his feet.

The warlock sneered, dark eyes full of hatred. "Tell me where my wife is, and I'll kill you so swiftly you won't realise your own passing," he offered, taking a step closer.

"If you don't leave, I'll torch this crow," Zilabeth replied, calmly. Although fear closed its bony hand around her heart, she fought not to show it. "I know it is part of you and you will suffer with the bird."

"You know nothing, pathetic human," he snarled, edging closer; slender fingers bunching into a fist.

More soldiers began to arrive at the entrance and Zilabeth recognised Pudding, Ben and Captain Brindle. Their rifles poking inside. She briefly glanced at them and gave a subtle shake of the head. Their bullets wouldn't do any good here. Dethtil would only be captured using her trap.

Zilabeth fanned the welding torch along the cage once again, the crow inside shrieking with pain as the intense heat briefly touched it. Dethtil hissed, his mouth pulled back in agony. The smell of singed feathers filling the air as smoke curled from the bars.

The warlock stepped closer, his torso rippling with anger, tendons standing out against the soft skin – she had him.

Taking a cautious step back, Zilabeth placed one foot behind the other. Careful not to disturb the fine god-created net on the ground. She was only feet from the sliding door, red dust wafting through on a wave of dry heat. The echoes of panicked voices reaching her ears from the Shadowlands as the escapees found refuge in the other world.

Her eyes never leaving Dethtil's, Zilabeth raised the blowtorch once again, filling the warehouse with the bird's cries. "If you want your crow back, come and get it," she jeered, lifting her chin in defiance. The gap between them now almost arm's length. She would not be cowed by this bully.

"Once I've relieved you of that man-made flame," the warlock spat as he stepped onto the fine net. "I will burn you until you're as black as my heart."

Another step and Zilabeth felt stone beneath her boots. She willed her antagonist to follow another pace. Just a few more inches.

Suddenly the cage was torn from her hands. The swiftness was so great that she hadn't the time to compensate from the sudden change in weight and she lost balance.

Staggering sideways, she barely had chance to register the grin on Dethtil's face before his fist connected with her stomach and sent her reeling in the shelving behind. Her teeth clashing together as her back slammed into the wall.

As she slid to the ground, the world spinning before her, she watched the warlock slowly approach. The blowtorch now held in his free hand and his promise of making her burn written in his posture.

She fought to remain conscious – she could not allow him to succeed, could not let the warlock pass beyond the net. This was their only hope of survival.

His boots creaked as he ventured closer, his heel scuffing the net and raising the material with his foot and he glanced down.

"What is…"

Before Zilabeth's lids drifted shut, she sensed a blur of movement from the corner of the warehouse.

Teaselberry growled as she pumped her legs for all they were worth. Her paws slapping the cold stone floor as she leaned into her attack. Tears prickling the corner of her eyes as she closed in on the beast who had struck her mistress.

Glancing at Zilabeth, her friend who now lay in a heap on the floor, broken shelving falling on top of her - she felt an animal anger rising from within. Wood trolls were known to be a passive creature, gentle and timid, yet little knew how ferocious their tempers could be when truly provoked.

Yanking the hammer from her utility belt, Teaselberry leapt at the warlock. She dug her claws into his back and scurried up onto his shoulder and began to strike him on the back of the head. Once, twice, three times. Each blow hitting the back of the cranium and issuing a dull thud with every blow.

Dethtil let go of the bird cage and it struck the ground amidst a chorus of squawks from the crow inside. With his free hand, he swatted at her, but she caught it between her teeth and bit down.

In his frantic attempt at dislodging her from her perch, Dethtil stumbled into the middle of the trap.

"Now!" Norgie yell from his hiding place.

She heard the whack of a mallet knocking the linchpin from a pulley. Then as the counterweight fell, the net rose, enveloping the warlock.

Spitting the hand from her mouth, Teaselberry jumped from Dethtil's shoulder as the netting came over his head and began to tighten.

The ground rushed up to meet her and she readied herself to land. Yet at the last moment she was yanked back, the air choked from her chest. One of the warlock's hands squeezed around her neck.

Blood rushed to her head, the pressure crushing her throat as she struggled in his grasp. She kicked out and raked her claws across his skin, but his hold was too firm.

"Release me," Dethtil screamed as he closed his fingers tighter.

The warehouse began to dim as Teaselberry gasped for air that wouldn't come. She was unable to no more than clash her teeth together. Then in the dimness she witnessed another body running towards her.

"Teaselberry," Gurple grunted as he slammed into the writhing body of the trapped warlock.

His claws tore into the man as he bit into the arm that held her. Digging his paws into the hand that throttled her and prised the fingers away. When that failed to work, the wood troll sunk his teeth into the pad of the palm and bit the thumb off.

Air flooded her lungs as Teaselberry was dropped.

She landed hard, striking her head against the stone floor. Yet she could breath.

Gurple reached for her and helped her up. Spitting the thumb from his mouth, he pulled Teaselberry into an embrace.

"Safe," he assured her soothingly as he stroked her back. "Safe."

And she did feel safe. Amongst the screaming, the thrashing beast in the net, through the cries of the crows as the human shape attempted to turn to bird before morphing to man and becoming something in between.

Above the clatter of feet as men rushed into the warehouse, amidst the confusion of gunfire that blasted from the doorways and explosions from within the Keep – she felt safe in Gurple's care.

Broken feathers fell through the fine weave as the net closed tighter. The silver thread digging through flesh, making small diamond shapes in the warlock's skin as he squirmed. A bone suddenly snapped and he screamed, eyes bulging, blood beginning to run from the criss-cross wounds that were appearing in his part bird, part human form.

"I...am...Dethtil," the warlock forced between splitting lips that had elongated into a grey beak.

"No," Norgie corrected as he placed the barrel of a pistol against the trapped man's temple. "You are dead."

His finger curled around the trigger and the gun jerked in his hand. The bullet driving through the skull of the feared warlock, leaving a tangle of blood, feathers and black downy hair.

Teaselberry pulled her gaze away from the horror and buried her head into Gurple's chest, feeling his heart beating from within.

"Tease?"

Teaselberry lifted her aching head from Gurple's chest to see Zilabeth, limp towards her, a stream of blood sticking her hair to her face. Yet her mistress was grinning.

"Tease, it worked," the inventor said, incredulously.

Teaselberry reached for her friend and the three of them embraced.

"I don't want to burst your bubble," Captain Brindle informed them from the doorway, his rifle trained out alongside that of Pudding's huge machine gun. "But the Keep has fallen, we've been overrun by the Empire."

Teaselberry felt herself being propelled towards the portal to the Shadowlands.

"Go," Zilabeth ordered, we'll be safe through there.

Flames ripped through the doorway, throwing the two soldiers across the floor. Pudding slamming into the tangle of Dethtil's remains while the Captain rolled to a stop against a bench.

Teaselberry and Gurple backed away from the gaping hole, where the doors used to be. Broken stone and splintered wood was all that remained of the frame.

"You're surrounded," commanded a voice from outside. "Come out with your hands on your heads."

Teaselberry turned to the Captain who was picking himself up from the ground. A fresh cut above his brow, leaking blood into a deepening frown.

"They'll kill us as soon as we step outside," he informed the rest.

"To the Shadowlands then," Zilabeth suggested, "we must give up Rams Keep."

She caught movement from behind as large shadows began to shift through the portal. Then two large grimbles stepped out of the red mist. Between their bulking forms, they carried a large chest, brass banding covering the wooden lid. Behind them a grumpkin scurried into view. The rubbery flesh from a skagwangle, in various states of deterioration, clung to his bones.

As he shuffled towards them, the grey tentacles wafted above the stone floor like a grotesque grass skirt. Teaselberry found his appearance equally as disgusting as the broken warlock.

"No, no, this grumpkins is not giving ups of the Keepsy," he said as he pointed a bony finger at the chest and ordered the grimbles to lower it to the ground. "This grumpkin will not give up my Queen's precious Ramsy Keep."

"Don't be a fool," Captain Brindle snapped. "It's already lost."

The grumpkin grinned and his entire face flopped forwards, his fat nose spilling over his rubbery mouth. He pushed it straight and held it in place, his swollen tongue working from beneath.

"You'se be forgetting Captain Brindley," he continued unperturbed by his sagging face. "That we are the Dark Army. And we is so much more than simple mans from the Empire."

He gave a single nod and the grimbles opened the chest to reveal a mass of clicking insects from within.

Tak…Tak…Tak. Pincers, teeth and barbed spikes rattled inside the chest. It was enough to make every hair on Teaselberry's body stand on end. There were thousands of them, crawling over each other.

"No," Brindle commanded, holding up an arm to the grumpkin. "Elora said not to use takwiches."

The grumpkin smiled, the hideous expression forcing Teaselberry to shudder. "Oh? This grumpkin says yes. This is what takwiches were created for. Elora says no, but my Queen, the daughter of Chaos, will like it."

He rubbed his fingers together in glee as he kicked the side of the chest. The insects rapidly began to scurry from inside, forming a dark blanket as they flowed through the gap and into the daylight.

Gunfire erupted. Bullets striking the ground and obliterating a few takwiches. But for every one that they hit, more took its place. And then the screams began.

Pudding leaned closer to his Captain. "Are you sure we're not the bad guys?" he asked.

Brindle turned to his subordinate, shaking his head as screams and shouts echoed from around the Keep, among a chorus of Tak…Tak…Tak. But it was the grumpkin that answered.

"We's are so much more than the baddie guys," he said, gleefully throwing a rotting arm around Pudding and pulling him into an embrace. Smothering him with the closeness of brothers. "We's is the Dark Army."

25

A Watery Tomb

Elora's boots squelched through the green and red seaweeds that clung to the steps and walls. Popping the air bubbles that were locked into the slimy vegetation and releasing a sickly aroma. Starfish hugged the coral materiel that formed the spiralling staircase while small crabs and silver fish skittered in the rock pools, darting away as her shadow passed over them.

She had no clue as to how far the staircase led down. Or where Neptula had gone, yet she could hear the Sea Witch's cackles as they echoed up to her, growing nearer with each bend she ventured around.

From above, the choked sounds of the spitfire's tortured engine ripped across the sky. The damage the fighter plane had been inflicted from the leviathan would soon bring it down. It was only a matter of time before Bray ditched into the water to the waiting jaws of the sharks and other sea creatures.

Beyond the whirring of the steam-powered engine, she could hear the roar of her dragon as Grycul tore through the ranks of water dragons. Aided by Zionbuss, the cannons of the Necrolosis booming above all other noises, except the booming of her own heart.

This was it. The final battle, the last fight. The decider of fates for Ethea. Would the land survive or is it a world doomed to be below the waves?

Salt water dripped from the ceiling and was sloshed through long slits in the walls with every wave that crashed against the Jewel. It poured forth in white foaming rivulets to wet her clothing and cling to her sword. Hissing and bubbling as her fiery blade reduced it to steam. This shell of a sea palace was surely a watery tomb. But would it be hers or Neptula's?

A tiny crab clipped along the step before her, its orange shell-encased body, blundering under her foot and before she could halt its descent, she accidentally crushed it beneath her boot. When she lifted it again, broken pieces of shell stuck to her sole, linked by sticky ichor.

Elora brought her gaze away, gripping her sword tighter as she wished the coming fight would be so easily done.

She scraped her sole along the ridge of the next step, rubbing the dead creature from her boot. She couldn't go into this battle with any doubts. Losing was not an option. If she failed, the world would fail and everything that had gone before, all the events that would lead to the future would be for nothing.

The porous sides of the coral staircase swept away to reveal a large bowl-shaped chamber. Shiny mother of pearl glistened along the outer walls. Pinks, purples, greens and reds shimmered as light shone through slits along the outer edge. Reflecting from the water at the chambers base to dance around them.

It was a pretty sight to behold, thought Elora, if it wasn't for Neptula sat on a coral throne. Her many thick limbs weaving and squirming over each other, partially hidden beneath the waves of the pool which stretched the full length of the chamber. The Sea Witch grinned, showing rows of white triangular teeth. Each point serrated and sharp enough to shred flesh from bones.

"Come, Elora," Neptula offered, curling a webbed finger to entice her closer. "I won't bite… much." The spines upon her scalp flicked up to spread the azure membrane that made up the fin on her head. Her grin widened and grip tightened around the large polished trident that lay across her lap. "Feel free to bathe in the waters of the mother sea, there are none finer than here."

"No thanks," Elora replied. "I'd rather bathe in your blood, after I've cut you open."

She dropped the final three steps to the base of the chamber. The water lapping over her boots to cover her feet.

On the far side of the room was a corridor. Two skagwangles filled the arched doorway, blocking the view beyond, but Elora got the impression that it led further down the Jewel, all the way to the seabed. Once she killed Neptula, she would be rushed by her loyal sea creatures. An ocean's worth would descend upon her. The chance of leaving this place alive, was close to zero. A fact that Neptula realised herself.

"The tide is turning, Elora," the Sea Witch offered, her tongue stroking delicately over her teeth as she looked her up and down with hungry eyes. "This chamber fills quickly."

Elora twisted her blade, the fire running along the god-created steel sparkling upon the water.

"I don't intend to take long," she replied, catching the movement of thick limbs below the surface. Strong tentacles curling and writhing as they prepared to strike.

Her smile widening, Neptula raised her trident and pointed it at the staircase which Elora had entered the chamber from.

A dull thunk, echoed from above and the light that fed from the stairway faded.

"I'm afraid, daughter of Solarius, that your time has run out. The way above is sealed," The Sea Witch explained, lowering her trident until the points were level with Elora's face. "But fear not, the Jewel won't become your tomb. Your body will be devoured soon after your passing."

Fighting the claustrophobic fear that began to grip her, Elora carefully planted her feet on solid ground and adopted a defensive stance. Deal with the witch first, then find a way out after - if she was still capable, she told herself.

"We will see," Elora said, glancing about the chamber, searching for anything that she could use to her advantage. Yet she found nothing. Instead she concentrated on her breathing and the sequences of her attack. "But first, you must die."

Neptula's grin spread like a crescent moon, from one side of her treacherous face to the other. Then without warning, she thrust her trident forwards.

The blur was so swift Elora failed to see the prongs sliding over her blade until the trident was twisted and her sword was wrenched form her grip.

Idiot! Elora scolded herself as she reduced herself to smoke. She slipped over and between Neptula's weapon, re-materialising on the other side of the chamber and caught her blade before it hit the water.

Yet before she had time to fully re-form, water crashed through one of the slit shaped windows, spraying her in a white foam. In the watery haze, her arm didn't merge back quickly enough and the soul reaver hit the water at her feet and almost sank from view.

Panic slapped Elora across her vision as another wave crashed through the opening. Yet somehow she managed to grasp the hilt of her sword and crouch back into a defensive position.

"I would strongly advise against becoming smoke in here," Neptula teased as she left her throne and began to circle around Elora, tentacles bunching and squirming like an octopus. "Smoke doesn't travel well through water. Neither does fire."

Finishing her last word, the Sea Witch launched into a vicious attack. Her trident flashing forwards while one of her appendages, coiled around Elora's ankle.

Ducking at the final moment, Elora avoided the sharpened steel but felt the wind from it upon her cheek. Her own blade slicing down and cutting through the water. She felt resistance as the steel found flesh and severed the end of a tentacle.

Green blood instantly filled the white pool with an inky cloud.

Neptula screamed in rage, the stumpy end of her limb spitting more blood as she thrashed it around, spraying the green liquid around the mother of pearl walls. Sharp teeth clashed together as she glared at Elora. Hatred burning from shark-like eyes.

"How many more legs do you have?" Elora asked cockily, although she didn't feel cocky in the least. "Is it eight?"

Neptula's screech bounced around the chamber as she rose out of the water. Anger forcing her to fight with overwhelming emotion. The spines on her head stretching so far that Elora thought the fine web between would snap.

Salt water splashed up as thick tendrils shot from the depths. Three tentacles striking high, aiming to pin Elora to the wall. One caught her blade and she parried down, the other two struck the chamber with enough force to fracture the smooth surface, showering her in pieces of mother of pearl.

When she saw that none of her lunges had made contact, Neptula screamed in frustration and bounded closer, splashing water in her haste to attack. Her trident was a silver flash of movement, darting, slashing and cutting. The metal clashing against the soul blade hard enough to jar Elora's shoulders.

She moved with the onslaught, pivoting the best she could on the uneven floor beneath the rising sea. The crashing of waves against the Jewel, roaring louder each time it battered the coral flute. More water pouring in through the slits in the wall as the chamber began to fill.

A tentacle suddenly wrapped around Elora's thigh and tore her from her feet. Her head slamming into the pool as she went under.

The icy chill of the water enveloped her, the world now one of salt and brine sought out every fibre of her body, breeching clothes and seeping into her mouth as she fought to breath.

Another tentacle curled around her shin and squeezed them together, the pressure so intense that Elora thought her bones might snap. Excruciating pain flared along her legs, her heart beating so hard it might rip from her chest. She attempted to drive her sword into her attacker but her arm moved sluggishly, the water slowing her down enough for Neptula to easily catch her wrist and coil another tentacle around it and then another tightened around her neck.

She was trapped.

The tendons in her throat burned as she struggled against the limbs the of the sea god. Her head filling with the dizzying rush of blackness, her surroundings shrinking, fingers growing numb, her body feeling less than her own.

With her free arm, Elora snatched her pistol from her thigh holster and pushed the barrel into the appendage about her neck, attempting to pull the trigger with a finger that she no longer felt. Her lungs screaming for air as she fought the gag reflex. If she opened her mouth, it was over.

Concentrating on the trigger, she leaned her head to the side and squeezed.

Sound worked differently under water. The blast from her handgun seeming more like a drowned zip than a bang. Yet the boom of Neptula's bellow, reduced everything else to an inconsequential flurry.

The pressure around her neck was released, as was that of her legs and Elora kicked to the surface.

A giddiness bound her to seek solid ground as she gulped in the air. Her oxygen starved brain making white flashes across her vision as she found the staircase once again. Fighting consciousness, she pulled herself up the steps until she was out of the water. The level now having risen halfway up the chamber and beginning to overlap the slit windows.

When she glanced around she saw that Neptula had retreated to the corridor entrance, holding her injured tentacle in her webbed hands.

"Kill her," she ordered the two skagwangles that had been on guard.

Tridents held before them, they advanced on her, cutting through the water with ease, while the Sea Witch watched with eager anticipation.

Steadying her breathing, Elora raised her pistol from the water and fired at the closer of the two. Her bullet piercing a hole in the rubbery head and ripping bone and blood from the back of his cranium. When she switched to the other and pulled the trigger, there was an empty click.

Seeing his chance, the skagwangle thrust his weapon towards her. She'd barely caught the three-pronged trident with the pistol, before he leapt out of the water.

His body coming down, she twisted her gun, so the trident spun with it, her attacker's arm folding out as she brought her foot between his chest and hers.

He opened his jaws, inches from her face. Foul fetid breath spewed from his mouth as his arm grasped her behind her back to bring them closer. Hunger filled eyes going wide, gills wafting like a frantic fan.

Elora yelled as she shoved her foot forward, flinging the skagwangle off herself. As he fell back into the pool, she swung her sword overhead and felt his skull split beneath the blade.

The skagwangle went still. His limbs becoming floating eels until she withdrew the soul reaver.

"Useless!" Neptula spat as she gripped the sides of the doorway. The fat suckers that covered her limbs bulging and relaxing in her frustration at the deaths of her guards.

Elora slumped back, sitting down hard on the steps. The cold and the fatigue from fighting had drained her, leaving her feeling immensely tired.

She undid the cloak that clung to her back, it made a slapping sound as it struck the steps.

"Then come and finish me, yourself," Elora taunted, opening her fingers and letting the gun slip from her hand. It made a splosh as it hit the rising water, sinking fast beneath the body of the guard its last bullet had killed. She wanted to present herself as an easy target, persuading the Sea Witch to stay and not vanish through the corridor to leave her to drown.

"I will," Neptula replied, raising her trident. "I'm going to tear you apart before feeding you to the low scum that crawl along the ocean's floor." She advanced into the room, swimming now that the sea was high enough for her to stretch her entire body. "They'll tear, rip and nip you as they feast…"

"Enough talk," Elora snapped, realising that time was now against her. "God of the sea? More like the god of wind, with all the noise that's coming out of your mouth."

Green blood ran into the scowl that formed upon Neptula's head, hatred setting her spines quivering again and she held her trident so firm that the silver shaft began to bend. Yet Elora had hatred of her own. A raw, hot emotion, burning with raging embers. Anger coursing through her veins, funnelling a fervour that made her shake. All fear falling away to be replaced by a tingling excitement.

Waves battered the Jewel, the crash of the ocean coming in rhythmic flows as the brine infiltrated the chamber. The water now inside swelling around its

Mistress as the god of the sea advanced. But to Elora, the sounds were changing, becoming a rush of whispers.

She shuffled back, allowing the darkness behind, to creep over her and the whispers clarified. A thousand voices speaking as one.

Elora…Elora…Elora.

An exhilaration rose within her.

Kill…Kill…Kill.

The soul reaver in her lap began to sing. The flames burning brighter, making steam from her drenched clothes. She wanted to destroy, to obliterate, to fill the Jewel with Chaos.

A tentacle curled around one of the floating skagwangles and Neptula flung his body to the other side of the chamber. His bones crunching on impact and leaving a green smear down the shining surface. Hatred drove the Sea Witch on. She was powerless to the all-consuming anger. Her body becoming an unstoppable storm as she cut through the water, making a V-shaped crest before her and leaving a white foaming wake.

Elora was smiling as she stood, levelling her sword to the side as she crouched low.

Kill…Kill…Kill.

The swelling tide struck the steps as Neptula attacked. Two tentacles slamming to either side of the staircase while two more shot forwards.

A chuckle escaped Elora as she witnessed blood leaking from the stump of one of the appendages. It looked comical as it crashed into the step at her feet, squirting green fluid and mixing with the salt water – leaving an odd pattern in the porous material of the

Jewel. She recognised that pattern, she'd seen it many times before. It was death, it was Chaos.

Stepping to the side, Elora stamped her heel down upon the tentacle, pinning it to the ground while she hacked with her sword.

Blade met flesh and the steel split the limb once again. Cutting it off an entire foot shorter than it already was.

I'll take you piece by piece if I must, Elora mused, just so long as I'm having fun.

She placed her free hand against the slick cold skin of Neptula's chest. Feeling the heat leaving her palm as smoke began to curl from beneath the contact.

The foul stench of cooking meat filled the room, meeting the echoes of the Sea Witch's scream. Elora pushed her hand deeper into the silver scales, watching the silver semi-circles blacken and fall away. When she withdrew her palm, she left a red welt in the shape of her hand.

Funny that. She had left a similar mark upon that gorgeous green-eyed boy.

Suddenly her smile faltered as she remembered the scene beneath the trees. That same boy, her love, was outside now, his plane failing him and close to death.

Shaking the thought from her mind she concentrated on the Chaos. It was what would defeat Neptula. Not the sentimental feelings of that weaker her.

Clenching her fist, she punched the Sea Witch across the jaw and watched her fall back into the water. The trident spinning away out of her grasp before it too disappeared beneath the frothing surface.

She was about to follow the god down into the depths of the chamber when there was a lull in the waves crashing against the Jewel and Elora could hear the sputter of Bray's spitfire, the pop-pop of the steam engine before it fell silent. Then felt the thrill of the kill leave her body as her mind went to her fiancée.

Bray pulled the stick back as far as it would go. Black steam chugging from both sides of the engine as it fought to keep turning. But it was clear that there was no fuel left to feed it. The leviathan that had attacked him, had ripped a hole in the liquid fire tank.

The entire plane shook violently, the glass in the cockpit windows vibrating so harsh that he thought they might shatter. Then the spitfire fell silent.

This was bad. Almost as sour as watching Elora follow Neptula into the bowels of the Jewel. His heart had leapt into his mouth when he had watched her disappear inside the finger of rock. His fiancée passing from view. It beat as hard now, yet the fear for his own life was dwarfed by the fear for Elora's

Air whistled over the sleek wings as the plane began to descend. He pulled back on the stick once again, seeing the flaps pivot up, but without the drive of the engine the craft glided lower and lower.

Ahead, a rank of water dragons changed direction. Sensing his distress and wanting to take full advantage of it. The long row of beasts forming a thick line as they headed towards him. Skagwangles riding high as they pointed arrows and spears, closing in for the kill.

Bray could do no more than press the trigger of the twin guns and watch as two lines of bullets tore a path ahead, although he was now no more than a passenger. Heading down to a watery grave.

The fighter picked up speed as it neared the sea, gravity sucking him down into his final plummet. His view filled up by the big blue and the millions of creatures that waited below the surface. Hungrily ready to receive him.

Grycul suddenly whooshed passed. Her large wings widening as she slammed into the row of water dragons. Sharp talons cutting into the ranks of flying beasts as she ripped, bit and spat balls of flames. She managed to open a path for him and he glided harmlessly though the rank of water dragons. Yet he thought it might have been better to die in a collision with the beasts than slam into the water and be torn apart and devoured by sharks.

In the distance the boom from the Necrolosis's cannons echoed through the empty sky. He had an idea that maybe he could steer the plane in its direction and with any luck, Zionbuss may come to his rescue. But the controls in his hand were useless. It was inevitable that he was to enter the sea.

The Jewel rose out of the water, several hundred yards ahead. Waves crashing into the sides as the tide swept across it, rising up the finger of rock, leaving less than half the tower visible – with Elora still trapped inside.

He glanced down at his thumb ring. The ancient runes glowing red as he spun it. Words from the eternal sigh filled the cockpit as he realised, that was probably the last time he would ever hear it.

With the sea rushing up to meet him, he closed his eyes and thought about Elora. Remembering how beautiful she was that day when he first saw her, how sweet her voice was when he first heard it in the fairy circle as she twirled his hair and how passionate their first kiss was. Shared in the forest outside Rams Keep. The memory brought a smile to his face. Which was swiftly broken as he hit the water.

He was flung against the controls, the steering stick jamming into his stomach as his chest collided into the controls. His head struck the windscreen and he felt something crack, and didn't know whether it was the glass or his skull. White waves spewed over the cockpit, momentarily blocking out the world.

When he slouched back into the seat, the plane had settled and bobbed with the rhythm of the waves. The sun glistening upon the rolling surface and for a moment everything seemed peaceful. Until the sea forced its way between the cracks in the door and through holes in the bottom of the cockpit. Within seconds the cold water had risen above his legs and the plane began to sink.

The twisted propeller broke away as the nose slipped under, the last trails of steam rising from the dead engine. The wings then disappeared from view and he could see the tide line climbing up the glass until the cockpit was fully submerged.

Bray struggled in the small space, pushing his mouth into the crevice above where he found a small pocket of air. This was the last time he would breathe. His ears began to pop as the plane drifted down, the immense pressure of the sea pressing in, fracturing the window as the rays of light which penetrated the surface, swayed with its own motion and lighting up the murky deep.

This was it.

He became light headed, his world beginning to shrink around him. Shadows passing by the cockpit.

Then the thud as something struck the plane. Another and the glass broke away, replaced by a thrashing mouth, sharp teeth gnawing at the frame as the shark tried to reach him inside.

Bray reached for his sword. Yet as his fingers opened the smuggler's pouch, he wondered why he should bother. There was no way out. His death was as sure as his love for Elora.

The spitfire groaned, strange underwater noises thumping around him as other sharks joined the frenzy. Attacking the plane from all sides.

It was a strange experience, knowing that the final moments of your life had come. He'd often wondered how it might end. Never had he thought it would end like this.

A shark worked its way inside the cockpit. It was a hammer head, thrashing its bar-shaped head from side to side, the strange black eyes opening and closing as it worked its jaws up and down, attempting to close on him; white teeth, pink gums and a large gaping hole.

Pushing himself as far back as he could, Bray reached for his blade. He would die fighting. Although with his body now starved of oxygen, he doubted that it would be much of a fight.

Elora heard the familiar whispers of the eternal sigh and when she glanced at her hand, she saw that her thumb ring was glowing. She spun it with her finger and watched the red lights flicker over the surface of the pool and shimmer up the walls.

"I love you too," she whispered, bringing the ring to her face and pressing her lips to the elven words.

Then from outside the Jewel she heard the whistling sound of something dropping rapidly from the sky. Followed by the crash of a heavy object hitting the ocean.

Instantly her thumb ring stopped spinning and she knew that Bray had ditched the plane.

"No," she yelled, biting her lip so hard she tasted blood. "No."

She heard nothing more from outside, only the waves that ceaselessly battered the Jewel.

"No," she repeated, sinking once more to the steps and burying her head in her arms. Her sword clattering beside her as she let it fall.

Thoughts of Bray drowning in the vast ocean, only a hundred feet from where she was filled her mind. She glanced above, to the staircase from where she descended but saw no way through. She couldn't help. "No."

From the pool, Elora heard laughter. A shrill cackle that worked its way to her core, piercing her heart along with the thought of never seeing Bray again. Never looking into those moss-green eyes and feeling the same love back.

"I might be mistaken," Neptula gloated as she drew nearer, "but I can smell a hint of blood in the water." There was a swish and scrape of a trident as it was collected from the bottom of the pool. "I do believe there is an elvish quality to it. A half-breed at least."

Elora felt numb and not just from the cold. Her entire body felt wrong, as if she was watching from above, not quite part of this world yet unable to break away. Her gaze settled on Neptula, concentrating on the smirk which was dissolving into mock sympathy.

"Oh no, I think…that Bray has become food for my children," she laughed, placing her hand over her chest and sticking her bottom lip out. "So, so sad. I wanted to dine on him myself. He looked simply ravishing the last time we met. I do hope the sharks have left me a piece. But I doubt it. You know what sharks are like."

The Sea Witch was so close now, Elora could feel her breath upon her bare arm and feel the coldness ebbing from the tentacles that were slowly coiling around her back. "At least I'll have you to dine on. The taste of a broken heart is so much sweeter."

Elora glanced away from those black eyes in time to see her sword slide from the step and sink to the bottom of the pool, along with the hopes of the world. She had been a fool to allow her feelings get in the way of killing Neptula. Now she had no weapons.

The coldness that was consuming her, chilling more with each breath she took, became icily cold as the water rose, lapping against her stomach, leaving only the upper part of her torso above. Her teeth began to chatter, clattering in time to her shivering body. She felt like death.

Neptula rested the prongs of her trident on Elora's knee, spinning the shaft slowly, teasingly. Tearing through the fabric of her trousers and cutting her skin.

Elora didn't resist as a bead of her own blood ran down the trident, flaming once before sizzling out. She met The Sea Witch's gaze and willed her to finish it. To make it quick. Even if it was painful, she didn't care - it was what she deserved.

Neptula leaned closer, her smirk returning as she brushed Elora's hair from her face, twisting the single golden lock around a webbed finger.

"Are you ready to join Bray?" she asked, gripping her hair tighter and twisting her head back to expose her neck. "Are you ready to leave this world, Elora. Ready to move onto oblivion?"

Elora nodded, letting go a deep sigh as she faced Neptula. "Yes," she whispered, seeing the reflection of her violet eyes in the black dead circles of the Sea God's. And watched them turn crimson. "But not before I send you there."

Elora clenched her teeth as she shoved both her thumbs into Neptula's eye sockets. Pressing them into the skull with all her might. Feeling the shark-like orbs bubble under the intense heat before dribbling down the shock-filled face.

Tentacles slammed into her from all sides. Crushing the air from Elora's lungs, squeezing the oxygen from every limb, yet still she held on. The water now rising above her neck but not caring.

She heard laughter once again. A crazy mad cackle that belonged to something not of this world. Not of any sane world. When she realised it was her own, Elora laughed louder.

Neptula screamed the wailing ear-splitting shriek of a siren. Yet above that, the whispers goaded her on.

Kill…Kill…Kill.

The water began to heat up and steam soon filled the top of the chamber. The surface becoming a bubbling caldron of boiling sea soup. Blisters formed on Neptula's flesh, swelling with clear liquid before splitting and popping. Mixing with the green blood that spewed from her skull where her eyes should have been.

The walls shook violently as the Sea God struck out with her tentacles. Striking the walls, the ceiling and Elora. Pain and panic driving her into a frantic rush of movement. The water now rising above their heads and making a mocking sound with the screams. Bubbles spinning and turning as they raced out of the flapping gills. They floated up as larger heavier objects began to sink down.

Chunks of rock fell from above. Large pieces of the Jewel dropping around them as the chamber itself began to crumble. The tiny creatures that were skittering along the floor were now hurrying through the flooded corridor as the Jewel began to collapse.

Elora pressed harder, her hands finding bone and pushing through the boiling flesh. Holding tight to Neptula, to her companion that would accompany her into the next life. Tighter than a dance partner as they twirled about the flooded, ruined chamber - tighter than lovers as the world crumbled around them.

Suddenly the ceiling collapsed and bore down. The weight pressing them into the bottom of the pool, pinning them, crushing them.

Any air that was in Elora's lungs was now driven from her chest, yet she was still smiling. Chaos had been delivered, oblivion was here and the whispers from the darkness were singing.

Neptula was dead. Her large ruined body finally going still, the life from within extinguished.

Elora had saved Ethea from drowning, yet couldn't save herself. But then, what kind of life would she lead without Bray.

The weight above, pressing her further into the Sea Witch's embrace. Elora closed her eyes and thought of her fiancé, his body not far from her own. At least they will die together. She would find him in the next life. They had an eternity with each other.

A memory of them at Rams Keep came to her mind. Their first kiss, that gorgeous face, those eyes…

26

Smoke on the Water

Bray broke the surface of the sea, his lungs burning with the effort and lack of oxygen. He gasped uncontrollably as he sucked in the air, his chest heaving with the effort. Every agonising muscle in his body screaming for rest. Yet he pushed it on. The Jewel, or what was left of it, was only ten feet away.

A rogue wave came from nowhere, washing over his head and slapping his face with salt water. Filling his mouth as the sea tried to claim him back.

He struggled to find the energy to keep afloat, his legs slowing, his arms becoming jelly, and he began to sink.

Something heavy nudged him from below and pushed him back up. The rough sandpaper skin from the hammerhead that had saved him, scraping against his hands as it guided his spent body to the rubble of coral.

Allowing the shark to take him, Bray concentrated on breathing. Thanking the Blessed Mother for sending him a saviour in the shape of a hammerhead. Or should that be the God of Chaos for creating the takwich which now controlled the shark.

It had come to his rescue. Breaking apart the cockpit of the plane and using its bar-shaped head, hooked him out. At first Bray, had tried to kill it, but as other sharks and water dragons came in for the kill, it viciously defended him. Biting and lashing out at anything with violent intent. Then others came to aid his escape. Two great whites and a swordfish. Creating a path for them to escape to the surface. Now all he needed to do was survive. Although, if his suspicions were correct, and Elora was dead beneath the ruins of the Jewel, his life wouldn't be worth living.

When they reached the rocks, the shark pulled away and Bray drifted into the solid mass. His body cried in pain as he clawed his way up the rubble, cutting himself on the sharp coral and broken shells as they dug into his flesh. He attempted to stand, but the effort was too great. Instead he crawled on hands and knees. Shaking with fatigue, he made his way to the top. Which was a good deal lower than it had been at the start of the battle.

There was no sign of Elora. Nothing to even indicate that she had been there, apart from the destruction which she had left in her wake. There was no life, just the empty shell of a broken step that led to a dead end. Water seeping up from below to form a rock pool, there was no coming out and no going down. If she was still beneath him, and had managed to defeat Neptula, then she would have run out of air long ago. He didn't want to think of her corpse laying feet below him, trapped forever in a watery tomb.

Bray slumped to the ground and rolled onto his side. Cold, wet and immensely tired. Fighting to stay conscious, he tried to shout Elora's name but all that came out was a choked rasping sound. It was no use, nobody could hear, especially not the dead.

His gaze fell on the horizon. The great shape of Grycul wafting her wings as she chased down the remaining water dragons and skagwangles. The rest had fled when they realised their god had died. Elora had rid the world of Neptula, saved the lands from being choked by the oceans, yet she couldn't save herself.

A shadow passed above.

Bray looked up and saw the belly of the Necrolosis. Its bone planking peeking through the souls of the green sea. A rope ladder was dropped, followed swiftly by Zionbuss. The demon landed hard, his horned face a mask of worry.

"Bray?" he said, coming closer and helping him into a sitting position. Propping him up against a boulder. He clicked his fingers and one of his skeletal crew produced a water skin. Delicately he placed it to Bray's lips and Bray drank deeply. "Where is my Queen?" Zionbuss asked, casting urgent glances about the broken Jewel.

Bray shook his head, clenching his teeth so hard his jaw hurt. He couldn't say the words. Couldn't even say her name. Instead he pointed at the ground, at the ruined staircase that was full of rocks and saturated by the ocean.

"No, it can't be," Zionbuss growled, his claws curling into fists as he sought a target to punch. "Elora!" he bellowed and began to rain blows into the coral, smashing great chunks of the ruined Jewel into smaller chunks.

"If there's any grimbles still alive, get down here and help," he ordered.

No sooner did he finish his command than two large grimbles landed, shaking the ground as they impacted.

"Dig!" Zionbuss yelled, pointing at the buried staircase.

Bray watched the three of them work. Huge muscles flexing and straining as bit by bit they lifted or smashed rocks, some as big as cars. He wanted to help, even though his body barely had the strength to stay conscious. But he knew he would be more of a hindrance and would only get in the way.

"Elora," Zionbuss repeated, as he squeezed his arm into a gap beneath a slab of coral and heaved the huge piece aside. It revealed an arm. The body it was attached to, bobbing below the surface.

It was thin and slender beneath the demon's huge hands. Parts of it charred black while the rest was cooked white. Steam rising from the hot water. But it wasn't Elora's.

"Neptula," Bray offered, "what's left of her."

Zionbuss dropped the arm and the grotesque shape sank into the murky depths of the chamber. Along with any hope Bray had left. Yet he would dive into the underworld, if it meant finding Elora.

He shuffled closer, dragging himself to the opening and pulled his legs behind him. Taking a few shuddering breaths, he dropped his arm into the hot water, grasping the remains of the step below and began to pull himself in.

Zionbuss caught the back of his shirt and wouldn't let go. "Wait," the demon ordered.

Bray struggled to free himself from Zionbuss's grip, but as his eyes caught movement, he paused.

Rising from the surface of the water, mixing with the steam, was smoke. Dark smoke. Grey particles of ash floating up, spreading out and thinning as it made its way towards the heavens. Coalescing around his face, almost caressing him as it travelled up.

"My Queen," Zionbuss whispered and sank to his knees. Large tears running down his scroll-worked face as he glared up at the smoke.

Bray followed the trails as they curled and weaved through the air, seeking any recognition of his love. He found none. But he did sense that the smoke was part of Elora.

"She has gone," Zionbuss said, heavily. Resting a hand upon Bray's shoulder. "Ethea will be less colourful without her in it."

"No," was all Bray could mutter as he lifted his arm out to the smoke, his fingers trailing through the warm particles. Was this all that was left of her?

His mind going numb, he absently spun the ring on his thumb. The gold band rang, the faint rasping sounds of the eternal sigh beginning to whisper. He felt like taking it off and throwing it into the sea.

He had lost Elora forever.

"Do that again," Zionbuss suggested. "Hurry."

Bray didn't understand why, maybe the demon found comfort in the sound, but he spun it again.

"There," Zionbuss exclaimed excitedly. "See?"

Bray searched at the spot where the demon was pointing, not seeing anything at first. Then he realised that the small grey particles of ash began to glow. He spun the ring again and watched the ash brighten to embers.

"It's her, it's Elora," Zionbuss laughed. "She is with us."

Feeling a tingle sparkle through his entire body, racing to the points of his fingers that were still trailing the smoke, Bray spun the ring again - faster now so that the words of the ancient elven song sang true.

The embers glowed red hot, throwing heat from the cloud of smoke. And as he watched, ethereal fingers began to form in his own. He felt the solidness of them, the familiar touch of fingers he had held many times before.

"Elora?" he whispered, choking on the lump in his throat. "Elora, come back."

The finger became a hand, the ghostly apparition spinning a band upon its thumb. The eternal sigh singing back.

Bray gripped Elora's fingers, holding tighter as they tried to slip through his grasp. He knew that if she left him now, she would never come back.

"Elora, please," he pleaded, raising his other hand to touch the disappearing smoke as he blinked back the tears. "Stay."

The embers burned hotter near his touch, swirling around his forearm, travelling up to his shoulder. They followed the contours of his chest, singeing black dots onto his clothes as they gathered around him.

"Bray?" came Elora's voice, sounding far away, yet he recognised it to be his fiancée.

"Yes, Elora. It's me."

The ascending smoke slowed, so thin now that it was barely visible. It teetered in the air, neither rising nor falling.

"We're to wed, remember?" Bray whispered, placing his lips against the spirit fingers. "We've an entire life to live together."

The smoke grew darker as it thickened. Slowly dropping as it flowed around him, touching him and becoming more solid. He could feel the weight of her arm draping over his stomach, a leg as it formed over his, and her head resting upon his chest; a warm smile appearing on her lips; violet eyes gazing up into his.

Bray feared moving, should she disappear again. Instead he returned the smile and gently rested the hand he held over his heart.

"You did it," he offered. "You've saved Ethea and everyone in it."

Elora breathed deeply, holding it inside her as if cherishing the air.

"No, we did it. All of us," she replied.

Bray felt confident enough that she wasn't about to suddenly vanish and so placed a kiss on her brow. "No more fighting, no more battles and no more enemies to defeat. We can live in peace now."

"Peace sounds nice," she muttered sounding as tired as he felt.

"And the wedding. You'll be my wife very soon and nothing will stop us. We can do it as soon as we return to Rams Keep."

Elora took another breath, a crease forcing a line across her smooth forehead.

"No," she told him, "first we've got one last problem to deal with."

27

Chaos is Unpredictable

Elora leapt from Grycul's back, high above the city of Rona. She plummeted through the white clouds, falling head-first and picking up speed. She trailed her hands through the cold vapour, laughing with the joy and exhilaration, finding simple pleasure with the thrill and the freedom.

Three days had passed since she had defeated Neptula and had returned to Rams Keep. Three days spent helping to put the place back in order, care for the injured and bury the dead. Sending out scraw-harpies to the south to ensure that Volcaneus kept to his deal, which he had – the god of volcanoes having disappeared leaving an empty vent in the Antarctic. On the second day, her friends from the north returned. Her Dark Army had dwindled with heavy losses in the battle with Hades and his demons. Sibiet and Hashim also told of brave heroism from the Vikings. Fighting against incredible numbers to kill the God of the Underworld. Grimwolf had killed him, yet it was clear that Jaygen had not returned with his mother and father. When Elora asked why, Ragna and Ejan explained that he had things to do in the north. They said nothing more about him and she got the impression that the story was a tragic one and best left unsaid for the time being.

Leaving the clouds behind, Elora rapidly gained more speed. The city of Rona rushing up to meet her. The spires of the palace pointing accusingly at her as she raced to meet them. The palace grounds becoming more detailed, the parade ground and pavilion, the guards on the walls and the squares of soldiers formed up in blocks around the perimeter, and many more through the city itself. It seemed the Emperor was feeling nervous, and so he should. The airship that had once belonged to the Emperor, the one she had stolen from him, now sat at the docking station, surrounded by Shades. Bray, Weakest and a large contingent of her army was already here, escorting Sibiet and Hashim through the grounds.

Elora smiled as she rotated her body, changing the course of her descent subtly, aiming for the main Imperial Building.

Moments before she hit the balcony, she reduced to smoke and landed gently outside the throne room.

From her hiding place, she could hear angry voices. Flek's mainly. Arguing with an older man while the twins, Quantala and Quantico added their opinions.

"She is not to be trusted," Flek growled. "You know already what she has done. And merging the worlds was only part of it. She's the daughter of Solarius, she will kill us all."

"But she defeated Neptula," argued the other. Elora tiptoed to the arched doorway and slowly peered around. The speaker was a portly man of middle age. His rich silk clothes and crown giving the impression of royalty. As did a number of others in the throne room as they watched the discussion.

"Chaos," Flek snapped, slamming his fist against the arm of the throne. "It's vicious, it's destructive and it will devastate the Empire. She won't be happy until she has reduced Ethea to ash."

"Yet it was her Dark Army that came to the rescue when the coast was under attack," suggested another, this one equally dressed in splendour. "And she hasn't attacked any part of my lands."

"Nor mine," agreed the kingly figure who was standing before Flek. "So I don't agree with you, that we should put all our forces into attacking her."

"You will," Flek bellowed, his face going a shade of puce. "You will because I command it. You may all be kings or queens, dukes or barons. But I am the Emperor. And you will do as I say or will be greatly punished along with your people."

"This is an outrage,"

Elora decided to choose that moment to reveal herself.

"I agree," she said, throwing the room into stunned silence as she stepped towards Flek.

"Elora?" The Emperor stammered, eyes becoming wide circles.

The twins reacted first, both drawing pistols from shoulder holsters and levelling the guns at her. They fired together, their weapons issuing twin clicks.

They repeated to squeeze the triggers, but they still wouldn't fire.

"You know," Elora offered as she casually slipped her blade from the smuggler's pouch. "A sword never runs out of bullets, or jams. And neither does it allow somebody to steal the working parts from inside.""

Chuckling to himself, Drifid stepped between the twin Shadojaks to stand beside Elora. He opened his hands and dropped the springs and firing pins from the now useless guns. They fell to the floor making a clatter against the polished marble. Then drew two pistols of his own and pointed them at the stunned pair.

"What?" They said in unison, each exchanging a look at the other before going for their swords.

"If they draw their swords, shoot them," Elora ordered.

Drifid's grin spread wider before he opened his mouth to speak. "Tak...Tak...Tak," he said.

Elora nodded. "Tak...Tak...Tak," she replied and watched the recognition pass between the brothers. They had been tricked by the takwich that possessed Drifid's body.

"Guards!" Flek screamed, "Kill her."

Elora bowed as the guards approached, yet her gaze was firmly fixed on the Emperor. "If I spill blood in this room today, Flek – it will be yours."

She crossed the room, momentarily becoming smoke as she passed through the guards to materialise beside the throne, the tip of her sword grazing Flek's chin. "We've been here before, haven't we?" She raised an eyebrow as he glanced the length of her blade, fear forcing his nostrils to flare. "Only this time I will not be tricked."

The gold gilded doors were suddenly flung open and Bray paced into the room. Flanked by Sibiet and Hashim and followed by Weakest and Ragna.

More gasps escaped the heads of states around the chamber as they looked on in sheer terror. And Elora had to admit, it was an impressive entrance.

"You cannot get away with this," Flek argued, regaining some composure. "I will not stand for it. The Empire will not stand for it!"

The guards watched as Ragna and Weakest stalked towards them and quickly withdrew, one of them even laying down his spear and raising his hands in surrender.

"The rest of the palace is secure," Bray informed her as he came to stand at her side.

"But the palace is surrounded," Flek argued, his face taking on the colour of beetroot.

"As I witnessed for myself," Elora stated, "whilst riding Grycul, high up above the city."

Flek's eyes darted towards the balcony and the sky beyond, beads of sweat breaking out upon his pasty brow.

"But…but…I am the Emperor," he squeaked.

Elora gazed around the room. Watching the other heads of states. The leaders of the countries that made up the vast Empire. They all looked on, some with pity in their eyes, other in stark terror but none came to Flek's defence.

"Is there any here who believe that Flek is the rightful Emperor? Any who would see him rule over Ethea?"

She exchanged glances with them all as they remained silent, even the small dog held in a lady's arms kept quiet, the lady herself, lips held firm only shook her head from side to side.

"So, what?" Flek addressed the room," You would have this evil creature, spawn of Solarius, take the throne? You will simply sit by and let the daughter of Chaos rule the Empire?"

His answer was only hard stares and a stony silence.

"But…"

Growing tired of his whining, Elora gripped Flek by his robes, yanked him from the throne and flung him on the floor at the feet of the twins.

"No, please," Flek sniffled from the floor, trembling hands gripping the trouser legs of Quantala.

Elora approached him, taking slow careful steps so the rest of the room could see what they had as an Emperor.

"Please, I yield, I yield," Flek pleaded as he sniffed back tears.

"You were right about one thing," Elora offered as she raised her sword above his head. "Chaos is vicious, it is destructive, and it can devastate."

She brought her soul reaver down in a single fluid slice.

Flek's god-created hand bounced several times before skittering along the marble floor, coming to rest under Hashim's foot.

"Yet, Chaos is unpredictable," she finished.

Flek opened his watery eyes and was as shocked as any in the room to find himself still alive.

"I will not start this day of the new Empire with a death," she continued, glaring at the others in the room. "The Empire is to be rebuilt on stronger foundations that don't rely on violence."

The portly king who had been arguing with Flek earlier, took a graceful step closer before falling to his knee and bowing low.

"May I be the first to show my loyalty to the new Empress. Roseland aligns itself and will be forever faithful to your rule."

Elora was shocked to see the King on his knees before her. And was even more surprised when other heads of states began to fall to their knees. All but one.

"Why?" A large, richly dressed king asked as he pushed passed his kneeling peers. "Why just give her the Empire? Why do we not take our lands back? Lands which are rightfully ours. She is a Shadojak as well as a demigod. She had no rights to the throne."

"You will kneel," Sibiet growled as he approached the outspoken monarch. "These things you speak are true. Yet you and the rest of Ethea are only alive, breathing the Blessed Mother's air, because of her actions."

Still riding the tide of astonishment, Elora slipped her sword away and stepped closer to the throne. Before she knew what she was doing her finger was tracing the intricate gold leaf, carved into the gold arm.

Empress? The most powerful being on Ethea. She couldn't get her mind around that. Less than a year ago, she was simply a girl who lived with her uncle on a barge. How her life had changed in so little time. She glanced to Bray, he nodded encouragingly, as did Ragna – the pair of them looking so proud.

Empress? Her?

She took a deep breath and withdrew her hand. "No," she said as she turned away from the throne. "The Empire should stay intact, for now anyway. At least until Ethea has settled from the merge. The Empire is still the only order amongst all the chaos that I have created. But I will not be the figurehead."

"Then who?" asked the first king who had pledged his allegiance.

"You will all return to your kingdoms and provinces. And will reconvene...let's say, a year from now and vote. The Empire will be a democracy where all have a say."

"And until then?" asked the king who had refused to kneel, his eyes firmly locked on the chair itself. "Should there not be a person in the seat, a caretaker to watch over the proceedings." He approached the throne, his greedy gaze soaking up the golden chair.

"You're right, there should," Elora continued. "That is why Sibiet and Hashim shall take joint responsibility. They are Shadojaks and that is their purpose. To reset the balance."

Elora glared at each of the kings and heads of state. "Any that oppose the Empire or attempt a coup, will be dealt with by the order of the Shadojaks. And less you forget, that includes me as well as my husband-to-be."

"Shadojaks are forsaken marriage," Quantico said snidely.

Elora stepped closer to the twins and made a show of drawing their soul reavers, before trusting them into Sibiet's care.

"They used to," she replied. "But today is a new dawn for all of us. New ways to live and new rules. Besides," she stood beside Bray and fed her arm through his. "Being a demigod has its perks." She kissed Bray on the cheek before bowing to the room. "Now if you'll excuse me, I have a wedding to attend."

"And what shall we do with these traitors?" Sibiet asked, pointing one of the blades towards the twins and Flek who was still sniffling at their feet.

Elora shrugged. "I'll leave that choice to you. I said there would be no blood shed today, tomorrow however…" and she shrugged again before steering Bray towards the balcony, where the large shadow of Grycul swept by.

The Wedding Day.

A light coat of frost dusted the courtyard, a warm glow from the morning sun glistening off all surfaces around the inn. The sky was clear and the wind still. A perfect day to get married.

Elora's footfalls crunched as she paced beside Ragna. Her arm fed through his and having to almost walk on tiptoe to keep her upper body level – he was so big. She had butterflies in her stomach and felt giddy with excitement. All her friends and family were waiting by the lake, along with her betrothed. She was looking forward to seeing him, it had been hard spending the night apart. Bray had been at the Keep with all the men, making merry and enjoying the stag night, while she remained at the inn. Ejan and her mother had organised a party involving a lot of games, chatter and alcohol. Her head was still a little fuzzy from the wine they had drunk, yet she couldn't wipe the smile from her lips. Moments from now, she would be a wife.

Her dress shimmered as they walked. The silky fabric catching the colours of the morning and returning it to the world with gleaming sparkles that shone all around her. It flowed, swept and swished with each step. An intricate pattern of diamond roses, woven from the hem, spiralling all the way to her neck line and spreading out down each arm. It was a gift from Grendal. The dress was hand-crafted from dwarf silver and spun by cotton fairies for an elven princess. How Grendal had come by the garment, Elora couldn't say, but it was the most beautiful dress she had ever seen. The veil that floated over her face was also made by the same fairies. It was so light that it had no weight, the tiny jewels which encrusted the material sparkling violet as they picked out the colour of her eyes.

Ragna was also dressed in fine clothes. The giant of a man wearing a silk shirt and velvet waistcoat, along with velvet trousers and polished shoes. He strolled with his chin held high, although Elora sensed that he felt less than confident wearing it.

When they passed the well, Elora gasped. The full presentation was before her. Hundreds of people had turned up to see her get married. Rows of chairs divided down the middle and arranged around an altar by the willow. A bright rainbow arced overhead, reflected in the still waters and casting an array of colours over Grycul who sat between the people and the lake. The Dragon Guard stood with shields held before them and spears resting at erect angles. On the other side were ranks of the Dark Army. Grimbles and grumpkins, bulworgs and men spread out in square formations and standing proud. They filled the grounds and Elora felt that they spread into the forest itself.

Beneath the willow, she let her gaze linger on Nat's gravestone. She felt a pang of sadness that he wasn't here himself, but took some reassurance that he was with her in spirit.

Everyone stood, their heads turned their way as they approached. When Otholo noticed them, he struck up the wedding march on his lute and the notes caressed over the body of water, which seemed to flow and ebb with the rhythm.

"Is there something in your eye?" Elora whispered to Ragna.

The huge Viking clenched his teeth, his nostrils flaring. "Nope," he said, swallowing hard. "I'm just a little tired."

"Tired?" Elora chuckled as she watched the tears he tried to blink away, fall into his beard. She hugged his arm tighter. "Thank you for giving me away."

"Hmmph," he said, sniffing back, keeping his stare locked ahead so she couldn't see his face.

She found it hard to hold back the emotion herself as they arrived at the rows of chairs and began to walk down the aisle. Everyone she knew was here. Everyone she had fought for, fought alongside or spilled blood with. Along with a few faces she didn't recognise.

Grendal was sat with her son. Captain Brindle and his platoon were seated to one side, Cathy was sat with Ben and his girlfriend, Genella playing at their feet with the baby. Ben had finally found a name for his son. They had decided on calling him Benn Junior, but with an extra n to stop confusion. Zilabeth was standing beside Teaselberry and Gurple. The two wood trolls watching her pass by, their paws interlaced within each other's, and wide toothy grins creasing their faces.

"You look beautiful," Thatch offered, his broad smile tightening his cheeks as she flowed on. Beside him stood Thud and between them was a greyhound. When Elora glanced down at the dog, Thud added, "Thatch found him wandering the Keep. He's got a soft spot for skinny dogs…"

"Shush," Thatch interrupted, nudging his wizarding partner. "She's getting married if you hadn't noticed."

Thud shrugged apologetically, but Elora had already moved on, her gaze having found Bray at the end of the aisle and the sight stole her breath away.

He was dressed in a dark green tunic with gold lace stitched into the sleeves and collar. It was plain but the effect of the tight-fitting suit, hugging his muscular frame, was extremely appealing. He was gorgeous, standing beside the altar. A crudely shaped arc that had grown from the branch of the old tree. Twisted willow intertwining with each other, covered in pussy willow which hung in great numbers like a thousand tiny beads of pearl. Elora glanced at the trunk and there was The Green Man's face, beaming back at her. Yet her gaze was soon drawn back to Bray.

As they neared, Norgie stepped away and stood beside Weakest, while Ragna lay a heavy hand on Bray's shoulder before he took Elora's in his other. Her own hand seeming childlike within his.

The Northman inhaled deeply, blinked away more tears. "She's yours now," he muttered quickly before tightening his lips. Leaning down he placed a kiss on Elora's forehead and then swiftly sat beside Ejan, before his emotions overwhelmed him.

"You don't scrub up too bad," Elora offered as she squeezed Bray's hand.

The world suddenly brightened as he smiled. "You don't scrub up too shabby yourself," he replied. He raised his fingers towards her head, ready to lift up the veil. Elora playfully slapped them away.

"Not until we've said the vows," she told him.

Glancing about, she couldn't find the vicar that was supposed to be marrying them. She was about to ask where he was when a young girl sauntered around the altar. A fine golden crown sat atop her golden curls.

"Minu?" Elora asked, unsure if she was seeing the god standing before her.

The girl smiled as she nodded, "Hello Elora. I hear that you did well in saving the world."

Elora felt her cheeks flush. "Erm…thank you." She felt worried that the god was here to give her another warning or impossible mission to complete. That's what she had been expecting ever since she first awoke. Something was bound to go wrong and spoil her day. She turned to her mother who was sitting beside Ejan. Athena was already dabbing tears from her eyes when she smiled.

"I said a few prayers last night," her mother explained. "It turned out that Minu had heard them."

"Yes Elora," the god confirmed. "I'm here to marry you. After all, you are the daughter of my brother. And as an aunt, I believe that I have some responsibilities."

Elora let out the breath she had been holding. She had never thought of the god Minu as being her aunt. It was made even stranger by the fact that Minu didn't appear older than twelve. *This day is just getting better by the minute.*

"Now if you will take each other's hand," Minu instructed.

Bray tenderly grasped Elora's fingers, stroking the back of her hand as they stared into each other's eyes.

"Bray, do you take Elora to be your wife? To love, keep and cherish for all of eternity, both in this world and the next?" Minu asked.

"I do," Bray answered, his gaze penetrating deep into Elora's as he placed the ring on her finger.

"And Elora, do you take Bray to be your husband? To also love, keep and cherish for ever, both in this world and the next?"

Feeling her heart skipping a beat, Elora swallowed the tears that threatened to run down her face and for the briefest of moments, her veil deepened to a shade of red, almost crimson.

"I do," she replied, willing herself to calm down, this was not the place for that other her. She struggled to push the ring on to his finger, but with a little pressure, it slipped on.

"Then as a god," Minu continued, "I grant with the will of the Blessed Mother, you to be man and wife. Bray, you may kiss your bride."

The butterflies in her stomach had now become a maelstrom of doves, battering emotions throughout her body. She felt breathless as Bray lifted her veil, his nose gently grazing against hers before he lowered his mouth. His arm curling around the small of her back as he drew her closer, pressing himself tighter as his soft lips touched hers.

Elora felt giddy as the crowd behind her suddenly erupted in a loud cheer. Yet Bray held her firm, his tongue softly touching hers and tasting of cherries. She became lost in that single time, that moment where everything around them shrank away, stripping the world to nothing but herself and Bray – her husband.

Then all at once he pulled away, leaving her legs feeling weak. "I guess we can wait until we're alone to do a lot more of that, Mrs Rona," he suggested.

"I'll hold you to that, Elf boy," she replied, locking her fingers within his.

They turned to face the people who were still cheering and made their way up the aisle. Still not fully trusting her legs, she allowed Bray to guide her as they made their way towards the inn.

"No," Elora instructed, steering Bray in a different direction.

Feeling a little more herself now, she ushered Bray towards Grycul. The dragon lowered her head to the ground and Elora gathered her dress in her hands and hitched it up.

"What are you doing?" Bray whispered.

Elora swung her leg over Grycul's neck and gestured for him to climb up. "We've spent the best part of a year, fighting, struggling and striving to survive. Through all that, we've never had time alone," Elora explained. "Call me selfish, but I'm not about to start sharing you now."

Bray grinned. "My thoughts exactly. But where are we going?"

"Some time ago, Zionbuss told me of this palace he'd built in the Shadowlands. It's secluded, quiet – abandoned really. But we'll be alone."

Bray's face lit up. "And we can spend months there and only a few hours would have passed here."

"Exactly."

Elora nudged Grycul's flank and the dragon sprang into the air. Huge wings buffeting the ground and showering the guests in the frost that was blown from the willow. The entire parade watched as they climbed high in the sky, waving and cheering while Otholo began to play a more jaunty tune. Leading the group back to the inn where they would begin the party in their honour.

Giving a final wave to her family and friends, Elora urged Grycul on and the dragon shrieked loudly into the day before the sky flashed into dusty red.

Epilogue

God of Winter

Peter stared up into the stars, attempting to work out where Polaris was, or Orion's Belt or the Great Bear – anything to take his mind away from the battles. The images in his head, the flash-backs, the memory of that day when he fought alongside the Vikings. They plagued him in his sleep; in his waking hours, stealing him back to the mud and the gore, to the blood and the violence.

"Keep still, fool," Shannog snapped, tapping his bare chest with her staff. "The spirits will not come if you insist on fidgeting."

Peter said nothing as he forced his body to remain motionless. Which was a job hard done while lying on a cold table out in the open with his shirt off and upper body exposed to the elements.

The wind picked up, stroking icy fingers over his skin and forcing his teeth to chatter. He was weak. The insulin having run out days ago, and he knew his days on this new world were numbered. That was why he had followed Shannog. Jaygen had mentioned that she might be able to help cure his illness. He had his doubts, but was willing to try. She certainly sounded as if she knew what she was doing. He'd spent the last two weeks in her shack, doing menial jobs for her while being fed a soup that tasted of foul bog water. Yet he was here now and if this ritual worked, he would have a much longer life than if he merely did nothing.

He closed his eyes and listened to the old crone as she continued speaking in that harsh tongue, repeating a strange incantation while dabbing ash over his belly. His mind wandered briefly to Jaygen and where he might be. His friend disappeared soon after the battle had ended, taking his fierce looking armour with him.

"I won't tell you again, keep still," Shannog spat sharply, her arms raising to the night, her incantation becoming louder.

Peter had begun to pick up elements of the language they spoke in the north. It was a simple dialect, but these words which the old woman was speaking seemed to outdate even Thea.

Then she abruptly halted. Her staff remaining high as her one good eye spun in its socket, her glances darting all about her as her wrinkles grew impossibly deeper.

"Something comes," she informed him.

Snow suddenly flew sideways as a harsh gust picked them up and began to spin them around the small circle. The flames in the torches blew wildly and almost gutted out, reducing the light to a small circle.

Peter sat up and hugged himself, attempting to protect his body against the elements. He saw nothing beyond the quivering flames, but sensed a foreboding presence in the darkness.

"What is it?" he asked Shannog, the old crone screwing her face tight as she sucked on her bottom lip.

"Inside," she ordered and hobbled from the table and into her log shack. Peter leapt up and rushed in behind her. Feeling the hairs on the back of his neck stiffen as she slammed the plank door behind him, sure that an evil creature was about to grab him once his back was turned.

Shannog leaned against her staff, staring at the door or at the flap of cloth which covered the only window. "He comes," she whispered, her gnarled and lumpy fingers squeezing the life from the twisted length of wood.

"Who?" Peter demanded as he reached for the sword he had kept from the battle. His hands shook as he pulled the bent length of steel from its worn scabbard, his nerves now as frayed as the belt at his waist.

Shannog didn't answer, instead her index finger pointed to the door. Then when she spotted him holding his weapon she knocked him on the head with her staff. "Idiot boy," she berated him. "You cannot hurt him with steel. Put it away."

The door suddenly slammed open. The wind howling like a banshee as it blasted inside, bringing with it snow, yet nobody was there. Then from the void, a large figure stalked out of the darkness, ducking his head to fit through the doorway, wide shoulders catching the frame either side and breaking off chunks.

Peter's sword clattered as it struck the rotten floorboards. The horror from the battlefields now returning to haunt him once more.

"You seem a little grimmer than last we met, Grimwolf," Shannog exclaimed, sucking thoughtfully on her bottom lip once again. "Perhaps next time you will heed my warnings. That suit is cursed."

Grimwolf stepped closer, his wolf-shaped head rising between the rafters and still he stooped, looming over them both.

"Odin may keep your warnings, Shannog," Grimwolf growled from behind his snarling teeth. "I've come for revenge. Where is the God of Winter?"

"You won't find the god in my house," Shannog replied.

Grimwolf glared around the small room, made particularly smaller by his presence. "I realise that, but where shall I search?"

"In the coldest, harshest of places," Shannog replied, pointing her staff out of the door. "In the high places, beyond the valley of the frozen spirits and above the giant ice glaciers. There you will find the oldest and tallest mountain in the north. There you will find Winter."

Peter thought he caught subtle movement from the wolf's helm – a nod maybe. Then Grimwolf turned and began to pace out of the room.

"Why seek Winter?" Shannog shouted.

Grimwolf halted by the door, turning his head to stare back at the old crone. "Because I will cut off his head."

Shannog thought over that for a moment before her creases smoothed and she began to laugh. An old throaty cackle which ended in a fit of coughing.

"Who said the God of Winter is a man? The stronger Gods are always women," Shannog explained once she regained control of her fitting. "And she won't be too easy to kill, not even for the likes of you. Winter is as cold and as harsh as her name. A lonely god maybe, but one as sharp as the Blessed Mother herself."

Grimwolf said nothing as he stalked out of the shack, leaving the door to the mercy of the wind.

Opening and slamming to its own accord until Shannog closed it and fastened the rusty latch.

"Fool, the world seems to be full of them," she muttered to herself.

"And me?" Peter asked as he hurriedly slipped into his shirt and grasped his old skiing jacket from a peg. "Am I to believe that you have fixed my illness with sorcery and dark magic?"

Shannog watched him as he stuffed his meagre items into a sack and threw it over his shoulder. Then she glanced at the door once again.

"Only trouble lies that way," she offered, pinning him with her one good eye. "Yet you are healed."

"I am?" Peter asked, feeling shocked. "The incantation and the painting of ash on my body worked?"

Shannog's face broke into a rare smile. "No," she cackled, "thems were just for fun."

Then realisation hit Peter. The odd tasks, the climbing down the mountain every day to fetch water from a certain stream, the black roots which he needed to dig up beneath a certain tree and grinding them to a powder on his return. "The soup?"

Shannog nodded, then passed him a bundle of the knobbly dark roots that had been drying above the fire.

"Dankgrub root. Take it sparingly and make sure you gather more before this runs out," she said.

"Thank you," Peter replied and tried to place a kiss on Shannog's cheek until she hit him with the end of her staff. Peter thanked her again as he stuffed the roots into his sack and opened the door.

The cold winter bit into him as he bolted from the shack, as if it thought him a fool for coming out in the open and attempted to usher him back inside. Yet a fool he was.

"Grimwolf?" he bellowed into the darkness as he ran in the direction of the heavy prints in the snow. "Wait for me."

The End

Acknowledgements

First of all, I would like to thank Paul Manning for the design and creation of the front cover. He has a wealth of knowledge and helped guide me in the right direction and has become a good friend.

Thanks also to my editor, Elizabeth Watkins (the Typo sniper), for having a keen eye and helping to spot the typos which had somehow slipped through.

To my children who gave me the inspiration, and my loving wife who had great ideas of her own and has kept me going on her home cooking.

And finally to the reader, for taking the time to read Ethea.

Printed in Great Britain
by Amazon